CATHERINE HART

Twice the winner of *Romantic Times'* Reviewer's Choice Award!

Critically acclaimed author of

SUMMER STORM

"Hart offers a gripping, sympathetic portrait of the Cheyenne as a proud people caught in turmoil by an encroaching world!"
—*Publishers' Weekly*

"Beautiful! Gorgeous! Magnificent!"
—*Romantic Times*

Author of FOREVER GOLD

A forever riveting, forever passionate tale of lawless love in the Old West.

FOREVER GOLD is Catherine Hart's sixth historical romance. In 1985 she received the *Romantic Times* Reviewer's Choice Award for the Best Indian Romance by a new writer (*Silken Savage*), and in 1987 she won again, this time for the Best Indian Romance (*Summer Storm*). She lives in Ohio with her husband and three teenage children.

BLAKE'S LIPS SWOOPED DOWN TO CAPTURE HERS.

"You are a priceless, precious treasure, *mi paloma*. A soft little dove with all the passion of a tigress." A final, lingering sigh shuddered through his large frame. "Oh, little one, what pleasure is hidden in your small, delicate body! Who would have guessed it?" His intense gaze captured hers again. "Tell me it was marvelous for you. Tell me you felt the world fall away from under you."

The wonder of their shared passion was still upon her, it and his spellbinding gaze combining to make the breath catch in her throat and her heart race in her chest. "It was wondrous," she breathed softly, her eyes a soft, luminous grey as she looked up at him. "It was like flying and drowning, being born and dying all at once."

He gathered her to him and held her tightly. "Oh, Megan, my Megan. What am I to do about you now?" His voice was gruff with his emotions. "How am I to get my ranch back from Kirk? How can I let you go to him now that I know what heaven there is in your arms?"

Catherine Hart

Leisure Books ✳ New York City

This book is dedicated, with much love, to my wonderful family:

First, to my husband and helpmate—
    a sweetheart and hero in every way.

To Sean—
    This is helping to pay for your future education, dear son, so don't laugh too hard at mother's work.

To Heather—
    Don't fret, daughter. One day soon, you'll be old enough to read my books and understand them.

To Brent—
    My young cadet, of whom I am so very proud. Good luck, son.

Last, to Sassy, my lively Siamese cat, who can turn beautiful script into Siamese gibberish with one pounce on my computer keys.—I can do very well without your "help."

I love you all very much!

A LEISURE BOOK

Published by

Dorchester Publishing Co., Inc.
6 East 39th Street
New York, NY 10016

Printed in the United States of America

1

The stagecoach bounced roughly into yet another hole in the rutted track. Inside, the seven passengers were jostled against one another, eliciting a chorus of groans. Megan Coulston stifled a cry as she flew several inches off her seat, the top of her pert little bonnet smashing into the roof of the coach. Down she came with a thud, her hat tilted crazily over one eye, as she caught at her mother's arm to keep from tumbling onto the floor.

"Oh, drat!" she muttered irritably, blowing a stray strand of cinnamon-colored hair from her flushed face. Gleaming grey eyes flashed from beneath long, thick brown lashes as she scooted back onto the seat and smoothed her rumpled skirt with slim fingers. A pear-shaped diamond winked from the third finger of her left hand. Though not large, it served to remind her of the man who awaited her at the end of this long, dusty journey, the man she was soon to marry, and the thought cheered her. A smile tilted the corners of her lips, lips that were naturally pink and just full enough to tempt a man into wanting to discover their lush softness for himself.

Lifting the crumpled hat from her head, Megan frowned again. A disgruntled sigh escaped as she fingered the broken stem of what was once a perky rose. Now it resembled a squashed strawberry. "Pooh!" she huffed. "This wouldn't have happened if we could have ridden from Abilene, rather than taking this horrid stagecoach all the way to Tucson."

"Now, Megan," Evan Coulston said as patiently as he could while suffering his own discomfort, "you know that wasn't possible. With all the things you insisted on packing, it is a wonder we managed to take the stagecoach. For a while there, I thought we would have to load it all in a wagon, or two—maybe even three. Between you and your mother, I was sure you meant to pack everything we own."

Jana Coulston eyed her husband with wry amusement. "Don't mind your father, Megan," she said with a hint of laughter in her voice. "He is still not adjusted to the fact that his baby daughter has grown up. If he had his way, you would always be his little girl, begging for candy and pennies at his knee. Now that you are about to become Mrs. Kirk Hardesty, he is suddenly realizing how old he is becoming."

Megan could not help but laugh at the irritated look her father gave her mother. "That's not fair,

Jana," he grumbled, "and not entirely true. I admit it was something of a jolt to have a young man approach me for our daughter's hand in marriage. It seems only yesterday that she was lisping her way through her first reader. Still, I know it had to happen someday. I just don't see why it had to be Kirk Hardesty. Why couldn't Megan marry some nice young man from Abilene, instead of someone who lives almost a thousand miles away?"

In that respect, Jana shared her husband's disappointment, though she hesitated to say as much to Megan. It hurt to think of her only child living so far from home. They would rarely see one another; they would be strangers to their own grandchildren in years to come. Still, Jana knew that, regardless of Megan's love for them, her heart was set on marrying Kirk. Without doubt, he was a handsome young man—almost too handsome, with his sandy brown hair, light blue eyes, and picture-perfect features. Lands, the fellow was almost pretty! Yet there was something about him that bothered Jana, though she couldn't put her finger on what it was exactly. Perhaps it was something to do with his eyes, so light a blue that they seemed to stare right through a person. Kirk's eyes were so light they were nearly colorless, and they seemed so cold and unfeeling that it actually gave Jana the shivers to look into them at times.

However, as much as Jana disliked Kirk's eyes, she had to admit that he treated her daughter like a queen, and would undoubtedly continue to do so once he and Megan were married. Kirk and his mother, Opal Hardesty, were wealthy landowners, owning a large ranch just outside of Tucson. Megan

had met him several months previously, when Kirk
had arrived in Abilene at the end of a long, grueling
cattle drive from Tucson. Within days, the girl had
been completely enthralled by the handsome, gal-
lant cowboy. He had lavished compliments and
gifts upon her as if money were as plentiful as his
flowery praises. Within weeks, the two young people were engaged, and only Evan and Jana's adamant insistence had prevented the two from
marrying in haste. No, if her only daughter were to
be married, it would be done properly, with a
decent engagement period, a lovely gown, an ade-
quate trousseau, and a beautiful wedding ceremony. Only on one point had they relented. The
wedding was to take place in Kirk's home. Thus the
trip to Tucson.

"I thought you liked Kirk, Daddy," Megan was
saying.

"I have nothing against the young man except
that he lives so far away," Evan assured her, though,
like his wife, he harbored a few unspoken doubts.
Evan felt he barely knew the man who was about to
take his only child so far from him. He and Jana had
owned and run their hotel for more years than he
cared to count, and in that time he had seen people
from all walks of life. In the process, he had
become a good judge of character, and there was
something about Kirk Hardesty that didn't quite
ring true. As much as he contemplated what it was
about Kirk that bothered him, the answer eluded
him. Whatever it was, he hoped it was something
insignificant, something that would not cause his
darling daughter to regret marrying him.

Maybe, as Jana had suggested, it was just that he resented Kirk for stealing his daughter from him, and for making him realize how fast the years were passing. It didn't seem possible that Megan was already eighteen, a beautiful young woman ready to start her own life and family. When had that petite little body developed all those womanly curves that young men loved to ogle, and that fathers regretted so much? Where had he been when Megan's delightful smile became devastating, when those gangly arms and legs had suddenly become graceful appendages? It had taken Kirk's proposal to shock Evan out of his blindness, and he couldn't honestly say he was grateful for this sudden revelation. In fact, he resented it heartily, while at the same time he wished that he and Jana had been blessed with more than one child in their marriage. Then perhaps the loss of Megan wouldn't have hit him quite so hard, wouldn't have made him feel quite so old or so sad.

Megan had settled into her own thoughts, most of which had to do with Kirk. Tomorrow she would see him again, after long months of separation. One more day of traveling in this dusty, dirty, bone-jarring, swaying stagecoach. One more day of eating grit and grime, of being covered from head to toe with dust that felt as if it were settling permanently into the pores of her skin. One more day of stifling heat that wilted her clothes and made her hair straggle into her face, that made her dress cling to her in wet patches and perspiration drip in itchy rivulets down her back. One more night of cramped quarters in a way station, of bathing out of a bowl with lukewarm water, when she longed desperately for a large tub full of steamy, fragrant bubbles.

While she thought with longing of a real bath and clean hair, she wanted even more just to be with Kirk again. It seemed ages since he had held her in his arms and whispered to her of his love as they stole kisses on the front porch swing. Once, he had even dared to brush her breast with his fingers, and a shock of hot, strange desire had shivered through her. He had often tried to get her to open her mouth when they kissed, but Megan had not permitted that intimacy, as she had not allowed him to touch her breast again. As much as she might have liked to, she was sure that nice girls would not do such things before they were married. Megan was not about to do anything that might make Kirk lose respect for her. She was taking no chance of losing him, for he was almost too good to be true.

From the first, Megan had been stunned by Kirk's good looks. That this handsome man should take notice of her made her absolutely giddy! When he professed his love, she had been struck nearly speechless with delight. It was a heady feeling to know that she had attracted this devastating man; that he, who could undoubtedly have any woman, had chosen her. For the first time in her life, she truly felt like a woman. To go to dinner on his arm, to have him sit next to her in church, to have her friends nearly drool with envy, gave her a sense of herself as a woman that was new and very wonderful. Megan had blossomed under his praise, her confidence growing by leaps and bounds as she witnessed for the first time the true extent of her untried feminine powers over a man. For that man to be rich and handsome was truly a girl's most treasured dream come true. She had eagerly accepted his proposal, and now, in a matter of days, she would be his wife. Surely, no young woman was as fortunate as she, even if the journey to Arizona was long, hazardous, and bruising. Megan thought she would surely have gone to the ends of the earth if necessary to marry him. Kirk was well worth the discomfort she was now enduring.

Megan had started to doze. Vaguely, she heard the soft conversation between her mother and father, and the louder snoring of the portly gentleman seated across from her. A young boy of seven sat on the smaller, extra fold-up seat between the two regular bench seats of the coach. His ever-swinging foot connected with his mother's shin, and she reprimanded him sharply. The poor woman's patience was being sorely tried on this journey. Wedged between the woman and the portly gentleman sat a tall, thin preacher. Unlike their jovial preacher back home, he had the sour, pinched look of someone ready and willing to sit in judgment on anyone he thought guilty of wrongdoing. Megan was glad that he spent most of his time reading his Bible, practically ignoring his fellow passengers. All her thoughts now melting away like mist, Megan drifted softly into sleep.

Megan awoke with a jolt. More than a mere jolt—she found herself sliding onto the floor of the stagecoach, unable to stop herself from tumbling into a heap. Her startled screech was barely heard over the shouts and screams about her. For a moment, as she glanced fuzzily about, she was sure she must still be asleep and dreaming. The young mother was clutching her son to her and crying hysterically. Megan's own mother was unnaturally pale, a look of fright tightening her fine-boned features. The preacher was praying fervently, his small eyes screwed tightly shut. Evan Coulston and the other gentleman were casting hasty, grim looks out the windows. Megan watched in bewilderment as her father drew his pistol from beneath the concealing panel of his coat. The portly man, at whose feet she had fallen, held a small derringer.

All this registered in her mind in a matter of seconds, as did several other facts. The coach was hurtling along at a breakneck speed, the drivers shouting at the horses and cracking the long whip. Then a chilling thought dawned on Megan. It was not the crack of a whip she had heard, but gunfire. No sooner had she realized this than another shot was fired from atop the stagecoach roof.

Suddenly everything seemed to be happening at once. Shoving his wife onto the floor with Megan, Evan shouted above the noise, "Stay down there, and don't get up until I tell you." To the frightened woman across from him and her wide-eyed son, he suggested the same. "All of you keep your heads down!"

All was confusion to Megan from that moment on. The stage was tearing across the rutted road at a terrifying speed. At one point, it bounced so violently that it nearly tipped over, causing Megan to hit her head so hard on the door of the coach that she literally saw stars. The men were shouting, the gunfire bursting all around, the coach bouncing and rattling. The racing horses were kicking up so much dust that it seemed impossible to breathe, let alone see. Above her head Megan heard a man cry out in pain, followed by a clatter on the roof.

"One of the drivers is hit!" she heard her father say.

"Damn! They're gaining on us!" the heavy-set man replied. "We'll never outrun them in this coach!"

Who "them" was, Megan could only guess, but she heard the preacher begin to pray even faster. Scared as she was, she fought the urge to giggle wildly. The sound of horses' hooves grew louder, and a gun went off so near that she jerked in fright, an involuntary scream catching in her dry throat.

The stagecoach slowed, then rolled ominously to a halt. For what seemed an eternity, no one moved—no one spoke. Someone outside the coach barked a gruff order in Spanish. Apparently his order was not followed, for he then repeated it in broken English. Through the window on the opposite side from her, Megan saw a shotgun fall from the roof of the stagecoach. A matching thud sounded nearby. Then came the dreaded, thickly accented command, "Everyone out of the stagecoach, your hands over your heads."

"Evan?" Jana whispered questioningly, gazing up at her husband.

"There's nothing else we *can* do, Jana," he sighed defeatedly. "There are too many of them."

"Don't worry, ladies," the chubby gentleman comforted. "They'll probably let us all go our way once they rob us of anything they deem valuable."

The stagecoach door flew open to reveal three masked bandits, all with their rifles pointed directly into the coach. "Throw out your guns first, then step down very slowly."

Reluctantly, Evan did as he was told. The other man also tossed his small gun out the open door. Once out, Evan turned back to help the ladies from the coach, but he was roughly pushed aside by one of the bandits. The robber looked into the coach, and upon seeing three women huddled together on the floor, laughed softly. "*Mujeres*, allow me the pleasure of helping you down." He extended his hand toward the young mother, who immediately shrank back with an ear-splitting shriek. The man merely shrugged and lifted the screaming woman from the coach. After shoving her toward Evan, he helped the boy alight, then Jana, and Megan.

Megan's legs were trembling so badly she barely managed to keep from falling as she stood beside her parents and watched the remaining two men climb from the carriage. While she and the rest of the passengers watched, their luggage was quickly ransacked, and two heavy trunks were tossed from atop the coach. A well-aimed shot broke the lock on the first box, and when the lid was raised, several of the bandits shouted their approval. The strongbox was filled with money, stack upon stack of green U.S. currency bound for the bank at Tucson. The second trunk, though smaller, held an even better cache, for it was brimming with shining, glowing gold.

Two of the bandits quickly loaded the stolen booty on the backs of their horses, while the other five stood guard over the watching, wary passengers and the two stage drivers. The driver who had been shot lay on the ground, clutching his thigh. His pantleg was bloody, and his face pale, but he had not been mortally wounded. Fortunately, a few days in the care of a Tucson doctor and he would be fine.

Now two more of the robbers came forward, leisurely approaching their small group of victims. Megan heard the laughter in his voice as one of them said, "*Por favor*, please to hand over your valuables now. Put all your money, your rings, watches, jewelry into this bag." Grimly the men began to do as they were told, though the preacher had little to contribute. Jana removed the ivory brooch at the neck of her dress and dropped it tearfully into the burlap sack. However, when the man gestured to her wedding ring, she immediately balked, curling her small hand into a tight fist. "No!" she wailed. "You can't take my wedding band! My God, what kind of animals are you?"

Megan watched fearfully as the man's face reddened with anger above his kerchief. If this creature dared to lay a hand on her mother, she knew her father would attack immediately, gun or no gun, and he would surely die for his efforts! Just as she was certain the man was about to strike her mother, a terse command came from one of the taller of the bandits, still seated atop his big chest-nut stallion. Megan could not understand the Span-ish words, but the content was clear, for the bully reluctantly backed down. He was going to allow her mother to keep her precious wedding band. Passing over Megan momentarily, he went on to the young mother, taking a cameo pendant and a small ruby ring, but again he let her keep her plain gold wedding band, though he glared at the other bandit as he did so.

At last he came to Megan. With a tearful sigh she released the pearl birthstone ring her father had given her just the previous week. The gold watch that had belonged to her grandmother followed it into the open sack. The odious man glared at her and waited. When Megan made no move to give him anything more, he pointed at the small pearl studs in her pierced ears. "*Los pendientes, señorita*, those also."

Megan glared back at him, muttering silent oaths to herself about greedy bullies, even as her hand rose to remove the earrings. Before she could take them from her ears, that deep, commanding voice cut through the air again. Angry words in rapid Spanish were exchanged between the two bandits, as Megan waited anxiously, not at all sure what to do.

"Come here, *señorita*," that same deep voice ordered suddenly. Megan's startled eyes flew to the taller man's face, what little she could see of it. His bandanna covered the lower half of his face, while the brim of his black hat rode low over his forehead to shield that portion of his features from view. "Now!" he barked, when she hesitated too long.

Megan turned pleading eyes on her father. "What should I do, Daddy?" she asked, lips trembling. The words had barely cleared her mouth when a coil of rope fell over her, binding her arms to her sides. A gasp escaped her constricting throat, her gaze flying once more to the face of the mounted bandit. "*Muchacha*," he said evenly, his voice a low rumble in his throat, "when I give an order, I expect to be obeyed." Step by trembling step, he calmly reeled in his shaken captive.

Her eyes are like soft grey clouds, so huge and frightened, he thought to himself. *She reminds me of a captive dove, so small and vulnerable*. He watched her try to control the fear on her face, but her quivering lips betrayed her. Small, even white teeth came down upon her trembling lower lip, a gesture that betrayed her even as she was trying to gather her courage in the face of this unknown enemy.

When she stood below him, he said, "What is your name, pretty *señorita*?"

Her small chin pointed upward in defiance as she craned her neck to face him. "Megan," she answered softly, her voice quivering only slightly. "Megan Coulston."

"Give me your hand, Megan." He loosened the lariat, and it fell to her feet, freeing her arms.

After the merest moment's hesitation, she slowly raised her right hand. "The other hand," he corrected.

With a suspicious frown, Megan complied. Long, strong fingers enclosed hers in a warm grip. Megan stood quietly until she felt his fingers tugging to remove her diamond engagement ring. "No!" she cried out. "No! Please! It is my engagement ring. Please let me keep it! Please!" Against his greater strength she tried to close her fingers, tried to draw her hand back from his firm grasp. When he would not release her hand, she began to struggle even more. Her right hand came out to push against his hard thigh as she twisted her body

away from him. The big horse shifted slightly, but
the man controlled his mount as easily as he had
wrenched the ring from Megan's finger, all the
while maintaining his hold on her hand.

With a flick of his wrist, he tossed the precious
ring toward the second bandit, the one with the
bag. "Here, *amigo*. You take the ring. I have found
something I like even better."

His soft, taunting laughter and cavalier attitude
toward the disposal of her treasured ring at last
ignited Megan's temper. "You arrogant beast!" she
screamed up at him, her grey eyes snapping now
like gleaming silver dollars. "Give me back my ring!
It's mine, and you have no right to take it from me!"

He merely laughed down at her, and in her
anger Megan gave no thought to the fact that from
this angle she could see his eyes, or the fact that
they were a deep, brilliant blue rather than the
brown of most persons of Spanish descent. His hard
fingers slipped down to clamp tightly about her
lower arm, just below her elbow, further restricting
her struggles. "Ah, so you *do* have a temper to
match your hair," he drawled softly. "I wondered
about that. That should make things more interesting still." His other hand snaked out to grab her
other arm, and before she had time to consider
what this meant, he had lifted her from her feet and
swung her up in front of him in the saddle.

After her initial squawk of surprise, Megan
bristled. "Put me down, you big bully!" she
screamed, oblivious to the hoots of delight from
the other bandits, who were watching with undis-
guised interest. It was her mother's frightened
weeping, and her father's exclamation of dismay

that finally drew her attention away from her captor.

"For the love of God, Megan, don't anger them any further," Evan admonished. "Let them have the ring. Kirk will understand."

Evan turned anguished eyes toward the man who held his daughter before him. "Please put her down now. You've got our valuables and you've had your fun terrorizing us all."

The tall man shook his head. "No, *señor*. I have decided to keep your little spitfire for a while. She should prove very entertaining. After all, we waylaid the stagecoach to take all the valuables, and what is more valuable than a beautiful, desirable young *señorita*?"

Jana's wail eclipsed Megan's immediate shriek, but not Evan's roar of anger. Bent on revenge, Evan started forward, stopped only by the hard thrust of a rifle barrel in his stomach. As he doubled over, Megan screamed, her small fists flailing at her captor. "Blast you! Don't you dare hurt my father!" Tears sparkled like raindrops in her eyes as she glared into the fathomless blue pools above her.

"Don't worry, Mr. Coulston," he said coolly, calmly capturing both small fists in one large hand. "Your darling daughter will be returned to you sooner or later, though I won't promise what condition she will be in by then. That depends on many things, not the least of which is how eager she is to do my bidding."

By now, the other bandits had mounted their horses, though their guns were still trained on the shocked passengers. "Please, if there is an ounce of mercy in you, let my daughter go!" Jana begged, tears streaming down her pale cheeks.

Megan was struggling and wriggling for all she was worth, cursing him between shrieks of rage. "Darn you, put me down! I'd rather be dead than go anywhere with you! Let go of me, you beast—you —you—bastard!"

"You won't get away with this!" the uninjured driver put in. "Kidnapping is a serious crime, even in these parts. The sheriff will see you hang for this."

"He'll have to catch me first," the man boasted, his manner as cool as ever.

"The Lord will see you pay," the preacher said. "You can't run and hide from Him. He'll see you fry in hell for all eternity for your crimes against this innocent young girl. You'll be forever damned."

His chest shook beneath Megan's back as he clutched her to him and laughed. "Preacher man, if I'm going to be damned, I'll sure as hell have fun sinning." With Megan held tightly before him, nearly immobile except for her mouth, he kneed his horse into a walk.

No matter how she twisted, Megan could not break his hold. The best she could do was scream vile epithets at him as they rode steadily away from the stagecoach and her parents. His arm tightened about her chest until she gasped for breath. "We're going to have to do something about that filthy mouth of yours, *querida*," he warned softly. As soon as they had crested the next rise, he took a moment to remove the bandanna from his face. This he promptly tied about her mouth, muffling anything further she had to say. He also took the precaution of tying her wrists before her, anchoring them to the saddle horn. "That should keep you fairly quiet for a while, my little spitfire," he chuckled, watching the fire blaze from her eyes.

Megan growled at him from behind her gag, hating him for frightening her, for kidnapping her, for stealing her engagement ring, for revealing such a ruggedly handsome face to match those laughing midnight blue eyes. Anyone this damned mean should, by all rights and reason, be ugly! It just wasn't fair!

2

When they had ridden perhaps three miles from the scene of the holdup, the other bandits veered off in another direction, leaving Megan and her lone captor to go their own way. He headed the chestnut toward the range of mountains that lay east of Tucson and settled the horse into an easy, even pace. He said nothing, gave his hostage no indication of where they were going or what he meant to do with her when they got there. If not for his hard arm banded so tightly about her waist, Megan would have thought he had forgotten about her altogether.

Megan's overactive mind was racing with unvoiced questions, imagining all sorts of horrible things too frightening to delve into too deeply, but too real not to contemplate. Where was this madman taking her? What awful fate awaited her when they reached their destination? Did he mean to harm her? Possibly to kill her? Why? Why her? Why now, when her life had barely begun, when she was on the threshold of marriage to the man she adored? Just this morning life had seemed so wonderful, so full of promise. Now the fabric of her dreams of marriage and children was being ripped apart by this blue-eyed demon who rode silently and unconcerned, his hard body holding her so close to his that she could feel the heat of him through the layers of clothing that separated them.

The longer they rode, the more his silence bothered her; and the more worried she became, the angrier she got. Finally Megan could bear it no more. Throwing her head back against his broad chest in order to see his face, Megan grumbled irritably at him through the cloth bound about her mouth, her expressive eyes shooting daggers at him. When he ignored her attempts to gain his attention, Megan resorted to more physical measures. Wriggling about in his firm hold, she threw herself sideways, until he was forced to pull her back into position before him in the saddle. Still he said nothing, until the hard heel of her shoe connected sharply with his shin above the protection of his boot.

"Ouch! You little hellion!" he objected loudly. "What the devil are you trying to do? If you don't sit still, you're going to dump yourself out of the saddle, and I'll be tempted to let you dangle by your arms from the saddle horn the rest of the way."

Megan's answer was an exasperated shriek beneath her gag and a sharp elbow to his ribs.

"Damn it, you little witch!" he yelled, pulling

his horse to a halt. Jerking her around to face him, he put his face, tight with anger now, close to hers. "I'm going to tell you one more time. Sit still and be quiet, or I'm going to pull you off this horse and beat your blasted bottom until it blisters!" He shook her so hard her teeth would have rattled in her head if not for the cloth between them. "Do you understand me now?"

Megan understood him perfectly, for his voice now held no trace of its former Spanish lilt. He had spoken in clear, unaccented English. The fury blazing from his dark blue eyes frightened her even more than his silence had. Prudently, she nodded her head, letting him know that his message was clearly understood.

"Good! Now behave yourself. You are fast wearing my patience thin." He shifted her face forward once more and they resumed their trek into the foothills.

Megan's mouth and throat were soon parched. Her lips felt as if they had become part of the fabric of the bandanna wedged between them. Even her ribs hurt from the restriction of his forearm pressed hard against them. For hours she sat upright, as far from his detestable body as she could manage, given the circumstances, but the ache in her lower back and across her shoulder blades was nearly unbearable from the constant strain. Finally, with a resigned sigh, she allowed herself to relax against his broad chest, though she refused to give in to the tears that stung her eyes and threatened to spill over at any moment.

On and on they rode as the afternoon waned into evening, the sun riding lower and lower behind them. They were well into the mountains now, following twisting paths lined with trees and rocks, crossing small streams that gurgled invitingly on their way down ever steeper slopes. For a while, though she could barely believe it, Megan dozed. The severity of the shock finally caused her tired mind and body to succumb to the lure of oblivion. Her stiff muscles finally relaxed, letting her captor support her limp weight, her head lolling back into the hollow of his shoulder.

Blake Montgomery shifted the young girl more comfortably against him. A sardonic smile creased his lips as he gazed down at the fiery hair and the innocent face it framed. He hadn't expected Kirk's fiancée to look so pure, so untouched, so innocent. He had thought she would be harder, more experienced. Could this young girl be as chaste and protected as she seemed? Stranger things had happened, he supposed. Still, it surprised him. Kirk had always shown a preference for women who had seen enough of life to know their way around and be able to handle themselves with skill in the bedroom. And with his looks, he'd had no trouble finding willing volunteers. What was Kirk doing with Miss Megan Coulston?

Inwardly, Blake shrugged. Maybe it was true what they said about men always wanting to marry a virgin, even men like Kirk. Blake had his doubts, though, that Megan's parents had been able to guard their daughter from his cousin's determined advances. Kirk's reputation with the ladies was almost a legend around Tucson. One devastating smile from those too-white, too-straight teeth, and women practically swooned. That this little girl could have withstood Kirk's practiced charm where wiser women had failed was too much to believe.

Megan was prettier than he had thought she would be. Oh, he hadn't expected Kirk to marry an ugly girl. His cousin was much too choosy. Yet Megan had a fresh natural beauty that appealed more readily to Blake than it ever had to Kirk. Kirk's companions were usually more sophisticated, with a more artfully contrived attractiveness about them.

Megan sighed in her sleep, drawing Blake's attention to her mouth, the lips almost hidden behind the kerchief. His grin twisted ruefully. Those lips—those perfectly delectable lips—must have been what Kirk could not resist. God, they were luscious! So soft and pink and tempting! Blake felt himself hardening at the thought of those lips beneath his, and he cursed himself for wanting her. His gaze searched her face for flaws; wanting, needing to find just one. Soft feathery lashes fanned her flushed cheeks. Her nose was small and straight, as were the teeth he'd seen when he thrust the gag between them. Her chin had a stubborn look about it even in sleep. She had one of those peaches-and-cream complexions that other women envied, un-usual for a redhead. Her hair wasn't a true red, however. It was a reddish-brown that reminded Blake of cinnamon, or nutmeg.

Blake chuckled to himself. That was amusing —nut meg—Meg—Megan. How appropriate! He wondered to himself if that was why her parents had given her the name. Maybe. Had they known she would have a spicy temper to match? He nearly laughed aloud. Then he remembered her eyes, and he sobered. They changed in color with her moods, obviously. He had seen them soften in fear and confusion to a misty grey, and become bright and clear, sparkling like frosted diamonds when she was angry. What would they look like in the midst of lovemaking, when desire ruled her senses?

Blake shook his head, as if to clear his mind of his wayward thoughts. It didn't matter that she was a beauty, that she had large dovelike eyes and the lips of a temptress. All that mattered was that he had stolen Kirk's intended bride, and if his cousin wanted her back, he would have to meet Blake's terms. Megan was Blake's means to an end, his trump card. He would have abducted her if she'd been ugly enough to scare the devil himself. Still, it might prove entertaining to have this lovely young thing around, instead of some homely creature. It might take a while for Kirk to comply with his demands, to take his threats as seriously as Blake intended them. Blake was sure Kirk would agree eventually, though. Who in his right mind wouldn't do everything in his power to retrieve this little beauty?

Megan had been dreaming that she was a little girl once more. Beneath her, the steady sway of the horse became, instead, the gentle rock of the rocking chair in her mother's parlor as Jana held her and read to her from her favorite storybook. The creak of the saddle leather became the comforting creak of the rocker rungs; back and forth, back and forth. Megan's head just fit under her mother's chin, and she could feel the warm breath stirring her hair as Jana spoke. Smiling, Megan snuggled closer into her mother's embrace. She felt the loving arm tighten about her, the hand that lightly brushed her breast and paused to linger. Warm, calloused fingers caressed the dimpled crest.

Calloused fingers! Megan's eyes flew open. No longer was she dreaming, yet the hand resting so intimately on her breast was still to be felt, and very real indeed! It belonged to none other than her captor! If that were not bad enough, against her bottom, situated so snuggly within the cradle of his thighs, she could clearly feel his arousal. Young she might be, but ignorant she was not!

Lurching upright and nearly spilling from his lap in the process, Megan cursed him thoroughly, if not clearly. One of her flailing feet slammed into the stallion's side, and the horse broke into a run. Before Blake could grab for her, Megan found herself sliding out of the saddle. With her hands still bound to the saddle horn, it was much as Blake had predicted. For countless seconds she dangled next to the racing horse, supported only by her arms, which felt as if they were being pulled from their sockets. How she managed to keep from being trampled beneath the pounding hooves, she didn't know, except that she was so short that the tips of her feet barely dragged the ground. The rope about her wrists burned into her skin, and she was unable to catch her breath for bouncing hard against the saddle and her captor's leg. Breath or no breath, a scream sounded behind the confines of her gag.

Suddenly she was being hauled upward, reeled in like a hooked fish. His hands felt like bands of iron about her upper arms. She heard his sharp curse, but by now she was beyond caring, beyond

anger. Huge sobs tore from her throat, and glistening tears rolled down her face. Megan had never
been one of those fortunate females who could cry
prettily. Within seconds her nose was red and she
was sniffing loudly. Unable to draw sufficient breath
through the kerchief across her mouth, she found
herself once more struggling to breathe. Just as a
grey, swirling mist was about to engulf her, the gag
was ripped from her mouth. Gulping in great
lungfuls of air, Megan willed herself not to faint.

"You stupid, willful female!" Blake ranted.
"You haven't the sense God gave a gnat!" Roughly
he wiped at the tears on her cheeks and pushed the
handkerchief to her nose. "Blow!" he ordered
tersely.

Mortified, but unable to do the chore herself
with her hands still bound, Megan obeyed. Finally
able to breathe properly, and able to speak for the
first time in hours, she lit into him. "If you would
kindly keep your hands to yourself, I would greatly
appreciate it!" Her voice was as gruff as a frog's.
There was something humiliating about trying to
scream at your abductor and having the words
come out in a croaking whisper.

"If you promise to keep quiet and not screech
like a cat with his tail caught in a door, I'll leave the
gag off," Blake offered.

"How awfully kind of you!" she retorted
hoarsely.

"Don't push your luck," he warned. "Your
choices are limited to my benevolence." He un-
corked his canteen and held it up to her dry lips.
"Drink."

She really had little choice. It was either drink

or drown as he proceeded to pour the tepid water down her throat. Sputtering and choking, she finally managed to turn her head away. Water ran down her chin and splashed the front of her dress. Again the handkerchief came forth to swipe at her face and dab at the wet spot on her chest. "Get your vile hands off me!" Megan hissed.

Grey eyes collided with those of deepest indigo. "Oh, hell! You'd think you had never been touched by a man before!"

The truth of his remark must have shown on her face, for he drew in a sharp breath and looked at her intently for several seconds. A crooked smile slanted across his face then. "Well, I'll be damned!"

"You'll be more than that if you touch me again, mister!" she threatened ineffectually.

Blake laughed outright. "Honey, you are in no position to be making threats, in case you haven't noticed."

"My name is Megan, not Honey," she sniffed indignantly.

"Yeah, I know. Like nutmeg, the color of your hair." His voice lowered to a gruff caress. "Sugar and spice and all things nice, is that what little Megan is made of?" he taunted.

Megan bristled. "Not for the likes of you," she retorted.

"We'll see about that. We are going to have lots of time to get to know one another. By the way, since we are going to be such close companions, my name is Blake—Blake Montgomery." Once more his eyes searched her face closely, but whatever he was looking for, he did not find this time.

"I don't give a hoot in hell who you are!" she answered daringly. "You are a common thief and low-down criminal. My parents and my fiancé will see you hang if any harm comes to me. Think about that before you assault me further, you kidnapping bully."

"Please stop, Megan," he said mockingly. "You are scaring me right out of my boots." Then he laughed that grating laugh again.

As he picked up the reins and settled her before him once more, he added, "You're a saucy little thing, though. I'll give you that much credit. Just remember, my patience and my sense of humor do have their limits."

The stagecoach barreled down the street, leaving clouds of dust and curious bystanders in its wake. It drew to a lurching halt before the Tucson Hotel. Before it had stopped rocking, the driver was shouting anxiously, "Get the sheriff! Find the doc! The stage has been robbed!"

A crowd gathered immediately about the coach. Someone ran to find the doctor, and the sheriff could be seen hurrying from his office a few doors down. Kirk Hardesty strode beside the sheriff, a frown marring his handsome features. "Damn it, Dick! Megan is supposed to arrive on that stage. If she has been hurt, there will be hell to pay!"

The two men shouldered their way through the crowd. "What happened? Who has been hurt?" Sheriff Brown barked out.

"Holdup!" the driver shouted back. "Pete took a bullet in the leg. They took the girl."

The white-faced passengers were being helped

from the coach. Kirk pushed his way to the front, nearly knocking a young woman down in the process. His pale eyes scanned the passengers and failed to find his fiancée. Spotting his future father-in-law, he grabbed the man roughly by the arm. "Where is Megan?" he demanded anxiously.

Evan Coulston turned stunned eyes to the man his daughter was to marry. "Gone," he croaked, pulling his sobbing wife into the supporting crook of his free arm.

"Gone?" Kirk shouted. "What do you mean, *gone*?" Kirk shook the older man as if to force the answer from him.

"Gone!" Evan answered gruffly. "Stolen. Taken away by that band of bandits who robbed the stage." Pain and sorrow lanced through him, making his voice crack and tears fill his eyes.

Beside him, Jana moaned pitifully, near collapse with worry over her daughter. "My baby!" she wailed. "My poor baby! God knows what those beasts are doing to her right now!"

A murmur went through the crowd of onlookers, pity and open speculation on their faces as they heard Jana's heartfelt cry. Sheriff Brown stepped to Kirk's side. "Why don't you take these folks inside and get them a room," he suggested curtly. "I need to question the drivers, then I'll want to talk with them. The lady looks about to faint, Kirk."

Kirk whirled on him, his face twisted with anger. "I'll take care of my fiancée's folks, Dick. You just tend to your own business—catching the animals that have taken Megan. I want their heads on a platter! I want them hanged and quartered!"

"We'll catch them, Kirk. I'll round up a posse, and as soon as I get some answers from the drivers and passengers, we'll be on our way. You comin' with us?"

"Wild horses couldn't keep me away. Let me get Megan's parents settled. I'll meet you in your office in ten minutes."

"I'm coming with you," Evan spoke up. When Kirk and the sheriff looked as if they might object, he said firmly. "She is my daughter."

It was pitch dark, somewhere near midnight when Megan and her abductor finally reached the small, hidden cabin nestled into the mountainside. Megan had long since used her last reserves of energy, and as Blake helped her from the saddle, her legs promptly collapsed beneath her. As she fell against him, Blake caught her, collecting her in his strong arms and carrying her like a babe against his broad chest. With his foot he kicked open the door to the cabin. Evidently familiar with the cabin, he walked directly to an unseen chair and deposited Megan on it. "Stay put until I get a lamp lit," he said.

Too tired to run if rescue were within inches of her, Megan waited. Seconds later, a warm light revealed the rough interior of the room. It was a single-room cabin, neat but small. The straight-back chair upon which she sat was one of three around a small square table. A rough stone fireplace was centered along one wall. Shelves had been secured to one side of it, some lined with canned goods, others with dishes and cooking pans. A small counter with pail, pitcher, and bowl served as additional kitchen workspace and dry sink combined. On the other side of the fireplace, toward the rear of the cabin, was an old rocking chair, its once-cheery pad now faded and worn. Next to the rocker, and butted up to the rear of the cabin, was the solitary bed.

To Megan's overwrought senses, the bed seemed to dominate the entire cabin. Her eyes quickly scanned the remainder of the cabin, noting the hooks on the wall, the additional shelves for clothes and linens, the coarse burlap used as coverings over the two small windows on either side of the single door. No, there was no other bed, not even so much as a small cot, only that one big bed that seemed to grow larger and more menacing with each passing minute.

Jerking her gaze from the bed, Megan caught Blake's mocking look as he said calmly, "It's not much, but it's passably comfortable, and it meets my needs nicely." As her eyes widened, he laughed. "The cabin, not the bed, Miss Priss, though you could add to my comforts if you like. I certainly wouldn't want to disappoint a pretty lady."

Fire blazed from her eyes as anger loosened her tongue. "Hell will freeze solid before I share that bed with you!"

His smile was arrogant and taunting. "You think so? Well, let me tell you a few facts. You, my dear Megan, are totally dependent upon me. Your well-being hinges upon my benevolence and my moods." His approach was silent and menacing as he closed the small space separating them. Muscled arms came out on either side of her, effectively trapping her in her chair. "When I say move, you'll

ask how fast. When I say jump, you'll ask how
high." His smile had become a chilling sneer.
"You'll be quiet when I want you quiet. You'll eat,
drink, and sleep on my command, and if you are
smart, you'll be damned quick about it when I tell
you to do something. In effect, I will be the master
and you my obedient, willing slave. Got the picture, princess?" he growled.

Fear tingled up her spine as his sapphire eyes
glittered into her. Instinct told her it would be
perilous to risk riling him further—at least just
now. She must use caution. She had to survive. She
had to use her wits, and perhaps her wiles, if she
were to survive, if she were to have any chance of
escaping this madman. Still, his words galled, and it
simply was not in her nature to be meek. A shiver
trembled through her, making her lips quiver, but
she met his gaze squarely with her own. "Whether
you like it or not, I have to go to the privy, and I
have to go now!"

He just stared at her for several seconds, his
nostrils flaring. "Well," he said, finally, a hint of
amusement in his deep voice, "even I can't argue
with nature." He drew her up out of the chair,
leading her toward the door of the cabin. "You'll
find the facilities a little crude, I'm sure. Not what
you are accustomed to."

Pulled along by her upper arm, Megan again
found herself in the dark night. A chill wind blew
strands of her hair into her face as she stumbled
along after him. At the edge of the small clearing,
Blake stopped. "Pick a bush," he said with a dry
chuckle. "Any bush."

Megan blinked up at his bulky frame. "What—

uh—what about snakes?'' she asked shakily.

Blake's teeth shone white as a demonic grin creased his face. ''If you're afraid, I suppose I could come with you and protect you.''

''Never mind,'' Megan grated between clenched teeth. ''I'd rather take my chances with your slimy relatives.''

''Try behind the big tree just to your left,'' Blake suggested, pointing her in the right direction.

Megan hadn't gone three steps when she remembered her bound hands. With a helpless sigh, she quickly backtracked. Holding her hands out before her, she waited for him to untie her.

''Ask me nicely, saucy kitten, and I might be persuaded to aid you.''

Swallowing her pride, Megan grudgingly asked, ''Will you please untie me?''

''Nicely done. There may be hope for you yet.'' Long, lean fingers dealt easily with the knotted rope. Giving her a shove toward the tree, he added, ''Be quick about it, and don't try anything. You wouldn't want to risk breaking your neck in the dark, now would you, darlin'?''

Megan thought it might be well worth the risk to be free of him, but first things first, and she really was in dire need of relieving herself. Her first surprise awaited her just behind the tree. Someone had placed a rough plank between two low tree stumps. The improvised seat rested over a shallow trench. Blake Montgomery had a twisted sense of humor, but at least she didn't have to squat in the bushes, and for this Megan was grateful. She truly was afraid of snakes, the very thought sending gooseflesh rippling over her.

"Talk to me, Megan, so I know you are still attending to business." The deep voice carried easily on the night air.

"Do you mind?" she spat back. "I'm not used to carrying on a conversation while—"

"While what, darlin'?" he baited, laughter lacing his words.

"Just shut up! I'll be out when I am ready, and not until. If you had any sense, you'd realize that you haven't given a thought to my needs all day."

"Captors rarely do, Megan. You would do well to keep that in mind in future. It might tend to soften your words a bit. The more obedient you are, the easier things will go for you."

Having finished, Megan vaguely heard his last comment. She was already picking her way carefully and quietly through the tangled brush away from where Blake stood waiting. If she could only lose herself in the dark, perhaps she could escape him. If she could find a place to hide until daylight, she could find her way off the mountain. Surely she could find someone to help her, someone to take her to Kirk's ranch and safety.

Behind her she heard Blake call her name, then again more loudly. A twig snapped beneath her foot, and Megan cursed silently. Her dress caught on a branch, nearly making her cry out in fright. Heart thundering madly in her ears, Megan stopped to listen. Blake was looking for her now, for she could hear the rustle of bushes somewhere behind her. Oh, God! She had to find a place to hide! Feeling her way almost blindly, Megan continued forward. Caution and the need for silence made her go slowly, though her mind was screaming for her to run. Ahead she could make out the shape of a large tree, and she headed for it, thinking to hide behind it.

Just as she came abreast of the tree, something large and furry leaped out from behind it, blocking her path. Megan stopped dead in her tracks, a scream trapped in her throat. Suddenly, without any warning at all, Megan found herself facing the most ferocious animal she had ever seen. A feral snarl curled the wolf's lips back to bare long, sharp fangs. A low growl held her motionless, her eyes wide with fright, her legs threatening to give out beneath her. Golden eyes gleamed wickedly at her in the darkness.

Megan's heart nearly leaped out of her throat as, behind her, a familiar voice warned, "Don't move, Megan. Just stand still and don't say a word. Lobo doesn't take kindly to strangers popping up out of nowhere to invade his territory."

Blake came up beside her, knelt down, and called to the animal. "Come, Lobo. It's all right, boy. Good dog." The wolf went immediately to Blake, sitting docilely at his feet, his long tongue lolling out as Blake scratched him obligingly behind the ears.

"Now, if you would just learn to obey as well as Lobo does. It was foolish of you to go dashing off in the dark. You're damned lucky it was Lobo that waylaid you. It could just as easily have been a cougar or a bear or a coyote."

Still frozen with fright, Megan could not answer. Her teeth clattered in her mouth, and every bone in her body was quaking uncontrollably. A weak moan escaped her constricted throat.

The wolf's ears perked immediately at the distressed sound, and he looked at his master inquiringly, the quick golden eyes darting from Megan to Blake. "Come, Lobo. Let's get the lady back to the cabin before she faints. She's not as light as she might look, believe me."

With Blake's strong arm looped about her waist, the animal following close behind, Megan let herself be led back to the cabin, her first small attempt at escape thwarted almost before it had begun. It occurred to her that she now had not one, but two captors to guard her every move, each a very capable, very dangerous beast in his own way.

3

Megan sat stiffly on the chair and watched as Blake fixed their supper. While he had gone to the creek for water, and to tend to his horse, Lobo had stood guard over her, and Megan had dared not move a muscle, let alone try to escape. She'd been afraid to even blink for fear the huge wolf would attack her.

Blake set a plate of beans and fried eggs before her and motioned toward the loaf of bread on the table. "It's not fancy, but it will fill your stomach. Eat."

Despite her hunger, Megan was not sure her trembling stomach could handle food just yet. She was tired and scared and next to tears. She sat staring at the food on her plate, thinking stupidly that the eggs looked like yellow-irised eyes staring unblinkingly back at her. "I said eat, or I'll stuff it down your throat!" Blake's rough voice broke through her weary stupor. "I've had about all of your stubbornness I'm going to put up with for one day,'' he continued harshly.

She turned tear-filled eyes to him. "I can't," she croaked pitifully.

A terse curse was her answer from him. There was no sympathy at all in the blue eyes looking back at her. "First the anger, and now the tears, huh, Megan? Well, it's not going to work, sweetheart, so forget it. Now, pick up that fork and start eating. Starving yourself will do nothing more than make you weak and sick, and I don't need an ailing female on my hands.''

Megan's chin came up belligerently. "You should have thought of that before you kidnapped me," she shot back. What kind of man held her prisoner? Was he concerned for her, or just worried about the inconvenience it would cause him should she fall ill? And what kind of captor told you his name, if Blake Montgomery was his real name? Since they had been out of sight of the stagecoach, he had not bothered to conceal his features from her. Shouldn't he be concerned that she could readily identify him? A shudder ran up Megan's spine. Maybe he never meant to turn her loose. Perhaps he meant to kill her after—after what? After whatever else he had planned for her.

Her soulful grey eyes reminded Blake of rainclouds, especially when two large raindroplike tears escaped to run unchecked down her cheeks. "Are you going to kill me?" she asked in a small voice that tore at his heart.

Blake hardened himself to her quivering lips and shimmering eyes. "Not tonight," he said gruffly, "so don't let it affect your appetite."

"What a cold, unfeeling beast you are! Your parents must be so proud to have a low-down snake like you for a son!" The words were out of Megan's mouth before she was aware even of thinking them.

If she'd thought him cold before, it was nothing compared with the look that came over his face at her words. His face hardened until the skin stretched tautly over his cheekbones and strong jaw. Those taunting, generous male lips thinned to a slash below flared nostrils. His eyes, such a warm blue before, were no more than cold, hard agates, sparkling with anger and contempt, icy as death. Fear shivered through her as he continued to glare at her through narrowed lids.

"Lady, you sure don't have much instinct for survival, do you?" he growled at last. When he leaned toward her, Megan jumped visibly. Laughing harshly, Blake picked up her fork and speared half an egg at one swipe. His calloused fingers wrapped themselves about her trembling jaw. "Don't say I didn't warn you." Prying her mouth open, he shoved the forkful of food between her lips, clamped her jaw shut, and ordered, "Chew, damn you." His blazing eyes dared her to defy him.

Half crying, half choking, Megan struggled to do as he bade, silently cursing him for the devil he surely was. During the next few minutes she somehow managed to swallow each man-sized offering Blake forced into her mouth. When he was satisfied that she had eaten enough, he put a cup of strong black coffee before her. "Do you think you can manage to drink that for yourself, or should I pour it into you?"

"I—I'll do it," Megan stammered. The first sip

of the steaming brew burned her tongue, but at least it was dissolving the lump of food still lodged in her throat. With luck, she wouldn't further humiliate herself by being sick all over the cabin.

Blake stacked the dirty dishes on the side counter. "There are some things I have to tend to outdoors. I suggest you use the time to wash up a bit. When I return I expect to find you undressed and in bed." Seeing the defiant look that met his command, he shook his head and smiled wearily. "Yes, Megan, you will sleep next to me in the bed, and not in all those layers of clothes women think are so necessary. I would hate to have to destroy the only clothing you have, but I will tear them off your back if I have to. Then what would you wear?"

Speechless as she was with anger and humiliation, he was gone before Megan could think of an appropriately scathing retort. She stood in the center of the cabin, a million thoughts whirling in her mind like a caged squirrel. She was across the room before she knew what she was doing. A low snarl brought her up short at the doorway. What little color remained in her face now drained away completely as she faced the huge wolf. "Oh, God!" she moaned, backing up slowly, her heart threatening to burst through her ribs as it thudded frantically.

Several more minutes passed as she debated what to do. Small, frightened whimpers escaped her trembling lips as she tried desperately to think, but no plan came readily to mind. Reluctantly, with suddenly awkward fingers, Megan unbuttoned her dress. She folded it carefully and laid it across the rocker, thinking that Blake would most likely have been cruel enough to rip it apart. She thought of all the clothes she had packed for the journey, all neatly packed in her trunk. Even now, her precious apparel would have arrived in Tucson with her parents and the stage. Little good the pretty dresses would do her now, hidden away in the mountains by an outlaw, guarded by a ferocious wolf!

Megan removed her shoes and stockings, thinking that she would have to launder her things sometime tomorrow, if Blake would allow her the privacy to do so. Otherwise, she would wear her soiled clothes until they rotted off of her, she thought rebelliously. Padding to the bowl of cool water, she found the cloth and sliver of soap Blake had left and proceeded to wash away the dust and grime of the long day.

As she finished washing, she spied the knife lying on the shelf. It was a long kitchen knife with a sharp curved blade, the kind used for everything from slicing bread to carving meat. Almost holding her breath, Megan picked it up, testing the eight-inch blade with her thumb. It was sharp, surely long enough and sharp enough to kill a man. Megan tried not to let the immorality of what she was contemplating bother her as her fingers curled around the notches in the well-worn handle. She had every right in the world to protect herself, didn't she?

"I wouldn't even think about it if I were you." Megan jumped as that smooth, deep voice sounded behind her. Whirling about, the knife clutched tightly, she faced him defiantly.

He stood just inside the door, not half a dozen paces from her. From all appearances, he was not overly concerned to find Megan holding the wicked weapon. Only the alert indigo eyes belied his casual stance. Once more Megan wondered how such a devastatingly handsome man could be a criminal. He should have been ugly as sin, as ugly as his hard black heart, as physically twisted as his evil mind.

At least his ebony hair matched his devilish soul. It fell now in damp midnight waves about his nape and forehead, one dark lock curling boyishly over his wide brow. His nose was razor-straight, with a noble look about it that went well with the high cheekbones that lent intriguing shadows to his lean face. The well-shaped lips were twisted slightly in a cynical smile, but not enough to entirely disguise their naturally sensual curve. Nor did they hide his straight white teeth. Then there were those piercing blue eyes. Those fascinating, knowing, twilight-blue eyes, fringed with thick black lashes that either highlighted or hid his thoughts according to his moods. Lines fanned out from the outer edges. Megan could not decide whether they were laugh lines or were merely caused by constant squinting into the bright Arizona sun.

Megan's gaze shifted away from his, seeking relief from his unrelenting stare, but relief was not to be hers. Now her eyes fell on his shirtless chest, covered only with a dark cloud of swirling black hair that tapered down into a line that bisected his hard stomach and disappeared beneath the waistband of his trousers. Beyond the nest of hair, Megan could see the muscles that banded his chest, broadened his shoulders, narrowed his waist. His skin looked so hard, yet so smooth. Megan guessed he must spend a lot of time outdoors without his shirt, for his chest and stomach were as dark as his tanned face. Goodness, but he was beautiful! But if the Bible were true, so was Satan.

"Trying to decide where to set the blade, Megan?" Blake's taunting words brought Megan's gaze jerking up to his. A hot blush stained her cheeks. In all truth she had been reluctantly admiring his blatantly masculine form, and she wondered if he knew this.

Swallowing hard, Megan shook her head at him, brandishing the knife. "Don't come any closer or I swear I'll use this knife on you."

"I don't think you have the guts, Megan," he told her calmly. "It's not quite the same as carving the Christmas turkey, you know. When you knife another human being, it does something to you. You feel the blade entering the body, tearing skin and scraping bone. You hear the agony you are causing; you see the blood spurting out of the wound, all over your victim, and if you are close enough, all over you as well. You see it and you smell it, as you smell the fear and see the pain of the person you are harming. It's not a pretty thing, Megan."

He took a step toward her, then another. "Give me the knife, Megan, or prepare to use it if you can." Another step, and he reached out his open palm for the knife.

"Stop!" she sobbed. "I mean it!" Blindly she slashed at his outstretched hand.

Drawing back a bit, he eyed her warily now. He could see the desperation in her eyes, making them wild and stormy. He could see the fear that was

making her act so rashly. Though he could have
used his superior strength against her, could have
knocked the knife from her shaking fingers within
seconds, he wanted her to give it to him voluntari-
ly. Just why he needed to have it this way, he didn't
know, but the feeling was there, too strong to be
ignored. Again he tried to reason with her.

"Megan, if you managed to wound or even kill
me, what good would it do you? Lobo would not
allow you out of the cabin. You would be stuck
indefinitely in the same room with a dead or dying
man." He saw an involuntary shiver go through her
and knew she was listening to his words. "Eventually you would die of thirst, if you didn't go completely mad first."

"Someone would come," she said shakily.
"Someone would find me."

"Not necessarily. This cabin is very isolated.
Besides, by the time you were found, Lobo might
have gotten to you. Animals sense death, and he's
very loyal to me. If he thought you had hurt me, he
would find a way to get in here. He would literally
tear you to pieces, and that's not a death I would
wish on anyone. Think, Megan. Think hard before
you try using that knife on me."

Again he held out his hand for the weapon. A
sob tore from her throat as she weighed all that he
had told her. Was there no way to win, no way to
escape this dark-haired demon? With a weary sigh
of defeat, Megan silently placed the knife in his
waiting hand. Tears streamed down her face, and
she bowed her head beneath the weight of her
misery. Her delicate shoulders shook with her
unsuppressed sobbing. Small white teeth bit into

her quivering lower lip as she awaited sure reprisal for her attempted rebellion.

A silent sigh of relief rippled through Blake at Megan's surrender, reluctant though it was. For a few minutes, he'd thought she was going to continue to defy him. He couldn't truly blame her for trying. For such a tiny thing, she had a lot of courage, and he found himself admiring that despite himself. Kirk's fiancée was turning out to be quite a handful; certainly not the docile female Blake had envisioned when first he had mapped out this revenge.

When she had stood before him, knife in hand, her eyes blazing silver flames, her russet hair in wild disarray, he thought he had never seen such a beautiful woman. His throat had gone dry, not in fear, but in desire, as he'd seen her breasts thrusting against her lacy petticoat, threatening to spill over the tops of their thin restraints with each agitated breath she took. Her quivering lips had been almost more than he could resist, and he had wanted desperately to quell their trembling beneath his.

Even now, her head bent before him, her face red from crying, he wanted her. Damn! This was not the way it was supposed to be when he had so carefully planned her abduction. He hadn't planned to feel such a burning desire for her, such admiration for her dewy beauty. God! He was actually feeling protective of her. What a joke! The abductor feeling protective of his victim! He even found himself wanting to protect her from himself! He applauded her courage, found himself looking forward to her next display of spirit, even though it made his self-appointed task harder. If he had known she was going to prove so stubborn, he would never have kidnapped her. In fact, he was sorely tempted, even now, to return the little spitfire to her parents and find another way to get at Kirk. Before all was said and done, Blake was afraid she might turn out to be more trouble than she was worth, especially if he could not keep a tight rein on these rampant longings he felt toward the lovely minx.

Blake deliberately made his voice hard as he told her, "Get to bed. I am going to bank the fire, and then we are both going to get some sleep. With any luck at all, you won't be half the trouble asleep that you are awake."

Hope and despair warred in her soft grey eyes, her gaze anxiously searching his for reassurance he did not give. Swallowing her trepidation, Megan inched her way toward the bed. Once under the covers, petticoat, chemise, and all, she lay stiffly, her eyes wide and wary.

Blake joined her all too soon. Sitting on the edge of the bed, he proceeded to remove his boots and socks, then stood to remove his gunbelt and hang it on the bedpost. As he unsnapped his jeans, Megan's hands balled into tight fists, her eyes screwed shut, but she could not stop the sudden jerk of her body when she heard his pants hit the floor. His soft laugh only increased her mortification, sending waves of color flooding into her face.

"Scoot over, honey, or you'll make me think you are anxious for my attentions."

Megan practically flew across the bed to hug the far wall. "When cows have two heads!" she muttered.

With another nerve-grating chuckle, Blake countered, "Yeah. You know, I saw one of those at a carnival show once."

Megan could only groan in dismay, wishing she had chosen any other example of her reluctance.

"Go to sleep, Megan. I am too tired to do either of us any good tonight. Besides, deflowering virgins takes more time and patience than I possess just now." A loud yawn came from his side of the bed as he reached over and turned down the lamp.

Darkness descended on the small room, saved from total blackness only by the banked coals of the fireplace. Megan lay stiffly, listening to the man breathing next to her. Though she was almost sick with weariness, she could not relax. Her violent trembling soon set the small bed to shaking.

Blake sighed in exasperation. "Megan. I assure you, I do not intend to harm you in any way, so just relax. Your life is not in peril. I may not be the most God-fearing, law-abiding person in the world, but I am not a cold-blooded killer. Nor do I intend to rape you. Now, will you please settle down so I can get some sleep?"

Megan thought a second about what he had said, then asked tentatively, "Then what *do* you intend to do with me? Why *did* you kidnap me?"

"You'll find that out all in good time, but you have my word that as long as you do not try to escape, and do as you are told, you will come to no harm. Now hush and lie still, before I am tempted to gag you again just to get some rest."

Megan did not know why she should believe this bandit, but she did gain a small measure of comfort from his words, enough to ease her trembling. Still, long after Blake had settled into sleep, his breathing deep and regular, she lay wide-eyed and stiff.

After what seemed an eternity, she finally lost the battle and gave in to the sweet oblivion of slumber. Only then did her muscles relax, her features soften and lose their fear-filled tension. Unknowingly, she turned from the hard wall, her body unconsciously seeking the solace and warmth of another living person, uncaring that the comfort came from the very man her conscious mind would have immediately rejected. In her sleep, she cuddled nearer, and when he turned and drew her close, she nestled into his arms as if she had always done so. With a soft sigh, she pillowed her head in the curve of his shoulder and slept soundly.

While Megan slept, her parents found no such solace for their troubled souls. The posse had gone back to the place where the stagecoach had been held up, and tracked the bandits for a short way. Then they had lost the trail. As luck would have it, a strong wind had kicked up sand to cover the outlaws' tracks. The posse returned to town, downhearted and discouraged, but determined to give it another try the next day.

Kirk had taken Evan back to the ranch with him, where they found Jana waiting for word of her daughter. The discouraging news brought no relief to the woman's tormented mind. Opal Hardesty welcomed them into her home, making them as comfortable as possible, but there was little that Kirk's mother could do to ease their heartache.

Kirk himself was enraged to have his bride

stolen away, practically beneath his very nose. "We'll find them, by damn!" he promised, pounding a clenched fist on the dining table and making plates and cups jump. "We'll find them and bury each and every one of those bastards!"

"I cringe to think what Megan may be going through at their hands," Jana sobbed. "My poor little darling! Oh, how I wish you could have found them today!" Her eyes wandered to the window, seeing only darkness beyond the pane. It had been dark for several hours now, and all she could imagine was her innocent young daughter being ravaged by those beasts.

"We'll find her soon, Jana. Perhaps tomorrow." Evan's words of comfort were for himself as much as for his wife.

"Yes, but it may be too late," Jana whispered despondently, voicing the fear each of them felt.

"As long as she is alive, it will not be too late, my love," Evan assured her.

His gaze locked with Kirk's for an endless time, willing the younger man to speak. "Er, your husband is right, Mrs. Coulston," Kirk answered finally, almost hesitantly. "Nothing else is as important right now as getting Megan back alive—safe and sound."

"I agree," Opal chimed in. "We can deal with everything else as soon as we have Megan back. Why, the poor girl must be scared stiff! I just can't believe such a thing has happened! Why on earth did they take Megan with them?"

As Evan and Jana shook their heads in mute despair, Kirk said, "That is what I would like to know, Mother." His cool gaze fell on Megan's parents. "Are you positive she did not do anything to cause them to single her out, to take particular notice of her?" Kirk's voice took on an accusing note.

"Certainly not!" Jana answered heatedly, glaring at Kirk that he would dare to suggest such a thing. "My daughter is a very proper young lady!"

Opal hurried to soothe wounded feelings. "Oh, Jana, dear, I'm sure Kirk meant no offense. It is just that we can't help but wonder if she might have drawn attention to herself by a misplaced word, something that might have angered them."

"The only thing she did was try to keep the engagement ring that Kirk had given to her," Evan explained tiredly. "The bandits were arguing among themselves, and had finally allowed Jana and the other lady to keep their wedding bands, but for some reason they refused to let Megan keep her ring. I still don't understand how it occurred. Everything seemed to happen so quickly. All I know is that one of the men decided he wanted to take Megan with them, and there was nothing any of us could do about it."

"Damn!" Kirk pushed himself away from the table and stood. "That ring set me back a pretty penny, too!" At Jana's gasp, he hastily added, "Of course, I won't care if we ever get it back, as long as Megan is returned to us safely. It is just that I chose that ring for her especially."

Evan's angry glare narrowed on the younger man, wondering once again what his daughter had seen in Kirk, beyond his obvious good looks. Any man who could be concerned about a ring when his fiancée's life was at stake did not deserve the woman's love. As upset as he was, Evan made up his mind to keep a close eye on Kirk. There was something that just didn't set right, here. More than met the eye. Evan was suddenly very sure he did not want Megan married to this man. If they got her back safely, he would do his best to convince her to go back to Abilene with him and Jana.

Much later, in the predawn gloom of their bedroom, having stayed awake with worry the night through, Jana confessed to Evan that she felt the same way. "I don't think Kirk really loves her, Evan. Not the way we love one another. He won't make her happy. He'll only break her heart. If we get her back, let's take her home with us."

"To tell you the truth, I think Kirk will be relieved if we do, Jana. As much as I hope otherwise, I honestly don't believe Megan will be returned to us unmolested, and Kirk doesn't strike me as the kind of man to accept a soiled bride. It will greatly surprise me if he is still willing to marry her."

"I don't care. All I want is Megan back, safe and sound—alive and well. I just don't want to see my baby hurt. Oh, Evan, we've got to find her— soon!"

Evan gathered her gently to him, his lips kissing the fresh tears from her face. "We will, love," he soothed, hoping and praying that this would be. "We have to believe that we will get her back safely."

Megan awoke slowly, her mind and body reluctant to give up the comforts of the bed. Grumbling irritably at the soft voice that urged her from her slumbers, she tried to snuggle deeper into the pillow under her head, but it refused to budge beneath her restless nestlings. When she attempted to wriggle into a new position, her legs seemed to be tangled in the bedcovers. The insistent voice called again, close to her ear, and Megan shook her head. "Go 'way," she mumbled sleepily.

Her pillow jiggled beneath her head. "C'mon, sleepyhead. Wake up," a voice much deeper than her mother's chuckled. Just as Megan's confused mind was identifying the owner of the voice, he said, "You've completely cut off the flow of blood in my arm, darlin'. I know your bloodthirsty little heart loves the thought of giving me pain, but could you take pity on me until after breakfast?"

Megan's heart nearly stopped altogether. Dreading what she would see when she opened her eyes, she took a deep breath and peeped out from under her eyelashes. The first thing in her sight was a section of tanned, hairy chest, rising and falling before her bleary gaze, the dark, curling hairs so close they tickled her nose. Hoping to avoid meeting his avid blue eyes just yet, Megan's gaze drifted lower, past his ribs, the hard, flat stomach. With a raw gasp of surprise, she acknowledged her mistake when she suddenly realized that the covers were down around their knees, and Blake evidently did not believe in modesty. He was completely nude. Megan was mortified. She had never seen a man without clothes before. Worse, she instinctively knew from that one brief glance that Blake was aroused.

Just when she was sure she would die of embarrassment, she realized that her petticoat had ridden up in her sleep and was now wrapped about her waist. The only thing that saved her from being completely exposed to Blake's view was the lacy chemise she wore beneath the petticoat. As if that were not bad enough, their legs were intimately entwined. A low moan of acute embarrassment escaped her lips.

"Kind of surprised me, too, to find you wrapped around me like a vine on a tree." Blake's wry comment brought her head up. For countless seconds, their gazes locked, amused blue holding shocked grey eyes prisoner. Then the laughter faded from Blake's eyes, his face tilting down to block all else from her view. His warm breath whispered across her lips a mere moment before his mouth captured hers.

The kiss was not at all what Megan would have expected from her arrogant abductor. It was soft, and sweet, his lips warming and seducing hers. The touch of his tongue was like a hot brand upon her lips, but when she would have drawn away, the arm beneath her neck curled tightly, preventing her from withdrawing from his embrace.

His lips teased at hers, his tongue tracing the curve of her lips, tasting, licking like a hot flame. "Let me in. Let me taste your sweetness." The soft, seductive tones were an invitation that Megan, in her innocence, could not refuse. Her senses already spinning, her lips now parted as with a will of their own.

His tongue investigated the warm cavern of her mouth, the sharp barrier of her teeth, then teased and taunted her tongue, until hers also moved, touching and testing in a tentative venture of her own. Had she been capable of thought, Megan would have been shocked at her boldness, but she was beyond thinking, existing totally on feelings. Wild yearnings such as she had never before experienced were assaulting her. Her heart was fluttering madly in her chest, like a captive bird, and there was a crazy quivering in the pit of her stomach. Fire curled through her veins, a wildfire that melted her bones, yet at the same time caused a tight burning between her thighs.

Blake's hand came up to gently cup one of her breasts through the soft material that shielded them from view. Instinctively her hands flew up to stop his, her fingers curling about his strong wrist. His hands caught hers, carrying them to his chest. "Touch me, Megan. Feel my heart beat. It's going crazy for want of you."

Megan's fingers threaded through the springy mat of hair. Then she was caressing him, loving the tickle of the dark curls against her palms, the hot satin skin beneath her fingertips. Her nails scraped lightly across the small male nipples, feeling them bud against her touch. Blake groaned in desire, the sound new and exciting to her.

When his hand caressed her breast with a touch as light as a butterfly's wing, Megan's moan blended with his. No longer did she think to resist him, or the strange and wonderful feelings he was eliciting. She barely knew it when he tugged the straps of her petticoat and chemise down to bare her breast, until his lips left hers to wrap about her pouting nipple. The gentle tugging sent a shaft of longing spearing through her most intimate parts, confusing and delighting her all at once. Her breath came in short pants, and she was sure she would faint at the hot pleasure coursing through her. In a move as old as Eve, she arched into him, glorying in the feel of his lips on her breast, his flicking tongue on the sensitized tip. At the juncture of her thighs, a liquid warmth was building as Blake continued his seductive assault on her untried body.

As his hands caressed her, charting the dips and curves of her slim figure, Megan's hands were on a journey of their own. Her fingertips were learning the feel of him, her hands measuring the breadth of his shoulders, her fingers kneading the muscles of his back and following the indentation of his spine. As she floated on a cloud of sensual pleasure, her fingers came up to sift through the dark hair at his nape, unconsciously holding his mouth to her breast.

It wasn't until his hand drifted up the sensitive skin of her inner thigh that Megan's hazy bubble of desire suddenly burst. Just as eagerly as she had held him, she now fought to push him away. "No! No! Oh, God, don't do this!"

Blake's head came up with a jerk, a look of sardonic disgust darkening his features. "I wondered how far the 'nice girl' would go until she decided to call a halt. Now I know." A ragged sigh tore through his chest. "You know, Megan, I can't decide whether you are an accomplished tease or an untaught virgin with a seductive siren locked away inside just aching to be let loose." Without waiting for an answer, Blake pushed her aside and rose from the bed. Tugging on his jeans, he ordered briskly, "Get up and get dressed, before I change my mind and decide to force my attentions on you whether you want them or not."

Her face averted, Megan tugged the straps back over her shaking shoulders. Shame colored her face as she thought how close she had come to losing her innocence to this villain, this dark bandit. How could she have melted in his arms as she had? How could she have submitted to his touch and felt such intense pleasure from those sneering lips and rough hands? She had a fiancé waiting for her, undoubtedly worried to death about her. She was promised to Kirk, whom she loved dearly, yet she had almost given herself to this rough stranger, with not a thought in her head of Kirk. She had thought only of the hot desire burning through her, only of the rapture of Blake's kisses, the promised ecstasy of his caress. Even now, in the midst of counting her blessings over a narrow escape, her body was trembling more with unfulfilled longing than with shame or fear.

Her troubled gaze shifted to Blake, now busying himself with building a small fire in the fireplace. How could she have responded to him so readily? What kind of woman was she to fall so easily into her captor's arms? True, he was a handsome devil, but a devil nonetheless. What kind of demon's spell had he cast over her, to make her act so boldly? What magic did he possess in those fascinating sapphire eyes, that smooth-as-whiskey voice, those wonderfully wandering hands of his? How had he managed, in a few hours, to overcome the morals and teachings of a lifetime, to breach barriers that no man, not even Kirk, had dared to cross?

Blake's voice cut into her worried musings. "See what you can do about some breakfast, while I get some fresh water for the coffeepot."

"I'm not your slave," she retorted sharply, her nerves severely frayed.

Blake noted the stubborn tilt to her chin. So she was back to being the spitting kitten so soon after nearly purring in his arms, was she? "I make the rules around here," he reminded her sternly. "Right now you can either take care of my needs in the kitchen, or in the bed. Take your choice."

Her eyes shot frozen fire at him. "You are despicable!"

"I'm a lot of things, but right now I'm hungry, so get your backside over here and start breakfast."

"I can't cook," she bluffed.

"Then I suggest you learn real quick, or I'll be teaching you more interesting things than how to fry bacon and eggs." Blake turned his back to her and walked toward the door.

A few steps brought her to the kitchen area of the small cabin. She didn't think twice before grabbing a plate and sailing it toward his hard head. It crashed into the doorframe inches from his head. "God, you're a witch in the morning," he said with a maddening grin.

"Brute! Beast!" she countered, sending a crockery bowl after the plate.

Shielding himself behind the open door, Blake chanced a glance at her. "That reminds me, fix a little extra for Lobo, will you?"

The iron skillet sounded like a gong as it hit the door. "I am not feeding your blasted animal! And the only way I'll cook for you is if I can find some arsenic to add to your food! And I'll be damned for all eternity before I let you touch me again!"

Between her rantings, she heard him say to the wolf, "The woman's mad about me, Lobo, simply wild for me." Megan's answering furious scream nearly shook the rafters.

4

After the rousing encounter with Megan in bed that morning, Blake took his time cooling his blood in the stream before returning to the cabin. Lobo was on guard to see she didn't go anywhere. Besides, it would give Miss Megan the opportunity to simmer down a bit herself. Lord, but the girl had a temper! Blake's ears were still ringing from the clang of the frying pan hitting the door behind him. When he finally returned to the cabin, Blake was not surprised to find Megan fully dressed and sitting in the rocker by the window, sulking. Neither was he surprised that she had not lifted a finger to prepare breakfast. Blake chuckled to himself. The lady was stubborn to a fault, but he had his own ways of dealing with Megan's sort of mutiny.

Saying not a word, Blake set about putting a pot of coffee on to brew. The aroma wafted through the small cabin, and when it was done Blake calmly poured himself a cup. Seating himself on one of the chairs at the table, he took out his knife and began whittling on a chunk of wood. Whistling softly to himself and ignoring Megan as if she did not exist, he waited.

Long minutes went by. From the corner of his vision, Blake saw Megan cast him several curious glances. Finally she rose and walked softly past him to where he had left the coffeepot warming over the fire. "Just what do you think you are doing?" he asked tersely, his voice shattering the silence and Megan's tense nerves at once.

Though she hated herself for it, Megan could not prevent her startled jerk at his words. Her chin came up defiantly. "It should be obvious. I am pouring myself a cup of coffee."

"No, you're not."

"I beg your pardon?"

"You can beg my pardon all you want, but I made the coffee and I am drinking it. Keep your fingers off it."

Megan faced him, hands balled into tight fists at her sides. "First you force me to eat when I don't want to, and now you deny me a cup of coffee. I do wish you would make up your mind, Mr. Montgomery."

His smile was downright demonic. "After our intimacies of this morning, couldn't you call me Blake?" he taunted smoothly. Before she could think of a properly scathing retort, he continued, "It is not *my* mind that needs deciding, but yours. When you get it into your stubborn head to behave and follow orders, things will go much better for you. If you had made breakfast as I told you, both of us would be eating. As it is, I had to make the coffee, and I will be the only one drinking it. Do you understand now, Megan?" His hard blue eyes stared into hers mercilessly.

Megan glared back at him, determined not to let him see how badly she was shaken, not only by his relentless attitude, but by his crude reference to that disastrous episode this morning. "Then I will fix my own coffee," she said with a saucy shake of her head, "and my own breakfast."

"Unless you've decided to fix my breakfast as well, you can forget it," he told her with an irritating superior smile.

"That's blackmail!" she exclaimed, forgetting her vow to herself not to let this ruffian rile her further.

Blake held back a chuckle, thinking she reminded him of a banty hen with her feathers ruffled. "What do you expect from a bandit? Those are my terms, and they are not negotiable. When you decide to follow orders, then you can eat. Sooner or later, Megan, you are going to get very hungry; and sooner or later you *are* going to cook for me. Besides," he reminded her, his eyes twinkling with wry humor, "I thought you said you didn't know how to cook. What had you planned to fix for your breakfast, or were you lying to me before?"

"Oh, just forget it! I'd rather starve to death than cook for you!" Megan stomped back to her rocker and threw herself into it. Another long span of silence reigned in the cabin, broken only by Blake's random, off-key whistling, which only served to irritate Megan all the more. Her stomach rumbled in hunger, but she wrapped her arms about her waist and tried her best to convince herself she was not at all hungry. However, the longer she sat there, the more desperate she became. Her traitorous stomach growled again, so loudly that Blake glanced up from his whittling, sent her a devilish wink beneath a cocked brow, and asked with a wide grin, "Did you say something, Megan?"

Megan thought she would sooner die than talk to that overbearing man.

Blake watched her and grinned openly. For a while he thought the stubborn chit would sit there until her stomach grew fast to her backbone rather than give in. He was tempted to fry a couple of eggs for himself just to tantalize her with the odor of cooked food. Instead, he bent his head over the wood he was whittling and waited for the inevitable.

"Uh, Mr. Montgomery." Her voice was so soft as to be almost inaudible. Blake pretended not to hear.

Clearing her throat, she tried again. "Mr. Montgomery."

When he failed to respond, she nearly shouted. "Mr. Montgomery!"

"If you want something from me, my name is Blake."

Megan was ready to explode, in more ways than one. Loathing herself and him, she forced her temper down. "Blake," she said quietly.

"Yes?"

"Was there something special you wanted for breakfast? I really am a very poor cook."

"Anything you can manage to fix will be fine," he assured her. Then he added for good measure, "Just don't forget to fix a portion for Lobo." The utter look of loathing and the mumbled oaths she threw his way as she retrieved the skillet from its resting place near the door convinced him it might be prudent to leave Megan alone to her cooking, before she tried once again to flatten his skull with the frying pan.

Blake gazed in dismay at the black lumps on his plate that resembled charred wood more than any recognizable food. It had been a mistake to leave Megan alone to her cooking duties, for he had come back to a cabin filled with smoke. Now she had the gall to present this mess to him and call it breakfast.

"Woman, what the devil do you call this?" he bellowed. "It certainly isn't anything edible!"

It was Megan's turn to hide a triumphant and slightly evil smile. "I told you I couldn't cook, but you wouldn't listen. Anyway, if I could eat it, it's not that bad. Go ahead. It won't kill you— unfortunately."

"I wouldn't bet on that," he retorted, eyeing his plate uncertainly. His glance veered to Megan's plate, empty except for a few remaining crumbs. "First tell me what it is supposed to be, since I don't recognize anything on my plate."

"That," she said, pointing to several long black strips, "is your bacon. Those are fried potatoes—"

"Fried, or charred?" he asked, wrinkling his nose. In truth, they *did* look like a heap of ashes.

Even Megan had to admit it, if only to herself. Luckily, Blake had stayed outdoors long enough for her to cook the breakfast, hurriedly eat her own well-prepared and delicious portion, and thoroughly burn what remained. Actually, Megan was considered a wonderful cook, having helped her mother prepare meals for their hotel guests for years. She would withstand torture before revealing that fact to Blake, however. She would not willingly do him any service. If she had to suffer, then let him suffer a bit, too. Even a little revenge was better than none, and it was doing wonderful things for her sagging morale.

She watched almost gleefully as he speared at a decidedly rubbery egg. It defied his fork and slithered off the plate and onto his lap. "Damn! If you hadn't cooked it to death, I'd almost swear this thing was alive." With a grimace, Blake plucked the offensive, greasy blob from his pantleg and flopped it back on the plate. "These, I suspect, are your attempt at biscuits," he muttered as he hefted what resembled a sooty rock. The thing weighed a ton. He shot her a suspiciously sickening smile. "Making your own weapons, Megan?" he sneered. "The army could use these for cannonballs with no problem, I'm sure."

Megan swallowed a snicker and managed a properly hurt look. "There is no reason to be so snide, Blake. I tried my best, and all you have done is criticize my efforts."

"All right, all right! Don't fly into tears!" With a valiant effort he mouthed a forkful of the potatoes, only to begin choking as he tried to swallow the awful stuff. He promptly spat it back onto the plate.

His eyes shot blue blazes at her as he carried the plate to the porch and gave the entire mess to the dog.

"Here, Lobo. I believe this is what is known as a burnt offering," he grumbled.

As Blake and Megan looked on, Lobo sniffed once at the charred food and promptly turned his back on it. "Good Lord, the dog won't even eat it," Blake exclaimed in irritation. "He's smarter than I am. He didn't even taste it!"

"He looks smarter than you do, too," Megan choked out unwittingly.

Blake wheeled on her, his eyes snapping angrily. "What did you say?" he demanded in a soft, threatening tone.

Megan sobered instantly. "Nothing. I didn't say anything! Honestly!" She gulped once and stepped back as Blake stepped toward her, then sighed in relief as he stalked past her to the fireplace. Not a word passed between them, though Blake threw her several disgusted looks as he prepared a decent meal for himself and ate his long-delayed breakfast.

When he had appeased his hunger, Blake tilted his chair back on its hind legs and calmly rolled a cigarette. "Tell me about your fiancé," he said finally. The intense look in his inky-blue eyes belied his conversational tone.

A startled, wary look crossed her fair features. Recovering quickly, she glowered at him. "I will not discuss Kirk with you. You aren't fit to clean his boots."

Blake hid his annoyance well, only a slight hardening of his jaw line showing his annoyance. "Is that so? Well, why don't you tell me what it is about him that makes him so much better than me?

Maybe I could model myself after him and become a better person. Don't you want to see me reform, Megan? Don't all women want to change what they feel is wrong about a man? Isn't it your Christian duty or something? Some unwritten law of womanhood since the time of Eve? Even she, though God had done his best work, thought Adam was imperfect. She thought Adam was a bit dull, so she took it upon herself to offer him a bite of that infamous apple and liven things up in Eden. Isn't there a little bit of Eve in you, Megan? Aren't you even a little bit tempted to try to make me see the error of my ways?"

He was taunting her again, and they both knew it. Still, there was a bit of truth to his words, and Megan began to wonder if it wouldn't be possible to get Blake to see how wrong he was to hold her hostage. Perhaps, if he had any conscience at all, she could make him feel guilty enough about his crimes to set her free, if not turn himself in to the law. It was worth a try. Almost anything was worth a try, if it resulted in her freedom.

"Come on, Megan," he wheedled. "Tell me about this man of yours. What is there about him that made you decide to marry him?"

"Kirk is a very nice person," she answered stiltedly. "He's kind, and thoughtful, and he respects me."

Blake rolled his eyes toward the ceiling and groaned. "So far he sounds dull as hell."

"You ought to know!" Megan retorted sharply.

Those sea-blue eyes narrowed suddenly. "Why do you say that?" Blake asked, a distinct edge to his deep voice.

Megan blinked in confusion, but refused to be

cowed by his look. "Well, if you're not the devil, you're his brother, and if anyone should know if hell is dull, you should."

Blake's features relaxed slightly. For a minute there he had thought that Megan knew more than he had suspected, that she knew he was Kirk's cousin, but she was just being her usual sassy self. He awarded her a crooked smile, his teeth flashing white in his tanned face. "Touché! Pray, tell me more of this fellow's virtues."

"He's very handsome. He loves me, and I love him."

Dark eyebrows arched sardonically. "Oh, handsome, is he? Does he have all his hair and teeth? Is that what makes him so appealing?"

"Of course, he has all his teeth and hair! He's not some old codger. Kirk is only twenty-three." Megan shot Blake a look much like a schoolmarm would give an extremely dense student.

"Is he tall? What does he look like?"

"Why all the curiosity about Kirk?" she wanted to know.

"Just curious about the competition," Blake answered with a smooth smile.

"The competition?" Megan was mortified that her voice came out in a raw squeak.

The leering look Blake sent her way was deliberate. He couldn't seem to keep from teasing her. "Of course, Megan. Don't women like to discover everything about the women their men knew before them?"

Megan's look was distinctly distrusting. "I can't really say, but I think this conversation has gone quite far enough."

Blake shrugged. "If you don't care to tell me more, I suppose we can find a more interesting way to pass the day." His glance cut to the unmade bed in the corner, then back to her reddening face. "Are you sure you wouldn't like to tell me all about this Kirk fellow? I believe you were about to describe his many physical attributes, my dear."

Taking the unspoken threat to heart, Megan continued. "He is not quite as tall as you, I suppose, though almost. He has light blue eyes and brown hair, even features—" As she spoke, she couldn't help but compare the man across from her to Kirk. Blake was tall and tan, with straight white teeth and a devastating, if teasing, smile. His shoulders were unbelievably wide, topping a broad, hair-matted chest. Yet he was not fat or flabby anywhere. He had a trim waist and hard stomach, and long, muscled legs. His arms, she had noted that morning, were banded by work-toughened muscles, and his fingers were long and lean. She'd never seen anyone with hair as black as his, so dark that it gave off blue highlights when struck by the sunlight.

Unaware that Blake was eyeing her curiously, or that she had stopped talking, she continued her study of him. Like Kirk, his features were even, except for the hint of a dimple in his left cheek. However, where Kirk was so stunningly handsome as to be nearly unbelievably perfect, Blake's handsomeness was of a rugged, rougher sort. If Kirk's face held the smooth, precise beauty of a statue carved of fine marble, Blake's might have been hewn out of granite, with that proud straight nose, those prominent cheekbones, and those faint lines fanning out from the corners of his eyes and around his mouth. His was an arresting face, made more so by the thin scar running over his left cheekbone and upward toward his temple, contrasting lightly with his tanned skin, and adding to the strength of his features.

If she had thought Kirk's eyes an unusual shade of blue, Blake's were still more striking. Looking into Kirk's eyes had been unsettling at times, like gazing into pale blue frozen pools. Blake's were a deep, dark blue, almost indigo. They reminded her of the color of new denims, or the blue background of the stars in the American flag. She'd seen them snap in anger, shooting hot blue light. She'd seen them sparkle with amusement, and soften to blue velvet when he had trapped her beneath him in the bed. Now those eyes were studying her with open merriment, almost as if he had been divining her private thoughts of him, and Megan could not prevent the hot blush that stained her cheeks a flaming pink.

"Lost in thought, sweet Megan?" he asked softly. "Now I wonder what thoughts could bring that flush to your face? It's really very becoming."

His remark about her appearance made Megan suddenly conscious of her dishevelment. In her rush to dress that morning, she had raked her fingers quickly through her hair as best she could for lack of a hairbrush, plaiting the fly-away tresses into a long, thick braid that hung down her back. She knew she had done a haphazard job of it to start with, and now she could feel damp wisps clinging to her nape and about her face. The heat of the day, even here in the mountains, was causing wet stains under her arms, and she was embarrassed to note that her dress was badly wrinkled and in need of freshening. Beneath her dress, her undergarments clung to her skin. Both she and her clothing could stand a good washing. She cringed to think how she would look and smell after a few days of wearing the same clothes in this hot climate.

"If I appear flushed, it is undoubtedly due to the heat in this cabin," she said in answer to his comment.

He gave a slight shrug. "I suppose I'm used to it. You would be a sight cooler, Megan, if you would unbutton that dress a ways, instead of having it fastened so close to your chin that it looks about to cut off the flow of blood to your head."

"I'd be a sight more comfortable if you would give me the benefit of a bath and a place to launder my clothing—and the privacy in which to do so," she countered sulkily.

That hateful grin she was coming to know so well creased his face. "How thoughtless of me. Why, any bandit worth his weight in salt would bend over backward to anticipate your every whim, I'm sure."

"Must you be so hateful all the time? All I want is a bath! I should think it a small request to be clean. And since it seems I am to be forced to share close quarters with you, you should be grateful that I prefer not to smell."

"Stink," he corrected nonchalantly, his blue eyes twinkling once again in merriment.

"Women do not stink," she answered stiffly, her small chin jutting out at him. "Skunks stink. Fish stink. Dirty socks and old boots stink."

"So do horse manure and women who don't wash," he added, waiting for her to correct him again.

She bit her tongue in an effort not to. It seemed he always had the last word in these verbal tauntings, always managing to get the better of her, no matter how hard she tried to remain calm. "Well, do I get a bath or not?"

Levering himself out of his chair, he said, "Why not? Grab a towel and the soap and follow me."

Neat brown brows knitted above grey eyes. "Follow you?" she echoed. "Where?"

"Why, to the stream, of course. Where else? It's a mite chilly, but it gets the job done. In case it has slipped your notice, this isn't exactly a royal palace. There are no servants, and I'm not about to act as one for you, even were it possible. There is nothing around that vaguely resembles a bathtub, and if there were, you would still have to bathe in cold water, since I'll bet you can't boil water without burning it. Now, let's get going, while the sun is still high enough to dry your clothes before dark." When she hesitated, he added, "Of course, if you want to run around stark naked this evening, that's fine with me."

Megan's teeth grated together so hard she was sure he heard them. "Lead the way, Mr. Montgomery," she muttered sourly. When he failed to move, she sighed heavily. "Please, Blake."

The dark head nodded. "You're learning, honey. Slowly but surely, you are learning."

Once at the stream, she balked again. "If you refuse to leave, or at least turn your back, I shall have to take my bath with my clothes on.''

"That would be a bit awkward, wouldn't it? And I'm sure you wouldn't get near as clean that way. Since I've agreed you should be clean, I insist you do it properly. Now, do you step out of those clothes yourself, or do I remove them for you?''

"And I insist that you turn your back while I do so!'' she shouted back.

"Ha! Why should I? So you can bash my head in with a rock? I may be a lot of things, but stupid is not one of them. Besides, I'm the one giving the orders around her, in case you've forgotten.''

"At least have the decency to close your eyes.''

"Since when have you credited me with decency?'' he mocked. Still, she saw his lashes lower over those intense blue eyes, long spiky lashes that framed his eyes so beautifully, lashes that any woman would have died to own.

She had the dress off and had unlaced the front of her petticoat when Blake's voice drifted lazily to her from where he sat in the shade of a nearby tree. "Enjoy your swim, Megan, but watch out for the snakes.''

"S-s-snakes?'' A quiver raced through her entire body, and gooseflesh rose on her arms and the back of her neck.

"Yeah. You know, those long round things that slither along in the water sometimes.'' He watched her from between barely slitted lashes, nearly laughing aloud at the look on her face. Her hands froze over the laces of her petticoat, and she stood stock still. "I don't hear any splashin' yet, dumplin'.''

"I—uh—I changed my mind. Maybe I could

manage better with a bowl of hot water in the cabin. Besides, I can't swim.''

"That won't get your clothes clean. And you don't have to worry, if you stay close to shore the water isn't that deep. Even if you did manage to get into trouble, I wouldn't let you drown. Why, I'd jump right in and save you, Megan, my dove. It would be a privilege and a pleasure.'' He couldn't quite hide the laughter in his voice.

"I said I've changed my mind! I can see that there is more than one kind of snake lurking here, and I don't trust either one of them any farther than I can spit!'' Megan had grabbed up her dress and was beginning to tug it back over her head. Through the rustle of the cloth, she did not hear him approach and was unaware of his presence until she felt his arms band about her, trapping her own arms above her head, securely caught in the cloth of her dress. Then she was being lifted into the air.

"You are going to bathe, Megan, and in the stream.'' With no further warning, he threw her into the stream, clothes and all.

It was a miracle that she found her footing so soon; another miracle that she managed to stand up and struggle out of the confines of the sleeves that bound her arms. Standing waist deep in the clear, cold water, her hair tangled and streaming in dripping strands about her face, she faced him with fury written in every feature and eyes like dark storm clouds.

"You rotten, slimy, low-down, no-good weasel!'' she shrieked. "You varmint! You clod! You beast!''

He stood on the bank, laughing so hard he could barely stand, thoroughly enjoying her tirade and the sight of her, dripping wet, her thin clothing nearly transparent from her dunking. "I get the picture, darlin'. In fact, the longer you stand there, the more enticing the view becomes. I can't decide whether you look more like a half-drowned angry kitten spitting at me or a deliciously semiclad mermaid."

His blue gaze shimmered and lingered on her thrusting breasts, drawing Megan's attention to her predicament. "Oh!" she exclaimed. Slapping her hand hard upon the surface of the clear water, she splattered him, then hastily ducked down until the water came to her chin. Before she could recover even a semblance of her composure, he hollered "Catch!" and the soap came flying into the water to splash her face again.

She wiped the water and wet hair from her face to find him standing with crossed arms, gazing down at her from the bank. "Now," he said, humor still lacing his words, "I am going to sit right here and guard against snakes and such, and you are going to shimmy out of those almost nonexistent clothes and get to washing. And if you're not quick about it, I'll just have to come in there with you and do the job myself."

Megan already knew enough about him to know he would do just that. Now the hateful jackass stood there watching, making no pretense of not looking, as she glared up at him. It was a wonder the water about her did not begin to boil, so hot was her temper as she tore the clinging garments from her body and tossed them on the bank. The soap had sunk to the riverbed and she had to nudge it nearer with her foot in order to retrieve it.

"Need some help, little mermaid?" he taunted, watching her trying to maneuver the soap without having to dunk her head into the water.

"I'll manage, thank you," she spat, her grey eyes filled with silver fury. Had he not been watching her every move in the crystal water, she might have enjoyed her bath, save for the chill of the water. For as warm as she had been before, she was fast feeling numb. The mountain stream felt like ice water. Loath to leave her hair dirty, she quickly lathered it, and in her hurry managed to get soap in her eyes. As she struggled to rinse it, her arms curved above her head, she unconsciously rose partially out of the water, giving Blake an unrestricted view of her firm, shapely breasts, the rosy nipples tightly budded against the chill of the water.

On the bank, Blake groaned. Maybe this wasn't such a grand idea after all. The little witch, petite as she was, had a perfectly tantalizing figure. Her breasts were full and lovely, her waist small, her hips gently flared and tapering into ridiculously long legs for such a short woman. What was he doing sitting here inflicting himself with searing torture? At this point he was not sure which of them was enduring more—Megan having to bathe before him in angry humiliation, or him watching with hot eyes and an even hotter body. If he had any sense at all, he would be in that water with her. That, or better yet, he should just saddle up, ride like hell to the ranch, dump the little hellion off on Kirk's hands, and be rid of her. However, she was necessary to his plans, so he was stuck with her for the time being. He hoped his scheme would pan out soon, for he wasn't sure how long he could remain in such close company with the little temptress and resist the urge to take her to his bed for more than sleep.

It was torture for both of them as Megan, wrapped only in a short towel, washed her clothing and spread it out to dry in the afternoon sun. When all but her dress was dry, and most of her body clothed again, he took her back to the cabin. There he left her, guarded by the ever-faithful Lobo, while he worked off his frustration by chopping enough wood to last the next three months. As he swung the ax into the logs with a vengeance, Blake was afraid that if he and Megan had to spend too much time together, he would probably end up with more firewood than he could burn in a lifetime, and denude the mountain in the process! Later, as he washed the salt and sweat from his tired body in the icy stream, he concluded that he would also have the bluest, most shriveled skin in history, and the largest, most permanent goose bumps on record.

5

"What are you doing in here?" Opal's sudden appearance and sharp tone startled Jana, who was dusting the bookshelves in the study. The late afternoon sun streamed through the windows, and for just a second, before Opal could recover herself, Jana caught a glimpse of intense dislike and something resembling suspicion on the other woman's face.

"Oh, my! You startled the daylights out of me!" Jana exclaimed, her hand going reflexively to her throat. "I finished polishing the furniture in the parlor, and I didn't think you would mind if I dusted things a bit in here. I just have to keep busy, you see, or my mind dwells too much on Megan. I can't bear to just sit and wonder when they will find her, or in what condition."

Opal's features relaxed into an expression of sympathy. "I understand, dear. If I was sharp with you, I apologize, but no one cleans in here except me. Kirk is very particular about where things are placed in this room, since he uses it as his office."

"Oh, I wouldn't move a thing, believe me," Jana assured her, reaching out to dust another in the line of books on the shelf. "It is just that I am not used to inactivity. I clean an entire hotel full of rooms nearly every day, with Megan's help, of course." Jana's face crumpled and tears sprang to her eyes as she spoke of her daughter. "Oh, dear! There I go again!" she cried, dabbing at her eyes with the edge of her apron.

As she reached for the next book, she glanced at Opal, wondering at the woman's sudden pallor. She could understand a bit of sympathy, even regret, from Kirk's mother at the disappearance of her future daughter-in-law, but this sudden blanching for a girl she had yet to meet?

Opal's hand came forward as if to stop Jana's. Quickly she walked over and laid her hand on Jana's arm. "Come help me with dinner, if you need to do something. This old room is depressing, and in your state that is the last thing you need." She tugged at her arm before Jana could dust another thing.

Jana stepped down from the low stool she had used to reach the shelf. "I've seen worse rooms," she commented, "though I couldn't help but notice those light spots over the fireplace where pictures used to hang. It is amazing what damage is done to our walls without our noticing, until we remove a portrait or wall hanging and see how the woodsmoke has darkened the rest of the wall."

"Uh, yes . . . yes, it is," Opal stammered. "There were three pictures hanging there until recently, one of them my brother's portrait. This used to be his home until Kirk inherited it upon Mark's death. We took the pictures down to clean them, and once I'd seen how badly the walls were in need of repair, I decided not to replace the portraits until I could get new wallpaper hung in here.''

"And your brother's name was Mark Montgomery?"

Opal stiffened noticeably, her lips thinning in her bony face. "Why, yes. How did you know that? Did Kirk mention it at some time?"

"No, I just recalled something Mrs. Higgins said about this being the Montgomery place. Kirk seemed upset that she still called it that."

"It has been two years. You would think people would start thinking of it as Kirk's by now."

Jana nodded. "Didn't your brother have a wife or children of his own?" she asked.

"Mark's wife died several years before he did, and Mark never remarried. He asked Kirk and me to come live here with him, and he taught Kirk everything he needed to know in order to run the ranch after his death."

"He must have thought a great deal of the two of you," Jana remarked.

A strange look, almost a smirk, came over Opal's face. "I don't think Mark ever really knew what grand opportunities he was handing Kirk and me, or how much we would put them to use," she said in a smug voice. "Oh, well, enough talk of the past. Let's get dinner started for when the men come back. Maybe they'll even be bringing your daughter back with them." Opal put a thin arm about Jana's shoulders. "And I don't mind your helping out around the house if it makes you feel better. Just promise me you won't go into the study again. Kirk considers that his private domain and gets so upset even when I go in to clean."

Blake had worked himself into a dark mood and was not inclined to put up with any sass from Megan when it came time to fix the evening meal. "It seems, if either of us are to survive, I'll have to do the cooking. However, I have decided that you are going to learn your way about a kitchen. Therefore I am going to teach you the basics. Stand over here and watch."

He proceeded to prepare the meal, tutoring her step by step, and Megan was hard put not to laugh. He taught her how to make light, fluffy biscuits, how to fry potatoes without burning them, the correct amount of grease to put in the pan, and the proper height at which to cook various foods over the fire. He even showed her step by step how to make a decent pot of coffee. "Tomorrow I'll show you how to make a pot of stew," he promised tersely. "How any woman managed to get to your age and not learn to cook is beyond me. Didn't your mother teach you anything? How were you going to get by once you married that fiancé of yours? You'd both starve within a month. Did you think you were going to live on love?" he asked derisively.

"Hardly!" Megan retorted with a sniff. "Kirk's mother lives with him, and I imagine she can cook. Even if she doesn't, they probably have someone to fix the meals. Kirk is not marrying me for my skills in the kitchen."

Blake snorted. "Obviously! He's in for a rude

awakening if he is." More conversationally, he asked, "Have you met his mother? How do you think you'll like living in the same house with your mother-in-law?"

Megan frowned thoughtfully. "No, I haven't met her yet, but I suppose we'll get on all right together."

"And what if you don't? What if she is a real harridan, bossing you around the house all day?"

"I guess I'll cross that bridge when I come to it. I really don't see any reason why I shouldn't like her, though. From what Kirk says, she sounds like a wonderful person."

"Like mother, like son?" Blake wore that familiar smirk again. "Has it crossed your mind, dear Megan, that Kirk might be a mama's boy, and that mama might rule the roost?"

Megan speared him with a cool look of her own. "I doubt that Kirk would allow anyone to dictate to him. He runs a large ranch, and from what he has told me, he does a very good job of it."

Blake pushed back from his empty plate and proceeded to roll a cigarette. "Prosperous, is he? You wouldn't be marrying him for his money, now, would you?" he questioned dryly.

Anger colored Megan's cheeks immediately. "How dare you suggest such a thing! Besides, what business is it of yours?"

A negligent shrug barely lifted his broad shoulders. "Maybe I'm planning to ransom you to him, if he's wealthy enough. How much do you think he'd pay to have you back, Megan? How much are you worth to him, do you suppose?" Blake looked up and snagged her gaze with his, his eyes hard and cold as they assessed her face, which had gone suddenly white. "Would he exchange his wealth, would he give up his ranch for you, would he pay all he owns and beggar himself for your return?" he went on relentlessly.

"And you, Megan. Would you still love him if he hadn't a dollar to his name?"

"Of course I would! I love him! I don't care how much money he has or hasn't got." Megan's voice came out in a hoarse whisper as she stared at the man across the table.

"That is where we differ, my dear. I *do* care how much money he has, how much property. Tell me, Megan, does your betrothed love you as dearly as you seem to love him?"

"Yes!"

"Good, then it shouldn't be too difficult to get him to meet my price." A derisive smile curved his lips, and the wavering lamplight cast shadows across his craggy features and made his eyes glow like sapphires. "I'm counting on it," he added.

"Is that why you are doing this? Is that why you took me with you?"

He didn't answer, just stared at her from across the table, watching her flounder as she tried to understand. A frown creased her forehead, confusion clouding her eyes. "How could you know if Kirk were rich or poor when you kidnapped me? He might have been poor as a church mouse. What would you have done then?" A sickening thought crossed her mind. "And what if he refuses to pay?" she added in a shaky whisper.

Blake's hand rose to caress her pale cheek. "What man wouldn't pay a king's ransom to have you back, Megan? He'd be a fool! But if he refuses, I might keep you for myself for a little while. You are very beautiful, you know.''

Megan jerked her face from his touch, her eyes blazing now. "Pretty is as pretty does, my mother always says. As evil as you are, I am amazed that you aren't as ugly as sin!''

His dark head went back as he laughed in genuine amusement. "Been admiring me, Megan? I'm not a vain man, but I would have had to be blind not to notice the looks you've given me.''

A furious blush colored her cheeks. "Those were looks of pure hatred, Mr. Montgomery.''

His blue eyes captured hers in a long look. "Little liar," he taunted softly. "You are attracted to me, like it or not, just as I am to you. I want you, Megan.''

"I don't want you!" She eyed him warily as he rose from his chair to tower over her.

"You wanted me this morning.''

Megan rose from her own chair and cautiously backed away from him. "That was unfair," she argued. "I was still half asleep. You caught me unaware. I didn't know what I was doing.''

She retreated further as he began to stalk her, a determined gleam in his devilish blue eyes. "You are wide awake now, and I could still make you want me," he insisted, following her step by step about the small cabin until her progress was halted by the wall at her back.

"Never.''

"I could make you burn for me as you never have for any other man, not even your oh-so-perfect Kirk.''

"No!"

"Yes." His arms came up on either side of her to trap her where she stood. "I'll prove it to you, my little innocent. I'll make you admit it gladly before we are done."

Blake's head lowered toward hers, his hand coming up to clamp gently about her jaw when she would have turned her head. The weight of his big body trapped hers lightly against the wall, just enough to prevent her from trying to evade his touch. His fiery gaze captured hers, and for the life of her, she could not look away. She stood there, frozen, watching helplessly as his mouth came nearer and nearer. As her vision began to blur, she shut her eyes tightly, blocking out the sight of those mesmerizing blue eyes. A shock jolted through her as his warm, firm lips met hers. "Kiss me, Megan," he murmured softly against her closed lips. "Part your lips and kiss me as if I were the only man in the world for you."

When she refused to comply, he simply chuckled. Then she felt his lips trail a string of kisses along her jawline, across her cheek, her eyelids, her brow; delicate touches dropped like precious pearls upon her sensitive skin. His wet tongue traced the curve of her ear, making her shiver and gasp. No sooner had her lips parted in quivering surprise than his covered them in a quick kiss, his tongue breaching the barrier of her teeth before she could prevent it.

With her hands, she wedged a small space between them, enough to push at his broad, granite-hard chest. Her head was spinning like a pinwheel, her heart trying to beat its way out of her chest. As he continued to torment her with his sweet kisses, swamping her senses, she instinctively fought him and her own growing desire. Her body twisted beneath his in a desperate bid for freedom, her small hands attempting to push him away; but it was like trying to move a mountain—a very big, very warm and determined mountain.

A sob, half fright and half desire, escaped her passion-swollen lips. "No, Blake. No."

"Yes, my sweet Megan," he insisted, his lips at last leaving hers to chart a path down her throat, stopping at the vulnerable hollow where her pulse was racing so madly. "God, you taste so sweet," he murmured, his breath warm and moist against her trembling flesh.

Then he was brushing her hands aside as his fingers dealt deftly with the row of buttons on her bodice. Her resistance was a fragile thing, soon broken beneath his greater strength and knowing touch. Despite her weak efforts, he soon had her dress undone and the cloth pulled down over her shoulders, along with the thin straps of her petticoat and chemise.

As his lips claimed hers to swallow her objections, he stepped back briefly, only far enough to allow the confining garments to drop to her waist. With a quick jerk, he had his own shirt tugged open, and when he leaned close again, Megan gasped to feel the soft furring of his chest hair against her bare breasts.

The fallen sleeves of her dress now bound her arms to her sides as effectively as any rope, rendering her helpless to fend off the hands that rose to caress her breasts. His calloused fingers found the rosy crests and urged them to hard, throbbing pebbles, and she could not hold back the moan of deep longing.

"Do you like that, my dove?" he whispered just before his mouth replaced one of his hands and captured a pouting nipple.

"Yes," she murmured, half out of her mind with the wild fires that Blake was kindling within her. If not for his body so tight against hers, she would have fallen at his feet, so weak were her knees. She wondered that he did not go deaf from the mad thundering of her heart beneath his dark head.

Suddenly he pulled back, and she gazed dazedly at him, her eyes wide and glazed with passion. "Oh, God, Megan. I've got to have you." As he spoke, his nimble fingers pushed beneath the waistband of her clothing, and a second later her clothing lay in a puddle at her feet. "I want to feast my eyes and my lips on your sweet body."

Even if she had had the presence of mind to protest, she did not have the breath. Before she could blink, he had scooped her up in his arms. Carrying her the few feet to the bed, he lowered her to the thin mattress. Several long, drugging kisses later, he had somehow removed her shoes and stockings as well as his own clothing, and was half atop her. His long body was hot and hard over hers, his skin like an inferno.

Their gazes locked in a searing look of shared passion, vivid blue to smoky grey. Yet, just beneath that sheen of longing, Blake sensed in Megan a shred of lingering uncertainty, a tiny flicker of fear mingled with the yearning that had her trembling

so sweetly against him. Once again Blake was
reminded of a dove as he held her quaking body
beneath his. Her heart was racing against his chest;
her eyes were large misty pools in her flushed face.
Those lovely lips were now bruised with the passion of his kisses and quivering temptingly. Her
skin was like warm satin, softer even than the
feathers of the bird to which he compared her.

She blinked and the spell was broken. His
mouth swooped down to capture hers once more;
his hand skimmed along her ribcage, then on to
discover the indentation of her tiny waist and the
curve of her hip. As his tongue delved once more
into her mouth, she felt the surge of him, hot and
hard against her thigh. The knowledge that she was
soon to lose her innocence was frightening enough
to pull her back suddenly from the web of desire he
was spinning about her. With a sob, she began to
fight him, her hands pushing him away, her head
turning in an effort to evade his magical mouth, but
Blake would not allow her to escape his silken trap
so easily. His mouth sought hers, his lips sliding
over hers in sensual enticement, his tongue dueling
with hers in a fiery dance. He held her firmly to him
while she squirmed and thrashed, his mouth robbing her of her breath as surely as the chest pressed
so tightly to hers. All the while, his hands were
coursing over her body, mapping curves and swells
and discovering the delights awaiting him.

Megan's small show of defiance was short-
lived. As she once again melted beneath him, her
quivering body welcoming his touch, his hands
caressed her silken skin with infinite care. His
tongue laved her love-swollen lips, as though to

offer a soothing balm. His lips came up to kiss away
the lone tear that seeped from between her lashes,
tasting the salt of it. "Don't cry, *mi paloma*, my
little dove," he murmured softly, his tongue tracing the swirl of her shell-shaped ear. A shiver of
delight swept through her, and he held her close
and whispered, "Don't be afraid of me, Megan. I'll
never hurt you. I want only to give you joy and
beauty."

Now his lips covered hers with tender care, his
tongue gliding in soft swirls against hers. His fingers
curled about her breast, softly exploring the tex-
ture of it, and when he fondled her nipple, he did
so with near reverence. When his lips had soothed
her mouth, they moved to trail easily across her
fragile cheekbone, revisiting her ear but briefly on
their way to the fragrant flesh of her throat. His
tongue dipped into the hollow of her collarbone
with the lightest of touches, as a bee might touch a
flower to collect the treasured honey hidden there.
"*Tan dulce*," he murmured in Spanish, as if English
were too harsh a language to express this moment.
"So very, very sweet." A shuddering sigh washed
through her, reverberating against the lips lying
tenderly against her throat.

Warm lips nibbled their way across the sensitive cord in the dip of her shoulder, causing her to
stiffen slightly, not in fear, but in delightful expec-
tation. She felt his lips curve in a smile against her
tingling skin. The searing heat of his breath announced the arrival of his mouth at her breast.
Then his tongue swept out to paint the flushed flesh
with hot lava. A moan escaped her parted lips as
Megan tangled eager fingers in his dark hair,

anchoring his head to her throbbing breast. His lips gently enclosed a waiting nipple, pulling it into his mouth with a rhythmic tugging that sent waves of desire coursing through her, and she arched into his sizzling touch. He was a wizard, casting his spell upon her, and she was helpless now to resist him. When he had thoroughly captivated one breast, he turned his attentions to the other, with the most delicate, devastating touch. Her breath caught in her throat at the beauty of it, at the strange longings that assaulted her, sending hot spears lancing through her blood to melt her very bones. A tight, warm tingling centered between her legs, making her tense with sharp desire.

Pure sensation had taken hold of her body and its movements. Now she arched into him, urging him nearer still. She writhed, not to escape, but for the feeling of her body moving against his, the soft abrasion of his chest hair against her sensitized breasts. As his lips suckled her, his hand soothed and excited her all in the same sweet motion. When his fingers curved about her waist, she sighed, and tensed only slightly as his hand splayed across her taut stomach.

Not until his touch wafted across the nest of hair guarding her womanhood did she begin to panic once more. His hand grew still until her resistance melted. Blake waited for her fear to subside, then, changing course, he let his hand traverse the curve of her hip, her thigh, down to the turn of her calf. Lazily he caressed her, slowly advancing up the tender flesh of her inner thigh until his fingers at last found their goal once again. All the while, he nuzzled her breasts, whispering

love words in a mixture of Spanish and English,
telling her how beautiful she was, how delicate and
enticing, how much he desired her.

She stiffened at the touch of his fingers on her
most private feminine parts, yet her body immediately betrayed her and arched into his touch. His
fingers moved against her, caressing her hidden
button of desire, and it was as if a volcano had been
lit within her. She was lost, thoroughly enchanted,
addicted now to his touch, a slave not only to his
whims, but to those of her awakening body.

Never had she known such fire as this. Never
had she desired anything as much as she craved his
magical touch. Her body lifted into his hands with
a will of its own, opening to his adoring touch as a
flower does to sunlight. A molten wetness coursed
through the heart of her femininity, and though she
gasped to feel Blake's long, lean fingers enter her,
she welcomed even this unfamiliar invasion, for it
helped to ease the feeling of emptiness that seemed
to come with the intense desire. She cried out in
wonder and crazed longing.

"What do you want, Megan?" he urged softly.
"Tell me, sweetheart."

"I don't know," she murmured, tossing her
head restlessly, searchingly. As his fingers teased
her, she gasped, "You. I want you, Blake."

Then he was over her, replacing his fingers
with his hot, probing manhood, and once again fear
fought for a foothold. "Shh, *mi angelina*, my pet.
Be still, *querida*, and let me love you." His warm
lips came up to caress hers, to still her fears. Gently
he introduced himself into her tight body, and
when she would have tried to squirm away, he held

her tightly, his mouth capturing hers in a long, intoxicating kiss. Then, his mouth still enticing hers, he took her maidenhood in one swift, merciful lunge.

The swift, sharp pain nearly jerked her from her enchantment, but Blake was there with soft words and tender kisses to lure her back into his spell. For long moments he soothed her, until she was once more pliant beneath him. Only then did he move again within her, slowly, carefully letting her take all of him into the wet warmth of her silken cavern.

She felt him moving above her, within her, stroking and filling her with himself. Megan felt as if she were floating in a magical land of sensual delight. After that one sharp pain, there came a melting warmth. And from that warmth sprang a hot well of desire, more intense than anything he had made her feel before. She was fire, she was air, caught in a swirling storm from which she had no desire to escape. He was the sorcerer who controlled the volcano now erupting within her, controlling her as well, and only he could appease these fiery sensations that threatened now to consume her with each silken stroke of his body in hers.

Encircled within and without in the hottest of flames, she clung tightly to him in the storm he had created. Her slim fingers wound themselves into the dark hair above hers, holding his mouth tightly to hers. Higher and higher she spun, like a cyclone of pure flame, until finally, with one mighty explosion, she disintegrated into a million fiery sparks.

She cried out with the force of it, her mewling

moan blending with the deeper tones of his as he joined her on the final flaming plunge. Then her quivering, boneless body was drawn close to his and held tightly. She could feel the frantic beat of his heart that matched her own, hear his own ragged breathing, feel the trembling of the hands that soothed her sweat-drenched hair back from her flushed face.

Her eyelashes fluttered, but refused to open, her lids feeling as if they were weighted. When she tried to speak, only a long, shuddering sigh emerged. She felt his kiss upon her eyelids, his lips feathering her lashes with the airy brush of a butterfly's wing. "Sleep, my love; my lovely dove," he crooned softly. "Sleep." And once again she was powerless to disobey him.

About to round the corner of the barn on his way to the house, Evan stopped short, halted by the sound of heated words being exchanged. He recognized Kirk's voice as one of the speakers. Ordinarily he would not have stooped to eavesdropping, but after having ridden with Kirk and the sheriff's posse for the past two days, and after having heard Jana's account of Opal Hardesty's strange behavior, he was certain that something odd was going on. If it concerned his daughter or her future as Kirk's wife, Evan wanted to know what it was.

"Now, Kirk, you know I've been doing everything possible to find the girl." This from Sheriff Brown.

"Two days, Dick, and not a trace! Don't you know a tracker good enough to be able to pick up their trail? Hell fire! By the time we find her, there isn't a chance those Mexs won't have raped her, or worse. It wouldn't be so bad if I didn't have her folks here breathin' down my neck. I have a ranch to run. If they weren't here, and you were doing your job the way you should, I would have time for my own interests here, instead of galavanting all over the countryside looking for my missing fiancée, who is probably dead by now anyway."

Evan blanched at Kirk's bald statement and his heartless tone of voice. It took tremendous effort not to step forward and plant his fist in Kirk's face.

"You really sound heartbroken," Brown commented sarcastically. "I suppose you'd rather find her dead than have a sullied bride on your hands."

"It might be better, yes," Kirk agreed nonchalantly. "On the other hand, Megan is a rare beauty. I suppose that's why they took her. I might be persuaded to overlook her lack of purity as long as she isn't carrying some Mexican brat in her belly. She could still serve her purposes." The sneer was obvious in Kirk's voice, and on his face. "There are still a lot of people around here who resent the fact that I own this ranch now, instead of my cousin. My standing in the community might improve immensely if I were to welcome my soiled fiancée with forgiveness and understanding. What a kind, wonderful soul I would appear, to still take the poor girl to wife after all that has happened."

The sheriff's laugh was as ugly as Kirk's. "Such a good man, indeed! You'd just better make sure Megan's parents don't catch wind of your deeds, past or future."

"That is precisely why I want Megan found soon. The longer they are here snooping around, the greater the risk. And don't forget, Dick, I can get you fired from your job as easily as I got you hired as sheriff. Your hands aren't exactly clean, either.''

"You do that, Hardesty, and I'll spill the beans about your part in everything,'' Brown warned spitefully.

"Thanks for the warning, sheriff. Do yourself a favor, if you do decide to start talking, and pay the undertaker ahead of time. Meanwhile, find Megan.''

Evan ducked back inside the barn as Kirk walked past with an evil smirk on his face. The older man longed to go after Kirk, to pound him into the ground for speaking of Megan in such a way, but he held back. He had heard enough to know that Kirk and the sheriff were in cahoots in some mighty shady dealings. Then there was the puzzling fact that several of Kirk's hired hands were not just average cowhands.

Now, why would an honest rancher need to hire gunslingers to guard the place? Evan was angry enough to want to find out. He sure as hell didn't want his daughter to go from the hands of one band of outlaws straight into those of another. After the things Kirk had said about Megan, Evan wanted to see him pay for every misdeed he'd ever committed.

"They say eavesdroppers never hear anything good about themselves.''

The slow, drawling voice startled Evan so badly that he jumped. The color fled his face as he turned to meet the chilling stare of one of Kirk's gunmen. "How . . . how long have you been here?''

"Long enough, Mr. Coulston. Long enough.''

The gunfighter ground out his cigarette with the heel of his boot, making certain it was completely out before he spoke again. "I'd be a mite more careful who caught me snooping next time. Could be someone who'd run straight to the boss."

"And what are you going to do—?" Evan's voice trailed off as he tried but failed to recall the man's name.

"Jake Banner, Mr. Coulston, and it's been a long time since I've been in short pants. I'm no schoolboy, to run tattlin' and tellin' everything I know."

No, Evan thought. This man was hardly a boy, probably hadn't been one even when he was young. He looked as if he had grown up the hard way, and fast. Jake's face was hard, his eyes old, as if he'd seen too much of life that was ugly. Though he couldn't have been more than thirty years old, this man had probably learned lessons too rough for most men to handle. His gunbelt hung low on his hip, identifying him as the gunfighter he was.

"I don't suppose you'd explain what it is I just overheard?" Evan ventured.

Jake smiled, but even his smile was remote. "I don't reckon so."

"I didn't think so."

"It isn't any concern of yours," Jake added. "Better watch out you don't put your nose in where it's gonna get shot off," he advised.

"If it concerns my daughter and her well-being, it is definitely my business, Mr. Banner."

Jake took a moment to think about this. He came to some sort of decision and nodded. "Then Kirk's study is your best bet. Have your wife try dustin' in there some more, but warn her not to get caught at it.'' He tipped his hat. ''Be seein' you, Mr. Coulston.''

The lanky gunslinger walked off, leaving an open-mouthed Evan to ponder how Jake seemed to know everything that was going on.

6

Warm lips were caressing hers ever so gently, but ever more persuasively, drawing her inexorably from forgotten dreams into wakefulness. A calloused hand was splayed possessively across her stomach, a hard, hairy thigh slung heavily over hers. Megan's moan was half reluctance at being awakened, half response to the immediate arousal of her body to his. His hand slid upward from the smooth skin of her belly to the even silkier flesh beneath her breast, and a ripple of gooseflesh followed its path. The delicious shiver caused the rosy tip of her breast to bud out in invitation of his touch.

Blake was taking unfair advantage, and he knew it. Still half asleep, Megan's defenses were practically nonexistent. She was as yet unaware of how warmly and willingly she was responding to his caresses. Her sleep-flushed body was pliant, smooth, and inviting. He buried his lips in her neck and inhaled the warm, sweet scent of her. "So soft," he murmured, "so sweet. I could lose myself in the smell of you, little dove."

Her answering murmur was muffled, drowsy, as she drifted dreamily in that netherworld just this side of sleep. Of its own, her head twisted, granting him access to the full length of her slim throat. "Yes, *querida*," he groaned, his lips grazing the delicate length of her neck, stopping to nuzzle the tempting pulse at the hollow of her throat. "Give yourself to me, give me all of you."

The deep, husky voice was seduction itself, vibrating through her in a series of tiny velvet-sheathed shocks. In her languorous state, it was impossible to deny the commands of that voice, those hands that were even now bringing her pleasure. Work-roughened fingers brought the tips of her breasts to hard peaks of aching anticipation. The warmth of his breath announced his advance mere seconds before his hot mouth claimed one waiting breast; tugging, pulling, dragging her through dark swirling mists of sensual enchantment.

An insistent knee nudged her thighs apart, clearing the way for his invading fingers to find the intense heat of her. Her eager body arched into his touch, unconsciously seeking the pleasure it had already learned to expect from him. Slender fingers tangled themselves in his midnight hair, pressing his face closer to her breast as a moan of delight escaped her parted lips. She was awash in sensual wonderment, her breath coming in short gasps. Her flesh was alive as never before, her skin afire and sensitive beyond belief. Against her thigh his rigid protuberance burned like a branding iron.

Untangling her fingers from his hair, Blake gently guided them toward that part of him that ached for her touch. "Touch me, Megan." The words were a whispered plea. "Feel what you do to me. Feel how badly I need you."

Adrift on a cloud of pleasure, she followed where he led. Her fingers brushed softly along the turgid length of him, so hot and hard and yet so very soft to the touch, like steel encased in satin. At her tentative touch, he groaned deep in his throat. The heat of him pulsed against her fingertips as if to leap into her hand. Surprised, she would have drawn away, but Blake's fingers wrapped hers about his throbbing member. "Please. Touch me. Know me."

Again she obeyed blindly, stroking him gently, coming to know the burning strength that could seem so formidable, so threatening, yet now responded to her touch with a vulnerability that registered vaguely on her stunned senses. For even as she was sending shafts of delight spearing through him, he was firing her passions, building the blinding yearnings to an almost unbearable point with his hands and his mouth upon her blazing flesh.

Then he was over and in her, filling her, stroking her within and without, and it was too much. She felt her body gather, center itself in her most intimate regions. Tighter and tighter, she was spinning into a tight ball of need, her senses crying out for relief from this strain of pleasure that was just shy of pain in its intensity. "Blake! Oh, Blake, please!'' She wasn't sure what she was begging for, and barely aware of doing so; only certain that Blake was the one who could help her, could end this tantalizing torture, this blissful agony.

Then, suddenly, she was spinning outside of herself. She was whirling inside a rainbow, a spectacular broken prism of color that revolved about her and within her at the same time, and it was wondrous and frightening and absolutely breathtaking. And Blake was with her, holding her tightly to him, and she was glad, for without his arms about her she was sure she would fly away and spin endlessly into eternity. Unconsciously, she clung to him, digging her nails into his shoulders, scoring his back as she felt herself swirling helplessly on a cloud of glorious, giddy rapture.

Megan came to herself slowly, reluctant to give up the splendor. On a deep sigh, she let her lashes drift open and found herself gazing up into cloudless, sky-blue eyes that stared down into hers. For countless minutes they lay there gazing at one another, both breathless with the depth of emotion that passed between them, wordlessly acknowledging the rare passion they had just shared.

Before the spell could be broken, Blake's lips swooped down to gently capture hers in a long, bone-melting kiss; wanting, needing to prolong this tranquil moment. ''You are a priceless, precious treasure, *mi paloma*. A soft little dove with all the passion of a tigress.'' A final, lingering sigh shuddered through his large frame. ''Oh, little one, what pleasure is hidden in your small, delicate body! Who would have guessed it?'' His intense gaze captured hers again. ''Tell me it was marvelous for you. Tell me you felt the world fall away from under you.''

The wonder of their shared passion was still upon her, it and his spellbinding gaze combining to make the breath catch in her throat and her heart race in her chest. "It was wondrous," she breathed softly, her eyes a soft, luminous grey as she looked up at him. "It was like flying and drowning, being born and dying all at once.''

He gathered her to him and held her tightly. "Oh, Megan, my Megan. What am I to do about you now?" His voice was gruff with his emotions. "How am I to get my ranch back from Kirk? How can I let you go to him now that I know what heaven there is in your arms?''

The magic bubble had burst. He knew it as soon as the words had left his mouth; even before he felt her jerk stiffly in his arms. "What did you say?" she asked softly—too softly. When he failed to respond, she pushed at his shoulders, trying to dislodge him from over her. "Answer me, damn you! What did you just say about Kirk and *your* ranch and me?''

Blake sighed heavily and raised his head to meet her angry gaze. "Me and my damn big mouth," he muttered. "Yes, I'll tell you! I would have told you sooner or later anyway. Kirk Hardesty, your oh-so-perfect fiancé, is my cousin, much to my everlasting regret.''

Megan's eyes were round grey saucers as she gaped at him in disbelief. "Your what! Your—your cousin? My God, Blake! What kind of man are you? What sort of foul game have you been playing? Did you know—?''

"That you were his fiancée?" he interjected. "Yes, Megan, I knew all along. I staged that robbery just so I could kidnap you without Kirk knowing who was behind your disappearance. It was no spur-of-the-moment decision to take you away with me."

"Why?" Tears clogged her throat, and it was almost more than she could manage to choke out the single word. Not more than five minutes before, he had made sweet, glorious love to her, and she had felt something soften within her, as if their souls had somehow touched for the briefest of moments. Now he was telling her that he had cold-bloodedly planned her abduction. Had it also been part of his scheme to rob her of her chastity? Had he planned that all along too? Suddenly she felt doubly deceived. "Why?"

Remorse darkened his eyes and hardened the line of his mouth. "It had nothing to do with you personally, Megan," he began, only to be interrupted by her shrill exclamation.

"Nothing to do with me? Nothing to do with me! You abducted me at gunpoint, you beast! You scared heaven and hell out of me, my parents, and half a dozen other innocent persons, not to mention robbing the stage and shooting one of the drivers!" Her temper was back in full force, her eyes blazing up at him as she pounded his chest with all the force she could muster behind her small fists. "You dragged me up this mountain, bound and gagged, then let that monstrous wolf of yours frighten me out of my wits! On top of all this, you seduced me, took what rightfully belonged to my husband alone. Yet you say all this has nothing to do with me?'' Hurt and confused, she eyed him warily. ''I think you owe me an explanation, Blake. I want to know the truth. Why am I really here?''

Megan's heart felt as if it were breaking. Why she should feel so deeply, soulfully betrayed by Blake, she wasn't sure. She knew she should hate him, should despise him with all her being, but there was a tiny corner of her heart that had begun softening toward him. Perhaps it was merely because he was her first lover, the man to teach her all the wonders of her own sensual nature. Megan only knew that this man had some strange power over her. Much against her better judgment, she was fast becoming very attracted to him, had wantonly and gloriously forfeited to him the precious gift of her purity. Somehow, quite suddenly and unexpectedly, she had begun to care very deeply for him, to hope that he was not such an awful person after all. *Please let there be a good excuse for all this*, she prayed silently, needing to believe in Blake's goodness. *Please let him be able to justify himself to me*.

He told her his side of the story over breakfast, though neither of them had much appetite. ''I told you the truth when I said I intended to ransom you to Kirk. That is why I abducted you in the first place.''

''If I might interrupt for a moment, why didn't you tell me that from the start? Why all the pointed questions about my fiancé?''

''Because I needed to find out how much you knew, how involved you were in Kirk's schemes.''

''What schemes? For heaven's sake, Blake, if

anyone has schemed, I'd think it was you!" she hastened to point out.

"If you will be quiet long enough and stop interrupting, I'll try to explain it to you. The ranch your dear fiancé is passing off as his has been in my family for several generations, passed down on my mother's side. My father came into the property only through marriage to my mother, and it was to be mine upon their death. A few years ago, my mother caught pneumonia and died. Then, a little over two years ago, my father died. It was then the trouble started.

"You see, after my mother died, my father's sister, Opal Hardesty, came to live with us, bringing her son Kirk. Aunt Opal acted as our housekeeper, and Kirk helped out around the ranch.

"Kirk never did like taking orders very well, not from Dad, and especially not from me, since we are so close in age. He resented the fact that I had so many privileges that he did not. I had been sent to Europe to finish my education, spent time in Spain with relatives of my mother's, visited family in Mexico where I studied ranching with my uncles on their large cattle *estancias*. I worked on our ranch as hard and long as anyone else, learning what I needed to know to take over when Dad was gone, but I also had a lot of freedom, respect as the only son, and no real financial worries. Kirk was jealous of me, but I never found out how jealous, or how devious he and Aunt Opal were until Dad died."

As she listened, a lot of things she had wondered about were coming clear to Megan. She had wondered why a common thief, a bandit, seemed so well educated. She gathered that Blake's mother's family hailed from Mexico and Spain, and that explained the fluent Spanish that flowed so easily from his tongue. The English was a product of his father's side of the family. Kirk, with his sandy brown hair and lighter complexion, certainly showed no signs of a Latin background.

Blake had been raised, if not in the lap of luxury, then in comfort. He was obviously used to fine clothes, if his expensive black leather boots were any indication. Though not compulsively neat, he did like things in order, and he was clean not only about his surroundings, but in his personal habits. Somewhere along the line, he had learned to cook for himself, so he must not be overly spoiled, but he did like his comforts. He was also used to having responsibilities. He took excellent care of his horse, saddle, and leather goods. And he was not a stranger to hard labor, for through the cabin window she had seen him chopping firewood, and could readily testify to the hard callouses on his hands. She wondered if his hard attitude was also a product of his childhood background, of being the only son of an affluent rancher, or if this was a result of whatever had happened after his father had died. She listened carefully, watching Blake's face as well as hearing his words as he continued his tale.

"The dirt had barely been shoveled over my father's grave when the trouble began. In fact, I came home from town the day after Dad's funeral to find my saddlebags packed and on the porch, and a strange lawyer in the parlor with Opal and Kirk."

Blake shook his head in disbelief at the memory, his dark blue eyes almost black with anger and pain. "I still don't know how they did it. Somehow Opal had gotten into the safe in my father's study. She had removed or destroyed Dad's will and some other important and valuable papers he kept there. She sat there like a vicious black widow spider, a smirk on her gaunt face as she presented me with what was, supposedly, Dad's most recent will. It bequeathed the entire ranch and all its holdings to her and Kirk. I don't think I've ever been so stunned in my life as I was at that moment, or so furious. I wanted to slap that victorious smile off her face. And Kirk was standing there with such a superior attitude, a sneer plastered on his face. I did try to rearrange his face for him before I left, for all the good it did me."

"You left?" Megan asked softly, forgetting her vow to remain silent.

Disgust and deep, dark anger narrowed Blake's eyes as he recalled the events of that afternoon and those to follow. "Yeah, I left. There was little else I could do at the time. Opal and Kirk and their fancy lawyer had seen to that, all right. They knew I'd never believe their ridiculous claims. They knew just how furious I'd be, and they were well prepared. In addition to the so-called new will, Opal had a letter she said my father had left for her. She took great pleasure in showing it to me. In it, Dad claimed that I was not his son, that my mother had already been with child when he had married her. Therefore he was leaving his property to his nearest blood relatives and not to me. They also had a signed document, supposedly written up before my mother's death, in which my mother legally signed the ranch over to Dad, to do with as he wished after her death. Nowhere did it say that he had to grant the ranch to me, as her only child, though the ranch had been in her family since they had first settled it a great many years before.

"Can you even begin to imagine how I felt, Megan?" Blake's hands were clenched into white-knuckled fists as he relived that terrible time, the darkest days of his life. His face was taut with anger and sorrow, his pain reaching out to her as he told her of his trials. His agonized eyes added their own eloquent plea for her understanding, her accept-ance, her forgiveness.

"I had just lost my father, whom I adored, the man I most admired in the entire world, the person I'd always looked up to and most wanted to model myself after. And he *was* my father, regardless of what anyone says. I believe that with all my heart, and somehow I will prove it. He *was* the man who sired me, and he loved me. There is no doubt that he loved me as much as I loved him. He is probably turning over in his grave at what Kirk and Opal have done."

Blake raked trembling fingers through his hair. "I have to give those snakes credit for one thing. They certainly knew when to strike—while I was most vulnerable. I was still paralyzed with the pain of Dad's death, still numb with sorrow when they callously ripped my heritage away from me. With their wild schemes and lies, they stole my home from me, Megan. The only home I'd ever known. It is the place where I was born and raised, where I spent so many happy years with my parents, two wonderful people who showered me with more love than most boys could ever hope to know. In a matter of minutes, Kirk and his mother had stripped me of everything I held dear."

Megan reached out and touched his arm in sympathy. "What happened then?"

"I called them all a bunch of greedy liars. I told them it would be a cold day in hell when they ran me off my own ranch. I told them to take their phony papers and get off my property." Blake gave a rueful laugh. "You know what happened then? They shoved their dirty documents in my face, called in several new ranch hands I'd never seen around the place before, and proceeded to pitch my butt off the ranch. But only after they'd roughed me up some so I'd take them more seriously in the future. Oh, I fought like a madman! I managed to break a few noses and blacken some eyes before I was done, but in the end they had their way. I woke up halfway to town, tied across my saddle with the few belongings they had seen fit to pack for me. Doc Shadley barely recognized me when I crawled into his office to be patched up. My face was a bruised and bloody mess, my jaw was fractured, and I had several broken ribs in the bargain. Needless to say, I was out of commission for a few days.

"I found out later that Kirk had fired most of the hands who were loyal to Dad and me, and replaced them with men of his own. That's why no one came running to my rescue that day. Then, before I had a chance to talk to our old family lawyer, his office caught fire and the old fellow burned to death with it. And to top it all off royally,

Sheriff Willis, who had known and respected Dad since they had both come to Arizona, got killed in a gunfight a few nights later. Convenient, huh? There I was, left with no legal documents to refute their claims, no old and trusted family lawyer, and a new sheriff, who was of course a close friend of Kirk's. They had everything very neatly tied up, and Dad wasn't even cold in his grave yet.''

Megan's head was spinning trying to assimilate all this new and confusing information. Not only was it an incredible story, but she could not reconcile this new, dastardly image of Kirk with the wonderful man she had agreed to marry. She could not believe that she and Blake were talking about the same man! Unlike the volatile outlaw who now sat before her, Kirk had always treated her with the utmost respect. He was generous to a fault. He was kind and courteous, had never raised his voice to her or her parents. He seemed to think highly of his own mother. In short, he was as near perfect as she could imagine any man being. If he seemed cold at times, she had thought it was because he was preoccupied with the responsibilities of running his ranch and managing his men. If he had seemed a bit opinionated, she had reasoned that he knew his own mind, was his own man, used to giving orders and using his own judgment about things.

Bringing her thoughts back to Blake, she said, ''What did you do next? Did you go back? Did you try to fight them?''

Blake gave a short snort of laughter. ''Of course I did, legally and otherwise. Not that I had much success! There was no way I could prove that Dad hadn't written that letter, or the will. I hired a new lawyer, but whoever forged my father's hand-writing did a pretty good job of it. I could tell the documents weren't written in his hand, but to almost anyone else they looked authentic enough. Even the judge they called in thought so. There was no way to prove otherwise, especially with Phillips and all the original documents burned, and Sheriff Willis dead. In fact, there was no record left of my parents' marriage or my birth, at least not anything that would hold up in court. No dates, no names, nothing.

"I thought maybe there were some papers left in the house, in Dad's desk or somewhere, but when I tried to get back on the place, Kirk had hired some pretty tough characters to guard the ranch. They ran me off on the business end of their rifles. When I tried to sneak back one night, I got a bullet in the thigh for my efforts before I even got near the house."

"So what did you do?"

"Among other things, I went down to Mexico to my mother's family for a while. I needed time to recuperate, to sort out my thoughts, to try to find some way to get my ranch back. It's mine, and I'll be damned if I'll let that greedy son of a bitch and his devil mother weasel me out of it!" Blake's fist hit the table with a resounding thud that nearly made Megan jump out of her chair. He sent her a wry smile. "You have to understand that it is more than just a ranch to me, Megan. It is my life, my birthplace and my birthright. My heart and roots are there. I have to get it back, just as I have to prove that Mark Montgomery was my father." A tortured sigh escaped him. "I could live with being labeled a bastard, if it were true," he told her. "But it is not, and I cannot let my mother's name be besmirched in this way, nor my father's. He was a proud man, Megan—proud of me, of my mother, of himself and his accomplishments. If he were alive, he would horsewhip anyone who dared say such things about his family. I've got to prove my right, not only to the land, but to my father's name—not just for my sake, but for theirs too."

He gazed at her solemnly. "You call me an outlaw and a bandit, but Kirk is the real thief, Megan. All I am trying to do is recover what was stolen from me; my rightful name and my land." As he watched the beautiful woman before him and saw the unveiled sympathy in her eyes, he deliberately hardened his heart toward her. "I will do anything to get them back," he told her with calculated coldness. "Anything. That is why you are here."

Though Blake hated himself for having to use her, to hurt her, he told himself it was necessary. He dared not let his softening feelings for Megan make him falter from his course. He could not allow himself to care for her, for it would ruin all his plans. Nor could he afford to give in to feelings of guilt over seducing her, when he still planned to exchange her for his ranch, should Kirk agree to his demands. He had no room in his life just now for anything that would interfere with his plans of revenge, especially a woman, and certainly not this particular woman. Instinctively he felt that Megan could be dangerous, not only to his schemes against Kirk, but to his entire life and his very heart if he were not careful. And he *would* have his revenge against Kirk. Whatever it took to accomplish it, he would do. He must not let this growing attraction for Megan, these soft, warm stirrings of his heart, prevent him from accomplishing his primary mission. If he collected regrets along the way, such as he was even now feeling in regard to Megan, he would have to live with them. The rewards would surely outweigh the regrets in the end; at least he hoped so.

"You see, Megan," he went on relentlessly, "I kept track of Kirk's activities through a friend of mine, and when I heard that his bride-to-be was soon to arrive, I came up with the idea of kidnapping you from the stage and holding you for ransom. I'm sorry I had to involve you, but I saw no other choice. If Kirk wants you back, he will have to sign the deed to the ranch over to me. It is a fair exchange, wouldn't you say?" he asked ruthlessly, his eyes boring into hers. "My own land for his beloved bride?"

After hearing his side of things, Megan's attitude toward him had softened quite a bit—until his last sarcastic comments. After the lovemaking they had shared, she had thought that Blake cared for her; she had begun to think she cared for him. Now it was clear that their passion had meant little to him. He obviously wanted to be rid of her as fast as possible. She was still to be used as a pawn in his game of revenge against Kirk, as he had planned from the start. It seemed that as far as he was concerned, nothing had changed; unlike Megan, who feared that nothing in her life would ever be the same after Blake.

Her pride was hurt, and she felt wounded to

the depth of her soul—used and soiled, and casually discarded. And she was angry all over again.

"How dare you involve me in this mess! Even if everything you have said is the absolute, God Almighty truth, you had no right to take your spiteful revenge out on me. And what about the others on the stage? You robbed them. And you shot that poor driver. What about that, Blake Montgomery? What about the agony you have caused my parents? You may have been innocently robbed of your heritage, or so you say, but now you are a criminal by your own actions. Have you considered that?"

He irritated her further by giving her that great lazy grin of his, as though he were not concerned at all. "But no one knows I was involved in the robbery, Megan. Are you forgetting that? And no one will, not if Kirk and your parents want you back in good health. Only their silence will guarantee your safe return. Don't fret, though, darlin'. I'll be contacting them soon about my demands. I'm sure they'll see reason."

She hid her hurt from his sharp gaze. "And what about that band of desperados that helped you stop the stage? Are you going to tell me they were all just a bunch of upright, church-going citizens?" she shot back.

He laughed outright at this, his teeth gleaming white in his dark face. "No, Megan. They really were what they seemed to be, for the most part. There was no way I could hold that stage up singlehandedly, honey. I'm good, but not that good. It's a pity the driver was wounded, but the wound wasn't bad and Doc Shadley will have him patched up as good as new by now. Besides, I didn't shoot him. Raul did. As for the rest of it," Blake gave a negligent shrug, "such are the hazards of travel in these parts. You will note that I didn't take so much as a coin for myself. The only thing I stole that day was you."

"And you think that makes you blameless? Lord, I don't believe you, Blake! You have got to be the most arrogant, self-concerned man I have ever had the misfortune to meet!" She leveled him with the most disgusted look she could manage, her small nose crinkling and her eyes as chilled as an Arctic day.

"Perhaps not completely blameless, but enough that the law can't pin anything on me. I thought this out very carefully beforehand, Megan. When I get my ranch back, I certainly don't want a price on my head. Only you, I, your parents, and my dear greedy relatives will know my part in all this, and I'm fairly sure none of you will be saying anything. Kirk and your parents won't say anything to jeopardize your welfare, at least until they have you back. Afterward Kirk will be too humiliated to say anything, even if I can't convince him to leave the territory. And I can't see you or your parents advertising what happened. It wouldn't do to have everyone speculating too much on just what went on between you and your Mexican bandit, would it, sweetheart?"

Megan wanted more than anything to slap that sneer off his hatefully handsome face. Her hands balled into small fists at her sides with the effort not to hit him. "So it doesn't matter who gets hurt, or how badly, as long as you get your precious ranch back! Is that a fair assumption, Blake? No matter that I will no longer go to my husband as a pure woman? No matter that my mother and father are sick with worry? Three innocent victims whose lives are ruined because of your schemes against Kirk!''

"Oh, for Pete's sake, Megan!'' he scoffed. "Be realistic. Your lives have not been ruined. Temporarily disrupted, perhaps, but not ruined. As soon as you are back with your family, your lives will go on as usual, none the worse for this brief episode. Even if Kirk doesn't marry you, you will go back to Abilene and marry some other fellow. Look at it as an adventure, something to tell your grandchildren about in years to come.''

Again she speared him with that frozen look, eyes like icy grey pools. "Whose grandchildren, Blake?'' she asked in a softly accusing tone. "Yours, Kirk's, or some other man's?''

Stunned silence followed her blunt query, until Blake said with a groan, "Megan, don't do this to me.'' He closed his eyes as if to make her words disappear, or as if he were in some pain of his own. When at last he raised his gaze to hers, she thought she saw a fleeting look of regret. "Don't do this to yourself,'' he said.

"Do what?'' she challenged. "Make you face the consequences of your ill-planned revenge, your uncontrolled lust?''

"You are trying to make me feel guilty for taking you to my bed. Well, sweetheart, you wanted it as much as I did, whether you admit it or not.''

"Oh, I admit it, Blake. I won't play the hypo-crite. I'll also be bold enough to tell you I enjoyed it immensely. That, however, is not the issue here. Now I want to know what you intend to do about it, should I find I'm to have a child as a result of our . . . our—"

"Lovemaking?" he supplied.

Megan frowned. "That term implies affection, Blake. Pray tell me, how can you possibly call it lovemaking when you intend to hand me over to Kirk like an apple that still looks good on the outside but has a worm in its center? Was seducing me part of your revenge? Was it in your plans all along?"

"No." He shook his head in denial. "I never intended to touch you, Megan. I never intended to like you, to admire you, to be attracted to you." At her look of surprise, he admitted, "Yes, I care what happens to you. Yes, I desire you, but nothing can come of it. I have chosen my path, and I must see it through. You are my means to an end, the only thing I hold that might force Kirk into signing over the ranch. I can see no way to regain my land and keep you, too, much as I might want to."

Megan's chin began to wobble, and she thrust it out defiantly, determined not to cry. "Not enough, evidently."

Blake's lips thinned in an effort to stem his irritation, at himself and her and the entire situation in which they now found themselves. "Can't you see how useless it is even to discuss this? If I don't get my inheritance back, I will have nothing to offer you or any other woman. I have no land, no home, no means of supporting a family. I don't even have the right to my own name, for God's sake, so how can I give it to a wife or a child?"

"But if you get your ranch back——" she suggested hopefully.

"If I get my ranch back, I will have traded you for it," he pointed out. "When I give my word, I honor it. I can do no less and live with myself. Not for Kirk's sake," he hastened to add. "I couldn't care less about my thief of a cousin or his mother, but for my own sense of honor I *will* return you to him, Megan, if he agrees to my terms."

"And what if he doesn't want to marry me, spoiled as I am by you? What if I no longer wish to marry him? What if I am carrying your child?"

Blake groaned. They had come full circle in their discussion. "We are crossing bridges before we come to them. We can only deal with those questions as they arise. I am telling you, though, that once Kirk discovers that I am the one holding you hostage, he will do anything for your return. He has always coveted anything I had. It is in his nature; he can't help himself. That is what I have been counting on to make this plan work. Besides, he'd be crazy not to want you back." *And I am crazy even to consider letting you go,* he added silently to himself.

"As crazy as I would be to want to stay here with you a moment longer than absolutely necessary," she shot back scathingly, her heart tearing apart in her breast. "I pity any woman you might marry, Blake Montgomery," she told him spitefully. "She will be getting a heartless man who is truly wed only to his precious ranch." If it killed her, Megan would not reveal to Blake how deeply he had hurt her.

7

Guilt flooded him, guilt he had been trying to deny since awakening that morning. Blake sat alone on the bank of the river and silently castigated himself. He should never have touched her last night, should never have taken things so far and made love to her, but she had been like a fire in his blood. She had been all innocence and flame, in the end so sweet and sensual, beyond anything he'd ever before experienced.

Now Megan's words echoed over and over again in his head. Blake could not seem to escape her quiet accusation. What if she were even now carrying his child? The very thought shook him to the soles of his boots. When he had concocted this crazy scheme, the idea of becoming attracted to Kirk's fiancée was the furthest thing from his mind, let alone getting her with child. Lord! He most certainly hadn't been using his wits! Of course, when he had first devised his plan, he had never dreamed that Megan would be a virgin. That just wasn't Kirk's usual style.

For that matter, it wasn't Blake's usual style either. When he wanted a woman, he went to town and visited one of the "girls" who kept rooms above the saloon, or one of those employed by the local madams in discreet but well-known houses about town. Oh, Blake had done his share of courtin' and kissin' with the local daughters of townsfolk, always within the bounds of propriety. But when he needed to relieve his frustrations with a good romp between the sheets, it was never with one of those sweet young innocents. No! There was always Cally, over at Iris's place, to welcome him; or Sal, who had a room over the Silver Spur; or one of the overpainted fillies in Blanche's talented stable. They knew their business, and the risks that went with it, and how to prevent unwanted complications. They never expected more than a man was prepared to pay for, they knew when to keep quiet; and if a man chose carefully, he could find a clean, pretty little companion for a night of hot, sweet pleasure with no awkward demands in the morning.

This situation with Megan was something entirely different, something Blake should have known to avoid from the start. He was twenty-six years old, not some green kid in his first experience with a woman. He never should have let his desires flare out of control! Sure she was pretty—no, she was more than pretty, she was out-and-out beautiful. With that cinnamon hair and those great grey eyes, she had knocked the pins out from under him.

Megan was an enchanting pixie, an alluring gamine with all the charm of a woodland sprite. She had a quick wit that amazed and drew him, an intelligence he had to admire, and a smile that would melt stone.

Beneath that fiery temper he had glimpsed the sweet young woman she tried to hide with her stubborn show of bravado. She was sweet and brave and darling, and Blake was falling more under her spell with each passing hour. There were times he wanted to reach for a bar of soap to tame her tart tongue. How she had ever acquired such a vile vocabulary, he would like to know, for he was sure her parents had not raised her to speak that way. The way she walked, sat, ate, all showed that she had been brought up to be a proper young woman. And she had been innocent before he had touched her.

"Damn!" Blake cursed himself for his stupidity. Sitting on the bank of the river, he momentarily considered tying a rock around his neck and drowning himself. Lord knew he deserved it. Absently, he skipped another stone over the ruffled surface of the water, his thoughts as disturbed as the rippling stream. He'd known upon first meeting her that Megan was not some tart to be trifled with. He'd suspected her innocence right then. What he hadn't expected was her sharp tongue, the million and one ways the little vixen would find to goad him, the sensual fires that lurked untapped beneath that veil of innocence.

Now he knew, but much too late. With a groan, he closed his eyes as if to shut out all thoughts of her, but her image came sharp and clear to mind.

He saw those lips that could spout curses to rival a sailor's best efforts, yet could lure a man to taste their honey and lose himself in their satin softness. Those wondrous grey eyes, so round and soft and misty in times of loving, snapping with all the fury of lightning when she was angered. Her fine-boned face rose before him, so delicate yet so strong, her chin raised in defiance. He envisioned her small hands, hands that could hurl dishes past his head one moment and stroke him into delightful ecstasy the next. Skin so silky, so sweet he could only think of burying himself in its satin folds. She was like no other female he had ever known; part urchin, part lady, part child, yet all woman.

A long, tortured moan escaped his clenched teeth. *Dios*, what a mess he had made of things! Just thinking of her had his body hardening in want of her. And this was exactly what had gotten him into this predicament. His desire for her had overruled his good sense, shutting down his brain until he could think of nothing but possessing Megan. Once he had tasted her sweetness, she was like loco weed in his system. Having taken her innocence, he had availed himself of her again, giving no thought to the consequences.

Now, because of Megan's words, he was being forced to face himself and his actions. Reluctantly Blake admitted that he was more than a little smitten with his beautiful captive. It would be difficult to hand her over to Kirk and walk away. Blake had a feeling his heart was already more involved than was wise. How could he turn her over to his cousin, when everything inside him urged him to keep her for himself, to take her and run to some distant, undiscovered corner of the earth where the two of them could live unbothered by the rest of the world. As appealing as that idea might be, he knew he could not keep her with him. He doubted, after all he had put her through, that she would have him, now or ever. Any speculations along these lines were useless anyway, for as he had told her, he would be honor-bound to return Megan in exchange for his ranch. Already, his conscience was bothering him for the agony he knew her parents must be suffering, not knowing if she were alive or dead or terribly hurt.

Even as he reluctantly reasoned that he would have to let her go, Blake knew that to calmly give her into Kirk's hands was becoming unthinkable, especially if she were to become pregnant with his child. There was no way he would be able to leave her then! His shifty, greedy cousin was the last person he would want to raise a child of his. He'd fight heaven and earth before he would allow that to happen.

What had happened to all his fine plans? Blake shook his head in despair. "Megan happened, you fool," he muttered to himself. "You blithely set out to capture an unknown woman, and ended up caught in the web of a wide-eyed elfin enchantress. Five feet nothing of the most exquisitely disguised dynamite you could hope to find. And it exploded in your unwary face." His teeth ground together in frustration. Megan was like good whiskey. She went down so smooth and fine, then hit you like a ton of bricks when your defenses were down. He hadn't even seen the trap springing around him.

The best he could do now was not to touch Megan again, no matter how badly he might want her. If Dame Fortune had not deserted him altogether, maybe Megan would not be carrying his child after all, and if he could keep his lecherous hands off her, all might end well. If he could resist her for long enough, perhaps her allure would fade. Maybe the more he avoided her, the less tempting she would become. Somehow, even as he thought this, he doubted it, but it was the only solution he could see, and he was determined to put his plan into effect immediately.

If Blake was filled with doubts and frustration, Megan was having an even tougher time of it. Alone in the cabin, with nothing to fill her time and thoughts but her own problems, she was nearly frantic. She'd been here, what—three days? Somehow it seemed more like a lifetime, so much had happened to change her safe, sane world into bedlam. Half a week with her enigmatic captor and suddenly she didn't know who or what she was anymore. She, who had her life and future happily mapped out, suddenly didn't know where to turn, who to believe, what to treasure close to her heart. Everything was confusion, a topsy-turvy tumble of feelings and information. It was as if she were in the center of a tangled ball of yarn, and the more she fought to unravel herself, the more she became caught in the ever-tightening strands of conflicting emotion. Her heart, her body, and her mind were all pulling her in separate directions.

"Think, Megan! Think!" she commanded herself. Under the present circumstances, it was nearly an impossible order to follow. If she were to believe Blake, then Kirk was a conniving thief. If she chose to believe in Kirk, then Blake was a liar and a criminal. One fact could not be denied: he had kidnapped her. It really didn't matter that there was a reason behind his actions—or did it? If what he had said was true, mightn't she have done the same thing in his place? "No! No, it's wrong, no matter how you look at it," she reasoned angrily. "He had no right to do this to me."

Her fingers twisted together painfully as she paced the confines of the cabin. A frown pulled her brows down over stormy eyes. Could she have been so wrong about Kirk? When she thought about it, she knew very little about the man she had agreed to marry. And everything she thought she knew about him had been from what Kirk had told her himself. Might he have lied? There were times, she remembered now, when Kirk had seemed so remote, so cold. Now she could recall how he had sidestepped certain questions her father had put to him. Was it possible that she had been so enraptured with him that she had failed to see the man he really was?

And what of Blake? In all truthfulness, Megan had to admit that he had not mistreated her. As much as it galled her to admit it, he had not forced her into his bed. No, he had seduced her, charmed her, enslaved her body in a remarkably short time, but he had not forced himself on her. Nor had he hurt her in any physical manner. He enraged her and infuriated her, but he had also bewitched her. He was breaking her heart.

She was his captive, but she had more freedom

than she had expected when he first abducted her. Another man might have kept her bound and gagged. She could have met a worse fate by far and found herself starved or beaten, but Blake fed her and gave her the small freedom of the cabin.

Still, he had used her for his own purposes. He had abducted her—torn her away from her family, just to wreak his vengeance on Kirk; and he would continue to hold her captive until he had his ranch back, if it had truly belonged to him to begin with. Could that incredible tale of his be true? On the other hand, could anyone have actually invented such a story? And why was she so tempted to believe Blake? Why did she feel such a desperate need to believe him? Megan's fingers massaged her throbbing temples. "Heavens, but this is all so confusing!"

More confusing yet were her feelings for the man. She would be the first to admit that he was a handsome devil, but a devil still. He had sweet-talked her out of her innocence. Much to her chagrin, Megan recalled all too clearly the sweet surrender in his arms. More than that, he had invaded her heart like a marauding conqueror, and she would never be the same again. He had brought her dormant body to life with stunning ease, teaching her the meaning of desire, showing her realms of ecstasy she instinctively knew she would never find with Kirk. "Why?" she wailed silently. "Why couldn't he have left me in blissful ignorance?"

If it were only her body he had captured, Megan might have been better able to console herself, but she was dreadfully afraid he had stolen her heart in the process. How and why this had happened, when she had thought herself in love with Kirk, Megan could not fathom. Yet with his teasing ways, his whispered words of need and praise and passion, Blake had done just this. She sensed a vulnerability in him that endeared him to her. How she could loathe the man, yet love him at the same time, was beyond her. "Love?" she whispered, the word trembling from her quivering lips, her eyes wide with despair. "Oh, dear Lord, how can it be? Please don't let it be!"

In a matter of days, she felt closer to Blake than she had felt to Kirk after weeks of knowing him. After all she had been through at Blake's hands, she trusted him more than she had trusted anyone in her entire life, though he had given her every reason not to. "It's the circumstances!" she reasoned wildly. "Only the circumstances! It's being cooped up here with no one else to talk to. It's being forced to abide his company, to live in such close quarters with him, that's all. Surely I can't really be falling in love with the man. I love Kirk!"

But did she? Had she ever truly loved Kirk? Megan was beginning to question this now. Kirk had been the perfect gentleman, the come-to-life ideal that Megan had always dreamed of someday meeting. Could she have attributed to Kirk all the qualities she wished to find in a mate? Could she have unconsciously blocked out any faults he had, wanting only to see the things she admired?

Kirk was, perhaps, even more handsome than Blake, in a cool, flawless sort of way. Yet the perfection of his face held less appeal, less character than the ruggedly hewn features of her captor. Then, too, even through the anger and trials of their short time together, Megan had come to appreciate Blake's sense of humor, though he often irritated her with it. Suddenly it struck her how staid and sober Kirk had been. In all the time she had known him, she could not recall Kirk having shown much humor. Oh, they had laughed together, but not the zany, witty laughter of shared humor. Kirk's eyes had never lit up with suppressed deviltry as Blake's were wont to do. Thinking back, Megan was willing to bet that Kirk did not have a playful bone in his body.

A shaky sob escaped her lips, and tears trembled like raindrops on her lashes as Megan faced the truth. She had been deluding herself to think that she had loved Kirk. If she were to be returned to him tomorrow—if he were still to want her after Blake had taken her—she could not wed him, for she did not truly love him. Blake had shown her this, whether he had meant to or not. Even if Kirk were the innocent one in this drama, she could not love him; just as she could not love Blake less if it turned out that he were the true villain. Blake might not want her love or deserve it, he might never return it, but it was his nonetheless. He might forever be her enemy, but he was now her beloved enemy, and there was nothing she nor he could do about it. Her heart had spoken, and her head had no say in the matter, regardless of how she might resist the idea.

Only one thing stood out clearly in her mind. She must find a way to escape him. She had to get away, before her feelings grew even stronger, while she still might recover from the blow of this startling discovery. Blake would still use her against

Kirk. He would still seek his revenge, and once he had achieved it he would abandon her without a backward glance or so much as a regret. Had he not already proved how relentlessly he was driven, to what lengths he would go? Had he not already advised her of his future plans and calmly stated that he would return her to Kirk and her parents?

Oh, he might feel a temporary twinge of guilt in the end, but he obviously did not return her feelings. Megan was fast learning that there was a vast difference between desire and love, at least where men were concerned. Want her he might, at least for now, but love her he did not, or he would not still be talking of returning her to Kirk; and Megan could not bear to think of staying with him and loving him more with each passing day, only to be dumped off on her parents in the end, like yesterday's garbage. It would hurt enough now to be parted from him, but how much more would it hurt if she came to love him even more; or if she found herself carrying his child, a constant reminder of their time together, a time that was coming to mean so much to her, yet meant so little to him? She had to get away! She just had to!

Torn with the realization of her feelings, so new and hurtful, Megan threw herself across the bed and gave vent to her emotions. Guilt, fury, and love combined in a strange mixture that had her wailing and thrashing in a flurry of tears and strangled sobs.

Outside, Lobo's ears pricked up at the awful sounds coming from the cabin, his head cocked to one side as if questioning Megan's odd behavior. Blake, who was just returning, could not begin to

fathom what had brought on this new storm of
tears, but he knew with certainty that he had
something to do with it. Had she been asked, Megan
could not have fully explained. With one foot on
the step, Blake turned and beat a hasty retreat,
self-recrimination etching harsh lines in his face.
Just now he'd rather face a tribe of wild Indians
than deal with Megan's accusing tears, and if that
made him a coward, he'd wear the name into
eternity, but he was damned if he could face her at
this minute.

Come bedtime, Blake surprised Megan by taking his bedroll and pillow and making a place for
himself to sleep on the floor next to the bed. The
shocked look she gave him brought a harsh chuckle
from him. "Now what is that look all about?" he
taunted. "Why, Megan, I'd almost swear I saw
regret on your face just now. Could it be you
actually want me to share your bed?"

Megan's chin flew up in a defensive reaction.
"Don't flatter yourself," she snapped back. "That
was relief you saw, pure and simple. I cannot tell
you how glad I am that you have decided to relieve
me of your crude attentions, no matter what your
reasons."

His teeth gleamed as he grinned at her. "Relieved or not, you are dying of curiosity, my little
cat. Aren't you going to ask me why I've chosen
new sleeping arrangements at this late date?"

Megan was nearly overcome with curiosity and
felt distinctly let down and rejected, but she'd fry
in hell before admitting it to this grinning devil.
"No, I am not going to ask. I am merely going to

thank God and all His heavenly hosts that might be responsible for my sudden good fortune." Crawling quickly beneath her covers and turning her back to him, Megan muttered a hasty "Good night" before Blake could see the hurt on her face or hear the strange tightening in her voice. It was a long while before sleep overcame her, a time fraught with longing and the struggle to hold fresh tears at bay. It seemed the more she tried to reason things out, the more confused she became. There simply was no figuring Blake or what he might do next, and if she didn't stop trying she would drive herself crazy in short order. She could only hope escape came before she lost her mind entirely and her heart irretrievably.

They were just finishing breakfast the next morning when Lobo began to bark ferociously and raced to the edge of the clearing. There he stood barking and growling, his big teeth bared and the hair on his back bristling. Though Blake's jaw tensed and his eyes narrowed into alert spears, he calmly set his coffee cup aside and pushed himself unhurriedly away from the table. With the same seeming lack of concern, he strapped his gunbelt to his waist, tying the rawhide thongs to his leg so that his holster rode low along his thigh. "Stay inside and away from the windows," he told Megan as he jammed his hat on his head and pulled the brim low to shade his eyes.

Megan watched apprehensively as Blake sauntered out onto the small porch. While part of her was worried for him, another part could not help but hope that help had come for her. Could someone have tracked them here? The sheriff? Kirk? Could rescue be minutes away? Who was coming, friend or foe? Whose friend, or whose foe—hers or Blake's?

Her heart was thundering in her chest as she stood in the center of the cabin, not daring to move, and looked past Blake toward the edge of the clearing. Just as she was sure she would faint from anxiety, a lone rider cleared the brush and rode slowly into view. Blake moved not so much as a muscle, but Megan's heart sank to her toes as Lobo ceased his growling and began to dance around the approaching horse, his tail wagging now in greeting. This alone told her that help had not come for her, but neither had harm come to Blake. If Lobo knew their visitor, so must Blake.

The stranger raised a hand in greeting and rode directly to where Blake stood waiting. A wide grin creased his face as he dismounted and bounded up the steps, Lobo at his heels. "For cryin' out loud, Blake! Can't you control that blasted animal of yours? First he wants a piece of my hide, and now he's liable to lick me to death!"

Though she could not see it from where she stood, Megan heard the answering grin in Blake's voice as he answered. "Now, Jake, what wolf in his right mind would attempt to bite into that tough hide of yours? It would be like chewing elephant hide, or at best buzzard meat."

The two men thumped one another on the back in greeting. "Well, Blake, did everything go as planned?" Jake asked. "You sure did stir up a hornets' nest back at the ranch. Kirk is fit to be tied."

"Does he have any idea yet who is behind his fiancée's disappearance?"

Jake chuckled. "Nope. Not a clue, and let me tell you, he's plenty worried, too. That pup is in for a big surprise right soon!"

"Yeah, well, I've had a few surprises of my own," Blake said cryptically. "So, do you think he's upset enough to give me what I want?"

"Oh, he's plenty concerned, but how he'll react when he learns you have his woman is anyone's guess," Jake answered with a shrug. "He does have the girl's parents breathin' down his neck, though, so that will help."

"I suppose the sheriff has been looking high and low for her."

"You suppose right, but you covered your tracks too well, and the sheriff has been chasing his own tail back and forth across the territory for the past four days with nothin' to show for it."

The two men shared a laugh at this. "Come on in, Jake, and I'll introduce you to Megan. I suppose she's anxious to hear about her parents and poor old Kirk." If Blake's eyes turned hard at this thought, Jake either didn't notice or thought it wise not to comment.

"I brought you some more supplies and food," the man said as he followed Blake inside. "Thought you might be runnin' low on a few things by now."

"That was mighty thoughtful of you, Jake. Thanks."

Megan stood as if nailed to the floor. Jake's appearance had lent an added reality to her situation, and she wanted to die on the spot. This was all too serious, too real. This was not some horrid dream from which she was soon to awaken. Nausea rose up to choke her, and any color she had once had in her face had fled, leaving only two huge grey circles of eyes to dominate. For one frightful moment she felt she might faint, and the only thing that prevented her from doing so was the mocking look Blake sent her way.

"Megan, I want you to meet a friend of mine. This is Jake Banner, the man who is going to deliver the ransom note to Kirk for me. Jake, may I present Miss Megan Coulston, the famed missing fiancée and the worst cook this territory has ever known."

Though his eyes grew round with suppressed mirth at Blake's last statement, Jake tipped his hat in polite acknowledgment. "Ma'am."

Megan collected her wits enough to nod in return. "I wish I could claim it was a pleasure to meet you, Jake. Under any other circumstances, it might have been."

Megan was not the meek little thing Jake had been expecting, and it took him a few seconds to recover from her tart comment. Shaking his head in amazement, he turned to meet Blake's amused, if slightly sour look.

"You see what I have had to put up with, Jake?" Blake complained. "Megan has a tongue as sharp as a razor, and a temper to match. She's given me nothing but trouble since I had the misfortune to steal her off that stage."

"If you had the sense God gave a goat, you would never have come up with such a fool scheme to begin with," she had the temerity to counter.

Blake gave her a familiar swat on the rear. "Cool that temper of yours, honey, and get Jake and me a cup of coffee, will you?'' His eyes were twinkling with deviltry again, knowing he was pushing his luck to the limit.

Megan met him look for look, her own eyes shooting silver flares. "Get it yourself, *sweetie*," she purred spitefully, "unless you want to wear it on your head!" With that she flounced over to the rocker and refused to look at either of them as she stared daggers through the dirty windowpane.

"Whooeee!" she heard Jake exclaim. "You've got a she-cat by the tail there, Blake, old boy."

"Don't I know it!" Blake answered in a disgruntled tone. "So far she's hissed at me, scratched me, and bit me, and damned near disfigured me. She's also thrown anything she could lift at my head and tried to lame me for life. Not to mention the fact that she screeches like a banshee and curses like a demented sailor. She's a regular little hellion."

"You don't say!" Jake chuckled, thoroughly enjoying his friend's predicament.

"By the way, Jake. When you come back up this way, could you manage to bring a few more dishes? Maybe some tin plates and such? The little witch has broken almost every dish in the place already."

It was several minutes before Jake could contain his laughter long enough to conduct business, and even then a guffaw would slip out from time to time. Even the warning glare in Blake's blue eyes could not tamp down Jake's mirth entirely.

8

Megan may have been stretching the truth some by telling Jake that under other circumstances she might have enjoyed making his acquaintance. Truth be told, she found him a bit forbidding. It wasn't so much Jake's looks, for he was handsome in a rough sort of way, his tall, muscular frame neither too thin nor too heavy. It was his stern, nearly haughty expression that was almost frightening. Even as he joked and laughed with Blake, there was a remote, wary way about him, as if he never let down his guard completely or let anyone close to him, emotionally or otherwise.

Megan knew that look. It was the trademark of a gunfighter just as surely as the tied-down, low-slung pistol on his hip and that peculiarly fluid way of moving. Had she thought about it, she would have been shocked to realize that Blake had those same traits, though they were not as pronounced as Jake's.

She was relieved when the two men went outdoors again, for Jake's dark eyes seemed to see right through her, and this made her uneasy, as if all her deepest, darkest secrets were being revealed and reviewed for flaws. It wasn't that Jake was unfriendly; in fact, he was very polite. He was just unsettling to have around.

The men talked in low tones on the porch for a few minutes, but Megan could not make out their words. Then Blake put his head inside the door and said, "Jake and I are going around back for a few rounds of target practice. I don't want you to become alarmed at the sound of gunfire."

Megan nodded. "I suppose you will leave Lobo guarding the door, as usual," she commented dryly.

He grinned. "Of course, darlin'. I wouldn't want you to wander off while I was entertaining our guest, now would I?"

"Heaven forbid!" she muttered, earning a hearty laugh from him.

The small piece of crockery shattered into slivers in midair. "You haven't lost your touch, I see," Jake complimented. "Been practicing much?"

"Not in the last few days. I've been too busy keeping Megan in line."

Jake chuckled and gestured to the pile of broken dishes they were using as targets. "From the looks of that, you aren't faring too well. Sure do make nice targets, though."

"Go ahead and laugh, Jake," Blake retorted with narrowed eyes. "Someday you are going to meet a woman who is going to knock you to your knees, and I hope I am there to see it.''

"Is that what Megan Coulston is doing to you, my friend?''

Blake scowled. "Yeah, and it's got me going in circles.''

"She's Kirk's woman,'' Jake reminded quietly.

"You aren't telling me anything I don't know. It is part of the same speech I give myself several times a day, the one reminding me that the last thing I need in my life right now is a woman, particularly this woman.''

"She doesn't cotton to gunfighters and outlaws, huh?'' Jake raised a dark brow. "I hate to tell you this, Blake, but very few nice ladies do. You should know that by now. We scare the daylights out of them.''

"More lessons, Jake? Just because you taught me to fast draw, doesn't make you my lifetime mentor. If I want a sermon, I'll find a preacher.''

Jake shrugged. "No more than a little advice between friends. Don't let the girl distract you too much. If you let down your guard at the wrong time, you'll find yourself pitching coal in hell before you know what hit you, even as fast and accurate as you are with a gun.''

"Megan doesn't know about my reputation with a gun, or that I've made my living by hiring out those particular skills for the past two years. I'd rather she didn't find out.''

Jake rolled his eyes in exasperation. "What do I look like, the town crier? This is the second time in two days I've had to tell someone that I'm not in the habit of blabbing everything I know, and it's getting real tiresome real quick.''

"Sorry, Jake. I didn't mean to insult you," Blake apologized with a crooked grin.

"Neither did Evan Coulston, but he doesn't know me like you do, either." That led to a discussion of Jake's talk with Megan's father.

"So," Jake concluded at last, "it seems Mr. Coulston isn't all that pleased with Kirk as his future son-in-law. It wouldn't surprise me if he takes his daughter and heads back for Abilene when this is over."

Blake nodded absently. "Do you think there is a chance they might find something in the study?"

"Could be. I've seen people so confident and so proud of their own evil deeds that they never bother to destroy the evidence of their crimes. It's like some sort of memento they keep around to gloat over. It's for sure Opal was about to have fits just finding Mrs. Coulston dustin' in there, like she was nervous she'd find something. I just wish them better luck than I had. The one time I managed to sneak into the house and have a look around, I nearly got caught. That she-devil aunt of yours sleeps real light. Since then they've gotten suspicious and don't let anyone near the house without a reason."

"Even so, do you think we could get Coulston to hand over whatever he may find?" Blake wondered aloud.

"Oh, for Pete's sake, Blake! Has that girl addled all your brains?" Jake growled disgustedly. "You're holding Megan hostage. It doesn't matter who you barter with, as long as you get your ranch back as a result. You just go ahead with your original plan, and I'll keep an eye on Coulston. If he finds anything at all, I'll take care of getting it to you. I'll also keep an eye on that shifty cousin of yours and his prune-faced mother. You know, that woman makes a black widow spider seem right friendly by comparison.''

Blake agreed. ''Makes me wonder if Uncle Bill died of yellow fever after all. Maybe she killed him in his sleep.''

''Ha!'' Jake barked skeptically. ''The poor man probably ran off or hung himself, having her for a wife. He should have strangled her and her son, and saved everyone a lot of trouble.''

Jake stayed overnight. Blake cooked supper as usual, after asking Megan if she thought she might manage to prepare a simple stew.

''Only if you want to chance an early death,'' she retorted sassily. ''On second thought—'' her eyes lit up wickedly.

''Never mind. You've already tried to poison Lobo and me once. I'd hate to subject Jake to your cooking.''

While Blake composed his ransom note to Kirk, Megan had an opportunity to speak to Jake about her parents. ''How are they, Jake? Are they terribly worried about me?''

Jake looked as uncomfortable with her questions as she was with his company.

''Tell me the truth, Jake. I know they must be nearly frantic, not having heard anything since the holdup, but are they both all right? Mother hasn't gone into fits or anything, has she?''

''Oh, no, nothin' like that,'' he was quick to assure her. ''They are both in good health, if that is your worry. Your mother doesn't eat much more than a bird, but she says she has no appetite right now; and your pa is sometimes up late at night, I noticed. Other than that, they are both tryin' to keep busy until they hear something. Opal Hardesty has let your mother take over some of the household chores, sort of busy work for her hands, you know. Your pa has been ridin' out with Kirk and naggin' the daylights out of him and the sheriff to do more to help find you.''

"Nagging must run in the family," Blake put in wryly, looking up from his writing to give Megan a grin.

Megan ignored him. "And how is the stage-coach driver who got shot?" she asked Jake.

"He'll be fine, ma'am. No need to worry. Doc Shadley patched him up almost as good as new." Jake offered a rare smile. "The widow Ellerby took him in until he's well enough to travel, and he seems right happy there. In fact, he's taken quite a shine to the widow and her famous peach cobbler. Wouldn't surprise me none if there's a weddin' come of all this one of these days."

This drew an answering smile from Megan. "Well, I'm glad to hear something good might come of all this, at least. They do say that the way to a man's heart is through his stomach."

Blake shot her a sidelong look and snorted. "You'd better hope that's not the only way to win a man, darlin', because your cooking isn't going to win prizes anytime soon. You just might wind up an old maid if that's what it takes."

Megan sent him a glare. "Might I remind you that I had a perfectly good fiancé practically to the altar before you came into my life and made a mess of things? And he didn't give two hoots whether I could cook or not!''

"He probably hadn't felt the sharp edge of your tongue yet either, or he would have run like hell in the opposite direction,'' Blake countered smoothly.

Megan gave him a disgusted look. "Just write your stupid letter and keep your opinions to yourself," she suggested tartly.

A few minutes later, as she was conversing with Jake, Blake walked over to her, his hand held out palm up. "Hand over one of your earrings, Megan.''

Her head jerked around sharply, and she frowned up at him in confusion. "My what?''

"Your earring. Just one of them will do for now.''

"Just what am I supposed to do with only one earring, Blake? For that matter, what do you need with one of them?''

"I am going to send it to Kirk, so that he has absolutely no reason to doubt that I am holding you hostage. I'm sure your parents can identify it as yours. We'll keep the other one. You see, just to make sure Kirk takes my threats seriously, I have told him that if he tries to double-cross me, I'll send him the matching earring next, with your delicate little earlobe still attached. That should get his attention soon enough.''

Megan could feel the blood congealing in her veins. Her eyes frantically searched Blake's face for some clue to his true intent, but his features remained bland. "Sure—surely you are not serious, Blake. Not even you would do something so horrible," she stammered. "Please, Blake! Tell me you would not really do such a thing!"

Blake felt like a heel. "Oh, hell, Megan! Of course I wouldn't. It's just a threat, something to hold over Kirk's head. You should know better than to even ask. Have I treated you so badly until now?"

Megan nearly sank to the floor in relief. Her knees were knocking beneath her skirt. With a shaky sigh, she lit into him. "Don't you ever scare me like that again, Blake Montgomery, or so help me God, I'll take the skin off your bones strip by strip!"

"You've tried that a time or two already, as I recall," he said with a wink. "Good grief, though, Megan! You must think I'm some sort of devil, if you really believed I would do that to you."

"I didn't think you would," she admitted sheepishly, "but you said it so seriously. Besides, what do I know about bandits? You are the first one I've ever had the misfortune to encounter, and you know you've set that blasted wolf of yours on my heels."

"As long as you stay inside the cabin, Lobo won't bother you. He's merely there to guard you when I am busy elsewhere."

"Yes, and he'd gladly chew my kneecaps off if given half a chance!"

"Ah, but who could blame him? You're such a tempting little morsel, Megan," Blake answered with a laugh.

They bedded down shortly thereafter, Megan alone in the bed and the two men on the floor in their bedrolls. If Jake was wondering about the strange relationship between Megan and Blake, he said nothing. He merely eyed both of them with curious amusement, shrugged, and settled down to sleep.

Jake left early the next morning with the ransom note, Megan's earring, and specific instructions from Blake. "I've warned Kirk in the note not to contact the sheriff about this, so keep your eyes and ears open, and get word to me if he does. Also, I've told him to send his reply in a sealed envelope, to be left at the hotel desk in my name. He'll be watching to see if I or anyone else picks it up. Wait at least ten days. Pick a time when the hotel is busy, maybe right after the stage comes in, or on Saturday night when the boys go into town for supper. It should be fairly easy to take the letter without anyone noticing then.

"I've told Kirk I will contact him later about the time and place to exchange Megan for the deed. I didn't figure he'd trust me enough to send the deed first."

Jake laughed at this. "You figured right. If not for Megan's folks pesterin' the daylights out of him, he might not even consider the exchange now."

"He might not yet, except I know he hates me enough to want to find me and make me pay for abducting his innocent bride."

Jake mounted his horse. "See you back here in about a week and a half. I still don't see why you don't head on up to that old gold mine of yours. Kirk is bound to remember this cabin sooner or later."

"Let's hope it is later. That old mine isn't safe anymore. I'd rather take my chances here."

After Jake left, Megan had some questions of her own. "What was all that about a gold mine?"

she asked curiously. "You haven't mentioned it before."

"No reason to. It's old and unsafe, and as far as anyone knows it is played out."

"Played out?"

"Yep, dry as old bones, no more gold to be found—played out," Blake explained. He laughed at her downcast expression. "Sorry to disappoint you, my dove. Why, for a minute there I could almost see you counting nuggets in your head. It's a nice dream, but so far that's all it is."

"So far?"

He nodded. "Maybe someday I'll give it a try, see if I can find a new vein. I have a feeling there just might be more gold hidden away up there, but it's not going to be easy to find. Then again, maybe it's not there at all. Who knows?"

A short while later, Megan thought to ask, "Why did you tell Jake to wait ten days before retrieving the letter?"

"Because by then, my sweet, Kirk and his boys will be getting lazy. They'll have started to wonder if I ever intended to pick up the letter, or if I have something else up my sleeve. They won't be watching the hotel as closely as they do the first few days."

"But why wait so long? Why did you wait until now to send the ransom note?"

"Two reasons. First, to make sure that no one followed us or follows Jake. It's better to let the dust settle a bit first."

"And the other reason?"

"Why, Megan, can't you guess?" he replied with a strictly evil smile. "I want to make Kirk sweat. I want his guts tied up in knots. The longer he has to wait to hear, the more time he has to think about what is going on, what awful things I might be doing to you, my dear. He'll be sweating blood before I'm through with him, and I am going to relish every moment of it.''

It chilled Megan to hear the hatred in Blake's voice as he talked of Kirk. ''You really hate him, don't you?'' she said softly.

''Yes,'' he hissed. ''If he and that bitch he has for a mother both dropped dead tomorrow, I'd dance on their graves.''

''Oh, Blake,'' she sighed sadly. ''I'm sorry for you, for all you have gone through, for what you are going through now. But don't you see what all this hatred is doing to you? It's eating you up inside. It is eating away at all the good inside you, destroying the man you are. If you let it go on, you'll soon be just an empty shell of yourself, with nothing to fill the void but your all-consuming hatred. That's no way to live, Blake. I don't want to see that happen to you.''

He offered her a wry smile, completely lacking in humor. ''I appreciate your concern, Megan, but as you told me earlier, kindly keep your opinions to yourself. I think I'm old enough to handle my own life without your advice. Besides, I expect that your concern lies more with Kirk than with me. Cheer up, honey. If all goes well, you'll be back in his arms in a couple of weeks. Of course, you won't be living on the ranch as you had planned, and he won't have much to offer you, but you'll be Mrs. Kirk Hardesty. That *is* what you wanted so badly, isn't it?''

His blue eyes bore into hers, wanting, needing

to hear her deny it. For the life of her, Megan could not seem to speak past the lump in her throat. As tears filled her eyes, she turned her gaze from his. Silence filled the room, broken at last by the echo of Blake's footsteps as he left the cabin.

Two mornings later they were roused from their separate beds by Lobo once again barking an alarm. This time Megan knew Blake could not be expecting whoever was approaching their lone cabin. Jake would certainly not be returning so soon. Clutching the covers to her breast, she watched as Blake slipped into his pants and quickly buckled on his gunbelt. He made a point of checking his pistol before shoving it into his holster. Not even bothering with his boots or shirt, he opened the door and stepped out onto the porch to wait.

"Better get dressed, Megan," he called back to her. "We have unexpected visitors." He whistled for Lobo, who came running and took up his position at Blake's side.

As if his words had released her from a spell, Megan bounded from the bed and shimmied into her dress, her fingers fumbling with the numerous small buttons in her rush. She stood barefoot, her hair straggling in her face, her dress still half-buttoned, when riders came galloping into the clearing.

"*Hola*, Blake, *amigo*. We have come to see how you and the woman are getting along up here by yourselves. Are you not glad to see us?"

"Not particularly, Raul," Blake said dryly. "How did you find me?"

"Ah, you need not worry that you left much of

a trail, *amigo*. If Santos was not half Apache, we would never have known where to look.''

Raul began to dismount, only to halt as Blake stated calmly but firmly, ''I wouldn't do that if I were you, fellows. Just stick your asses to those saddles until I say otherwise.'' All five reseated themselves. ''Now, why don't you tell me why you bothered to find me. We aren't exactly bosom buddies, and I do not recall issuing any invitations.''

''That is not very friendly of you, Blake,'' Raul said with a frown. ''We just thought we'd pay a social call on you and the lady.''

''Think again, Raul, and hightail it out of here. You and your men got all the loot off the stage. I didn't ask to get cut in on your shares, and I'm not inclined to share anything I have with you.''

Raul shrugged. ''All we want is a little time with your woman.''

''She's not here,'' Blake lied smoothly.

Raul's beady black eyes shifted from Blake to his men. ''Then you will not mind if we see this for ourselves,'' he suggested with a twisted smile.

What happened next was almost too fast for Megan to follow as she watched from the shadows of a window. On a silent signal from Raul, all five men drew their weapons. Blake fired five shots in rapid succession, as bullets whined in the air and hit the cabin with dull thuds. Before the thunderous report of the initial gunfire had faded, Raul and another of the bandits fell from their horses, dropping to the earth like felled birds. Blake was inside the cabin, Lobo close behind, almost before Megan could blink. As he slammed the door shut, she saw the remaining three outlaws scatter for cover.

With an efficiency that startled her, Blake reloaded his pistol. "Get away from the window, you little fool!" he growled, not really even looking at her as he reached for his rifle and checked its load.

"Let me have the rifle, Blake," she said, ducking as a bullet shattered the pane of the window where she had been standing just seconds before.

"Have you ever used one before?" Blake crawled to the opposite window and chanced a quick look outside. Immediately the glass disintegrated over his head.

"No, but I'm sure I could do it. It can't be that difficult." Megan jumped as another shot whistled through the window nearest her and buried itself in the headboard of the bed.

"Now is not the time for a quick lesson in target practice, Megan. Besides, I need the rifle for distance shots, and right now every shot counts. Those bastards aren't just funning with us. They mean business." He rose up and got off a quick shot before ducking down again.

"Then give me the pistol. I want to help. Please!"

"Not on your life, sweetheart!" he retorted between volleys.

"It just might *be* my life we are discussing here, you idiot!" she shouted as she huddled against the wall.

"Not likely. There are only three of them left out there."

"That's three too many by my count. What's the matter, Blake? Don't you trust me?"

"No offense, but that's about the size of it, and

I've got enough to handle without worrying about a bullet in my back.''

"No offense," she mimicked sarcastically as she crawled past him to reach the iron skillet on the open shelf. "Well I'll be boiled in oil before I sit here with no defense of my own."

He spared her a quick look and a chuckle as she crouched down with the frying pan clutched in both hands.

There were three windows in the cabin, two in front on either side of the door and one on the side wall opposite the fireplace. When Blake issued a sharp curse and muttered something about the outlaws spreading out to circle the cabin, Megan scuttled quickly to the side window, the only one with glass left in its pane. If Blake could cover the front, the least she could do was keep an eye on this side. Blake would need the warning, for anyone who might get a clear shot through this window stood a good chance of hitting Blake.

The gunfire was sporadic now, both sides considering their shots more carefully. Pinned down inside the cabin as they were, Megan knew what a treed raccoon must feel like, and it was not the most comfortable of positions in which to find oneself.

"Aha! Got one!" Blake shouted as Megan heard one of the bandits yell out in pain. "I think I might have just winged him though."

Just then Megan caught a glimpse of color through the window she was watching. Before she could shout a warning, the front door flew back on its hinges, and at the same time a man hurled himself through the window next to her. All was a blur. As Megan slammed the heavy cast iron skillet onto one man's head, Lobo lunged for the throat of the other. Though she only caught him a glancing blow on the side of the head, it stunned the man long enough for Blake's bullet to find his heart. There was no need for Blake to waste another shot on either intruder, for Lobo had successfully dispatched the second fellow. Megan turned away from the grisly sight, gorge rising in her throat.

That left only one outlaw unaccounted for, the one Blake thought he had wounded, and as Lobo ceased his unearthly growling, Megan heard the man call out to his friends. The only answer he received was from Blake. "They're dead, Paco. Give it up. Throw down your guns and come into the clearing with your hands over your head. That is the only way you are going to come out of this alive."

All was silent for an eternity of seconds. Then they heard the distinct sounds of a horse galloping away. Blake was on his feet and headed for the door before Megan could gather her wits. As she watched in stunned disbelief, Blake ran toward one of the bandits' horses and vaulted onto its back. He was going after the outlaw! He was actually going to ride off and leave her alone in the cabin with this mad wolf and two dead bodies!

"Noooo!" she screamed, hysteria clawing at her. "No! No! No!"

Halfway across the clearing, Blake wheeled the horse on its hind legs and raced back toward the cabin. At her shrill shrieks, chills of fear had rippled down his backbone. The only thing he could think was that one of the bandits still lived and now had Megan at his mercy. Throwing himself from the saddle, he dashed into the cabin, his gun drawn.

There she stood, huddled against a wall, her eyes huge and glassy in her pale face. Both hands were clasped over her mouth, stifling the squeaky little sounds that now emitted from her throat. A quick glance around proved to Blake that neither of the men inside the cabin had moved an inch. They were both quite dead, as were the two still lying outside on the ground. Megan was simply in shock. She had held up well all through the gun battle, but now, in the aftermath, she had succumbed to a severe reaction.

"Blast and damnation! This is all I need! Paco is getting away, probably to recruit more of his friends, and I have to calm a hysterical female." At that moment Blake could have chewed nails and spit them out. He was only one man, and he couldn't be in two places at one time, but he couldn't leave Megan in the state she was in. He would have to stay with her until she was calm again.

He would have to set Lobo on Paco's trail and hope to catch up soon. He was fairly sure he had winged Paco in the side, and that would slow the man down some. "Lobo!" he commanded. Pointing in the direction Paco had taken, he said, "Track, Lobo. Kill!" The beast gave one sharp bark and ran from the cabin, already on Paco's trail as Blake turned back to Megan.

Pulling her resisting body into the protective circle of his arms, he tried to calm her. "It's okay, honey. Everything is all right. It's all over with.

Come on, Megan. Pull yourself together, sugar." Bit by bit he could sense her body and mind responding to his murmurings, warming to his gentle touch. As her frozen senses began to thaw, great sobs shook her slender frame, and tears streamed unchecked down her fair face.

He let her cry it out, disregarding his own impatience to be on his way after Paco. When she was finally past the stage of incoherent hiccups and could speak without choking, she whispered accusingly into his shoulder, "You left me. You left me with that murdering animal and these mutilated bodies."

"No, darlin'. I didn't leave you. I'm here, aren't I?"

She nodded and gulped, but still did not look at him. Instead, she buried her face further into his shoulder. "You meant to leave, though. I saw you going. And you knew that Lobo would keep me here—here in this cabin, with no way out, no way to escape, penned in with dead men and blood all over." Her voice rose shrilly once more. "One of them still has his eyes open, Blake! One of them is staring right at me!"

Her small body was trembling like an aspen leaf in his arms. "Shh, baby, hush now. I'll take care of it. I promise." Sympathy rose up in him as he realized how ghastly this whole episode had been for her, how frightening. In his rush to catch Paco he hadn't thought of Megan's predicament, and she was right. Lobo would have kept her from leaving the cabin. She would have had to stay here with the bodies until he returned.

While a man would not have lost control, any

woman, no matter how strong she might seem, would have panicked as Megan had done. He had seen enough of life and death in his twenty-six years to accept such things when necessary, but he doubted that Megan had been exposed much to this darker side of life, even having been raised in a town as rough as Abilene could be at times. She had been sheltered by loving parents, until he, in his righteous fury, had torn her away from their protection, hurtling her into the midst of his own bloodthirsty, vindictive world. Megan had every reason in the world to be as upset as she was. More than that, she had every right to hate him for the havoc he had wreaked in her life.

Megan had soon calmed down enough so that Blake could settle her in a chair and go about the gruesome business of cleaning up the cabin. For now, he dragged the four bodies out behind the cabin. Later he would see to burying them. If he had not been so concerned with his own worries about Paco, Blake might have noticed how quickly Megan was recovering from her shock. He might also have taken note of the gleam of resentment lighting her clear grey eyes.

The longer she sat, the angrier Megan became. Regardless of how kind and gentle Blake had been in the past few minutes, the brute had nearly ridden off and left her to her hysteria. Only her frantic screams had stopped him and saved her sanity, for Megan was positive that, had Blake gone on, she would have lost her mind before his return. For this alone he deserved her wrath! He was thoroughly despicable, without a remorseful bone in his vengeful body, and she thoroughly loathed him at that moment. If anyone deserved revenge here and now, it was she! If she didn't get away from him soon, she truly would go crazy!

As she watched him kneel down to wipe a pool of blood from the floor, the realization struck her. Lobo was gone, sent after Paco. He would not return for some time. She was alone with Blake, and his back was to her. This was the opportunity she had been praying for, perhaps her only chance. He would never know what hit him! Without giving it further thought, before her conscience could stop her, she hefted the iron skillet and brought it down upon his bowed head.

Blake dropped like a stone. For one frightful second, Megan feared she had killed him, but when she bent down and felt behind his ear for a pulse, his heart was still beating regularly, which was more than she could say for her own at the moment. Gingerly feeling the top of his head, she felt a lump rising where she had struck him, but her fingers came away without a trace of blood. At least he would not bleed to death while she made good her escape.

Time was now of the essence. Knowing that Blake would wake up all too soon, Megan scurried to find her stockings and shoes. Running out the door, she found four of the outlaws' horses tied to the porch rail. Fortunately, they were still saddled. She grabbed the first in line and hoisted herself into the saddle. She did not stop to think that it would gain her time if she were to untie the remaining three, as well as Blake's own horse, and turn them loose. Nor did it dawn on her that she might have given herself further advantage if she had tied Blake up, hand and foot, or stolen his guns. All she could think of was getting away from the cabin as fast as possible. With one last look at Blake, lying unconscious inside the cabin door, she whirled the horse about and raced for freedom.

The fact that Paco had headed north from the clearing was to her advantage. Megan wanted to follow the river, which lay south of the cabin and ran westward. At least she need not fear running into either Paco or Lobo on her chosen route. As a twinge of guilt assailed her, she also conceded that it was very unlikely that Paco would return to the cabin. He would hightail it out of the area as fast as his horse would carry him, especially with Lobo hot on his trail. Blake would be in no immediate danger until he could regain consciousness.

Then it would be she who would have to worry, for Blake would have murder in his eyes when he awoke and found her gone! Megan did not doubt for one second that he would come after her, and if he caught up with her, there would be hell to pay! With that thought uppermost in her mind, Megan dug her heels into her horse's flank, urging it to a faster pace. She had to put as many miles between herself and Blake as possible in the short time allotted her.

9

"Megan! Megan! Answer me, you damnably stubborn female!" Blake's head threatened to split wide open with each shouted syllable. He'd awakened to a throbbing head and a lump the size of a goose egg, and he was in a foul mood. When he had discovered that Megan was gone, his first thought was that Paco might have doubled back and taken her. But that didn't make much sense once he'd thought about it. For one thing, Lobo was still gone, which meant the wolf was still tracking the outlaw. Secondly, if Paco had come back, Blake would have wakened to harp music and not a bursting head. Then, too, there was the skillet lying on the floor, mute evidence to the fact that Megan had clobbered him senseless.

Stumbling about, he had made a quick reconnaissance of the immediate area. Megan was nowhere to be found, but he had expected no less, with one of the horses missing. The puzzling thing was that Megan had not taken any of his guns; nor had she packed any food so far as Blake could tell. Neither had she stopped to release the other horses. All this told Blake that Megan was running in a blind panic, which might be the only thing in his favor now. Blake estimated that he had been unconscious at least an hour, and if Megan had left right away, she had a good head start on him. However, in her hurry, she would probably leave quite a trail and would be fairly easy to track.

Now he had been trailing her for several hours. He was sure he was closing in on her, but so far she had managed to stay just far enough ahead of him to go undetected. Blake had thought he would have caught up with her before now, but she was leading him a merry chase. First she had crisscrossed the stream several times, which showed that she was starting to put some thought into her actions. At one point she had ridden her mount downstream in the river itself for quite a while, and he'd had a devil of a time locating the point at which she had left the stream.

Blake was fast becoming desperate. In addition to his aching head and the unsolved problem of Paco, the sun was now setting. Already it was becoming difficult to see in the gathering gloom. If he didn't find her soon, there was a good possibility that she would escape him altogether. Blake ground his teeth in frustration, then groaned when the grinding caused his head to throb even worse. By God, Megan would pay dearly when he caught up to her!

Blake nearly missed the spot where Megan had

veered her horse away from the river to avoid a series of hills and cliffs that banked the stream along this stretch. The river ran swiftly over hidden rocks here, and continued to be rough water for a mile or so. There was no riverbank to ride on, and Blake breathed a sigh of relief that Megan had been wise enough not to attempt to take her horse to the water again along this particular area. She never would have made it through without drowning.

It was perhaps a mile farther on when, through the trees, Blake suddenly spotted the horse. Not daring to take his eyes from the animal ahead, he kneed his own mount to a faster pace. His blue eyes gleamed with anticipation. He had her now! And this time there would be no escaping!

Blake frowned. What the devil was going on? As he got closer he could see that the horse was standing in one spot, not moving away from him. He rounded the last stand of trees and drew his horse to a halt, confusion drawing lines across his forehead. The horse was grazing on a clump of grass, still saddled, and Megan was nowhere in sight. Dismounting, he approached Megan's horse. The animal nickered and shied away. It was then that Blake noted the bloody scrape on its right foreleg, and the limp.

"Hell fire and brimstone!" That was the mildest of the curses that issued from Blake's lips. Where was Megan? How long had he been tracking a riderless horse? He ran long fingers through his dark hair, mentally tracking her again, mile by mile. Lord knew he was not the most expert tracker, but he was not the most inexperienced either. Blake was sure he would have noticed the difference in the tracks if she had dismounted somewhere along the trail.

Suddenly it dawned on him. His palm came up, and with the heel of his hand he butted his forehead as if to knock some sense into his addled brain. The thoughtless action did nothing to ease his headache, but Blake was too relieved to care. "Of course," he muttered aloud. "Megan either dismounted when the horse became lame or she was thrown, and somewhere around here or I would have been tracking a limping horse. And I sure as hell would have noticed that." The only time he had failed to follow the actual trail left by Megan's mount was when he'd caught sight of the animal itself. Now all he had to do was find some sign of Megan on foot.

Glancing around in the gathering gloom, Blake frowned. He had to find her soon, before it was completely dark. Then he shrugged. How far could she have gone on foot? Surely not far. Then another thought came forward. He eyed the horse's foreleg with growing concern. What if Megan had been thrown? What if she were hurt? Cold sweat dotted his forehead, his eyes frantically searching what he could see of the surrounding area. "Megan! Megan, where are you?" he called out, every word growing in volume as his worry increased. Damn, but he wished Lobo was here!

Slowly he retraced his steps to where he had first glimpsed her horse. In the deepening shadows, he had to strain his eyes to see the animal's hoofprints. As he followed them through the brush, his despair deepened when he neared the edge of a steep cliff. "Megan!" he shouted, then muttered beneath his breath. "Blasted woman! If I find her in one piece, I'll beat the tar out of her for this."

"Megan! Answer me!" His words bounced back to him, echoing off the rocks. Then he heard it—or did he? He strained his ears. Again a mewling sort of sound, faint and indistinct. Blake shook his head. Where was the sound coming from? From which direction? "Megan! Can you hear me?"

The response was faint, barely heard over the sound of the water rushing over the rocks far below. It seemed to be coming from beyond the edge of the cliff. Walking to the edge, Blake peered over. Nothing. Then she called out once more, calling his name in a thready voice. "Megan? Where are you? Talk to me, honey. I can't see you."

"Blake! Don't go! Don't go away and leave me! I'm here!"

He heard the panic behind her words. "Where, damn it?"

"H-here! On the l-ledge!" She was sobbing now, afraid he wouldn't find her, afraid he would go away, afraid she would be left on the tiny ledge to die of exposure or starvation or both. "Please! H-help me, B-blake!"

Going down on his knees, Blake leaned out farther and peered down over the sheer cliff. Megan's sobbing drifted up to him. Then he saw her, just barely. She was huddled into a ball on a small ledge about fifteen feet down and to his right, all but hidden by the overhang of the cliff. "Holy hell!" he exclaimed, his head thundering as he leaned down and hollered, the blood rushing directly to the bump on his skull. "How in tarnation did you manage to end up down there?"

"I d-didn't exactly p-plan it th-this way!" she tried to shout back between chattering teeth. "My horse shied. Th-then he l-lost his f-footing." As long as she lived, Megan would never forget that frightful moment when she found herself flying headlong over the cliff, then skidding and tumbling over rocks, unable to find a handhold to stop her fall. Just when she was positive she was destined for a horrible death, her skirt caught on the branch of a small bush, breaking her rapid descent just long enough for her to grab onto the edge of the ledge. There she had clung for long, heart-stopping minutes, hearing the rush of the water far below, knowing that if she lost her small handhold, she would continue to fall several hundreds of feet straight down to a bone-crushing death. She had made the mistake of looking down and had nearly fainted, her fingers slipping ever nearer the edge, losing precious inches of grasp. Sheer panic and a desperate will to live had given her the strength to pull herself up onto the ledge.

She wasn't sure how long she had lain there sobbing in pain and panic. Loosened rocks had continued to fall about her, sending quivers of fright racing through her. For quite a while she could not stop crying or shaking, not even long enough to assess her situation. When she finally dared to look about her, there was nothing to encourage her. Her small island of safety was perhaps five feet long and two feet wide, balanced precariously in the middle of nowhere. There was no way off of it, either up or down. Worse, the tiny ledge was on a definite slant downward, and Megan found herself constantly scooting back away from the edge, for she tended to slide the moment she relaxed her guard.

She had managed to sit up, her back to the cliffside, her legs bent and her feet braced in front of her. Clutching her knees to her chest, she had rested her chin atop them and gazed about her in dismay. Had her situation not been so desperate, she might have enjoyed the view. From her precarious perch, she could see for miles. That cheered her not at all at the moment, for all she could think of was perishing slowly; alone, frightened, hurt, and hungry. She had wanted to get away from Blake. Well, she surely had done that! Indeed, she would be lucky if he, or anyone else, found her bleached bones years from now! How would he ever find her here?

Tears trickled down her face, stinging her scratched and scraped cheeks. That lone cabin seemed like a pleasant little haven by comparison. At this moment, she would sell her soul to the devil to be back there, safe and sound in Blake's keep. Would she ever see his dear face again? Hear his husky words of love whispered in her ear? Would she ever feel his hands caressing her, his lips so warm and enticing over hers? She would give the earth just to hear him yelling at her now! "Oh, Blake! I love you so. Please come after me. Please come and get me off of this rock!"

She had sat there shivering in shock and despair for what seemed like ten lifetimes. On her slanted perch she dared not move about too much, for fear she would lose her grip and tumble over the edge. As she huddled miserably into a ball, her various injuries soon made themselves felt. Though she had broken no bones, she had accrued quite a number of scrapes and bruises. The skin had literally been torn from her palms and fingers in her scramble to pull herself onto the ledge. Her shoulder ached abominably from the effort to lever herself upward, and there were several lumps arising all over her body where she had crashed into rocks on her descent. Her left cheek was seeping, she could scarcely bend her right elbow, and grit was ground into the raw flesh of both knees. Megan feared that the moisture trickling between her shoulder blades was not merely perspiration, and her left ankle was swollen three times its normal size. Even as she told herself she should consider herself lucky to be alive, pain gnawed at her; and she could not help but wonder if she would die here on this small ledge after all, perhaps not from her minimal injuries, but of starvation, thirst, exposure, or heaven forbid—some wild animal! Good sense told her no animal could reach her here, but fear was already making her thoughts unreasonable, panic swiftly gaining a foothold in her mind.

As the sun began to set, her fears grew. Hope of being found was flickering out, like a candle sputtering at the end of its wick. Shock was making her sleepy, and only fear kept her eyelids from fluttering closed. If she were to give in to her weariness, she was sure to tumble to her death, but how long could she stay awake? How long could a person go without sleep? As a child, she had sometimes dreamed of falling, only to awaken with a jerk to find herself in her own bed. If she fell asleep now, falling would not be a dream. It would be horribly real, and if she awakened, it would be to feel her body dashed upon the rocks far below. There would be no safe awakening from this nightmare!

She was sobbing softly to herself as the twilight deepened. Her crying nearly masked the sound of Blake's voice calling out her name. Stifling her sobs, she listened hopefully, praying that she had not merely been hallucinating. "Oh, please, God! Let it be him!" she thought wildly. "Let him find me!" Her voice weak and scratchy from crying, she called out to him.

When his face had appeared over the edge of the cliff, Megan nearly swooned with relief. In the gloom, she could not make out his features, but his voice was blessedly familiar calling down to her. Fear had gripped her again when he failed to see her there, and for a moment she thought he might give up and go away. Then he had spotted her. His cursing had sounded like a heavenly choir to her ears, and angry as she knew he must be, his face was more welcome than anyone's just now. "Blake, come and get me off of here!" she begged.

"Yeah, well I'm trying to figure out just how to do that, Megan," he called back. "You sure did get yourself into a pickle, girl. You couldn't have picked a worse spot to land in, could you?"

Megan shuddered just thinking about where she might have landed with a little less luck. "As a matter of fact, yes! Until I latched onto this ledge, I was on a fast ride toward the bottom of this little hill, and I doubt I would have survived the fall!" She could not believe she was now shouting at the only man available to save her. "Blake, please! I'm so scared!"

"Are you hurt?"

"Not too badly, I think."

"Okay, stay put and I'll be right back."

"Blake! Where are you going? Don't leave me here!" Panic threatened to overwhelm her again.

"I'll be right back, honey. I've got to get a rope. I'll only be a minute. Just sit tight."

"Sit tight," she grumbled to herself. "Where else would I go?" Megan curled her arms about her knees and waited for what seemed an eternity for Blake to return.

Blake could not believe the situation Megan had gotten herself into this time. He could not bear to think how he might have found her, her body crumpled and broken at the bottom of the cliff. Relief washed through him that she was not badly hurt. It was a miracle that he had found her at all, down there on that tiny hidden ledge.

Lord, he had surely had his share of problems since he and that woman had crossed paths! She was more trouble than a passel of wild Indians, and about as amiable. After nearly cracking his skull open with that skillet, he ought to leave her on that ledge for a while, just to teach her a lesson, but he knew he did not have the heart to do that to her. She looked so small and frightened huddled there. She had already suffered enough for her impetuous flight. Besides, angry as he still was with her, he was now uncomfortably sure that he was in love!

Blake led his horse near the edge of the cliff. Looping one end of a rope securely to the pommel of the saddle, he formed a larger loop at the opposite end. "Megan!" he called down. "I'm going to throw a rope down to you. Slip it about your middle, under your arms, and pull the loop tight about you. Can you manage that?"

"I-I'll try," came the answer.

"Don't try; do it!"

"Insufferably bossy man," she grumbled, every square inch of her body aching by now. She waited as he threw the rope over the edge of the cliff and dangled it down to her. It floated just out of her grasp, and she dared not lean out to grab it. "I can't reach it, Blake!"

He tried again, with the same result. The rope swung just so close and no closer, always just out of her reach. Megan wanted to weep again.

"Drat it, Megan! You're not trying! Grab the blasted thing!" Blake was becoming exasperated, not with her, but with the whole miserable situation. His head ached abominably, and he knew he wouldn't draw a proper breath until he had her safe once more.

"I am trying!" she wailed. "I don't dare move about too much! This sliver of rock is not very big, you know. Besides, I can barely see the rope to grab at it!"

"Well, what am I supposed to do, sweetheart? Should I set the damned thing on fire so you can see it more clearly?" he shouted down sarcastically.

"Don't shout at me!" she yelled back. On a quivering breath, she suggested more mildly, "Couldn't you climb down and get me, Blake?"

He wanted to scream with exasperation and helplessness. "Megan, my own," he answered as calmly as he could, "just do as I told you. There is no sense in both our lives being in peril. I'm not sure I could manage a feat such as that. You see, someone clobbered my head with an iron skillet. I have a lump the size of a mountain on my skull, and it's been all I could do to track you this far. Now, grab the blasted rope and I'll pull you up; or rather, my horse will.''

Fighting back tears, Megan finally managed to snag hold of the rope. ''I've got it!''

Blake heaved a sigh of relief. ''Put it around you and pull it tight.'' Several seconds went by with no response. ''Megan? What's the problem?''

The problem was trying to squirm about enough to loop the rope about herself without losing her balance. Megan's muscles were stiff and sore, not to mention the many abrasions and her aching shoulder.

''Megan? Megan, answer me!''

Megan had just managed to get the rope about her chest and both arms outside the loop when her foot slipped. Down off the ledge she went, nothing below her but a four-hundred-foot drop. Her scream echoed off the rocky wall.

Many feet above her, Megan's scream came simultaneously with the rope suddenly slipping rapidly through Blake's hands. Blake frantically grabbed at it, wrapping his bare hands around the rope in an effort to stop her fall. Still the rope whistled through his palms, burning them and nearly pulling Blake over the edge of the cliff for his efforts. Just when he was sure the bones in his hands would be crushed, the rope reached its end. Behind him, Blake heard his horse snort loudly as the rope pulled taut. Cow-trained as he was, the horse kept his head and his balance, taking the sudden weight at the other end of the rope with good grace.

"Bless you, Scoundrel," Blake breathed, even as Megan's second pain-filled scream reached his ears. Easing his torn hands from the coils of the rope, Blake leaned over, trying to spot Megan at the other end. It was too dark now to see her.

"Megan? Sweetheart, are you all right?"

"Oh, God, Blake," she moaned. "Pull me up. Please, hurry and pull me up." Tears clogged her throat, making her voice husky. "I think my shoulder is broken."

"Did you hit the wall? Are you near enough to it so you can push against it with your feet and help to guide yourself?"

"No," she groaned through gritted teeth. Megan was twirling dizzily at the end of the rope like a spinning top. Between that and the intense pain in her shoulder, she was becoming more nauseated and closer to fainting by the second.

"Grab the rope with your good hand, Megan," he instructed, already backing his horse slowly, step by step, pulling Megan toward the top.

"Aaargh!" Megan's gruff cry made him cringe for her. He could only imagine the pain and fright she was experiencing.

"Almost there, darlin'," he encouraged.

It seemed eons before he caught sight of her, longer still before he could grab hold of her extended arm and pull her to safety. Swiftly he undid the rope and hauled her into the haven of his arms. She lay panting and crying in the cradle of his lap. Blake stroked her bright head, relief pouring through him. After a while her crying ceased.

"God, Megan, you gave me such a scare," he whispered agonizingly. "I don't know what I would have done if I'd lost you.'' He kissed the top of her head. ''You are nothing but trouble, but heaven help me, I love you.''

There was no response from her. Gently he raised her bruised face to his. She had not heard his soft admission. For the first time in her life, Megan had fainted.

10

Megan rode in front of Blake on his horse, as she had when he'd first captured her. She was cradled in his arms, her head resting on his broad chest, as they made their way back to the cabin after spending the night in the hills.

Blake had made a thorough survey of her injuries. The worst had been her shoulder, which had been dislocated by the jolt at the end of the rope. After determining that it was not broken, he had popped her shoulder back into place. As near as he could tell, the muscles or tendons were not greatly damaged. Oh, she would be plenty sore for the next week or so, but she had been blessedly lucky. Her ankle was sprained and swollen, and her back and limbs and face bruised and scraped. Blake had tended to these injuries as best he could, carefully cleaning the bits of dirt and rock from her shredded palms and knees.

By the time Megan had awakened, her shoulder was aching and her various abrasions stinging. Her muscles were sore, too, but she was alive and safe and wrapped in a blanket by the campfire Blake had built. He had then proceeded to give her a tongue lashing she would never forget, starting with the fact that she had dared to clobber him with that frying pan and try to escape from him. He had gone on to list all the things she had done in their short time together to make his life miserable. He ended by bluntly informing her that he had been forced to shoot her horse because the animal's foreleg had been broken. Last but not least, he had told her that hell would freeze solid before she escaped him again.

By the time he had finished, Megan was well aware of how furious Blake was with her. She had no doubt that he would, in one way or another, make her pay dearly for her attempt to escape him this time, and if she ever tried it again there was no telling what he might do to her. In her heart, she was not positive she would not try again, but if she did, she intended to make a better job of it. For now, she was too grateful to be safe to contemplate much else. For now it was enough to be alive, to be warm, to be cared for, to have Blake here with her, angry though he was. It was all she could do not to tell him so, not to tell him how wonderful it was to see his angry face again and his snapping blue eyes, how much she had feared she never would again. It was all she could do not to tell him how dearly she loved him.

He had fed her, then prepared the bedroll for the two of them. Megan had fallen asleep in the warm, secure curve of his arms, her head pillowed on his chest and the secure sound of his regular heartbeats in her ear. She had awakened several times in the night, once when she had dreamed of falling from the ledge. Megan had awakened to the sound of her own screams, her body jerking violently. Blake had soothed her with gentle words in the dark velvet night; he had quieted her with his tender touch, his hands stroking her with infinite care until she at last slipped into sleep again.

The tenderness had seemed to vanish with the morning light, and they had ridden for hours now in silence. Blake was acting like a bear with a sore paw, and Megan was weary enough and wise enough not to aggravate him. She was much too sore to do much to antagonize him anyway. It was all she could do to grit her teeth against the pain that lanced through her shoulder at every jarring step the horse took. She got no sympathy from Blake, who merely threw her a damning look each time she moaned in pain.

In truth, Blake was angry at both of them. He was furious at Megan for all the trouble she had instigated, for nearly killing herself trying to escape him, and for the persistent headache that made his head pound and his eyes hurt. He was also angry at himself, for being so stupid as to steal her from that stagecoach in the first place, for endangering her life, for not having reached her before she had taken that hair-raising tumble down the cliff—and for caring about her as much as he did!

Yes, most of all, he castigated himself for having fallen in love with this little she-devil in angelic disguise. What good did it do to love her now? Even if she were to come to love him in return, he had nothing to offer her until Kirk agreed to the terms of the ransom. Then Blake would have to release her as his part of the agreement. Either way, he lost. Besides, after all he had put her through, what made him think Megan could ever come to love him? Sure, she enjoyed their lovemaking, but that did not mean she loved him. Even in the midst of their passion, she had never said anything about love. Perhaps she still loved Kirk, even after hearing the truth about him. Megan had never indicated that she believed Blake's side of the story or that she'd had a change of heart about Kirk. Blake sighed defeatedly. By involving Megan and then losing his heart to her, he had very neatly painted himself into a corner, and he had no one to blame but himself!

Though they had left the campsite just after dawn, it was nearly dark by the time they arrived at the cabin. By this time, Megan was sure she was about to die from her various aches and pains. Blake was not feeling much better.

The one thing that seemed to brighten Blake's mood was the fact that Lobo was there ahead of them. He was lying on the small porch, patiently awaiting their arrival.

Blake carried Megan into the cabin and laid her on the bed. "Don't move from this spot," he warned her gruffly, his blue eyes shooting angry sparks at her. "I'm going to have a look around, and I'll be right back." When he returned, he escorted her to the makeshift outhouse, heated a kettle of hot water for her, and fixed a quick supper for them while she washed the worst of the grime and horse smell from herself. He even grudgingly gave her one of his extra shirts to use as a nightgown, since her own clothes were dirty and torn from her misadventures.

Then, to her amazement and dismay, instead of making a bedroll for himself on the floor as he had done before, he climbed into the bed with her. At her astounded look, he said dryly, "If you think for one minute that I am going to put myself out for you, when I can sleep in comfort, you are seriously mistaken. I am going to sleep right here, where I can know exactly where you are, asleep or awake. From now on, I am going to know every breath you take. In fact, I'll have breathed it first."

"Really, Blake!" she retorted. "I'm not exactly in any condition to make a midnight escape just now."

He had the audacity to give her a nasty grin. "I know. That means I should have a good night's sleep for a change tonight." With that, he promptly turned his back on her, and within minutes his even breathing told her that he had fallen asleep.

When Megan awoke the next morning, Blake was already up and gone from the cabin. She lay there a few minutes trying to decide whether it was worth the effort to her sore muscles to try to get out of bed and get dressed. The thought of putting on those same torn and grimy clothes did not appeal, yet neither did running about clothed only in Blake's shirt. "What I would give for just one extra set of underclothes and one change of dress," she groaned in self-pity. To make things worse, in her fall she had lost one of her shoes, and Blake had had to ruin the other when cutting it from her swollen foot. Now she had nothing to wear on her feet. It was certain that Blake's large boots would never fit her small feet, even if he had an extra pair to offer her. Somehow Megan doubted he would offer them in any case.

It dawned on Megan that she was hearing a peculiar scraping sound from outside. Listening closely, she could not place the particularly rhythmic sounds. Curiosity finally got the better of her. Cautiously, with some pain and a bit of unladylike groaning, she pulled herself from the bed and hobbled to the side window. The sounds seemed to be coming from the area back of the cabin. She could hear them more clearly now, but could not see what was going on. Plucking the few remaining slivers of glass from the frame of the shattered window, she leaned out, careful not to jar her shoulder or put her weight on the injured ankle.

Megan was immediately sorry she had been so persistent. She finally had a good view of what was causing the bothersome noise. There was Blake, stripped to the waist, doggedly digging a grave for the four bandits who had been killed in the shootout. As early as it was, with the cool of the morning still upon them, Blake's labors had brought a sheen of perspiration to his skin. Sweat ran in rivulets down his bare back and dampened the waistband of his pants. As he turned to dump a shovelful of dirt away from the hole, Megan caught a glimpse of his face. It was grim and drawn, his jaw clamped so tightly that his lips were no more than a solemn slash across his face, his nostrils distended and his eyes narrowed into blue slits. It was obvious that he took no pleasure in his grim task.

Megan was careful not to make a sound as she

pulled back from the window. Conflicting thoughts muddled her mind. Blake had joined forces with these men in the robbery of the stagecoach, yet when they had come to the cabin—was it really only the day before yesterday?—he had readily protected her from them. Of course, he'd been defending himself also. He had fought these men and killed them, yet now he was taking the time to give them a proper burial. Why? Was it simply because he had to dispose of the bodies somehow? Perhaps he did not want anyone else coming upon the dead men's bodies near the cabin. Or maybe it was just in his nature to do what he considered proper. Was it out of necessity and caution, or out of a sense of propriety that he was laboring out there, digging graves in the morning sun?

Megan shook her head. Would she never know the ways of this man who had kidnapped her, then stolen her heart? One minute he was stern and forbidding; the next he was gentle or teasing. Which was the real Blake Montgomery, or were they all a part of the man? Was he good or evil, kind or hard-bitten, avenging angel or marauding devil —or a combination of all these things?

One thing she knew without doubt. He was the man she had fallen in love with; the one man she could not have and was much better off without. If and when she ever escaped him, she would leave a major part of herself with him. Her body would be gone from his, but her heart would remain within his grasp for a long, long time. The pity of it was that Blake would probably never guess that she loved him, and if he should guess her secret, most likely he would not care. His indifference would hurt most of all. That was why Megan would do all she could to keep him from knowing how deeply she had come to care for him. She could stand anything but his indifference, or worse yet, his ridicule.

By the time Blake finished his self-appointed task and returned to the cabin, Megan had managed to hobble about well enough to fix their breakfast. Blake entered the cabin to the enticing aroma of freshly perked coffee, delicately browned cinnamon rolls, and perfectly fried eggs, bacon, and potatoes. He stood in stunned disbelief as he eyed the meal steaming on the table. "What is all this?" he asked quietly.

Megan smiled sheepishly. "I—uh—well, I can cook after all, you see," she stammered.

Blake waved his hand over the table. "Why?"

"Why did I pretend not to know how to cook, or why have I decided to reveal the fact now?" she asked.

"Both."

"I lied before because I was hurt and angry, as well as scared. I didn't want to cook for you," she admitted, feeling perfectly justified in her previous behavior.

"And now?"

Megan's glance veered away from his, pain and embarrassment mixed on her face. "You saved my life yesterday. It's the least I can do to show my appreciation," she said shakily. When he continued to stare at her as if she were some strange mystery, she said, "Go on. Sit down and eat while it is still hot."

All through the meal, Megan continued to feel

his curious gaze. When he had finished, he complimented her on her skill. "Breakfast was very good,
Megan. Thank you."

"You're welcome. Thank *you* for coming to my
rescue yesterday. I really don't see how you managed to find me, but I am so very glad you did."
With effort, she forced herself to meet his avid gaze.

Was it wry humor or curiosity that made his
eyes glisten so? "Are you, Megan?" he questioned
softly. "Forgive me if I don't quite believe you. You
went to a lot of pain and trouble to escape me, and
all for nothing. I very much suspect that you are
like the thief who was brought to trial — sorry only
that he was caught, but not really repentant of the
deed."

Megan had the grace to blush, but still she
defended her statement. "Of course I mean it,
Blake. If not for you, I would still be sitting there on
that ledge, unable to climb off. That, or I would
have fallen to my death by now. How could I fail to
be grateful to escape such a fate?"

"Ah, I see," he jeered. "The lesser of two evils.
Life is preferable to death, even if it means that I
have you back in my evil grasp once more?"

Her chin tilted up in that telltale gesture of
hers. "Something like that," she conceded haughtily.

"And now that you have revealed your true
culinary skills, am I to continue to be rewarded
with decent meals?" he prodded. "After all, your
life must be worth more than one uncharred breakfast."

"I pay my debts, Blake. From now on, I will
cook our meals." She was frowning at him now. He

was not being gracious about this at all, and she had
been trying to make it up to him for all the trouble
she had put him to yesterday.

"Decent, edible food?"

"Yes!" she hissed. "Now, will you stop bela-
boring the point? Sweet heaven, I'm sorry I ever
brought the matter to light. I swear you have got to
be the most exasperating man God ever set breath
into. Didn't anyone ever tell you not to look a gift
horse in the mouth?"

He favored her with that crooked, half-devious
smile of his. "Oh, but unlike the poor Trojans, I am
too suspicious to be led merrily down the garden
path by either a sudden gift or a pretty face. You
may be nearly as beautiful as the famed Helen, my
Megan, and like her you were brought away against
your will; but unlike her, there will be no rescue
for you until Kirk delivers the deed to the ranch
into my waiting hands—no tricks, no false promises, just the restoration of my birthright."

"And what if Kirk doesn't agree?" she queried
hesitantly.

Again that decidedly wicked smile. "Then
you'd better measure the windows and place an
order for material for curtains the next time Jake
comes up this way, because we are both going to be
here until he does agree, little darlin', no matter
how long it takes."

A short time later Blake collected his rifle,
called Lobo to his side, and informed Megan that he
was going in search of Paco. "Since Lobo returned,
I think it is safe to assume that Paco is dead, but I
just want to be sure. Since I need Lobo to lead me to

him, I have placed the other horses out of your reach. If you should manage to get out of the cabin, which I shall lock on my way out, you'll never be able to find them. Besides, I doubt you can walk ten feet without breaking your neck, so I'd advise you to remain inside until I return. I wouldn't try to climb out any of the windows, if I were you. The only reason I haven't boarded them up is because I feel confident that you won't manage a sudden, miraculous cure in the few hours I will be gone, and I thought you might appreciate the fresh air.''

"How awfully kind of you!" she retorted snidely. "And have you given any thought to what I should do if Paco is not dead and has decided to return while you are gone? What if he has friends who are even now looking for him and show up in your absence? Aren't you even going to leave me a gun so that I might defend myself?"

He didn't even try to stifle the hoot of laughter that erupted. "You really take the cake, Megan, to think I would be fool enough to arm you! You never stop trying, do you?"

"Well, what if something happens to you and you can't get back? What if someone does come? One locked door certainly won't stop them, particularly when they could climb right in the open windows! What am I supposed to do? How would I defend myself?" she argued insistently.

Blake walked calmly to where the skillet lay on the table. Picking it up, he nonchalantly tossed it toward her. It landed at her feet with a resounding clang. "Use this," he commented dryly. "You seem to be uncommonly handy with it."

On his way out the door, he turned. "Remember what I said about staying put, Megan. After yesterday, you should know how dangerous this territory is. You wouldn't get too far in your condition before I caught up with you, but you never know what might happen in the meanwhile. I might remind you of the wild animals out there."

"You remind me of one in particular," she said. "A skunk!"

"I'll remind you of a much more dangerous animal if I come back to find you gone again," he promised. "And I won't go so easy on you a second time." With one last measuring look he walked out and barred the door from the outside, as Megan looked on in dismay. Then she watched miserably from the window as he mounted his horse and rode off, Lobo loping along at his side.

For a while, Megan moped about the cabin, sulking and pouting in her anger. She sat in the old rocker at the window and rocked until she was almost dizzy, until the rockers on the ancient piece of furniture nearly smoked in protest of her frenzied movements to and fro. When she could stand her inactivity no longer, she gathered the ingredients and prepared two loaves of bread, setting the pans of dough on a sunny windowsill to rise. Sick to death of Blake's nourishing but boring stews, she found soup beans and smoked ham hocks among the supplies Jake had brought. Luckily, Blake had thought to bring a sufficient supply of water into the cabin to start a pot of soup. She even took the extra effort to make dumplings to add to the bean soup.

That done, Megan was still restless. Had her

ankle not pained her so, she would surely have paced the cabin in frustration. Instead, she located several badly wrinkled but usable apples, which she pared and made into a pie. Then she took up thread and needle and attempted to repair the damage to her clothing.

It was hopeless. Whole sections of her dress and petticoat were nearly in shreds from her tumble over the cliffside. The material was so strained in places that it would not hold the stitches. Megan held the cloth up and shook her head in dismay. The dirt was literally ground into the weave, and the scrubbing it would take to clean the garments again would further strain the weakened fabric. Even if she could get the dirt out, she doubted she could thoroughly remove the dried bloodstains left from her various wounds.

In the end, the only garment she could properly repair was her chemise. Her petticoat looked like something her mother would use for a dust rag, and her dress was so tattered and soiled that no poorhouse resident would be caught dead in it. Still, she had no choice but to wear the clothes. It was either that or go about in Blake's shirt for the duration of her stay with him. Granted, the shirt hung on her, covering her from beyond the tips of her fingers nearly to her knees, but that still left an awful lot of leg showing. Blake had already proven to be a very sensual man, and the last thing she needed now was to arouse his virile nature. No, it would not do to throw temptation in his path! With that thought firmly in mind, Megan resignedly dressed in her tattered attire.

It was late afternoon when Megan heard the

sounds of an approaching horse. It was with much relief that she saw Blake ride into the clearing. He was alone, save for Lobo. If he had found Paco, he had not brought him back, dead or alive.

Megan met him at the door. "Well?" she asked.

The look he gave her told her his dark mood had not improved since morning. "I found him," he said shortly.

"And?"

"He was dead."

"I noticed you didn't bring the body back with you."

"No."

Getting information out of him was like pulling teeth from an alligator. "Did you bury him?" At his questioning look, she admitted, "I saw you through the window this morning when you were burying the others."

"Yes, I buried him." *What there was left of him to bury after Lobo finished with him*, he added to himself with a hidden shudder. "Any more questions?"

Megan shrugged and turned away, trying to keep the hurt from registering on her face. "Megan, look. I'm sorry, but it has been a very trying couple of days. I'm tired, dirty, and hungry. It's making me a little short-tempered. Did you have any trouble here while I was away?"

"A lot you care! You are not the only one who has spent a few rough hours lately." Try as she might, Megan could not control the quiver that crept into her voice. "I ache all over, I'm filthy from head to toe, my clothes are ruined and I've lost my shoes! And I burned my darned thumb on the blasted pie tin," she hastened to inform him. The events of the last few days had caught up with her. Her nerves were thoroughly frayed. She loved a man who would only break her heart, and her one attempt to escape him had nearly meant her death. All at once it was too much to bear. Tears came suddenly, rolling down her cheeks in salty tracks as he swung her about to face him.

He pulled her gently into his arms, easily overcoming her token resistance. "Don't cry, *pequeña*," he crooned. "Tell you what. Let's take a quick trip to the river. The water will help to ease the stiffness in your muscles, and you will feel like a new woman once you are clean again. Then we will come back and eat the delicious dinner you have worked so hard to prepare."

She sniffled against his shirt. "I didn't think you had noticed."

"Of course I did. It's been a long time since I've come home to the smell of freshly baked bread and apple pie. And if my nose does not fail me, there is also the aroma of ham and beans in this room." He lifted her chin with lean fingers until her face tilted toward his. His smile made her knees go weak. "It's a nice feeling to know that someone went to all that trouble just to feed me. Thank you, sweetheart. Now, how about that bath?"

"Okay." She managed a shaky smile in return.

His grin turned devilish, his eyes now lighting with roguish delight. "I might even be persuaded to tuck you in and tell you a bedtime story, if dinner is half as good as it smells," he added. He gave her a mischievous wink. "And I tell a heck of a bedtime tale, little darlin'!"

11

Was it just the moon, spreading its fragile light upon the water like a sheer wedding veil; or the stars, so big and bright in the clear Arizona night that they seemed close enough to touch? Or was it the warm evening breeze that caressed the skin like a lover's touch—like Blake's touch as he gently washed her, careful not to jar her tender shoulder? It might have been a combination of all these and more, for the water felt like satin lapping at her sensitive skin as Megan stood in the stream and let Blake minister to her. The night had taken on a magical quality, like something out of a favorite fairy tale where the witch miraculously became a princess once more and the handsome prince fell madly in love with her, taking her away with him to his castle where they lived happily ever more. At any moment Megan expected to see woodsprites dancing merrily on moonbeams, so enchanted did the moment seem.

Blake had led the way to the river, where he had cajoled her into removing her dress and petticoat. Clad only in her combination, which she called a chemise but was actually chemise and drawers in one garment, Megan then obediently stood in the water as Blake proceeded to wash her hair. Oh, how sinfully delicious it had felt to have his long fingers gently massaging her scalp! How pampered she felt. Except for directing her to tilt her head this way or that, not another word was spoken between them.

Now Blake had finished with her hair, and his hands were ever-so-lightly cleaning her body, easing the stiffness from her injured shoulder with strong, knowing strokes. The buoyancy of the water seemed to carry her body closer to his, and she could feel the heat of his skin. As his fingers brushed aside the shoulder straps of her chemise, a flush rose through her and she was glad she was not facing him at that moment. Yet when she might have voiced a protest, no words came from her parted lips. It was as if he and the night had consorted to cast a spell upon her, willing her to comply with his wishes.

The bodice of her chemise fell away, baring her breasts to the night breeze, and as Blake's hands followed the material to the curve of her waist, gooseflesh rose on her flesh and her nipples puckered in response. As he pushed the cloth over her hips to float lazily toward her feet, he felt her stiffen slightly, though no murmur was forthcoming. Still, sensing her confusion, he whispered, "Let me adore you, *mi paloma*. Let me."

His words, spoken softly against the responsive flesh of her bared neck, sent yet another thrill through her. A part of her knew she should not be placidly allowing this, should be protesting. It would only compound her problems, deepen her feeling for him at a time when she was most vulnerable. It would only mean greater heartbreak later, but she couldn't seem to forget how horrible it had been to think that she might die and never feel his touch again, never know his body within hers once more.

She tilted her head even further back, allowing him better access to her throat as his lips now sought a path to her ear. Sharp teeth nibbled tauntingly at her lobe, making her shiver, and when his hot tongue swirled inside the shell of her ear, Megan's knees threatened to give way beneath her. Only Blake's strong arms about her waist prevented her from sinking beneath the water. Of its own, her body sought the warmth and support of his. Even through the sodden material of his denims, which he had left on to appease her modesty, she could feel the proof of his rising passion. The mat of damp curls that covered his chest tickled her bare back.

As his hands moved up along her ribs on a course to her breasts, Megan found herself holding her breath in anticipation. Then his hands, cool from the water, yet strangely warm, cradled the underside of each waiting breast. When his thumbs came up to brush the puckered crests, her breath released in a throaty moan. "Give to me, Megan, my dove," he murmured low. "Give to me freely of your sweet love, your warm honey. Give me all of you there is to give a man, and I will take you tenderly. I will show you a world of such splendor it will make you weep with joy to behold it." He turned her in his arms so that she was facing him, her breasts pressed tightly to his furred chest. Looking deep into her wide grey eyes, eyes that shone like silver with the reflection of the moonlit water, he implored, "Share this with me tonight, *querida*. Here, now, for I need you as I have never before needed any woman. Share the golden splendor with me."

Her answer was there in her eyes, in the arms that rose to wrap about his neck and pull his lips down to meet hers. This time it was her lips that melted onto his, her tongue that parted his sharp white teeth to seek entrance to his mouth. It was her tongue that met with his in a heated duel that fueled their passion, her fingers threading through his ebony hair to hold his lips to hers. When, at length, their moist mouths parted, she whispered breathlessly, "Love me, Blake. I want you. God knows, I want you more than my next breath."

His arms tightened about her as he held her close to him, her breasts branding his chest. Diamond-blue eyes filled with desire stared down into hers for a long, enchanted moment. Then his hot, firm lips were tenderly ravaging hers, his long fingers delving into her shining wet tresses to cradle her head as he took his fill of the delights of her mouth. There, with the heat of their longing warming the cool water, his broad hands relearned the curves and contours of her silken body. With a touch as light as a whisper, as caressing as the water lapping gently about them, he again found her breasts. His calloused palms and fingers teased her yearning flesh, the rosy nubs that thrust themselves invitingly into his hands.

She quivered like a flame in his arms, his name trembling from her lips as her hands now sought his flesh, seeking to return the pleasures he was giving her. Slender shaking fingers brushed lightly against the cloth of his trousers, unerringly finding his swollen manhood, and Blake thought he would explode with longing. His hand joined hers there, clasping her fingers to his heat, then guiding them to the fastenings of his denims. For just a moment she faltered, then acceding to his wordless command, she struggled to push the heavy buttons through the wet cloth that bound them. It seemed an interminable time, to both of them, before the task was finally accomplished. With burning impatience, he helped her push the trousers past his hips, then kicked free of them at last.

Their naked bodies came together like iron to a magnet. Slick, hot flesh sought its match as limbs twisted together and moist lips slid heatedly to give pleasure wherever they might. For endless minutes they held one another in sweet torment, until neither could withstand the torture further. Lifting her in shaking arms, he twined her legs about his waist. Beneath her hands she felt the muscles of his shoulders bunch and quiver as they took her slight weight.

Then she was sliding down his slick belly, slowly lowered to be impaled upon his stiff spear. As she felt him enter her, the breath left her body in a rush. Her back arched against the band of his arms as she sought to accommodate him further, to take all of him within her warm, waiting sheath. Her moan of sheer pleasure mingled with his on the night breeze. He filled her completely, momentarily assuaging that empty yearning that had tormented her. Tiny tremors seemed to radiate throughout her body, tremors centered where Blake now rested within her.

Blake thought he would lose his mind as he felt her slight convulsions about him, telling him just how much she wanted him, how more than ready she was for this joining. "So tight," he murmured. "So warm and wet and silken." As he held himself tightly within her, his lips sought her thrusting breasts, first one, then the other. The budded crests unfolded within the warmth of his mouth, like flowers to the sun, then sprang forth even more boldly as he suckled upon them. He reveled in her immediate response, her silken muscles tightening about him, drawing him even further into her body, pulling him to the very depths of her, until he felt himself touch the mouth of her womb. That she felt it too was evident as she tightened about him, quivering and mewling his name in a voice weak with desire.

She wanted to hold him there forever, but already her body was issuing more urgent instructions. Of their own volition, her hips rotated upon him, teasing and pleasing him at once. He answered her unspoken taunt by withdrawing from her, then plunging deep within her once more, then again and again. Their bodies danced the dance of fire and flame, their passions rising higher and higher, blinding them to all but their violent needs. The flames rose, consuming them, fusing them body and soul, until, when they thought they would surely die of the pleasurable torment, they burst together in a furious blaze that hurled them into a world of glowing, golden glory. Shimmering lights danced about them, showering them with unbelievable beauty, twirling slowly about their entwined beings.

Megan clung dizzily to Blake's muscled shoulders, the molten weakness sapping her strength. Her head found the cushion of his chest as he shifted her into his arms and carried her wordlessly to the cabin. In her benumbed state, she barely realized that her shoulder had ceased to ache, or her ankle to throb. She no longer felt the numerous abrasions from her fall. She was completely relaxed, warm and comfortable and totally at home in Blake's arms. She let the feeling of rightness wash over her, welcoming it as she had welcomed Blake.

The feeling remained as Blake gently laid her on the bed and joined her there. The warm glow continued as his lips scattered reverent kisses upon her face and he gathered her body close to his as she drifted off to sleep. And the glow was still there when he awakened her in the night to make love to her once more, and then again before dawn began to tinge the morning sky in shades of pink and gold.

The bed was empty when Megan awoke the next morning, her arm reaching out to encounter the bare spot where Blake's warm body should have been. She stifled a yawn, as her eyelids drifted open. Then she saw him. He was standing in the open doorway, looking out at the early morning. As she watched silently, his hand came up to rake through his midnight hair in a gesture somewhere between impatience and weariness. She saw more than heard his deep sigh, his bare shoulders rising and falling with his breath. He seemed troubled, and Megan could not help but wonder if it had something to do with their repeated and tender loving the night before.

In the light of morning, Megan was not entirely comfortable with the situation herself. What had taken hold of them last evening? Was it moonlight madness that had swamped their senses, making them lose themselves in one another's arms? Megan blushed warmly as she recalled their wild, uninhibited loving—the things he had done to her with his hands and his mouth—the things he had enticed her to do to him in return. She had lost count of the number of times she had been forced to bite her tongue to keep from crying out to him how much she loved him.

Blake was having similar thoughts. God, but he did love this woman! Still, he should have kept his vow to himself; he should never have touched her again, should never have succumbed to the temptation to make wild, wonderful love with her. It would only make it harder to give her up. There was no future for them together. Not now—not yet—perhaps never. But he couldn't seem to hold himself back from her. He needed her sweetness and soft sighs like drought-stricken land needs rain. He had never needed another living person as much as he needed Megan.

He turned to find her still watching him. For a moment they watched one another warily. Then his gaze swept over her disheveled form, from the one breast nearly bared beneath the rumpled bedsheet to her tangled mass of cinnamon curls, and his lips curved in a reluctant grin. His hungry eyes again met hers, his feet already carrying him back to the bed. As Megan shyly returned his smile, he shucked his britches, and when he made to join her on the bed, she scooted over to make room and lifted the sheet to admit him.

The next hour was spent in joyful pursuit of the glorious gratification they now knew they could share together. If either of them felt a twinge of guilt, they quickly buried it. There would be time later for regrets. Now, while they yet had time together, both silently vowed to make the most of it.

In the next few days, whenever Blake was away from the cabin, Megan began a campaign to win Lobo's trust. As frightened as she was of the huge animal, she knew it was her only chance. If she could befriend the wolf, perhaps he would one day allow her to leave the cabin, despite Blake's instructions. Then again, her efforts might prove all in vain, but it was worth a try. She still intended to try to escape at the first opportunity, as much to save Blake from himself and the dangers to his life as for all her other reasons.

She began by sneaking Lobo bits of food. At first the wary beast would not venture near the tempting tidbits she offered. Wryly, Megan wondered if he remembered the charred meal she had first cooked. These offerings were much more enticing, however, and gradually Lobo's twitching nose overcame his wariness. She only fed him small amounts each time, only what he could quickly eat, for she feared what Blake might do should he discover her trying to befriend his faithful pet. To think he would be angry was a gross understatement, she was certain.

Megan was much too scared of Lobo to try to feed him by hand. Instead, she at first threw the offerings onto the porch where Lobo would sit guarding her. After several times in this manner, she garnered the nerve to calmly set the food just outside the door of the cabin, letting Lobo come closer to gain his choice bits. Finally, she even left the door open, both wolf and girl watching one another as he crept up and sampled her offerings.

It was several days before she dared to offer Lobo a piece of meat from her hand. Megan had to force her hand not to tremble as the huge wolf sniffed at the food in her fingers. When his sharp white teeth bared and reached out, it was all she could do not to back away or drop the meat and slam the door. As he finally bit into the thick chunk of rabbit, Megan nearly screamed, fearing he meant to take her fingers in the process. But Lobo very gingerly plucked the meat from her fingers. So neatly was it done that his teeth did not even graze her flesh.

So stunned was she, and so scared still, that Megan did not immediately draw back her hand. Therefore, when Lobo's long wet tongue suddenly lapped at her open palm, she nearly fainted in fright. She looked down to find Lobo gazing up at her with limpid eyes. "Good doggie," she managed to croak, forcing a wobbly smile to her lips. "Good Lobo." His furry tail thumped once on the wooden floor of the porch. Then both he and Megan backed off from one another. Shakily she shut the door. So far, so good. She still had all her fingers. With luck, one day soon Lobo would trust her enough to allow her out of the cabin.

When Blake was there, he and Megan spent long hours together. In unspoken agreement, they took advantage of their truce, new and fragile though it was. Each tried to avoid subjects that would anger the other or cause bad feelings. Neither wanted anger or sadness to intrude on their time together. If there were times when the thought of leaving him brought tears to her eyes, Megan valiantly blinked them away. If there were moments when guilt ate at him, he shoved the thoughts aside. For now, he wanted only to love her, and she him.

Blake found he liked having Megan near, even when they were not making love, now that she was not constantly screeching at him. When he was engaged in some task just outside the cabin, he often invited her to join him. She sat in the sunlit yard and watched as he patched cracks between the logs, readying the cabin for winter. Sometimes they went for walks, or sat together on the small porch, Megan in the old rocker and Blake on the rickety steps, Lobo faithfully at his side.

There were moments when he angered her still, or she him. When Blake decided to repair the leaks in the cabin roof, he did not allow her outside with him. Megan took offense to this, especially when Blake calmly pointed out that he could not watch her while he was occupied at this task. Nor could he chase her from atop the roof. Megan stomped back into the cabin. "I hope you break your fool neck!" she called out to him, slamming the door in her wake.

By the time Blake had finished and come in to supper, Megan's temper had cooled. She smiled sweetly at him, and Blake was certain that all was forgiven. They sat down to an excellently prepared meal of baked quail, potatoes and gravy, with baked cinnamon apples for dessert. Blake ate double servings of everything, complimenting Megan lavishly on her cooking skills.

Sated, and feeling very good about himself and the world in general, Blake sat back in his chair to enjoy a last cup of coffee, which Megan had insisted upon refilling for him. He took a generous mouthful of the steaming brew, but before he could swallow it, his mouth began to twitch uncontrollably. Unlike his previous cup, this coffee was unbearably bitter. Even as he attempted to spit it out, his cheeks contracted, pulling in toward his teeth. His lips pursed out, and his tongue curled up in his mouth.

As the coffee splattered from his pursed lips, Megan erupted in laughter, despite her best attempts not to do so. Glaring at her, Blake noted the devilish twinkle that lit her eyes. "Megan! What have you done!" he accused. Unfortunately, with his mouth so twisted and malformed, his words came out sounding rather like "Mgn, woot uv oo doon," thus destroying their effectiveness. This sent Megan into fresh peals of mirth, tears streaming down her face as she held her sides and rocked back and forth in her chair.

"Dmut, Mgn!" he tried again, only managing to amuse her further. Pushing himself up from his chair, toppling it in the process, Blake stomped to the water pail. There he managed to spill half the contents on the floor in an effort to drink, but he did manage to consume enough water to make his jaw work partially once more. With effort, he managed to form understandable words. "Whut did you put 'n da coffee!" he muttered threateningly.

"A-a-alum!" she stuttered between gales of laughter. "Oh, Blake! You look so funny!" Spasms doubled her over once more as another fit of giggles ensued.

"Ulum! Why you windictub witch!" he roared, his eyes flashing blue flames.

"That's 'vindictive witch,'" she corrected mildly, "and you deserved it after the way you acted today. In truth, you deserve more than a mild dose of alum, which will not harm you in the least, and which effect is even now abating."

Something about the tone of her voice and the smug look on her face warned him there was more to come. "Whut else hab you done?" he asked warily.

Megan stared back at him, her lips pressed tightly together as she fought not to laugh again. Her eyes watered with the effort, gleaming up at him impishly. "Just—just a bit of castor oil in your gravy," she admitted with a slight grimace. As his face took on a thunderous appearance, she added hastily, "Not enough to harm you, Blake. Just enough to keep you hopping, my love." She backed away as he began to stalk her, her hands held out in front of her to ward him off. "It will clean out your system, darling. Honestly, it will make a new man of you." A giggle slipped out, even as she began to wonder if she had carried her small revenge too far.

Blake's roar nearly undid the repair work he had done to the roof. "You wicked, nasty little cat!" His temper had finally loosened his tongue from its kinks. His hands grabbed for her, but she deftly eluded his grasp. She scampered to the opposite side of the table from him. "You'd better run, Megan," he agreed, "for when I catch you, I'll teach you a lesson you won't soon forget!"

His long arms reached across the small table, but before he could conclude the movement, his stomach began to cramp horribly. Clutching his aching gut, Blake glared hard at her, then ran out the door, heading for the privy as fast as his long legs would carry him.

On and off all through the night, Blake made repeated trips outdoors. In between trips, his stomach ached too badly to allow him to reprimand Megan in any way but with damning words and threats. By morning he was through the worst of it, but his face was pale and he was weak from the cramps. Finally, he fell asleep, but only after making Megan crawl into bed between him and the wall, so that he would be sure to awaken if she attempted to rise. His last mumbled words were "Rotten wench!" as he clutched a handful of her hair and drifted off.

The next morning, Megan felt remorseful about her little trick, and she feared that Blake might truly be angry enough with her to make her regret it further. When Blake finally awoke late that afternoon, she apologized profusely. She voiced her

apology so repentantly and repeatedly that Blake at
last relented and accepted her plea for pardon, as
much to silence her as anything, for he had a
terrible headache as a result of his tumultuous
night. They struck a bargain for peace between
them once again. One thing was certain. Blake
would walk a bit more softly around Megan's fiery
temper in future. Her means of retaliation were
devious, to say the least, and Blake wasn't certain
he wanted to experience another example of her
brand of revenge anytime soon.

"Blake? . . . *Blake*!" Kirk roared, so upset that
he didn't even think to lower his voice. He stood
staring incredulously at the ransom note Opal had
found just minutes before. He waved it at his
mother, who was sitting at the kitchen table, as
thin-lipped and stunned as he. "Blake has Megan?
That bastard was behind the whole thing?"

"Lower your voice, Kirk," Opal advised tiredly, "unless you want the whole ranch to know
about this. It might be a little difficult to explain to
some people, you know." She quirked her head
toward the upstairs bedrooms where Megan's parents were still asleep.

Kirk continued to rave. "I'll kill him for this!
We should have killed him before and had it done
with. I knew just kicking that son-of-a-bitch off the
ranch would mean trouble someday."

"Hush, I tell you," Opal hissed. "Just calm
down. We have to think what to do now. That note
specifically said not to tell anyone about this, or he
would kill the girl."

Opal's words still hung in the air as Evan burst
into the kitchen, Jana on his heels. Shaving lather

still blotched his pale face, his shirt half-buttoned. Behind him, Jana's eyes were wide with anxiety, her hair uncombed and her wrapper held haphazardly together with trembling fingers. Upon hearing Kirk yelling Mcgan's name, they had come running, sure that something dreadful had been discovered at last.

"Kill who?" Evan gasped, having overheard Opal's last statement. "Have you had word of Megan? Is she alive? Is she all right?"

Opal threw Kirk a disgusted look that clearly said, *Now see what you have done*? "Sit down, Evan, Jana. Yes, we've had word. We received a ransom note this morning."

Jana breathed a shaky sigh of relief. "Then Megan is still alive?" she asked weakly. Her eyes begged for reassurance of that fact.

"So far, I guess," Kirk grumbled, earning another warning look from Opal.

"Where is she? How soon can we get her back?" Evan blindly accepted the cup of coffee Opal set before him.

When Kirk would have spoken, Opal gestured for him to remain silent. "I'll handle this, Kirk." She handed Evan the earring that had been included in the note. "Is this Megan's earring?"

Evan stared at it blankly. It was Jana who took it from his numb fingers and studied it. "Yes! Oh, yes!" she cried, tears streaming down her face.

"You're sure?"

Jana nodded. "Evan and I gave these to her on her last birthday. I even remember the bandits fighting over whether or not she could keep them. Yes, this is Megan's, but where is the other one?"

Opal had the grace to look uncomfortable with her news. Without a word, she handed Evan the ransom note to read for himself. He nearly choked upon reading the part about the matching earring and Megan's possible mutilation if the demands were not met.

"Who is this animal?" he groaned, raising tormented eyes from the note. "And why is he demanding the ranch in exchange for my daughter?"

"He is my brother's bastard stepson, and he has been trouble since the day he was born," Opal explained. "Why my brother ever allowed him to live here all those years, I'll never know, but Mark was a fool for that wife of his. Even when she died, Mark let the boy stay on. When Kirk inherited the ranch, Blake was furious. For some reason he felt it should have gone to him instead. We had to forcibly remove him from the property."

"And now he is using Megan to try and steal it from under us," Kirk said vengefully. "Well, the crazy bastard has another think coming if he imagines I'll sign over this ranch to get her back." When Kirk saw the flames shooting from Evan's eyes, he hastily added, "We'll think of some other way to rescue her, now that we know who has her and why."

"What about the sheriff?" Evan wanted to know. "The note says not to contact him or let anyone outside the family know, or he'll kill her. Would he do that?" He watched as Opal and Kirk exchanged a private look.

Opal chewed her lip anxiously. "I don't know. In fact, we can't actually be sure Megan is still alive.

The earring by itself means nothing, except that Blake took her. We only have his word that she is alive, for what that is worth.''

"I think we should let Sheriff Brown know," Kirk decided.

"No!" Jana leaped from her chair, frantic at the thought. "You can't destroy the only chance Megan might have to survive this terror! Not while there is still hope. Maybe he has someone watching! For God's sake, Kirk, don't jeopardize my child's life!"

"I agree." Opal surprised even Kirk. "We need to keep this as quiet as possible. No need to take chances with Megan's safety, and no need to stir up more gossip in town, either." She speared her son with a quelling glare. "Dick Brown hasn't been much help to us so far, anyway. Not that I can see. We'll handle this ourselves."

"But how?" Jana asked on a whisper. She realized, as did Evan, that it would be unfair for Kirk to have to relinquish his ranch, but the fact remained that their daughter was in the hands of a madman. "How?"

It was a question they all asked as they stared at one another across the table.

Evan chanced upon Jake Banner later that afternoon. The big gunfighter's cool, knowing gaze irritated Evan beyond caution. "What do you know about this Blake fellow who has my daughter?" he blurted.

"Enough to keep my mouth shut and my eyes open," Jake answered enigmatically. "Some folks in these parts think Blake Montgomery should have inherited this place from his father."

Evan was caught up short by Jake's announcement. "His father? I thought Opal said Blake was Mrs. Montgomery's bastard son. Are you saying he was actually Mark Montgomery's son?"

Jake lifted a big shoulder. "Kind of puts a new slant on things, doesn't it?"

"I don't care who he is, he's still an animal! No decent man would hold an innocent young woman for ransom as he is doing. It is insane! It's the act of a criminal!"

" 'Judge not, lest ye be judged,' so the good book says," Jake quoted. "Maybe this is the only way he has to regain what is his."

"It's still wrong to involve Megan. She has nothing to do with all this, no matter whose ranch it is. Besides, what does a man like you know of right and wrong? You live by the gun, not by the Bible. I'm surprised to hear you know it exists, let alone quote from it."

Jake's smile was not a smile at all. "Oh, you'd be surprised at some of the things I know, Mr. Coulston. I'll bet with a little more snooping, you and your wife could learn a lot yourselves—maybe uncover the whole ugly truth about what's going on here. I'd be careful who I trusted with the information, though, if you catch my drift. Real careful."

Once again Evan was left to ponder Jake's vague warnings.

12

"Megan! Megan, come out here a minute!"

Megan pulled her sticky fingers loose from the mass of bread dough she was kneading and wiped them on the damp towel she was using in lieu of an apron. When she reached the door she saw Blake on his knees at the base of a tree. Lobo was dancing about him, more excited than Megan had ever seen him, and emitting sharp yelps. As Megan approached, Blake yelled at the wolf to back off and behave, for Lobo was intent on getting past Blake's guard to whatever Blake was protecting.

Sighting her, Blake waved Megan forward. "Come see what I have found."

Megan peaked over his shoulder, not knowing what to expect, and was delightfully surprised. There, nestled in a pile of pine needles, was a little chipmunk. It was the tiniest, most darling creature Megan had ever seen, with its soft brown fur and white and dark stripes. "Oh, Blake, he's so sweet! However did you find him?" she cooed.

"I didn't. Lobo found him. I just rescued him." He pulled her down beside him for a closer look. The chipmunk appeared to be just a baby, and it was obviously frightened. The poor thing was shaking all over, its little head bobbing this way and that as if looking for an avenue of escape.

"He's quivering so badly it's a wonder he doesn't shake his stripes loose, the poor baby." Megan gave in to temptation and reached out her hand to touch the furry animal. She squealed in surprise as the chipmunk, taking her hand as an escape route, scampered up her arm. For a moment it stopped on her shoulder to peer about, then tunneled through her thick hair to hide in the curve of her neck. "Oh! Blake! Do something!" she shrieked. "Oooh! Help me! It—it tickles!"

Blake was rolling on the ground, convulsed in laughter, while Lobo was barking his head off. Neither of them was worth his weight in salt to her. Squirming about, Megan finally managed to capture the elusive little creature herself. Cradling it in her cupped palms, she brought it down from its perch and studied it balefully. "Okay, scamp. Enough is enough," she told it. It sat there in her hands blinking up at her, then promptly snuggled into a tight ball and cuddled further into her palms, its tiny tail wrapped about its face.

"Well, I'll be hornswaggled! I think he likes you," Blake exclaimed in amazement, finally done with his fit of laughter. He swatted at Lobo, who was still trying to get to the chipmunk. Lobo bounced back once, then leaped forward for yet another attempt.

"Lobo, if you so much as harm one hair on this chipmunk's head, I'll knock you into the next territory," Megan snapped, glaring at the huge wolf with fire in her eyes. To everyone's surprise, Lobo hung his head, tucked his tail between his legs, and slinked off to hide under the porch.

A feather could have knocked Blake off his feet, so surprised was he. His shocked gaze traveled from Megan to Lobo and back again. "And I've left that quivering coward to guard you all this time?" he asked, shaking his head as if this must all be just a bad dream. "I don't believe this! My God, it's a wonder the blasted animal didn't guide you off this mountain and straight to the ranch. He probably would have if you'd merely have asked."

"My mistake. I should have asked," Megan muttered, torn between laughter at Blake's stunned look and the fact that her plans for escape had just been thwarted. Now Blake surely would not trust Lobo to guard her. "Drat!"

Blake eyed her skeptically. "How did you do it, Megan? How did you win Lobo over?" The wolf had never obeyed anyone but Blake, unless instructed by Blake to do so. Lobo always did exactly as Blake commanded. He never disobeyed and he'd never trusted anyone else before, so far as Blake knew, and he'd had the wolf since it was a pup. Now, it seemed, Lobo had split his loyalties, and Blake was both angry and astounded.

Megan was all innocence as she turned wide grey eyes on Blake. "Why did I have to do anything, Blake? Couldn't the animal just like me? I am a very likeable person, you know."

"You are a witch!" Blake shot back. He indicated the baby chipmunk now asleep in her hands.

"You bewitch everything you come into contact with. Wild creatures sleep nestled in your palm and eat from your hand. I don't understand it." He shook his head in bewilderment. "Jake likes you, Lobo obeys you, that chipmunk trusts you, even stone-hearted Kirk proposed to you. And to top it all, you've even had *me* dancing to your tune."

Megan turned sad eyes to his. "Have I really, Blake?" she asked softly. "If that is true, then let me go. My parents must be sick with worry."

His features hardened, his eyes like blue chips of ice. "No. I will not release you, Megan. Not until Kirk meets my demands." In his heart, a small voice added, *And I wish I didn't have to give you up then. I wish you could be mine forever.*

Megan took the chipmunk back into the cabin to protect it from Lobo, and soon the little fellow decided he liked both the cabin and Megan and took up residence there. He scampered about each day, poking his tiny nose into every nook and cranny. He shadowed Megan's footsteps, often perching on her shoulder or head to watch her clean or cook. True to Blake's prediction, he even ate out of Megan's hand and chose to sleep on her pillow. Megan had been well and truly adopted! She adored her new pet, promptly dubbing him Scamp. Even Blake was taken with the cute fellow. Lobo barely tolerated Scamp, but knew better than to try to harm him. Megan would have hung Lobo out to dry, and the big wolf knew it.

A creature of another temperament soon paid them a visit, much to Megan's dismay. She had gone down to the river to get water for the morning meal, Lobo in attendance, when she suddenly heard a tremendous racket in a nearby thicket. Instantly alert, Lobo sniffed the air, his hackles rising. Suddenly the bushes parted to reveal an immense, terrifying bear, at most, twenty feet away from her.

With a scream that froze the blood in Blake's veins as he stood in the yard outside the cabin, Megan tore out of the trees, running for all she was worth toward the cabin, Blake, and safety. Blake stood rooted to the spot, wondering what possessed her.

"Blake!" she shrieked. "Blake! Oh, God! Get the gun!" The words weren't out of her mouth when she launched herself into his arms, shaking and crying and screaming.

"Megan!" he choked, prying her arms from about his throat. "Tell me! Quickly!"

"A b-b-bear!" she stammered, her eyes as huge as ponds. "A b-b-big one!" He looked in the direction of her pointing finger just as Lobo backed out from the trees, followed immediately by the bear. As the big grizzly rose up on its hind legs it stood nine foot tall or better, and at a quick glance Blake guessed it weighed at least a thousand pounds. It was truly an awesome sight, its teeth large and gleaming as it roared in anger at Lobo, who was desperately trying to hold the bear at bay. The bear's paw was as large as the wolf's head. Its head was enormous.

"Get into the cabin and don't come out, no matter what!" Blake ordered. Giving Megan a hefty shove to start her on her way, Blake dashed around the corner of the cabin to retrieve his rifle. His training had taught him always to keep it loaded and ready, and he was never so glad as now. Running back to the front of the cabin, he was relieved to see that Megan had done as he had told her. He caught a glimpse of her frightened white face inside one of the windows, but then his attention was captured by the bear once more.

Lobo was still valiantly trying to defend his territory and his master from the monstrous intruder. As Blake watched, trying to draw a bead on the bear for a fatal shot, knowing that one shot might be all he would get, the bear swiped at the dog with a huge paw, catching Lobo a blow along the ribcage. The big wolf flew through the air like a dandelion puff, yelping in pain. He landed with a thud and did not get up.

The bear let out another spine-tingling roar, looking about with his small, close-set eyes for his victim. Though his side vision was very poor, once he had his quarry sighted straight on, the grizzly could see just fine. This Blake knew, as well as the fact that the bear's senses of smell and hearing were remarkably keen. When the grizzly turned in his direction, Blake knew that the bear had realized his presence. His heart was thudding so hard in his chest that he wouldn't have been surprised if the bear had located him by the sound alone.

With an ominous growl, the bear came down on all fours, and Blake knew that it was going to charge. Blake had time for one shot, and he prayed it would be perfect, for nothing this side of hell matched the fury of a wounded grizzly. If he missed his mark, Megan would witness a gruesome sight indeed. There wouldn't be much left of him after the bear got done mauling him.

The bear charged at unbelievable speed. Taking careful aim, Blake pulled the trigger. The explosion of the shot was echoed by Megan's frantic scream. Blake watched in terror as the bear still came on, straight toward him, rage blazing from its red-brown eyes. Blake was preparing to meet his Maker, certain that a swift but painful death was imminent, when the grizzly suddenly faltered. Not three feet from where Blake stood, the huge bear suddenly stopped, gave a queer quiver, and fell dead before Blake's disbelieving eyes.

His pent-up breath exited Blake's lungs in a gush, and he sank slowly to his knees, weak with relief. Hanging his head, he gave a short, fervent prayer of thanks to God, for he felt sure he had just looked death in the face and lived to tell of it. He was still shaking with glorious relief as Megan came barreling off the porch, the infamous cast-iron skillet still clutched in her hands. She rushed to his side, knelt down before him, buried her face against his chest, and cried as if she might never stop. For long moments they clung to one another.

Megan lay against his chest, thankful for the steady beat of his heart beneath her ear, knowing how close she had come to losing him. And Blake held her there, clutching her tightly to him, grateful to be able to hold her in his arms, to feel her tears wetting his shirt, to smell the clean scent of her hair tickling his nose—grateful just to be alive to enjoy this moment.

It was several minutes before either of them thought of Lobo, but then they both seemed to do so at once. Blake stood, pulling Megan to her feet. First he cautiously approached the grizzly, Megan close behind him with her handy frying pan. After satisfying himself that the big bear was truly dead, Blake walked to where Lobo lay in the dirt. Skirting the bear, Megan trailed behind. Blake stooped down and laid his fingers alongside the wolf's throat. Surprisingly, he found a pulse. With a light, tentative touch, he examined Lobo for injuries. He found a lump on the wolf's head, and his right front leg was either badly sprained or broken. This was the least of Lobo's injuries, however. Blake soon determined that three of the wolf's ribs were broken, and he could only hope that none had punctured any vital organs. Also, there were five long, bloody gashes gouged along Lobo's side, where the bear had swiped at him with his enormous paw.

"Is he alive?" Megan asked hesitantly.

Blake nodded. "Yes, but he's pretty badly beaten. I'll carry him inside. You clear off the table. Get some water heating and find the sewing kit. I'll dig out some salve and tear up a sheet for bandages."

Between them, they managed to patch the poor animal up a bit. Lobo awakened and whined pitifully while Megan was stitching his side, but Blake held him firmly to the table all the while. At least the wolf had remained unconscious while Blake had set his ribs. Then they disinfected his wounds with the salve and bound him with strips of clean cloth. Lobo was a sorry sight when they were done, but at least he was alive, and with luck he would fully recover to fight another day.

Later that night, as they lay cuddled together in bed, Megan's head snuggled into his shoulder,

Blake asked, "Were you actually going to attack that bear, armed with nothing more than a frying pan, Megan?"

He felt her nod her head. "Stupid of me, wasn't it?" she conceded in a tiny voice.

"Very." Blake shuddered to think what might have happened if the bear had only been stunned and not killed. "It was also the most courageous thing I've ever seen," he admitted. "But if you ever heedlessly disregard any order I give you in future, especially when it means your safety, I'll paddle your bottom until you can't sit for a week. Do you understand me?"

"Yes." Again the small voice and the nod.

"Good. Now kiss me."

Megan propped herself up on his chest, a mischievous smile lighting her face. "Is that an order, sir?"

He fought an answering grin and said gruffly, "It most certainly is."

"Yes, sir! Right away, sir!" She gave him a mock salute and brought her sweet lips to his for a kiss most men only dream of.

Two days later, with nary a bark of warning from Lobo, still too sick to move from the porch, Jake rode up to the cabin. "Afternoon, Megan," he said, tipping his hat and nodding. "Hello, Blake."

Megan knew what poor Marie Antoinette must have felt on her way to the guillotine. One look at Jake and her heart sank to her feet. Even Blake didn't look as thrilled to see Jake as Megan would have thought.

"Come on in, Jake," Blake responded.

"Megan, heat up some of that coffee, will you? And maybe fix Jake a bite to eat."

Blake led the way inside. "You hungry, Jake? Megan can fry you up a bear steak if you like."

"Bear steak? You go bear huntin' while I was gone?"

"More like the bear came hunting here," Blake replied, and went on to explain their scare of two days before.

"Sounds like you've got more luck than you have sense," Jake commented upon hearing, not only about the grizzly, but also about the bandits' attack. Megan noticed that Blake more or less made light of her attempted escape.

"Well, what news do you have for me?" Blake asked at last, bringing the conversation back to the point of Jake's visit.

Jake reached inside his vest and drew out a sealed envelope. "I haven't opened it, so I don't know what it says, but I'd guess it's not what you want to hear."

Megan held her breath while Blake opened the letter. His face grew grim as he read, his jaw tightening until a nerve jumped along its edge. "Damn him!" he said at last.

Megan couldn't stand it a moment longer. "What does he say? It is from Kirk, isn't it?"

"Oh, yes, it's from your beloved fiancé all right," Blake barked. "That stupid jackass *would* risk your life by calling my bluff."

"What exactly does that mean?"

"It means, my dear Megan, that Kirk refuses to pay your ransom. He obviously does not take the situation seriously enough. That, or he simply does

not value your skin as much as he does his stolen
land.''

Tears rose to Megan's eyes, making Blake's
stern face float before her. "Well," she croaked out,
sobs rising fast, "that makes two of you, doesn't it?"
Before her tears could fall, she dashed from the
cabin, ignoring Blake's shouts that she come back.

She ran down to the riverbank, where she
threw herself into a heap and lay sobbing as if her
heart were broken. She didn't bother to answer
when Blake called out to her, or when she knew for
certain that he had joined her there. She continued
to weep until there were no more tears to cry. Still
she lay there on the ground, her face cradled on her
arms, refusing to look at Blake.

"Are you finished with your crying?" he asked
finally.

"Go away, Blake. Just go away." Her voice
sounded as utterly weary as she felt.

"I can't do that, Megan, but I can tell you how
sorry I am."

"I know exactly how sorry you are!" she
retorted with a sniff. She threw a red-rimmed glare
at him. "You are a truly sorry excuse for a human
being!"

He had the grace to look abashed. "Megan, I
know you are angry and hurt, and I honestly
apologize for my part in all of this. If there was any
other way to get to Kirk, I would have done it and
not involved you, believe me." He paused a long
moment, then added more quietly, "I never meant
to hurt you, Megan. I guess I didn't realize you
really loved him that much."

Megan's mouth flew open and words tumbled

out before her brain had a chance to analyze them first. "Love him! Love him!" she screeched. "If I had that lousy, no-good, penny-pinching sonofagun here right now, I'd shoot him! I'd hang him from the tallest tree! I'd break every bone in his worthless body, and then I'd tie a rock around his neck and throw him in the river!"

In her anger, she didn't take note of the huge grin that stretched across Blake's face at her words. "How can he do this to me?" she raged on. "Why, you'd think I was some dance-hall girl, or some common floozy, the way he's acting! You'd think, if he really loved me, I'd be worth at least a bit of negotiating before he refused flat out to pay my ransom! Holy catfish! Where are the man's brains? Where is his compassion—if not for me, at least for my poor parents? Why, for all he knows, you could even now be slitting my throat and hiding the body! My God! What kind of man puts that low a price on a human being's life? And to think I almost married that—that—"

"Bastard?" Blake supplied readily.

Megan nodded, then blinked as the reality of her situation suddenly hit her. "Oh, my God!" she said weakly, sinking back down to sit on the bank from which she had risen during her tirade. Her teeth sunk into her bottom lip, and she closed her eyes tightly for a moment as she gathered her courage. Finally she looked back at Blake, fear and hope mixed in her eyes. "What are you going to do with me now?" she asked so softly that Blake had to strain to hear her words.

"For God's sake, don't look at me that way,

Megan, as if you expect me to strangle you at any moment." Blake shook his head in dismay and denial. "I'm going to keep you here with me and send Kirk another message—this time a bit stronger—and hope he is more convinced this time."

"And if he isn't? Will you let me go then?"

"We'll cross that bridge when we come to it."

Blake led her back to the cabin, where Jake sat waiting and looking extremely uncomfortable. Megan pulled herself together to fix them all a meal, surprising Jake by preparing a tasty dinner when Blake had sworn she couldn't boil water without burning it. "Oh, Megan's just full of surprises," Blake said cryptically when Jake commented on the fact. "There is never a dull moment around her, believe me."

Blake wrote another ransom note to Kirk, then followed Jake outside when it came time for his friend to leave. Within minutes he was back in the cabin. "I need your dress and petticoat, Megan," he said. "And your other earring."

"What!" Megan stared at him in dismay. "What are you going to do with them?"

"I'm going to send them to Kirk, of course. Your clothes are so torn and stained he's sure to think the worst. At the least he will believe I'm beating you regularly."

"And what am I supposed to wear around here? For pity's sake, Blake! Those are my only clothes. It's not as if I have a closet full of them to choose from."

"I know that, and so does Kirk. That's just the

point. The thought of you running around naked up here with me will drive him mad. It just might be the edge I need.''

''Has it occurred to you that the man might not care? If he knows—er—if he thinks,'' she corrected with a blush, ''that you and I have—uh—been intimate, he might not think I'm worth having back at any price, let alone that precious ranch you two are feuding over.''

''It's worth a try. I'm willing to bet his pride won't allow him to give anything to me freely, especially not his intended bride, regardless of her virtue. He'll probably want to find you more than ever, if only to kill me.''

''There you may be right, but I'll still be the one running around with not so much as a pair of shoes to my name!''

''I'll let you wear my shirt,'' Blake offered with a grin.

''How gracious of you. And what do you need with my other earring? If memory serves, you told Kirk you would send it with my earlobe attached.''

''It needn't be yours, Megan, though Kirk won't know that, of course.''

''Then whose?''

''You don't really want to know that, darlin'. Just trust me.''

With four dead bodies buried behind the cabin, it didn't take much imagination to guess what Blake was suggesting. ''Oh, Blake!'' she groaned sickly. ''You didn't!''

''Don't think about it,'' he advised.

''How can I not?'' she retorted. ''Have you any

idea what this will do to my poor parents? They'll be frantic!''

"Honey, if there were any way to ease their worry without letting Kirk know, I would do it." Blake took her into his arms, trying to soothe her with his touch. "Maybe Jake can do something. We'll see."

When the second earring was delivered, Megan's mother fainted. Kirk stormed out of the ranch house in a fine rage, taking his frustrations out on his poor horse. Opal turned several shades of green and retired to her room with a headache, after seeing to Jana. Evan went out behind the barn and vomited.

Jake found him there. "Things aren't always as they seem, Mr. Coulston," he said cryptically. "Often our own eyes deceive us."

Evan glared at the gunfighter. "What are you trying to say, Banner? You know more about all this than you let on, don't you?"

"Now, I wouldn't want that to get around, and neither would you if you are smart," Jake drawled. "Let's just say that I'd like to think your daughter is not harmed in any way." Jake smiled smugly. "Maybe gunfighters just have more faith than most other folks."

"Are you saying that is not Megan's—er—" Evan could not bring himself to say it.

"You'll have to draw your own conclusions about that, Mr. Coulston. Just don't believe everything you see at first glance."

13

"Trying to make love to you with a chipmunk running up and down my backside is distracting, to say the least, Megan," Blake complained with a grimace and an exasperated sigh. "Can't you do something with that little terror for a short while?"

Megan looked up at Blake and giggled, her grey eyes twinkling like sooty stars. "What would you suggest I do with him?"

Blake grinned in devilment. "Boil him in oil; skin him and make a change purse?"

"Blake!"

"All right," he relented. "Sew him into an empty flour sack and let him chew his way out. Put him in a cooking pot and slam the lid on him. Anything! Just get rid of him for a while. Do you know what it is doing to my nerves, just waiting for his sharp little claws or teeth to wander where they would do the most damage?"

An impish smile lit her face. "Maybe I could

train him to attack on command,'' she suggested slyly.

"You would, too," Blake concluded, shaking his head in mock disbelief. "I haven't had a truly peaceful moment since we've met."

"And whose fault is that?" she countered.

"Yours, of course. If you had been the meek, mild type of woman I assumed you would be, I wouldn't have had half the problems I've had with you."

"Just goes to prove that it isn't wise to assume too much about persons you know nothing about." Her smile was as old as Eve, his answering kiss as old as time itself.

"What will you do if you can't get your ranch back from Kirk?" They were sitting in the shade of a big old oak tree, Megan cradled in the curve of Blake's legs, her head resting on his chest.

Blake sighed, half in the contentment of the moment, half in response to her query. "I don't know. Maybe I'll go back up to the mine and have another try at finding the vein." He shrugged. "I haven't been up there in a long while. That old mine hasn't been worked since my grandfather's day. When it played out, *Abuelo* shut it down."

"You must think there is still some hope of finding gold, though."

"Yes, but finding it will take more luck than skill. If it is there, it's probably hidden deep in layers of rock."

"Is that why no one else has tried to find it?"

Another shrug. "That, and the fact that no one else seems to believe there could still be gold in that long-abandoned site. Dad used to tease me unmercifully every time I brought the subject up."

"Does Kirk know about the mine?"

Megan felt Blake stiffen at the mention of Kirk's name. "He knows about it, but if he has any interest in it, he's never shown it. He always treated it as a joke, like everyone else. It wouldn't do him any good, in either case, because my grandfather willed the mine directly to me on his death, not to my mother or dad. There is no disputing my sole ownership of the mine."

"How long has it been since you were last there?"

"About a year. I poked around up there for a while, hoping to strike it lucky. Lady Luck hasn't been looking my way since Dad died, though. It's a wonder I didn't kill myself exploring all those old shafts. The bracings are rotten in more places than not. It really isn't safe, and I didn't have the funds to make it so. It didn't take long for me to realize the futility and danger involved, so I abandoned the idea and set about trying to find a way to get my ranch back. Ranching is a lot safer, and the profits are fairly steady."

He grinned down at her upturned face. "Who knows? Maybe everyone is right. Maybe I'm kidding myself to think there is gold still hidden away up there, but it has been a nice dream nevertheless."

"What would you do with your riches if you did discover gold?" Megan asked. "Would you buy a new ranch? Start over?"

Blake shook his head, his sky-blue eyes studying hers. "And let Kirk have what is rightfully mine?" he asked softly. "Let bygones be bygones? Is that what you would do, sweet Megan? Would you let someone steal from you, and turn the other cheek; repay their malicious thievery with good-will? Don't you see that it's not just the ranch? I have to clear my name and my mother's—even Dad's. To think that even one person would believe their lies! God, Megan, it hurts more than I can tell you! They have blackened my good name, my mother's, my family's integrity. They have stolen more than my material inheritance; they have stolen my right to my own name.''

Megan could scarcely bear the pain in his eyes. Her own misted over with tears as she twisted about in his arms and pulled his head down to hers. "*I believe you, Blake,*" she whispered, her lips softly caressing his.

His hands came up to frame her face, his eyes searching hers. "Do you, Megan? After all that I have put you through, you can tell me this?"

"I believe you," she repeated softly, meeting the intensity of his look. Her heart added silently, *I love you too much not to believe you.*

"You can't know how much that means to me, my sweet Megan, my little dove." His arms tightened about her, his lips coming down to cover hers as softly and tenderly as a butterfly's wings. Moments later the kiss became a cry of need, and Megan answered that need with her own. Desire flared between them, and beneath the spreading limbs of the old tree, the two lovers found blissful moments of peace within one another's arms, a twining of souls.

It was a time out of time—their time, even with thoughts of the ranch and Kirk dangling over their heads. They were creating a special bond, not that of captive and captor, not even that of mere lovers, but a bond of friendship as well. They talked to one another of wishes, of dreams, of childhood remembrances, of private hopes and fears they would not think to tell anyone else.

And yet, even with this new and precious closeness, neither spoke of love, or of a future life together. It seemed a forbidden subject, a futile one for each of them. Megan still thought of escape, believing it the best and only solution for her, since Blake was still intent on revenge against Kirk. Blake could see no way but the one he had chosen, could find nothing to offer Megan if his plans fell through, no honorable way out of his predicament if Kirk acceded to his demands. Megan could not be his. Even while both nurtured secret hopes that the other might return their love, neither truly believed it possible. It was simply too much to hope for.

"And then there was the time I snipped off Peggy Smith's pigtail with my new school scissors in second grade," Blake recalled with a sheepish laugh.

"You didn't!" Megan gasped in amused horror. She could just imagine what a darling little rascal he must have been at that age, his blue eyes sparkling with mischief. "You must have been a terror."

"Oh, I was. Dad tanned my hide more times than I can count," he admitted.

"Did you carry frogs in your pockets and hide snakes in the teacher's desk, too?" she prompted, intrigued with the vision of a young Blake.

"Worse. I once hid Miss Appleton's eyeglasses

for three days. The poor woman ran around blind as a bat and nearly broke her neck before she finally found them.''

"And later, when you went away to school, was that the end of your pranks?''

"Hardly. Actually, the older I got, the more inventive the pranks became. Of course, I had plenty of other fellows to consort with.''

"I know what you mean. That was about the only thing I really enjoyed about going East to finish my schooling. I missed my parents terribly then.''

"You went to a girls' school?'' This was something of a surprise to Blake. Unless a girl's parents were wealthy, young ladies rarely left home to go to school, and Blake was fairly certain that Megan's parents were not wealthy. She had told him that they owned and ran an hotel in Abilene, and though they made a good living, they had lived fairly moderate lives on the whole, according to Megan.

"Yes. Mother said she wanted me to grow up to be a fine lady. Though she did her best, she could not seem to curb my tomboyish ways on her own. She was sure Miss Abernathy's School for Young Ladies was the answer.''

"Was it?''

Now Megan laughed impishly. "Where do you think I learned most of my more colorful vocabulary, foolish man?''

Blake blinked. "There?'' he asked incredulously. "I thought you picked it up from hanging around the hotel clientele.''

"Oh, I picked up enough there to contribute my share to the clandestine classes at school, enough to make me fairly popular with the other girls, but most of it came from the 'young ladies' of my acquaintance at school.''

''Sweet Jesus!'' he whistled, shaking his head. ''Remind me never to send my daughter, should I have one, away to school.''

An awkward silence followed his thoughtless statement, as Megan and Blake stared at one another in dismay, then looked away. ''Forget I said that,'' Blake mumbled at last. ''Stupid of me.''

''Rather,'' she murmured thickly, excusing herself a few seconds later. Blake did not follow her into the cabin, sensing they both needed time to gather their thoughts and get control of their feelings separately.

Megan was getting dressed, if donning one very thin chemise and one floppy shirt could be termed dressing. Blake had just gone out to get firewood for the morning fire from the woodpile at the rear of the cabin. She barely heard his curse amid the crash of tumbling firewood, and she smiled to herself. Usually she was the one to awaken in a foul humor, but Blake's morning was evidently not starting off well this day. She wondered how long it would take him to restack the fallen logs, or if he would leave that chore until after breakfast. Just as she was deciding what to fix for the morning meal, she heard several successive thuds, accompanied by grunts and more wood tumbling. A series of sharp barks from Lobo added to the symphony of noise.

''What in the world is going on back there?'' she wondered curiously. Her brow furrowed as she heard the horses add their loud neighs and stomping to the din. She had just decided to go investigate for herself when Lobo raced into the cabin, barking like mad. He ran up to her, tugged on her shirt tail, then raced for the door again. When she did not immediately follow him, confused at Lobo's actions, particularly since the animal never entered the cabin without being told he could, Lobo ran back to her. This time he grabbed her hand between his huge jaws and tugged impatiently, not hard enough to hurt, but firmly enough that she could not pull her hand from his grip.

"Okay, fella. All right! I'm coming!" Megan followed the wolf around to the back of the cabin, afraid to guess what she might find. Never in her wildest imaginings did she expect to find Blake leaning weakly against the rear wall, the headless remains of a rattlesnake dangling from his hand.

The blood rushed from her head at the grisly sight. "Oh, dear heaven! Blake, throw that hateful thing away!" she shuddered. "I wondered what all the ruckus was about out here. I guess *that*," she pointed at the offensive reptile, "answers my question, though I still don't know why Lobo dragged me out here. Little help I would have been. Snakes scare me silly. Thank God you killed it!" She was jabbering, but her fear of snakes was all too real, and she couldn't help it.

"The damn thing bit me," Blake rasped, staring at the snake with incredulous eyes. "Twenty-six years I've lived and worked out here, always aware of the possibilities, seeing others get bitten, but always avoiding it myself—until now!" He gave a gruff laugh. "Until now," he repeated.

Megan's eyes grew huge as she began to comprehend what he was telling her. "Blake?" she queried hesitantly, frightened at what she was hearing, wanting him to tell her it was all a bad joke.

His eyes met hers, and the dismal truth glared out at her. "Don't panic on me now, Megan. I need you."

Her fearful gaze traveled his long form, seeing no evidence of blood. "Where?" she managed to squeak out.

"My back. Not the easiest of places to reach by oneself. You are going to have to help me, Megan. Can you do that, honey?"

She nodded slowly, noting how pale his face was becoming already. "You'll have to tell me what to do. I've never had to do anything like this before."

Blake let the snake slither from his fingertips, and Megan shivered violently. Slowly he pushed himself from the side of the cabin. "Let's get inside."

As Megan helped him into the cabin, she was frightened further by how wobbly Blake was becoming already. Though ghostly pale, he was perspiring profusely, and by the time she had him seated on the edge of the bed, the mild activity had greatly increased the rate of his heartbeat. "What do I do first?" she asked worriedly.

"Help me off with my shirt." Blake's hands were shaking so badly that she brushed them aside and unbuttoned the shirt herself, easing his arms out of the sleeves. With great trepidation, she steeled herself to view his back. Megan gasped aloud, unable to help herself, as she looked in dismay at the two distinct puncture wounds high on his right shoulder. Already the skin around them was an angry, swollen red, spurting fresh blood with his every heartbeat.

"Listen, Megan. I'm feeling a little fuzzy already. I don't know how long I'm going to be able to remain conscious."

"Oh, dear God, Blake! Don't pass out on me! I need you to tell me what to do!"

"You—you'll have to get some water boiling and sterilize some rags for bandages." He shook his head as if to clear it and gave a short, humorless laugh. "No, first you'll have to build the fire. Sorry, but I never did get the firewood for you, did I?"

"I'll get it. Don't worry. What then?" Megan had a definite suspicion she'd better get the rest of the necessary instructions from Blake while he was still coherent enough to make sense.

"Sterilize the blade of the sharpest knife you can find—not in the water—use the flame. It's faster and better." His breathing was becoming more rapid, his voice weaker and more thready. "Do you have any open cuts in your mouth or on your lips? Any teeth that have been bothering you?"

"What has that to do with anything? Are you sure you are thinking straight, Blake?"

"It's my shoulder and my arm that are numb, not my brain. At least not yet," he replied with effort. "You are going to have to lance the punctures with cross-cuts. If you can manage to squeeze enough of the venom out by hand, you won't have to suck it out. If not, you will have to use your mouth, but not if you have any cuts that will absorb the poison into your own system." He disregarded her involuntary quiver. "And for God's sake, don't swallow any of it! Rinse your mouth thoroughly when you are done. That is very important. You *do* understand, don't you?''

She was all too aware of the dangers, as well as the amount of valuable time that was passing so rapidly. ''Yes, yes! Anything else?''

''Use some of that alum you're so fond of after you cleanse the wound. It will help to draw out any remaining poison and reduce the swelling. Once the wounds are clean, just bandage it and let me rest. Don't be surprised if I run a fever. My body will be fighting the poison.''

''That's all? Nothing else?''

Blake shivered, fighting the nausea that threatened him. ''That's all you can do. The rest will be up to me and nature.'' His words were becoming slurred, his vision fuzzy.

Seeing that he was about to fall over, Megan urged him onto his stomach. ''Stay with me, Blake. Stay awake as long as you can. I'll hurry. I swear I'll hurry.''

It took every ounce of courage Megan possessed to approach the woodpile for kindling. She gagged as she stepped timidly over the dead snake, and she was thankful for Lobo's presence at her side as she quickly gathered an armload of wood and scurried back into the cabin. She had a fire lit and water boiling in record time.

As she cautiously applied the heated knife-blade to the puncture wounds on Blake's back, he groaned in agony, and Megan nearly cried aloud for him. Only Blake's stern admonition kept her from biting down on her own lip as she helplessly caused him even more pain. She would almost have traded places with him rather than hurt him this way. It was even worse when she compressed the skin around the wounds between her fingers and squeezed as hard as she could. Sweat dotted her brow and ran in stinging rivulets into her eyes, but it was nothing compared with the agony Blake was enduring. He was drenched with perspiration, and shaking so violently that Megan could scarcely keep her grip.

"This isn't doing much good, I'm afraid," she told him, not sure if he could even hear her now. "There is not enough give to your flesh." With a silent, fervent prayer, she set her lips to the wounds, first one, then the other, sucking out as much of the venom as she could. She had to fight the reflexive urge to swallow, and an even greater urge to vomit. With much effort, she forced her mind away from thoughts of the snake, forced her concentration solely on her task. Somewhere in the midst of her efforts, Blake lost consciousness. By the time she had the wounds cleaned and bandaged, he was already feverish, his face flushed.

All that day and throughout the night, Blake fought for his life. Megan never left his side except to fetch more water from the stream to cool his feverish flesh. Lucid moments were rare; more often he thrashed and moaned and rambled incoherently about the ranch and Kirk and sometimes about Megan, mostly disjointed phrases that made no sense to her. The only thing his garbled words proved was that Blake had been telling her the truth about Kirk. Surely a man this sick and out of his head would not be spouting lies!

Just after dawn the next morning, Blake's fever

broke, and he fell into a deep, natural sleep, his breathing much less labored. One final time, Megan bathed his body with cool, refreshing water. Then she lay down beside him to sleep.

But sleep would not come. Her tired mind refused to allow her weary body rest. Her brain kept repeating one phrase over and over again, *"Escape. Escape. Escape,"* until she thought she would scream. Finally she stopped fighting the urgings of her mind and opened bleary eyes. Sunlight filtered across the bed, highlighting Blake's pain-worn features, the unshaven jaw, his sinfully thick lashes and the thin scar along his left cheekbone. Her fingers reached out to caress the small imperfection on his rugged face, and she wondered silently how he had come by the scar. She had never asked him about it, and now she would probably never know what had caused it. With a deep sigh she acknowledged the fact that she had unconsciously reached her decision. Now that he would live—before he could awaken and try to stop her—she would flee.

Slowly she eased herself from the bed, careful not to jar him. She filled a glass with fresh water and set it within his reach for when he awakened. She had to stop herself from taking time to make broth for him so that he would have something light yet nourishing to eat. He would make do somehow, she was sure. Taking only a canteen for herself, she left the cabin, taking one last, long look at her sleeping lover, the man she had come to love with all her heart.

Lobo did not try to stop her when she saddled one of the horses and started to ride away. Rather, the big wolf seemed to want to follow her, and she had to firmly instruct him to stay with Blake and guard him. "Don't let anything happen to him, Lobo," she said on a sob. "I love him as much as you do."

This time Megan took the same faint trail Blake had used to bring her to the cabin. It was much faster and safer than the river route she had attempted before. It was mid-afternoon, and she was halfway down the mountain, when she stopped, unable to go further. All along the way, her heart had been warring with her mind. What if Blake's fever returned? What if he awakened and, finding her gone, tried to follow her? He was too weak, too sick, to survive such an attempt. What if someone came to the cabin while he was unconscious? Someone intent on harming him? What if Lobo could not defend him? What if Lobo had followed her instead of staying with Blake? What if Blake were too weak to care for himself properly when he awakened? What if he died there in that secluded cabin, all alone, all because she had deserted him when he needed her most, when he was most helpless?

A ragged sob tore from her throat, and she wheeled her horse about and headed back for the cabin and Blake. It was long past sunset when she at last rode into the clearing, to be greeted by Lobo's joyous barking. Brushing the tears from her eyes, she sighed with relief at having reached the cabin, for several times she had thought she had lost her way in the dark. Disregarding her stiff muscles and aching backside, she raced into the cabin, only to find herself facing the business end of Blake's pistol. Megan stopped short, unsure of her reception.

Blake's hand shook as he slowly lowered the gun. "I thought you'd left," he said weakly.

Megan slowly approached the bed, biting her lower lip to keep it from wobbling. Finally she stood beside him. "I did," she admitted in a near whisper.

His piercing blue eyes gave her no mercy as he asked gravely, "Why did you come back?"

Tears rolled freely down her face as she surrendered her pride. "Because I love you, Blake. I love you more than my freedom—more than my life. I—I tried not to, but it's no use. I can't convince my heart otherwise." She fell to her knees at the side of the bed, her face buried in the edge of the thin mattress, and wept.

His hand trembled as he stroked her tangled tresses. "I know, Megan. I've been losing the same battle with myself," he confessed in a husky voice laced with tears. "I love you, too, *querida*. More than is wise, more than I ever intended to, and I don't know what in heaven or hell to do about it."

A tremulous smile lit her eyes as she raised her face to meet his gaze. "Truly?" she asked. At his answering nod, she sighed with joy and relief. Then the gravity of their situation struck her anew. "What do we do now?"

"We'll work it out somehow, my little dove, *mi paloma pequeña*. Together we will find a way," he promised softly. "Just say you'll stay with me."

"I'd rather die than leave you again, Blake. It would be worse than death not to be near you always."

14

Four days later Jake came racing into the clearing as if the hounds of hell were on his heels. Before he had reined his horse to a full halt, he was out of the saddle and bounding up the steps of the small porch. "Blake! Kirk and about twenty of his best guns are on their way here!" He stopped briefly to gasp for breath. "They can't be more than half an hour behind me! You've got to get your gear and get the heck out of here pronto!"

Blake cursed fluently in two languages. "How did they find out where we were?" he questioned through grated teeth.

"He doesn't know for sure that you are here," Jake said. "I just happened to overhear them making plans to ride out this morning, or I wouldn't have had any idea. I guess they have exhausted nearly every other location in their search. When someone mentioned the mountains, Kirk suddenly remembered this cabin. He seemed to think there was a good possibility that you might be here, because he immediately ordered twenty of his men to be prepared to leave within the hour. Five of us were supposed to stay to guard the ranch. I didn't even bother making an excuse for leaving. I just threw a saddle on my horse and got here as fast as I could to warn you.''

Blake was already stuffing necessities into his saddle bags. ''Thanks, Jake. Would you saddle our horses for us?'' To Megan he tossed an empty gunnysack. ''Pack as much food as you can manage into this, nothing perishable. And hurry! We're pulling out in five minutes at most. I'm going to fill the canteens. Be ready to ride when I get back.''

''Wait!'' Megan caught up with him at the doorway, clutching at his arm. ''Blake, you are in no condition to ride yet, especially a mad dash over these mountains with Kirk on your heels.''

''Well it doesn't look as if I have any other choice at the moment, Megan,'' he said with impatience.

''Can't you talk with him? Try to reason with him? Surely, if I say that I came with you willingly, there is nothing he can do to you!''

Blake shook his head in denial. ''Megan, my love, I can't believe how naive and innocent you are at times. First of all, your parents know you did not come with me of your own free will—''

''Yes, but if I were to say that I stayed with you willingly—'' she interrupted.

''It wouldn't matter, Megan. Not to Kirk. You are a fool if you think he would stop long enough to listen to anything you said. The man is on his way

here with twenty of his hands. He isn't coming to
tea. He's out for my hide, any way he can get it. He's
gunning for me, sweetheart. His fondest wish is to
see me six feet under with dirt on my face.''

"But why do we have to run? Isn't there some
way to settle things here and now? Some way that
no one would get hurt? Maybe you could send me
out to talk with him when they get here? He
wouldn't harm me.''

"Ah, but then he would have you safe and
sound in his clutches, and I'd kill him where he
stands before I'd let him have you now. And the
only thing that would gain me is self-satisfaction.
Aunt Opal would still have control of the ranch,
and I couldn't very well go gunning for her, now
could I? Even a hard-hearted bandit like me has
some code of ethics, some morals.''

"Why not fight it out here, if you two are so
intent on killing one another? Why wait? Why put it
off any longer? You fought off those five bandits all
by yourself. With my help and Jake's, the odds
would be no worse. After all, Jake is a gunfighter,
isn't he?''

"Megan," he sighed in exasperation, "these
are no ordinary cowhands he's bringing with him.
This is Kirk's select group of gunmen—sharpshooters. Even with Jake's help, we wouldn't stand
a snowball's chance in hell holed up in this cabin.
Yes, I would love to settle things face to face with
Kirk, but Kirk isn't about to face me man to man.
He's too much of a coward to do things that way.
He's got to have his roughnecks along to do his
dirty work for him. Don't you see that? Kirk has a
yellow streak a mile wide, and a twisted mind

almost as devious as his mother's. They cheated me out of my inheritance by fraud. They didn't stand a chance using honest means. They wouldn't recognize honesty if it stood up and bit them! And you can bet your life that if I beat Kirk in an honest fight, he'd have a dozen witnesses to testify against me. Even if I killed him, which I would hate to do, Aunt Opal wouldn't rest until she saw me hang. In fact, I would be willing to bet that you will witness an old-fashioned lynching if we don't get moving within the next few minutes."

"Isn't there any other way?" Megan was still trying to find another solution.

"None. We've got to go. Now!" Even as they spoke, Blake had been filling the food bag. "Are you with me or not?" His eyes speared her, hard and gleaming, reminding her without words that just a few days past she had sworn to stay with him.

"Of course I'm coming with you, even if I'm not entirely convinced that this is the only way." She followed him out the door, accepted his helping boost into the saddle of the horse Jake had waiting for her.

Blake reached up to cup the back of her neck and pull her face down to his. His lips covered hers in a swift, possessive kiss before he vaulted onto his own horse.

"Where you heading?" Jake asked.

"South. I'm not really sure where we'll end up."

"Then I'll head north and try to lure them away from you."

"Much obliged, Jake."

"It's the least——" Before Jake could finish his

thought, the air was alive with gunfire. Blake grabbed for Megan's reins, urging her horse and his into the cover of the trees toward the back of the cabin. Jake did likewise, taking only enough time to fire off an answering shot as he covered their retreat.

"That's Kirk and his boys," Jake said, though Blake was well aware of the fact, and Megan had already guessed as much. "They'll try to double back around us and cut us off."

Blake nodded in agreement. "We'll pick off as many as we can, then hightail it out of here. I'm just glad we had enough warning to get out of the cabin. We'd have been like trapped fish in a barrel in there."

Blake glanced at Megan. Her face was pale, but she gave him a quivery smile. "You all right, darlin'?"

"Fine. Blake, if you have to, why don't you and Jake use me for cover? I won't mind, and Kirk wouldn't dare shoot if he thought he might hit me."

Blake was stunned that she would even suggest such a thing, but proud that she would care enough to offer herself as a shield for his protection. "I'd never bet your life on that, honey. You don't know Kirk the way I do." Once again words came to a halt as a new volley of gunfire was exchanged.

They dismounted now, in order to present smaller targets to their enemies. Megan watched helplessly as Blake and Jake fought side by side, taking careful aim and always trying to ensure that one had reloaded his gun before the other took the time to do so. The barrage of gunfire seemed to go on forever, but it was actually just a few minutes before silence fell once more.

"Send Megan out, and no one needs to get hurt!" Megan recognized Kirk's voice ringing out over the clearing that separated them.

"Come and get her, Kirk!" Blake called back. Megan shook her head in despair. One suggestion was just about as ridiculous as the other. What was the sense in all this useless talk? Did these men just naturally enjoy antagonizing one another?

"Megan, honey! Can you hear me?" Now Kirk was talking to her. "I'm here, dearest. I've come to take you home. That scum will never lay a finger on you again. Answer me, Megan. Do you understand me?"

Megan exchanged an odd look with Blake. "Should I answer him?" she whispered, "or let him think I've lost my wits and my hearing along with my purity, as he seems to believe?"

Blake chuckled, and Jake nearly choked upon hearing her blunt comment. "Go ahead and answer him. Let him know you are all right."

"I'm here, Kirk, but I do not want anyone hurt. Promise me."

"Are you protecting my cousin, now that he is your lover, Megan?" Kirk called in reply. "Tell me, did you give yourself to him willingly, or did he force you? I'll gladly kill him for you, Megan. You don't have to be afraid of him any longer."

"Did you bring the deed, Kirk?" Blake broke in. "That was the deal. No deed, no fiancée."

"I'm not a fool, Blake. I told you I would never agree to that. No woman is worth that much, not even one as lovely as Megan, especially since you have ruined her for me.''

"Then why are you here?'' Blake asked, watching curiously as Megan's eyes shot angry flames in Kirk's direction. "If you don't love the woman enough to trade your ill-gotten gains for her, why do you still want her back?''

"She's mine! You may have had her first, but she is still mine.''

"What if she won't have you anymore, Kirk, after having felt my brand on her?'' Blake taunted.

Kirk's hate-filled laugh cut the still air. "She'll have me, cousin. No woman in her right mind would chose a beggarly bastard like you over me! Besides, she has little choice in the matter, even if she has changed her mind. No one else would have her now. She'll consider herself lucky that I still want her.''

"In a pig's eye!'' Megan hissed furiously, her voice carrying across to Kirk. "I wouldn't marry you now if you were the last man on earth! You are a self-centered pig, Kirk Hardesty! I pity the woman who ever does marry you!'' Megan grabbed the rifle from Jake's grasp. "Marry this, you braying jackass!'' With no more warning than that, she raised the gun and fired at Kirk. For someone who had never fired a gun before, her aim was uncommonly good. Kirk ducked and yelled as his hat flew off his head, a hole in the center of it.

"Nice shot,'' Blake said with a grin, as Jake let out a roar of laughter. The battle was on again, fast and furious.

It was several minutes before the three of them

finally made a run for it. In that short time, four of Kirk's men had been injured, and Jake had taken a bullet in the arm. When Blake managed to nick Kirk, temporarily causing havoc among Kirk's men as they hovered anxiously over their boss, the three friends saw their chance and took it.

As they raced their horses through the sparse cover of trees, dodging around rocks and hills, Megan had never felt so scared, and yet so strangely exhilarated. The blood sang in her veins. Her eyes sparkled like frosted diamonds as she shared a brief, triumphant gaze with Blake.

About two miles from the cabin, they stopped to confer. "You once mentioned an old aunt of yours in Santa Fe," Jake said to Blake. "Do you think she still lives there?"

"If she's still alive."

"Could she help you prove your case against Kirk?"

"Maybe." Blake thought a minute, then smiled. "Yeah, maybe she could at that. She was there when Mom and Dad were married, and I think she stayed with them until after I was born. Maybe she has some documents or something."

"If she could even sign some sort of sworn statement, it might help," Megan offered. "You could take it to your lawyer and see."

"Then let's ride."

"I'm going with you," Jake told them. "I can't go back to the ranch with a bullet hole in my arm. If they haven't already guessed, they would know for sure that I was up here with you. My father's ranch is just outside Santa Fe. We can stay there while you locate your aunt. Besides, I couldn't help noticing that Megan could use some clothes, and my stepsister is about her size.''

''Just don't notice much else,'' Blake warned lightly. ''I would hate to shoot a good friend just because he couldn't keep his eyes off my woman.'' Megan glowed at his possessive words.

''Don't worry. I've got one hole too many in my hide now. Before we reach Santa Fe, we may be glad they didn't hit my gun arm.'' Jake grimaced as he flexed his injured left arm.

''As soon as we are far enough away to be sure we are not being followed too closely, we'll stop and have a look at that wound,'' Blake promised.

They rode all that day, stopping only to tend Jake's arm. Luckily the bullet had gone all the way through the fleshy part of his upper arm, not striking bone on its path. They kept a steady pace for the most part, pushing their mounts when they had to cross open areas where they could be seen from a distance. Once or twice they spotted what might have been Kirk and his men, but they could not be sure from so far away. Blake was taking no chances either way. At each of the few streams they crossed, they rode their horses up or downstream for a distance, leaving the water at the most unlikely area. They avoided extremely rocky or soggy areas where their horses' hoofs would mark their trail.

Finally, lack of light forced them to camp for the night. Even then they had to eat their food cold, knowing that a campfire could be sighted for miles.

Megan cuddled next to Blake in his bedroll, tired and cold and sore from the long hours of continuous riding. She was also somewhat embarrassed to be sharing Blake's blankets, with Jake mere feet from them, but Blake had been adamant. There would be no lovemaking between them with Jake so close, but he insisted she would sleep in his arms and nowhere else.

Lobo snoozed peacefully several yards away. The wolf had caught a rabbit for his own dinner, but for the humans, supper had consisted of a can of cold beans and a strip of tough jerky. There was only whiskey or water with which to wash it down, and Megan had opted for the water. Now, as she lay shivering, trying to absorb some of Blake's body heat through their clothes, she wondered if the whiskey might have been the better choice. At least it might have warded off some of the night's chill.

"How long will it take to reach Santa Fe?" Megan asked softly, not wanting to wake Jake.

"Seven, eight more days depending on how hard we ride and what kind of problems we encounter."

"What kind of problems? Kirk and his friends?"

She felt him shrug. "That, or Indians, or desperados. Any number of things."

"You don't think we'll run into any Indians, do you?" she asked tentatively.

"It's hard to tell, darlin'. Maybe. Maybe not."

"I hope not," she whispered on a shiver.

He gave her shoulder a comforting squeeze. "Don't borrow trouble before it happens, Megan. We've enough to deal with as it is."

They were both too tired for further conversation. They had pushed themselves to the limit. Jake was wounded, and Blake was not yet fully recovered from the snakebite. They were both nearly asleep when Megan mumbled sleepily, "Blake, quit pulling at my hair."

At the same moment, Blake grumbled, "Honey, stop scratching my chest with your fingernails. We've got to get some sleep."

Simultaneously, both answered, "I'm not."

There was another definite tug at her scalp, another scrape at his chest. Two sets of eyes sprang open. As Megan felt something tangling itself in her hair, she let out a shriek and sat up, jerking the covers from both of them in the process. With frantic fingers, she batted at the wriggling "thing" in her hair. "Get it out, Blake!" she screeched. "Get it off me!" All she could think was that it was a bat or a scorpion or a huge spider.

When Blake finally managed to grab the squirming creature amid Megan's wildly flailing hands, and got a look at what he had captured, he groaned aloud and burst out laughing, much to Megan's confusion. Whirling about, she glared at him, until she too recognized the small animal. A silly smile tilted her lips as she saw the distinctive white stripes and chubby cheeks of none other than Scamp, her ornery chipmunk.

"Scamp! You little devil! Where on earth did you come from?"

"If he answers you, Megan, you are both on your own, because I'll leave both of you right here," Blake warned with a deep chuckle.

Megan threw him a disgruntled look. "Don't be silly, Blake. But how on earth did he get here?"

"My guess would be that he was either in the

food sack when we packed it, or he crawled into the bedroll as I was tying it. Whichever, we now have the little rascal to contend with once again, and I was hoping I'd seen the last of him in our bed.''

Now it was Megan's turn to laugh. ''Ha! This little fellow knows when he's well off, and he's here to stay!'' With that, she lay back down, pulled the covers back over them, and perched Scamp in the center of Blake's chest.

By mid-morning of the following day, it was obvious that something had to be done about Megan's lack of clothing, and soon. Blake winced in sympathy as he viewed the chafed skin along the insides of her legs. ''You should have said something sooner, Megan,'' he told her, tossing his extra pair of denims at her.

''Would it have done any good? Jake has more sympathy for me than you do.''

Blake's indignation turned to amusement as he watched her wriggle into the denim jeans, struggling with pantlegs way too long for her. ''You look like a circus clown,'' he laughed.

Megan threw him a look that should have burned. ''If you could manage to stifle your laughter long enough to help me before I trip and break every bone in my aching body, I would greatly appreciate it, Blake Montgomery!''

He was still chuckling as he finished rolling the cuffs. Ten bare pink toes peeked out beneath the bulky bottoms. ''You would swim in my boots, even if I had an extra pair, but I could part with a pair of socks, I suppose.''

"So kind of you to offer," she returned dryly, pushing her voluminous shirt tail into the overlarge waistband.

The end result had Blake chuckling anew. "You look more like a little brother than my lover. Maybe I should start calling you Morgan instead of Megan." He nearly choked on those words a few seconds later as Megan hoisted herself into her saddle. From the back, with her shapely derriere firmly encased and explicitly outlined by the stiff material, there was no mistaking her for anything but the woman she was. Her more rounded hips and bottom filled the denims quite nicely in the seat. "We most definitely need to find you a dress soon," he muttered fervently to himself, fighting down a rush of desire.

Kirk and his men galloped into the ranchyard at a dead run. Even from a distance, anyone could tell that Kirk was mad as a hornet. He threw his reins to a waiting ranch hand and stomped to the house, murder in his pale blue eyes.

"That lousy little bitch shot at me," he shouted, tossing his hole-riddled hat at his mother.

"Megan did this? Why? What happened?"

Kirk proceeded to explain, only his version of what happened was decidedly one-sided, in his favor. At the end, he said, "She evidently prefers my worthless cousin to me. Believe me, when we find them again, she'll pay dearly for that. And Blake will pay with his life."

Opal cast a glance behind her, curious as to why Megan's parents had not yet come running to hear the latest news. "What are you going to tell the

Coulstons?'' she asked in a secretive tone.

Kirk had been too angry to consider this as yet. Now, watching his mother's face, he stifled his anger and considered what he would do next. ''I think perhaps it would be better not to tell them anything more than the fact that Blake got away from us, with their darling daughter.'' A devious smile curved his lips. ''Let them think I still intend to marry their daughter when we rescue her from Blake's clutches.''

''Do you?''

''Perhaps. We'll see. One thing is for sure. Whether I marry the bitch or not, I will devote myself to seeing that she spends years in misery for choosing Blake over me. She'll wish she were dead when I am through with her!''

Meanwhile, in their upstairs bedroom, Jana was showing Evan what she had discovered. ''Look at this, Evan! It's a will—Mark Montgomery's will. I did as you suggested and sneaked into the study again. I found this tucked into one of the books on an upper shelf, the very shelf I was dusting when Opal nearly had fits that day. Why, I was reaching for this exact book when Opal nearly jerked me off of the stool I was standing on.''

Evan took it from his wife's hands. Upon reading it, he was just as excited as she. ''This gives all the property that Kirk now claims as his to Blake Montgomery. It says right here, 'To my son, Blake Montgomery.' '' Evan's eyes scanned the document. ''Nowhere does it say anything about Blake being his stepson.''

''No, it doesn't. In fact, it implies very strongly

that this Blake was a very beloved son. And look here——" Jana took the will from him. "Mr. Montgomery bequeaths almost everything to his son, and he leaves Opal and Kirk only a small cash settlement. 'To start a new life on your own,' it says, as if he was almost sure they would not want to stay here once Blake owned the place. What do you think, Evan?"

Evan shook his head. "I don't know, Jana. The Hardestys must have had some kind of new will or something in order to get this place from Montgomery's son. I wonder how they made everyone think he was only a stepson?"

Jana frowned and said, "My guess would be that was Opal's doing. Evan, I have yet to meet a woman who strikes me as more devious. If they did indeed steal this ranch from Montgomery's son, what else might they do? I wouldn't see Megan married into this den of thieves now for all the world!"

"My worry now is for Megan. Is this Blake Montgomery just as evil as Kirk and Opal, I wonder? Oh, I can see how angry and desperate the man would be, having his inheritance stolen from him by his own relatives, but just how much of a devil is *he*? Is he just a decent man driven to desperate measures, or is he the kind to really harm her?"

Opal gazed up at him with hope shining from her eyes. "We have already decided that Megan has not been harmed, thanks to that Banner person It really was quite kind of him to soothe our minds that way."

"You haven't said anything to Opal or Kirk about that, have you?" Evan asked.

"No, and I'm not about to, either. No more than I am going to tell them what I discovered in the study."

"You'd better return this before they miss it." Evan handed the document back to Jana.

"Must we? Isn't there someone we should give this to, someone who will see that Kirk and Opal pay for what they have done?" Jana was replacing the will in its envelope when she noticed two more very thin papers in the envelope. "What's this?"

Carefully she removed the aged papers and unfolded them one by one. "Why, Evan, look here! It's Mark Montgomery's marriage certificate." Quickly she scanned the other. "And this is a record of Blake Montgomery's birth and baptism. Look at the dates! The boy was born a full year and a half after his mother and father were married!"

Evan glanced over her shoulder, reading carefully. "This clearly lists Mark Montgomery as the boy's father."

"Evan, we must do something. Even if Blake Montgomery is a horrible person, he has a right to his property. No doubt he is justified in his retaliation against Kirk. Perhaps he sees this as the only way to regain his ranch."

Evan groaned and pulled his wife into his embrace. "Jana," he sighed. "Oh, Jana, why do you have such a soft heart? The man has stolen our daughter from us. There is no telling what he has done to her! True, that gruesome earlobe was not hers, but the torn and bloody clothes were the same ones she was wearing the day of the holdup. How did they get in such condition, Jana? And what is she doing for clothing? For all we know, she may be naked and ill. He may have beaten or raped her. How can you feel sympathy for the man who is holding our daughter hostage?''

Tears filled her eyes as she gazed up at him. ''I have to believe she is all right, Evan,'' she told him softly. ''She may not be able to come to us, but she is alive and well. I know it. My heart refuses to believe otherwise. He won't hurt her, Evan. He won't hurt our Megan.''

''I pray you are right,'' he answered quietly.

''What are we going to do with these papers, Evan? We can't take them to the sheriff, not if he is in on all this with Kirk.''

''We are going to have to be very careful, my love. Kirk has some dangerous characters working for him.''

''What about that gunfighter, Banner? He has certainly seemed to be prodding us along in the right direction all this time. Do you suppose he knows where Blake Montgomery is?''

''You are right. If we take a chance on trusting anyone, maybe it should be him. Hide those papers someplace. Maybe we can even trade them to Montgomery for our daughter, if it is proof he needs.''

It soon became evident that Jake Banner had not returned with the others. No one seemed to know where he had gone, or if he was coming back. Kirk was very suspicious of Banner's disappearance. On a chance, Evan lied, telling Kirk he thought Banner had said something about a personal emergency elsewhere, before he had rid-

den out. Evan could only wait and hope that Banner
showed up soon, before Kirk or Opal discovered
the missing documents. If they should discover the
papers gone, perhaps Banner's absence would lead
them to believe he had taken them, and they would
not think to accuse either Evan or Opal.

15

"You are not welcome here, Jacob, not as long as you are still wearing that gun-for-hire." The old man pointed a gnarled finger at Jake from his wheelchair. "The day you strapped on that gun, you ceased to be my son. Take your friend and your whore and leave my house."

Jake returned his father's glare. "I never was the son you wanted, old man, and we both know it. Don't give me all this bullshit about gunfighters. We couldn't stand one another from the time I was born, and I sure as hell wasn't wearing a gun then."

Megan glanced uncomfortably from Jake's hard face to that of his father. Standing in the shelter of Blake's arm, all she wanted was to leave this house as quickly as possible and find someplace to lay her weary head. They had traveled for nearly a week, hardly resting, and she was bone-tired and grimy with sweat and dirt from their ride.

"We're staying, old man," she heard Jake state firmly. "You don't have to like it, but you will be civil to my friends, especially the *lady*." Jake stressed the last word forcefully as he glowered down at the older man.

Blake was just as pained by the situation as Megan. Jake's problems with his father were his own, but when Mr. Banner had called Megan a whore, Blake had gone rigid with anger. "Megan and I will find another place to stay, Jake," he said, aiming a harsh look at Roy Banner. "Someplace where a lady gets due respect."

"There's no need for that. This house has plenty of empty rooms, and if my *father*," Jake nearly sneered the word, "doesn't want to be bothered with us, he can keep his distance easily enough." A wry smile curled the corners of his lips. "Not exactly the return of the prodigal son, is it?"

"Damn you, Jacob! This is still my house, and—"

Roy Banner's words were cut short as a woman sailed into the room. After one quick look about, her dark Spanish eyes locked on Jake and she burst into a radiant smile that made her age-lined face glow with beauty. "Jake! Oh, Jacob! You've come home!" Her skirts rustled about her as she rushed to his side and threw her arms about him in delighted welcome.

Blake and Megan watched in horror as Jake staggered under the woman's exuberant embrace. Jake grunted in pain as she connected with his injured arm. "Carmen," he ground out through clenched teeth. "I don't know whose greeting is worse, yours or the old man's."

She backed away, instantly alarmed. "Jacob! You're hurt!" Carmen did not wait for a reply. She could see for herself the red stain already seeping through his shirt. Her arms came about him more gently as she guided him to a chair. "Sit," she ordered softly.

As Jake sank into the chair, his father commented acidly, "Probably got less than he actually deserved. Wouldn't surprise me if he's wanted by the law, him and his friends." Roy nodded at Megan and Blake, who were still standing, watching as Carmen's fingers made short work of the buttons of Jake's shirt.

For the first time since entering the room, Carmen was reminded of her guests. She threw a quick look over her shoulder. "*Por favor*, please have a seat, and feel welcome in my home." She shot a condemning glare at Roy Banner. "Please forgive my husband's bad manners."

Jake almost grinned as his father exploded. "Bad manners! My God, woman! He shows up out of nowhere, after nearly three years, without a word of warning, dragging his rag-tag friends with him, and most likely a bounty on all their heads—"

"Enough!" Carmen's voice sliced the air like a sharp knife. "No more, Roy," she warned. "Not one more word." When Roy opened his mouth as if to argue, she said, "I mean it. He is your son, and he is hurt, and even if you truly did not care for him, which I know is a lie, I *do* care. This is my home, too, and Jacob and his friends are welcome here for as long as they care to stay."

Roy Banner graced them all with a sour look, then swiftly wheeled his wooden wheelchair from the room without another word. Only then did Megan heave a sigh of relief. The animosity between Jake and his father had been awful to witness. Even now the air reverberated with the tension of their confrontation. Blake, too, was still wary. "We appreciate your kindness, ma'am, but perhaps it would be better if Megan and I stayed elsewhere," he suggested.

Carmen Banner did not look up from her examination of Jake's wounded arm. "Nonsense. Now sit down before you fall down. The two of you look almost as bad as Jacob does. As soon as I tend to this arm, I will see to a decent meal for all of you and have one of the servants ready your rooms and baths. You have ridden hard, no?"

Jake grunted as Carmen prodded at his wound. "*Sí, mamacita.*" Carmen glowed at the loving title. "Blake, Megan," Jake said with obvious pride in his voice, "I want you to meet my lovely stepmother, the woman who has been my own dear *mamacita* since I was ten. Marrying Carmen was the smartest thing my father ever did."

"Blake Montgomery, ma'am, and this is Megan," Blake acknowledged with a nod. "It's a pleasure to meet you."

"*Con mucho gusto, Señor* Montgomery. I hope you and your pretty wife will be comfortable here, in spite of my husband's surly attitude."

"Oh, I'm not—" Megan began, only to be cut short as Blake interrupted.

"Don't be modest, darlin'. Of course you're a pretty little thing, isn't she, Jake?" Blake's eyes shot a warning. If Mrs. Banner thought he and Megan were married, then he was willing to let it seem so to spare Megan any unnecessary embarrassment. It would also curtail a discussion of separate bedrooms later, which Blake was not about to allow under any circumstances. Though Megan had assured him that she would stay with him, he was not yet completely sure of her, and was taking no chances. She was his now, completely, and he meant to see that she remained his.

"I'm glad Megan has you so bewitched, my friend, or I'd be leery of having you meet my little sister," Jake answered. "Tori is quite a beauty herself."

"Victoria," Carmen corrected out of long habit. "Such a lovely name I chose for her, and you insist upon calling her Tori."

"Speaking of Tori," Jake said with an audacious wink at his stepmother, "where is she? I thought she would have come running to greet me before the dust had settled in the ranchyard."

A fleeting look of distress crossed Carmen's face and was quickly hidden. "It is late, Jacob," she said softly. "Tomorrow is soon enough."

Within an hour, after devouring a delicious meal, Megan and Blake were tucked away in the privacy of their own room. Blake lay on the bed, a sheet draped over his splendid nudity. Propped up on one elbow, he watched with lazy interest as Megan lingered in her bath. She lay her head back against the rim of the tub, luxuriating in the warmth of the water, in the novelty of being clean again after days of dusty travel. Her hair straggled in damp strands from the loose knot she had hastily fashioned on the top of her head. "Mmmm," she sighed contentedly. "You have no idea how much I've missed this. I think I could stay like this forever, it feels so good."

"Think again, my little wet dove," he said with a sensual growl in his deep voice. "I have better plans for our time."

Megan's smile was almost as wicked as his. "Such as?"

In a flash, he was off the bed and dragging her glistening body from the water. "Such as drying every silken inch of you with my tongue, for a start," he promised huskily, carrying her swiftly to the bed. Heedless of the damage to the sheets, he followed her down, pinning her naked, squirming form beneath him.

She arched tauntingly into him, her eyes alight with love and desire. "Is that a threat or a promise?" she asked, seduction in every word, every movement. Her tongue came out to curl into the dark mat of hair on his chest, finding and teasing a flat male nipple.

Fire curled through him at her bold quest. "Both." He enjoyed her sweet tongue a few seconds more, then abruptly took command of things. Lacing his fingers in hers to still them, he sipped lingeringly at her lips. Only when her lips quivered with longing beneath his did he take them fully, deepening the kiss until she shook with the intensity of it. The clean warmth of their aroused bodies created an erotic scent that rose to enclose them in its musky essence. When he had conquered her mouth, invaded and ravaged its sweet secrets thoroughly, his mouth abandoned it for waiting territory.

Megan's mew of regret soon turned to moans of longing as he set out to prove his previous claim. He began at her damp brow, then on to her temples, her eyes, her cheeks, along the bridge of her nose. Not an inch of her face escaped his searching tongue, interspersed by the most alluring of kisses. She squirmed, torn between laughter and desire as he turned his attentions to the ticklish shell of her ear. "You've lived with that wolf of yours too long, Blake!" she giggled. "You are acting just like him."

Blake growled playfully, nuzzling the tender flesh of her neck until she bared the area he wished to explore. There was a deep intensity to his voice as he informed her, "Wolves mate for life. Did you know that, my sweet Megan?"

All laughter was gone from his azure eyes as he gazed down at her. "Do they really?" she whispered shakily, searching his face for a clue to the feelings behind his words.

"Always. They are unerringly faithful, and fiercely protective. They will fight to the death to defend their domain against intruders, as I would do for you. You are mine now, forever. You *do* realize that, don't you? You could not run far enough or hide well enough that I would not find you and claim you again." His face was fierce, the skin pulled taut across his cheekbones.

Megan tugged her hands free of his and framed his face gently between them. "There will be no need," she assured him tenderly. "The only direction I shall ever want to run is toward you." As if proving her words, she brought her mouth to his. "Love me, Blake. Love me and never let me go."

When he at last released her lips once more, he

continued on his original course. Her shoulders, and then her breasts knew the wet, warm enticement of his lips, his tongue, his teeth. He followed the curves of her body over her hips, her sleek stomach, down the length of her long, trembling legs. Megan turned to liquid fire beneath him, emitting incoherent little sounds of desire that seemed to inspire him further. Just when she was sure he would end the delicious torment and come to her at last, he turned her onto her stomach and proceeded to lave her back and buttocks, tracing intricate patterns on her heated flesh. Shivers chased through her as his mouth followed the indentation of her spine. Down her thigh, past the turn of her calf, his mouth left a wet trail. When he teased the back of her knees, she wriggled beneath him, caught in the spiral of desire her lover was so deftly spinning about her, wanting him with all her being, yet caught helplessly beneath his enchanting mouth.

Megan's eyes flew open wide and she gasped in a wild shock of desire as Blake flicked wetly along the arch of her foot. Instinctively she tried to pull away from his ticklish, tormenting touch, but he clasped her ankle firmly between strong fingers. A deep chuckle floated up to her just before he wrapped his lips about her small toe. She lurched beneath his touch, and as he suckled on her toe, she thought she would surely die of the savage longings swamping her. His mouth pulled gently, his teeth grazed the unbelievably sensitized flesh, and his tongue lapped repeatedly until she was writhing in a nearly mindless state, entirely at his mercy as he treated each toe to the same endless torture.

She was panting breathlessly, weakly crying out his name over and over, when he turned her to her back once more, and still he was not yet done. Blake's devil-tongue snaked up the inside of her pale thigh to that beckoning feminine delta, his ultimate goal. Beneath the burnished curls it delved, past the smooth protective folds, to the delicate flesh so hot and damp and trembling. A shaky cry escaped Megan's lips as his tongue toyed with her there. Her hands clutched wildly at his dark head, trying both to pull him nearer and to push him away as her passion mounted to unbelievably high plateaus. Her hips lunged upward to meet his relentless mouth, then writhed in an attempt to escape the wondrous torment. Then she was flying on wings of fire, her body convulsing violently, a glad cry echoing through the room.

Even as the tremors shook her, Blake joined their bodies, becoming one with her. She wrapped herself around him, her soft body enfolding him, welcoming him, sharing the wonders of her mad flight. It seemed impossible to fly higher, yet when Blake came into her, that is exactly what she did, until she felt deliriously dizzy. As he continued to love her with a frantic rhythm, she sought helplessly for something solid to cling to. Her legs bound him to her, her hands clinging to his massive shoulders. As ecstasy exploded about them in dancing colors, her nails scored his broad back, her small teeth sinking into the hollow of his shoulder. "No more," she whimpered faintly. "Oh, love, no more or I shall surely die.'' She lay limply in his arms as the world spun crazily about her, waves of rapture swirling endlessly, on and on and on in miraculous splendor as she sobbed his name with her every breath.

Long minutes later, her head cradled upon his chest, he murmured, ''I have heard it called 'the little death,' and if dying is as beautiful as loving you, I won't mind so badly if I can do it in your arms, but only after a million years spent alive with you.''

It took three days of searching before Blake at last found his aunt. Meanwhile, they stayed at the Banner ranch, and tried to avoid seeing Roy Banner. Carmen Banner was as charming and courteous as her husband was not. She saw to her guests' needs and to Jake's recuperation, though he insisted she was overdoing it. He was healing very quickly now that they had ceased traveling at such a grueling pace. Carmen's nutritious meals must have helped, too, and simply being home again.

The older woman was very gracious. The morning after their arrival, she cheerfully donated a lovely selection of her daughter's clothing for Megan's use, urging Megan to take what she needed and not to worry about returning any of it. Megan was thrilled to have decent clothing again, not to mention at least one change of everything! She was wondering about the girl whose clothes she was borrowing, whether she would meet Victoria soon and have an opportunity to thank her.

Her curiosity over Jake's younger sister, who was actually his stepsister, was roused even further later that morning as she heard Jake shouting the girl's name. Megan was admiring the abundance of beautiful flowers in the central courtyard of the house when she suddenly found herself witness to another confrontation, this time between Jake and Carmen as they unknowingly carried their argument to her.

"She couldn't have!" Jake shouted. "Damn it, she wouldn't have!" His face was twisted with painful emotion. "This was the old man's idea, wasn't it?" he accused.

Carmen shook her head sadly. "No, Jacob. He agreed with her, but it was Victoria's decision."

"Why? For God's sake, why?" Jake's voice was plaintive as he dragged lean fingers through his thick, unruly hair.

"Perhaps it *is* for God's sake, or at least His will. She felt called to this, Jacob."

"To be a nun? Why not a teacher? Or a missionary? Or a—a—anything else!" To Megan's eyes, as she stood watching unobserved, Jake looked stunned, thoroughly shocked and bewildered by his stepsister's actions. He was actually pale as he questioned Carmen.

"Jacob! It is not a crime to want to serve God!" Carmen said firmly. "Victoria has always been a good girl. She has always enjoyed going to church, even when the rest of you were complaining about having to attend. The last couple of years, she has helped the sisters teach the little Indian children who come to the mission. She loves it; she always has gotten such comfort from her faith. Why should this come as such a surprise to you?"

Jake stared at Carmen as if ready to beg her to

refute her words, and Megan, half-hidden by a flowering bush, thought she heard a sob lurch from his throat as he tried to speak. The big man blinked and cleared his throat noisily. His voice was husky with emotion when he finally spoke again. "Tori was always such a little minx, such a sweet little terror. All long legs and flying braids, so coltish and bouncy, always into more trouble! I can't count the times I saved her from disaster or took the blame for her so Dad wouldn't know. I paddled her behind more than once. I just can't see her doing this, not the Tori I remember."

"She is no longer a child, Jacob," Carmen tried to explain. Her hand reached out to touch his arm in a soothing gesture. "In six years, this is only the second time you have come back. Victoria has grown up while you were gone. She is a young lady now. Three months ago, she celebrated her seventeenth birthday."

Jake nodded. "Did she get the gifts I sent? Did she like them?"

A sad smile trembled on Carmen's lips. "Yes, Jacob. The hair combs were lovely, the most beautiful she has ever owned."

As if her thoughts were his own, Jake clenched his big hands into fists. "She couldn't take them with her, could she?" he almost groaned. "They've cut off all her long, beautiful hair, haven't they?"

He reached out and gathered his stepmother into his arms. For long minutes they stood sharing their pain and loss with one another, and Megan wanted to cry for them. She wanted to melt quietly away, wished she had not overheard all this, but her only way out of the garden was past them, and she was loath to disturb them in this private moment.

"Is she happy?" The big gunfighter's voice sounded rusty with unshed tears. "Is this truly what she wanted?"

Carmen brushed the tears from her cheeks and tried to smile. "*Sí*, Jacob. I could not bear it if I thought otherwise. I miss her so much, it is as if a great hole has been torn in my heart, but I let her go and I pray for her daily. Now you, too, must learn to let her go and be happy for her."

"I'll try, Carmen. I'll try."

Jake walked slowly from the garden, his broad shoulders hunched and his entire body a portrait of despair. Carmen sighed and sank down on a stone bench, her face buried in her hands. Raising children was rarely easy, but letting them go was heartbreaking.

As if sensing someone's presence now that Jake was gone, she raised her head and glanced about. When she spotted Megan standing quietly in the corner of the garden, color rushed to her cheeks. "Oh, my! What you must think of us! Always fighting and squabbling! I am so sorry, *Señora* Montgomery."

Megan came forward. "It is quite all right, Mrs. Banner. Please don't apologize or feel embarrassed. All families have their problems. I understand." She sat down on the bench next to Carmen, instinctively knowing that Jake's stepmother needed to talk to another woman.

"How can you possibly understand?" Carmen shook her dark head. "How can I explain?"

"There is no need to explain anything, especially to me. Blake and I are only guests in your

home. In a few days, we will be gone, and you can
forget that we were ever here.''

Carmen raised tear-filled eyes to Megan's. "You
are kind, *Señora*. You remind me in that way of my
Victoria.''

"You miss her very much, don't you?" Megan
asked, seeing the sadness in Carmen's face. "What
is she like? Jake says she is very beautiful.''

"I have to admit that I, too, think she is
beautiful, even if she is my daughter," Carmen
admitted shyly. "I have no modesty where Victoria
is concerned. She has been the light of my life since
the day she was born. Already she is taller than I,
and she has a serene loveliness about her. She was
always such a cheerful child, even in the worst of
times, always smiling, always sharing her joy with
the rest of us. Oh, she has a terrible temper when
she wants, and she can pout for days on end to get
her own way." Carmen sighed. "I suppose she will
learn to curb those traits soon enough in the
convent.

"She has her father's eyes, the most lovely
gold-green, an unusual color for someone of Mexican blood, and such thick, long eyelashes. Her
friends always envied her for her lashes. Her hair is
dark like mine, the deepest of browns; it hangs—it
used to hang," Carmen corrected with a shake of
her head, "in waves all down her back. Jake loved it
so. When she was small, he would sit on the porch
in the evenings and brush it for her until it shimmered like sunlit sable. He was always so good with
her, and she adored him. She cried for days when
he left. She was only eleven then, and she didn't
understand why he had to go. For a long while she

blamed Roy, and I suppose she was right to do so in many ways.''

"How old was Jake then?''

"He had just turned twenty, and he was her idol, her handsome beloved brother. Though he is actually her stepbrother, she has always thought of him as her real brother, since I married Roy when Victoria was just a few months old; and I have always loved Jacob and Caroline as my own children.''

"Caroline?'' Megan asked, confused by the new name.

"She was Jacob's older sister. She was killed when Jacob was twenty,'' Carmen explained sorrowfully.

"Is that the reason Jake became a gunfighter?''

"I suppose they all have their reasons,'' Carmen sighed, "but yes, Caroline's death was Jacob's reason. He was mad for revenge, determined to avenge his sister's death.'' Carmen's gaze sought Megan's for a moment, then dropped away. "I've never asked him if he caught the men who killed her and her baby and husband.'' Her voice was almost a whisper and she twisted her fingers together in her lap as she confessed, "I think I am afraid to know what he did to them. I am a coward that way. One part of me hopes he made them pay for their crime, but another part shies away from the very idea of violence. I go to Mass and I light a candle for Caroline and her family. Then I light one for Jacob's soul. I pray that Jacob and his father will one day resolve their differences, but I have never been able to bring myself to pray for the souls of Caroline's murderers.''

Megan covered Carmen's shaking hands with her own. "Jake is very lucky to have someone who cares for him as much as you do."

Carmen returned the gesture, patting Megan's ringless fingers restlessly. "Your young man is also fortunate to have you to love him, for I can see that you do love him very much. Stand by him, Megan, for he will need a love as strong as yours. Do not despise him for what he does; do not desert him. He needs you very much, and he loves you. I can see it in every look, every word and touch. Love such as yours comes but once in a lifetime. I knew it with Victoria's father, and it was a wondrous thing. Marry for love, and hold him dear to your heart each day."

"You've known all along that Blake and I are not married, haven't you?" Megan said on a soft gasp.

"*Sí*, but I have also seen the love you share. It is a rare gift. Do not squander it, for only God knows how long you will have one another in this lifetime. My first husband died before Victoria was born. We had only been married a few months, but not a day of my life has gone by that I have not missed him or thought of him. I married Roy because I needed someone to provide for me and my new baby, and he had two children who needed a mother's care. That was over sixteen years ago, and I have come to care for Roy in many ways, but not in that same glorious way that I loved Francisco. When your man asks you to marry him, follow your heart, even if your head tells you differently, and you will not regret it. When I go to church, I will pray that things work out well for you, even as

I pray that something will turn Jacob from the life he now leads."

"And what if Blake does not ask me to marry him, Carmen?" Megan questioned softly, sadness and fear in her own face now.

Carmen smiled gently and squeezed Megan's hands. "Are you not already wed to him in your heart, Megan? Is that not what really matters? As Victoria would say, 'have faith.' Love can perform many miracles."

16

Megan pondered Carmen's words over and over in the next couple of days, not truly understanding some of the woman's vague references to Blake, but too shy to ask what she meant. In time, she supposed, it would all make sense. In the meanwhile, she was simply pleased to have another woman to converse with, nice clothes to wear, wonderful meals, and a soft bed to sleep in.

She liked Carmen, and wished she might have met Victoria. Roy Banner was another story entirely. When she chanced to pass him in or outside the house, he glared holes through her. He never greeted her in any way; in fact, he seemed to go out of his way to avoid her, Blake, and especially Jake. Still, Megan could not help pitying the old man. He was surly at best, but she imagined that anyone would be out of sorts being confined to a wheelchair day in and day out. She learned that he had suffered a severe stroke three years previous, and that Jake had returned home for a short time then to take over the running of the ranch until Roy improved enough to handle things once more. When his father had recovered, Jake left again, and had not been home since—until now.

Megan also learned that Jake and his father had never gotten along. They had been at odds since Jake was a child, at least as long as Carmen could recall. It was such a shame! Megan could not imagine growing up with a father like Roy Banner. Her own father was such a dear, and Blake cherished the memory of his father. She felt sorry for Jake, and for Roy, too. It must truly be awful to take no pleasure in the small things that made other people smile, in one's own children; and Roy had been disabled in that aspect long before the stroke had taken the use of his legs from him.

The afternoon of the second day, while Blake was out trying to locate his aunt, Megan spent some time altering one of Victoria's dresses to fit her. While most of the clothing fit fairly well, this one dress, which Megan thought the prettiest by far, needed a tuck here and there.

She was sitting on a bench in the far corner of the courtyard garden, which had fast become her favorite place, when Roy Banner wheeled himself into the courtyard. Megan was amazed at how well he usually maneuvered about in the portable chair. It was crudely built, but sturdy, with large wooden wheels that Roy pushed into motion with his hands. Three years of this had given the man a great deal of dexterity with the chair, in addition to well-developed muscles in his arms and hands. She had noted how irritated he became whenever he required help with his chair. He was fiercely independent, and would rather cut out his tongue than ask for aid. The house had been remodeled, with wooden ramps at the doorways, and most of the time Roy got along fine.

Megan knew that the man had not noticed her, sitting as she was in the far corner. She watched as he wheeled himself along the worn stone path that led from the house to the barn. Suddenly, as she watched, the chair lurched off the path. Immediately Roy began to curse, jerking angrily at the wheels of his chair. "Damn, blasted, infernal contraption!" He swore and scowled, and beat on the chair with his fists, but he could not get the chair back on the path again. The wheels were stuck in the newly turned earth that the gardener had worked just that morning.

Putting her sewing aside, Megan reluctantly approached him. "Would you like me to help you, Mr. Banner?" she asked softly, already knowing his answer and dreading it.

Roy Banner's head jerked up in surprise and agitation. "No, I would not!" he spat out between clenched teeth. "There is nothing I need from the likes of you!"

Megan bit her lip in an attempt to stem her anger. "Then I suppose you do not want me to summon help from the house, either, sir," she said tartly.

"What I want is for you and your lover to leave my house and take my gunslinger son with you when you go." Banner glared at her, and Megan thought herself fortunate that the man could not rise from his chair or he would surely strangle her.

She stood her ground, her arms folded across her chest, and stared back at him. "We'll be leaving soon. No sense working yourself into another stroke over it, Mr. Banner." She paused, then added conversationally, "You know, at first I thought it was just me you disliked, or perhaps Blake or your son. Now I realize that you are just naturally mean-natured. I don't believe I've ever met a man quite as irascible as you. You are just plain ornery, and too cranky for your own good. It makes a person wonder how you ever fathered a man as fine as Jake."

Roy Banner puffed up like a banty rooster, his face rose-red and contorted with anger. "You wouldn't know *fine* if it bit you on the nose!" he roared. "*Fine* does not make a living by his gun. *Fine* does not consort with outlaws and prostitutes. *Fine* honors his parents and respects the law."

"No, Mr. Banner," Megan argued, shaking her head at him. "In my book, a fine man is one who meets his obligations to friends and family, who does everything within his power to right a wrong. A fine man earns the respect of others and stands by his friends. He gives his word honorably, loves his family, and inspires trust in those close to him. Your son is a fine man; Blake is a fine man; my father is a fine man." Left unsaid was the thought that she did not put Roy Banner in that category.

So furious he could barely speak, Banner managed to sputter, "And what do you consider a fine lady, I wonder? One who rides about the country with gunfighters, giving her favors to any man who can afford them or who smiles at her twice?"

Fire flew from Megan's eyes, but she gave him a frosty smile. "I am well aware of what you think of me, sir. You have made it clear that you consider me a tart. You have gone out of your way to avoid me, as if I would contaminate you. I have seen you flinch in anger and despair that I am wearing clothes that belong to your stepdaughter."

"She is an angel, sweet and fine and pure!" Banner railed, fury in every line of his dour face. "I am only glad that she is away at the convent now, safe from your reach, safe from Jake's influence. Victoria is everything that you are not and can never hope to be. Yes," he hissed, "I hate seeing you in her clothes, sleeping with your lover in her bed! I'll burn the damned thing when you leave!"

"And disinfect the house with lye soap?" she suggested wryly. "Well, let me tell you something, sir. Your Victoria might well be the next thing to a saint, but I do not consider myself a fallen woman. I was raised to be a lady, and that is exactly what I am today. I would proudly admit my love for Blake to all the world, without qualm. I am not, nor will I ever be, promiscuous. I belong to one man, and one man only, and I will not have that love belittled by you or anyone else.

"I feel sorry for you, Mr. Banner. You are a mean, narrow-minded old man. You judge everyone by your own measure, and cannot admit that you just might be hasty or mistaken in your opinion. It matters not that others might be hurt by your stringent attitudes. You have even driven your own son away with your hard-hearted, mule-headed hatefulness."

Megan drew a quivering breath. "I should let

you sit out here until you turn blue," she told him sharply, "but I won't. My mother taught me better manners than you seem to have learned in all your years." With that, she yanked the chair loose from the mud and set it straight on the path once again. "Have a pleasant afternoon, sir." She started to walk away from the man, who sat there staring after her in speechless ire. On second thought, she stopped and looked back at him. "Oh, and a smile now and then will not crack your face, sir, regardless of what you believe. With practice, it might even improve your sour disposition!"

To everyone's surprise, Roy Banner chose to join them at the supper table that night. He was not exactly congenial, by most standards, but neither was he obnoxious. He said very little, practically ignoring his fellow diners, but he did not glare and glower at everyone quite as much as was his usual habit. One thing thoroughly shocked everyone. At the start of the meal, he requested that Megan ask the blessing on the food. Perhaps he was testing her, perhaps it was his way of recognizing her presence at his table, an apology of sorts. Megan could only guess at his reasons, while the others looked at one another in mute wonder. Hiding a grin, she managed a respectable prayer with admirable aplomb. Afterward she flashed the old man her most winning smile, and lo and behold, he almost smiled back! He even spoke a few decent words to his son, perhaps for the first time in years.

On the third day, Blake located his aunt at last. Josefa Ramirez resided in a little house on a quiet

street not far from the main plaza, and she promptly
invited them to stay with her. By dinner time, Blake
and Megan had moved into her one spare bedroom,
and by bedtime it was quite evident that dear *Tía*
Josefa, the oldest of his mother's siblings, was in
her dotage. She was a sweet, generous old soul, to
be sure, but she was just a bit batty. Twice during
dinner she forgot Blake's name, and she lapsed into
reminiscences of her girlhood several times that
evening, all of which had to be interpreted by
Blake, since Josefa spoke not one word of English
and Megan knew no Spanish.

When Blake questioned her, she clearly recalled being present at his parents' wedding, but
could not remember the date. Then she referred to
his father by the wrong name, which further dis-
credited her story. She seemed quite sure that she
had attended Blake's mother during his birthing,
then commented on what a darling daughter
Angelina had born.

"Oh, hell!" Blake exclaimed in frustration
when they were at last ensconced in their bedroom. "*Tía* Josefa is as nutty as a Christmas fruit-
cake! What do we do now?"

"I know how disappointing this is to you,
Blake, but perhaps she can still be of help. Maybe
she has better days when her memory is sharper."

"And maybe you are wishing for the moon, my
love. Sweet of you, but just as hopeless as my dear
old aunt." He joined her in the bed, lying with his
hands laced behind his head as he stared up at the
ceiling. Beside him, Megan finished brushing her
hair.

"There is still a chance she might remember

something of worth, or that she might have some papers of use to you," she suggested hopefully.

"If she can remember where they might be," he answered dryly. "Even if she had any, she might have thrown them out years ago. That, or used them in the bottom of one of those twelve birdcages."

Megan bit back a giggle. "She does have quite a menagerie, doesn't she?"

Blake cocked a dark eyebrow in Megan's direction. "Is that what you call the eight cats, fifteen birds, the pet lizard, and the fountain full of goldfish? I wonder how she keeps them from eating one another," he asked in amused amazement. "We certainly didn't help things by adding a wolf and a chipmunk to the collection, did we?"

Megan could not hold back her glee any longer and burst into laughter. "No, darling, we didn't. If you will keep a sharp eye on Lobo while we are here, I'll try to keep Scamp out of trouble. It is the least we can do for the dear old lady."

Blake rolled from his back and gathered her into his arms. "Say that again," he implored, his eyes blazing into hers.

"It's the least we can do—" she repeated.

"No, *querida*." His warm, hard body pressed hers into the mattress. "The part where you call me darling. That has to be the sweetest word on earth when it comes from your lips."

"Darling," she whispered softly, gazing up at him with all the love in her heart. "My dearest, beloved darling."

As it turned out, Aunt Josefa had saved every letter, every note, card, or piece of correspon-

dence she had ever received. She had stacks of old
newspaper clippings she had decided to keep for
reasons known only to herself, more books than
most libraries, and several collections of recipes
handed down from generation to generation, all
crowded into every nook and cranny of her tiny
house in no particular order. Interspersed erratically in all this were her more important papers.

With Josefa's permission, Megan and Blake
began sorting through half a century of collected
paper. Working steadily, it took the better part of a
week. Stuck in the flyleaf of an old history book
they found Josefa's will. Amid a stack of recipes
they found her marriage certificate. Late Uncle
Jorge's will was in the back of the family Bible, and
recorded in the front of the Book were his death
and the birth and death of their only son. The dates
of the births and deaths of Josefa's parents, and
those of her brothers and sisters, were also carefully noted, but not their marriages or the births of
their children.

The title for the small house and the lot on
which it stood was located under a stack of old
mementos in a trunk in the tiny attic. Also in the
trunk were Josefa's wedding gown and veil, old
roses and bouquets she had dried and saved from
the days when Jorge was courting her, a stack of old
love letters bound in pink ribbon, a pair of blue
baby booties, and her son's christening gown.

Nowhere could they find anything of aid to
their cause, until Megan happened to notice that
many of the church documents had been signed by
the same priest, and that the ceremonies had been
conducted in the same church. She grabbed Blake

and went in search of Aunt Josefa.

"Oh, yes, dear," Josefa confirmed. "Father Miguel served the mission church for years and years, as far back as I can recall. Why, he married my parents, and all my brothers and sisters, and most of my cousins. He has christened over fifty of our babies, and buried more of our relatives than I care to remember."

"The mission church in Santa Fe?" Blake asked, excited at finally having discovered something. "Is it still there? Is Father Miguel still there? Did he marry my mother and father?"

"Well, I am sure he did," Josefa said, though she sounded a little vague on that point. "He must have. And the church is still here. I attend almost every Sunday. Part of it had to be rebuilt after the fire, of course, but that was a long time ago. It is really quite a lovely church. There are others more ornate in Santa Fe, but this one has always meant so much to me. It is not fancy, but it is so serene; it makes one feel so close to God. You must go with me someday soon."

"Yes, yes, of course." Blake was nearly frantic with the wandering of the old lady's thoughts. "What of Father Miguel?"

"Old Father Miguel is no longer there," Josefa said with regret. "Now we have a younger priest, Father Romero. Oh, he's such a nice young man, so kind and caring, but it is just not the same without Father Miguel." Josefa was already beginning to digress again, as was her habit these days.

"Did Father Miguel die?"

"No." Josefa shook her head and frowned slightly in concentration. "No, I do not believe so. I think he went someplace else, perhaps among the Indians." Josefa's frail little hands fluttered fretfully. "Oh, dear!" she wailed. "I simply cannot remember! Perhaps you can ask Father Romero. Maybe he knows." She turned rheumy brown eyes toward her nephew. "I am sorry, but I cannot remember," she apologized.

Blake patted the old woman's hand gently. "It is all right, *Tía*. Please do not upset yourself over this. I'll go and talk with Father Romero first thing tomorrow morning."

"I have not been a great deal of help to you, have I?" Josefa said, a woeful expression on her small, wrinkled face.

"You have been more help than you know, and I cannot thank you enough." It was a small lie, but worth it when Josefa beamed up at him with a wobbly smile.

As they were about to leave the house the next morning, Jake came by, and Blake invited him to go along with them. On the way to the church, Blake filled his friend in on their morning's mission. "I am hoping to find some record of my parents' marriage in the church books," he told him. "If not, perhaps we can find Father Miguel, if he is still alive. He could at least verify the date that my parents were married. I doubt if he would have any verification of my birthdate, since Mother and Dad were living on the ranch when I was born."

"Would that be recorded in the church in Tucson?" Jake asked. "If you could get proof of the date of marriage here, and that of your birth in Tucson, you would really be making progress."

"Even the date of your christening would help," Megan added.

"The game would still not be won, since I am still lacking Dad's original will. I don't even have anything with his signature on it, to prove that the false will that Opal and Kirk presented is a forgery."

"You would still be closer to proving your claim than you were before," Jake pointed out.

"What about the bank?" *Tía* Josefa asked in her vague way.

Three heads turned toward her, two of them wondering if Josefa were off on some thought of her own or actually contributing to their conversation. "The bank?" Blake asked. "What about the bank, *Tía*?"

Josefa gave him a disgruntled look as if he were the one who was daft. "Did your father do business at the bank? Surely they would have his signature on some kind of papers, if that is what you need."

Blake translated quickly for Megan's benefit, a wide grin splitting his handsome face. He nearly cracked the poor woman's ribs with the great hug he gave her. "Bless you, *Tía*! You are an angel! An absolute angel!"

Megan was laughing aloud with joy, and Jake looked sheepish. "Now why didn't we have the brains to think of that?" he grumbled good-naturedly. "Now that your aunt has mentioned it, couldn't he have signed for feed at the feedstore, or for tools or fencing at some of the other stores around town? I know it has been a while, but maybe one of them still has a note he signed."

Megan was frowning thoughtfully. "There is

something I don't understand here, Blake. Why couldn't some of your friends or neighbors have testified in your behalf? Surely there are people around Tucson who were there when you were born, who know that you are Mark Montgomery's son."

"There are, and they did testify before the judge. However," Blake grimaced as he recalled those dark days, "for every person who swore in my favor, there was someone to swear differently." At her befuddled look, he explained, "They were paid by Kirk to lie, Megan. It all came down to my word against theirs. Weighed against the documents they showed, and the proof I could not produce, the judge ruled in their favor; and I am still not convinced that the judge was not bought off, too."

"Then even if we do find proof that the will was falsified, that the ranch really should be yours, we have to find a different judge to hear your case, an honest judge," she said.

"Yes, and we will undoubtedly have to notify the U.S. Territorial Marshal to back us up, since Sheriff Brown is Kirk's man, too."

"Right," Jake agreed, "but Kirk and Brown have had their own differences lately. You nail Kirk's hide to the barn door good and proper, all legal-like of course, and Brown will fold like a house of cards in a spring breeze. Tucson will be looking for a new sheriff."

Blake grinned. "Sounds good to me. You interested in the job?"

"First we have to get your ranch back, and for that we have to find Father Miguel, or at least his book of church records. I'll have plenty of time to consider what I want after that.''

In the end, they found neither. Father Romero was very sympathetic to their quest, once *Tía* Josefa had introduced everyone, but he warned that their answers might take some searching. First, because of the fire several years ago, he explained, many of the records dating previous to the last ten years had been destroyed. Those that remained had been water-damaged in the same rainstorm that had produced the fateful bolt of lightning that had caused the fire to begin with. They were welcome to sift through the damaged church records if they wished, now stored in a musty back room.

"Father Miguel has been gone from the mission church for twelve years now," he told them. "The last I heard, he was still alive, traveling from camp to camp, trying to convert various Indian tribes. I believe he was working with the Chiricahua Apache just last year, in the area around San Carlos. He might still be with them."

"That would be Cochise's old band of Chiricahua, now led by his son, Naiche. Didn't they just relocate to the San Carlos reservation a few years back?" Blake tried to remember what he had heard.

"Most of them did, but some have since deserted," Jake put in. "Victorio just escaped his reservation at Tularosa, and some are thought to have joined up with him. No one knows for sure where they are now. Some say Mexico, but others claim that Victorio is still in southeast Arizona somewhere. They are not on the warpath yet, but they are supposedly raiding pretty heavily.''

"Then let's hope we can find what we need from the old church ledgers. The last thing I need is to have to traipse over some of the roughest territory in Arizona in search of Father Miguel, especially with Megan along.''

Father Romero showed them to the small, dank room where the old church records were stored. Huge volumes were stacked around the four walls from floor to ceiling, in no particular sequence. "I'm afraid you have your work cut out for you,'' Father Romero explained with an apologetic wave at the large books. "After the fire, the records were all transferred to this room. We tried to be careful in handling them, since many of them were old even then, and most were soggy from the rains. With a church to repair and a thousand other things on our minds at the time, I'm afraid we were rather careless of the order in which we stacked the books. We never have managed to find time to sort them all out again.''

Blake and Megan shared a look of dismay. "Are you any relation to *Tía* Josefa, by some chance?'' Blake mumbled under his breath.

17

When Father Romero discovered that Megan did not read Spanish, which put her at a disadvantage in searching through the record books, he offered to get one of the Sisters from the convent to help. "It will make the work go much faster with four persons looking," he said. "Since this will help us to put our records in order, which we should have done years ago, it is also our responsibility. I wish I could be of more help personally, but my duties are too heavy just now. I am sure the convent can spare someone to assist you, however."

The young postulate that the convent sent was known as Sister Esperanza. In English, her name meant Sister Hope. She arrived shortly after Jake left to escort *Tía* Josefa home, for the older lady tired quickly. Sister Esperanza spoke both English and Spanish, which helped tremendously, and she and Megan got to work right away on the first of the volumes that Blake hefted onto a tabletop for them. Esperanza quickly showed Megan what to look for in the record books, and they settled down to seriously searching through the handwritten data.

As she worked beside the young woman, who was very near her own age, Megan could not help admiring the girl's natural beauty. Unlike the concealing headgear of the older nuns who had completed their vows, this young woman wore a square headpiece made of white lace over her dark hair, which was drawn back into a tight knot at the back of her head. The severity of the hairstyle only served to emphasize the fragile loveliness of Esperanza's face. The smaller white collar that ringed the neckline of her coarse black dress also designated her as a postulate, a young woman newly come to the convent who had yet to take her vows as a nun. Later, when she had completed her training and taken her vows, she would wear the larger, heavier collar and the full white headdress with the black veil overtop.

Even then, with her hair completely covered and only her fair face exposed, Megan thought Esperanza would never be able to conceal the glowing beauty of her flawless complexion or the lively intelligence that made her green-gold eyes sparkle. Esperanza's features were almost unbelievably perfect. Esperanza glanced up from the ledger before her, and for a moment, as Megan looked into her large, dark-fringed eyes, a forgotten memory tapped at Megan's mind. It was gone before Megan could place it. As strange as it seemed, she felt she should know this young woman, though Megan was sure they had never met.

They had been working steadily for an hour when Jake returned to help. He stopped in the doorway of the small, shaded room, lighted only by the dim sunlight filtering through the one high window. "How is it coming?" he asked.

"Not that well," Blake answered gloomily. "Find a chair and grab a book, friend. At the rate we are progressing, we may be here quite a while." Blake shoved a dusty volume out of the way to make room. "You can work at this table with me while Sister Esperanza helps Megan."

Beside Megan, Sister Esperanza stiffened. Megan, caught suddenly in an attack of sneezing, did not notice the other woman's reaction. Megan's fit claimed the men's attention, and they both turned toward her, laughing. "That is not the most flattering greeting, Megan," Jake said jokingly. "I hope it is the dust that has affected you, and not me."

"Achooo!" Megan shook her head and waved her hands helplessly in the air about her. "No— uh—uh—achoo! S-s-sorry!"

Jake's eyes were crinkled with laughter. He glanced idly at the young Sister seated next to Megan. Suddenly he froze; the half smile on his lips melted away, and he stared at Sister Esperanza with a stunned expression, half hope and half despair. The poor man looked as if he had been poleaxed. His throat worked spasmodically, and when he finally spoke, his voice came out as gritty as sand. "Tori!"

Megan and Blake watched in silent wonder as Jake slowly approached the woman who had been

introduced to them as Sister Esperanza. Jake's big
hand was shaking as he reached out toward her.
Tori leaned back slightly to avoid his touch. "I am
Sister Esperanza now, Jacob," she said softly. Only
her wide green-gold eyes told of her pleasure at
seeing him; they also held what might have been an
apology.

"Why, Tori? Why?" he croaked, even as he
reached out and caressed her cheek. "Help me to
understand."

She smiled sadly up at him. Her hand came up
to enfold his, then gently put it away from her. "It
is what I want, Jacob. How else can I explain it to
you? It gives me peace, it soothes my soul, it makes
me feel useful and needed."

Jake shook his head. He looked like a man
caught in the midst of a nightmare. "No. No. I can't
accept that. The Tori I remember wouldn't need to
join a convent to find peace. She was a lively, happy
girl, so filled with life and laughter that it made you
smile just to watch her. What happened to that girl I
knew? Did Dad force you into this? Did he chase
you into hiding, with his gloomy attitude and
violent moods?"

"Dad had nothing to do with my decision. It
was my choice entirely." Tori glanced about her
guiltily. "Oh, Jacob, I shouldn't even be talking
with you. It is against the rules to have any contact
with my former family. I am supposed to be adjust-
ing to my life away from home, not clinging to my
past."

"Forget the blasted rules!" he ground out.
"You could have stayed at home and felt useful. If
you needed more, why not get married and have a

family? That is enough to make most women feel wanted and needed." His hands came up in a helpless gesture to rake through his hair. "Why this, Tori? You must have had proposals of marriage. You are a beautiful young woman. What can they offer you here that you can't find with a husband and children? What about love? What about children? Won't you yearn for a family of your own one day?"

He came around the table to kneel at her feet. Both of them were unaware of Megan and Blake, who silently tiptoed from the room to afford brother and sister privacy. "Oh, honey," Jake groaned, taking her small hand in his. "I know we weren't much of a family, but don't you see that we were never the average family? Most families don't fight the way we did; normal families love and respect each other. You could have that. It doesn't have to be the way it was at home, with Dad and I at one another's throats all the time, and Caroline wanting to leave so badly that she married the first man to ask her, and you running off to find some peace at last. You could have it all—a husband who loves you, children at your knee. Don't forfeit all that for a life of solitude, angel."

Her smile was a little wobbly. Tears shimmered in her eyes. "You used to call me that all the time when I was small," she said shakily, "but I am not a little girl any longer. I am a grown woman, with a mind of my own and needs of my own."

"And do you think a life here will meet those needs?" he asked a bit harshly. "Who here will love you the way your family will? The way a husband and children would? How many will understand that wild streak of yours when it surfaces?''

"I am trying to learn to curb my temper, Jacob,'' she answered wryly. "I am beginning to learn the meaning of patience and understanding and devotion to a higher cause than my own wants. Contrary to what you seem to want to believe, I am not hiding here. I am not running away from anything; rather, I am running toward something.'' Her voice softened as she looked at him imploringly. "I will be a bride one day, Jacob. Once I take my final vows, I will be a bride of Christ, and who could ask for a better, more loving or understanding husband? The mission children will be my children, and the other Sisters will be my family. The church will be my home. I will lack for nothing, dear brother. Please believe me, and try to be happy for me.''

"I don't know if that is possible, Tori, but I'll try, if this is truly what you want.''

Her gold-green eyes took on a devilish twinkle quite in contrast with her angelic demeanor. "Jacob, I didn't give you this much trouble when you left home, and you must admit that mine is the more acceptable vocation. Not that I blame you for what you felt you must do. Nor have I ever stood in judgment of you. I am simply asking for that same acceptance from you now.''

"It is just such a change to think of you like this, instead of the little hellion who was always in some sort of trouble,'' he admitted. "You must know I'd rather think of you racing across the ranch on your horse, as wild as the wind, your hair streaming out behind you. It is a much better picture to carry with me in my mind than that of you kneeling in prayer on cold stone floors for hours on end, until your knees are numb and your back aches, or scrubbing convent walls until your hands are raw.'' Again he reached out, this time to caress her hair. ''At least they have not cut off all your glorious hair.''

She could not hold his look, her eyes shifting away from his. ''Not yet, but soon, Jacob. When I take my first true vows and wear the white veil of a novice, then I must relinquish all signs of vanity, just as I have already given up all material things from my former life.''

''As well as the family that loves you,'' he added tersely. ''When will these all-important vows take place, Tori?''

''In a few months, as soon as I have learned more about what it means to be a Sister.'' She placed her small hand on his tense arm. ''Jacob, please do not be bitter over this. You have chosen your life; allow me to choose mine as freely. I do not want to go into this with regrets for having hurt you.''

He shrugged her hand off. ''Yet you will do so, regrets or not, won't you? Whether I approve or not, whether your mother misses you so terribly that she cries at the mere mention of your name?''

The tears that Tori had held back now flowed down her cheeks. ''It is hard enough without you making it more difficult for me, Jacob,'' she whispered, swallowing a sob.

Her tears were his undoing. ''All right, angel. You win. But if you ever change your mind, don't feel too embarrassed to admit it and come home. Dad might holler a while, but you know he has always loved you, better than he ever loved Caroline or me, and he will welcome you back." Lean brown fingers brushed the tears from her cheeks, and before he rose from before her, he leaned forward and kissed her lightly on the forehead.

As he walked quickly toward the door, his own tears not far from the surface, she called after him in a voice hoarse with emotion. "I love you, Jacob Banner."

He turned sad eyes to hers. "Yeah," he sighed. In a voice too low for her to hear, he muttered, "Just not quite enough, I guess." She blinked and when she looked again he was gone.

When Megan returned to the room, Tori, or Sister Esperanza as she was now called, had turned her tear-stained face back to the record book. She appeared to be working diligently, but Megan noticed that she was not turning the pages, nor were her fingers following the fine handwritten lines as they had before. Though hesitant to interfere in Esperanza's private affairs, Megan asked quietly, "Is there anything I can do, Sister Esperanza?"

The woman did not look up, but merely shook her head. "No," she murmured. After hesitating a moment, she said, "Not unless you could talk to Jacob for me, try to get him to understand that this is what I want to do with my life. I am afraid I have hurt him dreadfully."

Megan did not know quite how to answer. "I really don't know him very well, Sister Esperanza. I've only just met him through Blake."

Something in the tone of her voice must have alerted Esperanza, for she looked up and eyed

Megan oddly. "Are you afraid of Jacob?" she asked in surprise. "Is it because he is a gunfighter?"

Megan floundered for a reply. She answered as honestly as she dared, hoping she would not offend Jake's sister. "No, I'm not afraid of him, exactly. I'm not sure how to explain it. He's just so solemn, so—so hard sometimes."

To her amazement, Esperanza laughed. "Oh, don't let that rough exterior fool you. Under that forbidding face, Jacob is a lamb in disguise." When Megan gave her a doubtful look in return, Esperanza giggled. "It is true. I swear it. Would I, about to become a nun, lie?"

"I don't suppose so," Megan replied with a sheepish grin. "But you *are* his sister, so you might be somewhat prejudiced in his favor. You two were very close, weren't you?"

"Yes, we were." Esperanza's face glowed with her memories. "Jacob taught me to ride my first pony. According to my mother, it was toward him that I took my first baby steps. Caroline was older; I suppose everyone expected her to help look after me, and she did when Jacob would let her. From the start, he just sort of claimed me as his personal possession. Perhaps it was because he and Dad were always at odds with one another. I know he was lonely for someone to love, someone who would love him back without conditions, no matter what, and I did. I still do, for that matter."

Esperanza sighed sorrowfully. "I haven't hurt him purposefully. I would never hurt him if I could help it. He has been through so much heartbreak already for one man, for a man as good and sensitive as he is inside. If he seems hard, it is because he has had to be in order to survive what life has dealt him. I hope one day he can find peace within himself, as I am seeking here. Maybe then he will lay down his guns and be able to enjoy life for once."

Later that evening, when Megan and Blake were alone, he said, "Did you see the look on Jake's face? He loves Tori so much."

Tugging her dress over her head, Megan answered, "Of course he does. She's his sister."

"No, not really." Blake came to her and swiftly unlaced the ties of her chemise, as if he had been doing this service for her for years. "Esperanza, er, Tori, is his stepsister. There is a world of difference there, Megan, my dove."

Dumbfounded, Megan stared up at him. "Do you mean that Jake loves Esperanza as a man loves a woman, not as brother toward sister?"

"That is precisely what I mean. Sad, isn't it? I've only known Jake a couple of years, but I know him well enough to be sure that he does not give his affections lightly. He has known very little real love in his life, and a lot of sorrow. His mother died when he was six or seven. When his father wasn't berating him, he was ignoring him. His older sister and her family were killed when Jake was twenty. Carmen took him under her wing, and he adores her, but Tori has been the real joy of his life. Now, because of her choice to become a nun, she has been taken out of his reach, too." Talented fingers peeled her chemise from her. Her pantalettes joined it on the floor. As she stood naked before him, Blake proceeded to shed his own clothing.

"Poor Jake," Megan said. "He probably feels so deserted, so rejected just now. No wonder he took it so hard, especially if he loves her in the way you suggest." For the first time, she could really sympathize fully with the man.

"Oh, Blake!" Megan pulled him close in her embrace, holding him tightly to her. "Do you realize how truly fortunate we are to have discovered one another? Others go through their entire lives searching for a love such as ours. What we have found is more precious than gold, more rare than the most perfect of pearls."

"Then let's not waste a moment of it." He carried her the few steps to the bed, then took his place over her. But tonight, filled to overflowing with the wonder of their shared love, Megan had other ideas. Pushing him from above her, she shoved him onto his back. Then she took the dominant position. "Tonight," she murmured, her voice a sultry promise in itself, "I will make love to you. Let me show you how very much I love you, how much I want you. Let me make you need me as badly as I need you."

He gazed up into her smoky grey eyes and was lost. "With pleasure, *querida*. I am yours to do with as you wish."

She ate him with her eyes, she adored him with her mouth, she tasted every inch of his beloved body with her tongue, from his head to his toes and everywhere in between. Blake watched through a haze of passion as Megan seduced him, and in the process, she herself was seduced. She hovered over him, her delicate nostrils flaring as they caught the musky scent of arousal, her head thrown back in abandonment, thoroughly enjoying her power over him. Then her tousled hair was a cinnamon curtain about their faces as her lips sought his. Their lips melted together; their tongues tangled and mated, hers dueling expertly with his as she led him in the kiss.

When her warm breath sang in his ear, her teeth nipping ever so lightly at his earlobe, she felt the intense shiver that echoed through him. Her tinkling laughter held an edge of devilish delight to it. She teased, and she tantalized, until Blake thought he would go out of his mind with wanting her. Her hands found him, fondled him, and when her warm, moist mouth closed over him, he groaned with the building pressure, the quivering arrows of sheer longing that speared through him. "Yes, oh, yes, my sweet love, *mi pequeña paloma*," he groaned in encouragement. "Touch me. Feel me. Yes, like that. Oh, yes. So sweet. So good."

Megan was deliriously drunk on her own feminine prowess. Every moan of delight she wrung from him went straight to her head like fine wine. She knew she held him in her spell in those moments, and even as her own desires mounted to fever pitch, she was reluctant to relinquish her new-found powers over him. She wanted to prolong this sweet torment as long as she could, forever if that were possible.

All too soon, the fires grew too hot to endure any longer. The flames of desire were consuming them both. Suddenly she needed to have him within her, needed to feel him filling her with himself, making her complete where emptiness was gnawing at her. With agile grace she straddled him, and when he came into her, she welcomed him with a glad cry of joy. His hands on her hips steadied her, guiding her into the rhythm of love. When his hot lips wrapped themselves about a turgid nipple, she felt the pull all the way to her toes as he suckled her.

She was engulfed in a tidal wave of pure passion. She was riding high on the crest of a giant wave, and Blake was with her all the way. The wave built higher and stronger, gathering power as it raced toward uncharted shores. Then they topped the crest, and for heart-stopping eternal moments, they balanced precariously, deliciously on the edge of ecstasy. Timeless seconds later, they plunged together into the pounding surf. As she tumbled forward into a rapture so profound that she could scarcely bear the splendor of it, she heard a high, keening sound in her ear, never realizing it was her own voice calling out in wordless wonder.

They washed ashore gently, enfolded tenderly in a gold-sparkled mist of foam that slowly, gradually dissolved like bubbles in a crystal goblet of rare wine. With a sigh of absolute contentment, Megan rested her damp head on Blake's heaving chest and listened to the sound of his heartbeats thundering in her ear, until finally the beats calmed in accord with hers. The muscles in her thighs trembled against his, their languid limbs still entangled. If she were to die this very minute, Megan knew that heaven could hold no greater glories than that which she and Blake had just embraced.

Jake did not join them when they continued their perusal of the church records the next day.

He made some excuse about having some things to attend to for his father, but it was clear to Blake and Megan that Jake simply could not bring himself to go near the church again, knowing that Tori would be there, so near and yet so far from his reach. Sister Esperanza was a mass of nerves herself. With each footfall outside the door of the room where they were working, she started visibly. She spilled things, she dropped things, she knocked things over, until finally Megan took pity on the poor woman. Unobtrusively, she took Esperanza aside and told her that Jake would not be coming to the church that day. Only then did Sister Esperanza calm down enough to be of more assistance than she was hindrance.

It was late in the afternoon, when their eyes were watering from the strain of deciphering Father Miguel's spidery-fine writing, that they found what they were looking for. Esperanza was sure that it was only by God's good grace that they had not all gone blind already. They had finally located two volumes that encompassed the approximate years of Angelina and Mark Montgomery's marriage, since Blake had not been sure in which year his parents had wed. Megan and Blake had each taken a book and were scouring it wearily but determinedly. Esperanza had chosen a volume that had no yearly dates clearly printed on it, but had been stacked between the two that Blake and Megan were now examining, in the hopes that it was the one dating between the other two.

Megan was nearly falling asleep from the monotony of the task when Esperanza suddenly gasped aloud, then groaned in dismay. In the hush of the room, her quiet exclamation sounded like a cannon being fired. It brought both Blake and Megan rushing to her side.

Then they saw what Esperanza had seen. The particular book she was searching through had been badly damaged, both from the fire and the rain. The binding of the book was rotting away, the cover badly burned. The edges of the pages were charred, some so badly that half the page was gone. Water had soaked through many of the thin pages, and some had become stuck together as they dried. The open pages before her had not gone unscathed.

Esperanza pointed to a line a third of the way down the right-hand page. Just barely legible were the names of Angelina Francisca Magdalena Ruiz y Pizarro, and Mark Anthony Montgomery. The rest of the line was completely obliterated where the ink had run and flames had licked at the paper. The all-important date was smeared beyond legibility. In fact, nowhere on numerous pages both before and after were the dates clear enough to read.

On a page near the front they finally found a date, but it meant little, since the frugal *Padre* had often run one year into the next in his records, choosing not to waste space by using a separate book for each year. Some of the huge books encompassed five years or more. The page this date was on was so far ahead of the one designating Blake's parents' wedding that it could have been the same year or three years before, depending on how many entries the priest had made in a year's time. They had no way of determining this. Thus, all their diligent efforts had gone for nought.

Megan could have wept, and she knew that Blake felt the same. "I am so sorry," Esperanza murmured, as if she were personally responsible. "At least this proves that your parents were married in this church by Father Miguel. Does that not help?"

Blake sighed and rubbed a hand over smarting eyes. "All it means is that we will not be searching for Father Miguel without reason. He did marry my mother and father. Now all I can do is hope that we find him, that he is still alive and sound of mind, and that he can recall the date, or at least the year, of their wedding. No one has ever doubted that my parents were married, you see," he went on to explain to the downcast young Sister. "It is just the date that we need so desperately now."

"So you will go in search of Father Miguel."

Blake heaved a dejected breath. "Yes, we will go in search of the good *Padre*," he confirmed wearily. "If I never prove my parentage or get my land back, God knows it certainly will not be for lack of trying. We will leave tomorrow, the day after at the latest. Thank you for all your help, Sister Esperanza. If ever there is anything we can do to repay your kindness, please do not hesitate to ask."

"You are very welcome, both of you. I was glad to do it. I only wish it could have been with better result." When she left them at the entrance of the mission, she said simply, "*Vaya con Dios, mis amigos,* and good luck in your quest. I will pray for your success. Please, if you will, say goodbye to Jacob for me, and tell him I will remember him always in my prayers and in my heart."

18

It was decided that they would look for Father Miguel first at the San Carlos reservation in the southeastern Arizona territory, since that was where most of the Apache nation was now head-quartered. A brief shopping trip was in order before they could leave. Not only were there supplies to buy, but Megan needed several more items of clothing for the ride.

With *Tía* Josefa as her guide, Megan took a fast tour of the shops in Santa Fe. According to Blake's instructions, Megan purchased two split riding skirts of durable material, three serviceable blouses, and a pair of riding gloves to protect her hands from further abuse. They had to visit the boys' section of one store in order to find a Western hat to fit her, since Blake had declared the more fashionable ladies' bonnets as next to useless. He said he preferred that she not buy a regular bonnet, either, since a Western hat such as his would be much more practical under the circumstances.

The same applied to the jacket he told her to purchase, and the rain slicker. They may not have been the height of fashion, or what a lady was used to wearing, but they would keep her far more warm and dry than anything she could have bought in one of the ladies' stores. He assured her she would be glad to have them before their journey was done. Luckily, the bootmaker had a pair of good leather riding boots in a size to fit her, again in a boy's size.

Then Megan turned her attention to more feminine items. She bought an extra set of underthings, several hair ribbons, pins, and a comb and brush of her own. She even included a bar of lavender-scented soap for good measure and her own tin of tooth powder.

Finally, she bought a white lace shawl to wear with the prettier clothes that Carmen had given her, not because it was on the list of things Blake said were necessary, but because it was so beautiful that she simply could not resist it. Blake had warned her that she could bring only what would fit into her saddlebags or rolled up in the bedroll he was buying for her, but she would make room for the lovely shawl somehow. Perhaps her vanity was showing, but somehow she felt the need for just one thoroughly delightful, feminine article all her own, something that no one else had worn before her. She justified this by recalling all the beautiful new clothes that had been left behind when Blake had stolen her from the stagecoach. Let Blake yell if he wanted; he owed her this much, at least!

They said goodbye to *Tía* Josefa the next morning. "It has been so good to see one of my family again," she told them tearfully. "You must promise to come again soon. I find I am lonely now, living here all by myself. How often I yearn to see my family again, but I am getting too old to travel so far alone."

"We will be back again, *Tía,*" Blake promised. "Perhaps the next time I go down to Mexico to visit, you can come with me."

Josefa brightened at this. "Oh, it would delight me so to see Juan again, and Felipe and Honora and all their children." Blake explained to Megan that Juan and Honora were Josefa's younger brother and sister, who had returned to Mexico to live. Angelina, of course, had moved to Arizona after her marriage. She and Rosa had died, but another of their brothers was a priest, now living in California. Of all the close family, only Josefa still lived in Santa Fe.

Before they left, Josefa drew Megan aside. She handed Megan a small package and gestured for Megan to unwrap it. Inside, Megan discovered the beautiful christening gown that had belonged to Josefa's only child. "Oh, no, Josefa," she exclaimed. "I cannot take this! You have saved it all these years." Megan was touched to tears, but handed it back to Josefa.

Josefa shook her head emphatically and pushed the gown firmly back into Megan's hands. "*No! No! Es un regalo para su niño.*" When Megan still failed to understand, the woman laid her hand gently upon Megan's stomach. "*Su niño,*" she repeated. "*Su infante.*" She made a cradle of her arms and rocked them back and forth as one would do with a baby. Then she made a large circle in front of her with her arms, mimicking a large tummy, then pointed at Megan's stomach again. "*Bebé,*" she said.

Now Megan shook her head. "No, Josefa. No baby," she answered, though Josefa's words gave her pause for thought. When *was* the last time she'd had her monthly flow? It had been in the midst of packing for the trip to Tucson, a good week before they had boarded the stage. That would place it approximately a month and a half ago, Megan realized with a jolt! She should have gotten her flow two weeks before, by her calculations.

Suddenly Megan felt weak at the knees. Could it be? She had been with Blake for over a month now. Even so, she reasoned to herself, women were known to be late when under stress, and she had certainly been that. Surely it was only the unusual circumstances that had occurred this past month, all the travel and tension.

Still, her hands went instinctively to her belly, and Josefa nodded affirmatively. The old woman chattered away in rapid Spanish, gesturing toward Megan's cheeks, her eyes, her hair. "*Si, un bebé,*" she repeated. "*Es verdad.*" Josefa seemed so certain, despite any objections from Megan. It made Megan begin to wonder if there were something different about her, something the older woman could see or sense even before Megan could discover the truth for herself.

Deep inside, Megan hoped that Josefa was right. Just the thought of carrying Blake's child within her made her giddy with joy. *Oh, let it be,* she thought to herself. *Let it be true.*

Yet when Blake asked her what Josefa had wanted, Megan kept their strange communication to herself. She wanted to savor the idea a little longer, her own personal hopes and dreams. She did not want to inform Blake prematurely, lest it not be so. Also, she was not sure how Blake would take the news if Josefa proved correct. While she knew he loved her, impending fatherhood was another matter. Blake had said nothing as yet about wanting to get married, and privately Megan thought that he wanted to get his ranch back first, or at least prove his right to his father's surname. She would wait a short time before mentioning it to him, at least until she was positive of it herself. In the meanwhile, she would be especially careful in the coming days, just in case, for Blake had warned that the country through which they would be traveling held many dangers.

After leaving *Tía* Josefa's house, they met up with Jake at the Banner ranch. Jake would be traveling with them as far as the San Carlos reservation. Then, if they did not succeed in finding Father Miguel there, Megan and Blake would continue the search for the priest while Jake went on to Tucson to find out what had been happening there in their absence.

They bid a quick farewell to Carmen and Roy. The latter surprised them by inviting them back. "But next time you sleep under my roof, you will either do so in separate beds or be married." He speared Blake with a sharp look. "If you have any brains at all, you'll marry this girl and make an honest woman of her. I like her," he said gruffly, as if his opinion were the only one that mattered.

Blake smothered a chuckle, but could not quite hide his quick grin. "I do, too, sir," he assured Jake's father. "I'll give your advice some serious thought."

"You do that, boy," Roy growled. He wheeled his chair about and threw Megan a conspiratorial wink behind Blake's back.

The first leg of their trip was almost luxurious compared to the rest of it. They paid fare for themselves and their horses on the spur line of the Santa Fe Railroad that ran as far as Albuquerque. This saved them about two days traveling time, and the longer Megan could avoid torturing her posterior with hard saddle leather, the better she liked it. They stayed overnight in a small hotel, and were up bright and early the next morning to catch the stage that ran from Albuquerque to El Paso, Texas, following the Rio Grande.

Megan wasn't as thrilled with the idea of taking the stagecoach as she had been with riding the train. She still hadn't forgotten the adventures of her last stagecoach trip. "Why are we taking the stage?" she asked, almost sulkily.

"Are you that eager to be in the saddle again, Megan?" Blake teased with a chuckle, eyeing her behind with a wicked gleam in his eye.

"No, but we won't save any time this way, will we?"

"Believe it or not, we will, simply because the stage will stop every fifteen or twenty miles for fresh horses. Even though our horses will be tied to the back of the stage, they'll stay much fresher, since they won't be carrying our weight all day, and the rest stops at the way stations will save our provisions, which we will need more later. I figure we'll save at least another day this way, too. By mid-morning tomorrow we should be at the rest stop in Socorro, and that is as far as we want to go south. We'll ride west from there on our own.''

"That is where the trail gets rough, after we leave the Rio Grande," Jake went on to explain as they watched their gear being loaded into the boot of the stagecoach. "We'll pick up the old Gila River Trail, such as it is, heading into Arizona. Actually, it's no more than an old Indian trail this far east, but I guess it's better than nothing."

"What about Lobo?" she asked. "You had a hard enough time getting them to let him on the train. Surely they won't allow him on the stage?"

Blake shrugged. "He'll keep up," he said, not at all worried about the wolf.

Megan had noticed the strange looks she and Blake and Jake had received from other people, both on the train and in Albuquerque the evening before. The three of them were getting some of the same looks now from their fellow passengers, and the disapproving looks had nothing to do with the tiny chipmunk nestled peacefully in Blake's vest pocket. Upon first noticing them, other people tended to stare, then shy away, almost in fearful fascination. Folks readily made way for them, and Megan got the distinct impression that it was done more from caution than from friendliness, especially when she caught some of the sidelong glances thrown in Blake and Jake's direction.

When she thought about it, she could see why. Both men looked rather formidable, with their guns

strapped low on their thighs and their hats shading
their watchful faces. They looked rough, tough,
and ready for any kind of trouble. Blake looked
every bit as much a gunfighter as Jake, and Megan
felt a shiver of ice run down her spine at the
thought.

Megan was getting her fair share of looks, too,
and not the most respectable she'd ever received at
that. As they boarded the stagecoach, the other lady
passengers pulled their skirts aside, as if the slightest contact with Megan was to be avoided at all
costs. Megan's polite smile dissolved at the obvious
rejection, and she knew that if she were to speak,
they would act as if they had not heard her. For her
association with Blake and Jacob Banner, she was
being snubbed! Nothing like this had ever happened to her before, with the exception of Roy
Banner's reaction, and she could not help but be
hurt, though she did her best to hide it. As she sat
silently beside Blake, her small chin jutted out
defiantly and her eyes shot silent daggers at her
fellow passengers. Let them think what they
wanted, the narrow-minded prigs! As long as she
had Blake at her side, that was all she needed.
Certainly she did not need the approval of these
snobby strangers!

Still, she found it interesting to note that while
the women shunned her, they were surreptitiously
casting admiring glances from beneath their lashes
at both Blake and Jake. Likewise, the so-called
gentlemen of their little group were not beyond
sending Megan sly looks when they thought her
escorts were not watching. Megan glared back,
seething with indignation. *Self-righteous hypo-*

crites! she thought angrily. *Given half a chance, any one of these "good ladies" would throw herself at Blake's head in a second and then claim it was all his fault; and any of these "proper gentlemen" would be beneath my skirts in a blink, if they thought they wouldn't get shot for their efforts!* Megan's chin came up a bit more.

Blake must have sensed her hurt, for a few minutes into the journey, his hand found hers beneath the folds of her skirt. His warm fingers wrapped tightly about hers, offering comfort. His dark head leaned toward hers, and he whispered low in her ear, "I'm sorry, darlin'. I just wasn't thinking, I guess."

Turning her face toward his, she saw the apology echoed in his eyes. At that moment she would have moved the earth to erase the regret from his face. She mustered her most radiant smile to bestow upon him. "I love you," she told him simply. Then, before God and everyone, she leaned forward and kissed him on the lips.

Her mouth curved under his in a smile as she heard the lady nearest her gasp and hiss loudly, "Blatant hussy!"

The poor man who was presumably her husband whispered back, "Hush, Mildred. Good God, do you want to get us all shot?"

Blake's mouth mimicked hers in a return smile, and on the other side of her, Megan was sure she heard Jake choke back a chuckle, while the man across the way inhaled on his cigar a little too heartily and went into a fit of coughing. About this time, Scamp wriggled out from Blake's pocket. He scampered up to perch on Blake's shoulder, where he rubbed the sleep from his shiny little eyes and looked around grouchily. Then he let loose with a spate of angry chattering, as if berating everyone for waking him.

The other two ladies went into shrieks of hysteria, as if a snake had been set loose in their midst. The men merely stared, then began to laugh. Blake gave a disgusted grunt, and growled, "Lord, you'd think they'd seen a gila monster at the very least."

The young Easterner sitting across from them asked hesitantly, "A gila monster? What's that?"

Blake did not have the opportunity to reply to the greenhorn's question, for the stagecoach driver, alerted by the women's screams, was rapping sharply on the coach roof and calling, "What in tarnation is going on in there?"

Jake leaned out his window and yelled up, "Nothin' to get excited about! The lady just has a bee in her bonnet!"

Megan dissolved into giggles and hid her face in Blake's shoulder.

When the ladies could not be calmed, Jake suggested wryly, "Give the little varmint to me. I'll take him with me up top for a spell. It's a bit too stuffy in here for my nature anyway." With that, he stuffed Scamp under his shirt and pulled himself deftly through the door window and onto the top of the rocking stagecoach, much to the amazement of the young greenhorn.

Things quieted down considerably after that. Blake stretched his long legs out in front of him, pulled the brim of his hat low over his eyes, and proceeded to nap. After a few minutes, Megan leaned her head against his hard shoulder and did the same. Blake was by her side, and for the moment all was right with the world.

Later that afternoon, after the noon stop and a change of horses, the greenhorn's curiosity got the better of him, overcoming his initial trepidation. All of a sudden he was as talkative as a magpie, and full of questions about the West and its inhabitants. "Are you—er—are you a real gunfighter?" he asked Jake, who was once again riding inside the carriage. Even Megan gaped at his blunt question, and she felt Blake stiffen next to her. It grew so quiet in the coach that you could have heard a pin drop in the heavy silence.

"I reckon I'm real enough," Jake replied smoothly, leveling a cool stare at the young man. "If your next question is how many men I've killed, don't ask it."

The Easterner gulped. "No sir," he answered timidly. "But I was wondering why you tie your holster down to your leg like that."

"It makes a faster draw. Any other questions?" Jake drawled.

"Yes. Is there really such a thing as a gila monster, and what is it?"

"Oh, they're real enough, too. They are a kind of poisonous lizard around these parts. Ugly as sin! They look like some kind of shrunken dragon, and when they hiss, you'd swear they are gonna spit fire right in your eye. Grow to better than two foot long."

Megan shivered, even though she had an idea that Jake was embellishing his tale just to scare the fellow. She could only hope they would not see any of these terrible creatures on their travel. She had a suspicion she would be no more fond of gila monsters than she was of snakes.

That hushed the fellow for a while, but soon he cleared his throat loudly and said, "I—er, I hope you won't take offense, but I noticed that you two gentlemen have exceptionally fine teeth." His hesitant gaze traveled from Blake to Jake and back again. At their suspicious looks, he hastened to explain. "I'm a dentist, you see, so I notice these things, and most of the men I've seen while traveling West have had the most awful teeth, all brown and broken. I can't help wondering why yours are so straight and white."

Megan bit back a chuckle as she waited for their reply. "Milk," she heard Blake mumble.

"What's that, sir?" the young fellow asked.

"I said, milk," Blake grumbled. "Milk and knowing when to duck in a fistfight."

Jake gave an elaborate shrug. "That might have worked for you, and I agree with the part about avoiding a swinging fist, but I hate milk—always have."

"Then what is your secret, sir?"

"Whiskey and wild women, son," Jake assured him with a serious face, though his eyes twinkled with wicked delight as the young dentist turned red from the neck up. The other women gasped in outrage, and Megan hid an embarrassed blush behind her hands. The other gentlemen just stared, no doubt wondering if Jake was serious or not. Blake just shook his head in resignation. He knew from experience that there was nothing Jake enjoyed more than joshing an unsuspecting greenhorn, and this one was an especially willing target. "Of course, too much of one will make you crazy," Jake went on straight-faced, "and too little of the other is just plain bad for a man's health. The trick is to figure which is which before it's too late."

As was the usual arrangement in a small way station, the women all bedded down together in one bedroom while the men made do with whatever other beds were available—cots, tabletops, bedrolls on the floor and in the stable loft. That night Megan found herself sharing a room with the two haughty ladies with whom she had endured the stagecoach ride. None were thrilled with the arrangement, but Megan told herself she could put up with them for one night.

Obviously, the other two women felt differently. The bedroom had two double beds in it, and when Megan returned from a brief wash in the small washroom down the hall, each of the ladies had claimed a bed entirely for herself, lying right in the middle and leaving Megan no place to sleep. When Megan stopped short in the doorway, the women both looked through her as if she were not there, then shared a smug look between themselves. *Well, we'll see about this!* Megan thought stubbornly.

As if she had noticed nothing unusual about the arrangements, Megan proceeded to undress. She had a twinge of regret that she had not thought to purchase a nightgown, but she quickly shrugged that off. She could sleep just as well in her chemise and underdrawers for one night. If she'd brought a nightgown, she would not have had room for the shawl, and a lot of use she would have for the nightgown after tonight, anyway! She would be sleeping fully dressed on the trail.

When she had finished shedding her clothes, folding everything neatly away, she turned toward the other women. Standing between the two beds, her hands planted firmly on her hips, she announced loudly, "Now, whichever of you two ladies has the warmest feet is about to have me for a bedmate, so make up your minds quickly. I'm too tired for much quibbling."

When both of the women just lay there gaping at her, she strode over to the bed where Mildred lay, whipped the coverlet open, and snapped, "Move over, dearie. I do hope you don't snore."

Mildred was dumbfounded as Megan crawled in beside her and nudged her over. "Well! I never!" she huffed.

"Well! I should hope not!" Megan retorted as she doused the lamp. "And don't steal all the covers, either."

Mildred cringed on her side of the bed as Megan settled down for a good night's rest, a self-satisfied smile tugging her lips upward.

By the time the stagecoach reached the noon way station the next day, Megan was ready to bid a hearty farewell to all her coachmates. They would have the noon meal here, then she and her two companions would go their own way. She and Blake were still seated at the table, finishing the last of their meal, when the relief stagecoach driver pulled into the yard. Jake had already gone outside to saddle their horses and see to the transfer of their belongings from the stage, a chore for which he had volunteered so that Megan and Blake could have a few moments to themselves.

The door opened and the new driver came into the main room, laughing at something the other driver was telling him. Something about the man caught Megan's attention, and when he walked by her, she looked up. The breath caught in her throat, and she thought surely she would choke on the piece of pie that lodged there. "Oh, my lands!" she exclaimed softly.

Blake looked at her questioningly, but before she could explain, the driver turned and said to those in the room, "Stage leaves in ten minutes, so do what you have to do, folks," His eyes roved the room as he added, "That means you ladies especially. I don't make no unscheduled stops along—" his voice fell away as his gaze lit on Megan. "You!" he hollered, pointing his finger at her. "You're the gal that was taken off my stage on the Tucson run!"

"No! No, I'm not," Megan lied, even as she stood and blocked the man's view of Blake. "You've mistaken me for someone else, mister."

"In a pig's eye!" the man fired back, starting toward her. "You're that Coulston gal or my name ain't Joe Landy!"

"Of all the damned luck," Megan heard Blake mutter from behind her. Then he was standing, pushing her toward the door, only to find Joe Landy blocking their way, not only to the front door, but to the path leading to the kitchen and the rear door, too. The only way left open to them was the stairway to the second-floor bedrooms. They ran for it.

Pulled along behind him as Blake bounded up the stairs three at a time, Megan's feet barely touched the steps. Her shins, her ankles, her knees all hit several times, but her feet never made contact, she was sure. After hearing Joe yell, "Stop, or I'll shoot!" she didn't care how she got up the stairs, as long as she made it alive. They had barely rounded the corner at the top of the stairs when chips flew off the banister behind them. With her heart thundering in her ears, Megan never heard the gunshot. She just kept running.

Blake dodged into the first bedroom, found there was no lock on the door, and dashed for the second room. This one was the way station owner's and his wife's, and there was a sturdy lock on this door. Yanking Megan inside, Blake slammed the door and locked it. Then, hearing several pair of footsteps pounding up the stairs in pursuit, he dragged a heavy dresser in front of the door for good measure. Megan hadn't yet caught her breath when Blake hauled her toward the window, threw it open, and yelled for Jake. Before she knew what was happening, he was stuffing her legs out the open window.

"Blake!" she shrieked. "What are you doing? We're on the second floor, for pity's sake!" She was sitting on the windowsill, her arms braced on the frame on either side of her, facing a sheer drop to the ground. Her fingernails clawed at the wood in panic.

Blake's head came through the window at her waist. "Now is not the time to quibble, Megan," he told her shortly. "Here comes Jake. Now, when his horse is directly under the window, I want you to jump. He'll catch you.''

"Jump?'' she screeched over the sound of shouts and heavy pounding on the door behind them. "I can't!" She craned her head to see his face. He was perfectly serious. "I can't! If Jake misses me, I'll break every bone in my body!''

"No you won't. Look, we don't have time to argue, love. You are sitting only fifteen feet from the ground right now. The blasted horse's back is five feet high. I can lower you practically into Jake's arms. You'll drop four maybe five feet at most.'' As he spoke he was prying her hands loose from their grasp, wrapping his big hands about her wrists. Behind them the door shuddered beneath the weight of several men's bodies. Blake's thigh nudged her bottom off the windowsill.

Megan hung in midair, suspended only by Blake's hands as he carefully lowered her. "Blake, if this harms our baby, I'll never forgive you!'' she shrieked.

He lifted her until their faces were even with one another's, though his was upside down. At least she hoped his was the one that was upside down. At this point, she was so scared she couldn't be sure. "What baby?'' he asked stupidly, a silly grin on his face.

"The one I think I may be carrying.''

"Now you tell me!'' Blake shook his head in wonderment. "Your timing could stand some improvement, darlin'.'' He gave her a swift kiss and dropped her.

19

They escaped the tiny town of Socorro by the skin of their teeth. They circled and backtracked, and soon lost the few riders who had first followed them. They headed west, counting themselves lucky that none of their fellow passengers knew their destination; they had been extremely wary lest anyone overhear an ill-timed conversation. At the least, their true direction of travel would remain a secret, and perhaps Jake's identity.

When the immediate danger had passed, Blake leaned forward and captured the reins of Megan's horse, pulling her mount to a halt. "Okay, little darlin', let's hear more about this baby of ours you've neglected to mention until today."

Megan eyed him uncertainly, trying to judge his reaction to her news. Scared as she had been, she was certain she'd seen him grin, and had thought he was pleased with the idea, but now she was less sure. "I'm really not positive, Blake," she hastened to explain. "That is why I did not say anything sooner."

"But you think you might be carrying my child?"

She nodded. "I believe so; I hope so."

She watched closely as he drew a deep breath and closed his eyes for a brief moment before answering. "It will complicate things, no doubt of that, but I hope so, too, *querida*." His sapphire eyes caressed her face lovingly, then dropped to her still-flat stomach. Megan was glad that Jake was far enough ahead of them to afford them a measure of privacy as Blake said intimately, "I want to see you grow round with my child, to feel him move within you. I want to see the glow of motherhood upon your cheeks, to watch your breasts fill with milk; to witness each little change in you, no matter how small, and to know that our love has created the life within you."

He reached out and laid his hand upon her belly, and she felt the heat of his touch clear through her clothes. Their horses shifted restlessly, but that did not deter him as he leaned toward her and kissed her tenderly on the lips. "I love you, my dove, and I will love any and all of the children we might create together."

"Oh, Blake! I love you so much; and I am so glad that you feel the way you do. I was worried that you might not like the idea, especially right now. This is not the most desirable time, I know, with everything else so unsettled."

His rough knuckles caressed her cheek. His eyes smiled into hers. "I don't think you or I have much control over such things, honey. Nature will take its own course, in its own time. When will you be sure about the baby?"

A wild blush stained her cheeks. "In two or three weeks, I suppose. Each day I go without —uh—"

Laughing at her flustered state, he said, "I know what you are trying to say, sweetheart. Don't be embarrassed. You never have to be shy about anything with me, Megan. You are going to be my wife."

Pure joy lit her face, and at that moment she was more beautiful than Blake had ever seen her. "Truly?" she breathed, as if this might all be a dream, and she was fearful of disturbing it lest it shatter into reality.

"As soon as I can arrange it, we are going to be married," he assured her. Then his face took on a more serious, determined look. "If I have to make copies of all the legal documents recording our marriage, the baby's birth, our wills, property deeds—whatever—I will. Our children will never go through what I have these last few years. No one will ever have cause to doubt this child's parentage, or his right to his own heritage. This I swear to you, Megan. Neither will anyone ever besmirch your name or your reputation; not while I draw breath. My only hope is that we can prove my right to the Montgomery name before this baby is born. I want him to bear that name, legally and rightfully. I want it, and I know Dad would want it as well."

It took all of Megan's courage to speak her next words to him. His very touch made her ache for his arms about her. His voice alone made her quiver with longing and overwhelming love for him. She had to force the words from her reluctant lips. "Blake, you don't have to marry me just for the sake of the baby. I don't want you to—"

His face could have been carved of stone as he stared at her. His hands came onto her shoulders, and he nearly shook her out of her saddle. "My child will not be born a bastard!" he ground out from between clenched teeth. "Don't even think about it, Megan. You are going to marry me, come hell or high water, and nothing this side of death will prevent it. Do you understand that?"

She met him glare for glare. "I hear you," she announced stubbornly. "Now you understand something, Blake Almighty Montgomery. I will not have a husband who feels forced to marry me for the sake of my child or my reputation! If and when I wed, I need to know that the man I am about to devote my life to is marrying me because he loves me, because he cannot bear the thought of life without me, not because of some horrid sense of obligation!"

Blake had the audacity to laugh—not just a chuckle, but a full-throated, straight-from-the-belly laugh. "Oh, Megan, you are a sight to behold when your dander is riled. Your eyes spit storm clouds and lightning, your cheeks glow like ripe cherries, and your mouth is the most delectable thing since Eve's apple."

His hands framed her flushed face as his eyes held hers. "Don't you know by now how much I love you?" he asked sincerely, all trace of humor gone. "You hold my world in the palm of your hands, my future in your next breath. Nothing on this earth could force me to marry you if I did not want to, and I definitely want to, my love. More than anything else, I want to make you my wife, to hold you close to my heart always and in all ways. I need you, *querida*. I need your smile to light my days, your sighs to soften my nights. Without your quick temper and sharp tongue, my life would be too dull to bear. Never doubt that I adore everything about you, even when I am so angry with you that I could beat you.''

The smile on her face was at once radiant and the slightest bit smug. "You can't beat me, Blake. Not while there is the chance that I carry our child."

"Then I'll have to find another way to make you pay for your transgressions, won't I?" he rebutted with an equally satisfied grin. "Oh, and the name is Andrew Matthew, by the way."

"I beg your pardon?" Megan shook her head in confusion.

"You have it."

"Blake! Whose name is Andrew Matthew?" She nearly shouted in exasperation.

"Mine, of course. Blake Andrew Matthew Montgomery. Mother was a devout Catholic, and she was proud of me as only a mother can be, but even she would never have named me anything as grandiose as 'Almightly.'"

"If she had known at the time how impossibly overbearing you would grow to be, she might have considered it." Catching up her reins, Megan spurred her horse and left Blake staring after her, shaking his head and laughing. No, life with Megan would be one surprise after another, but it would never be dull.

They followed the Gila River Trail through forests and mountains, winding their way out of New Mexico and into the raw Arizona Territory. Their route was the most direct, but certainly not the smoothest of traveling. Neither, however, was the area that was their destination. The San Carlos Reservation was situated amid the most barren, devastated land Megan had ever set eyes upon. As she looked out upon the desolate landscape, she shivered. "It looks more like the devil's handiwork than God's," she breathed in absolute awe. "Why would He ever create something so lifeless, so forsaken as this? How can the government expect anyone, even the Indians, to live here? Surely nothing can survive upon this wretched land for long."

"Precisely their reasoning, I believe," Blake answered disgustedly.

"It's not right," Megan said, shaking her head sadly.

"No, it's not," Blake agreed. "Most of my mother's people managed to live hand in hand with the Indians in relative peace for many years. They traded for land, for horses, for goods; but they also respected the Indians' right to the land of their birth. Others could have done the same. That is not to say that all Mexicans came to this territory with such tolerance. Many were just as greedy and corrupt as the Americans. History proves how ruthless and devious Cortez was in his dealings with the

Aztec Indians in Mexico. The U.S. government seems to have taken a page from Cortez's book in its own dealing with the American tribes.

"Still, progress will not be halted, and someone must always pay the price. The white man was determined to explore and expand, casting his eyes westward toward more fertile lands. My own ranch was once Indian land, some of it bought and paid for in blood, both Indian and white. My family is just as guilty as the rest, if blame be placed for this." His hand swept out in a broad arc, indicating the barren land that was now the home of the once-proud Apache nation.

"Perhaps, but at least you take no pride in the Indian's sad plight," Megan pointed out. "You don't gloat as many others do."

"No, if anything, I pity them, though I'm smart enough not to admit it to any one of them. They are a proud people, and they would sooner slit a man's throat than accept his pity."

From the time they rode onto reservation land, they could feel eyes upon them. Though they saw no one, they sensed they were being watched and followed. As they made their way across the vast, desolate land toward the community of San Carlos, headquarters of the San Carlos Reservation, it took all of Megan's willpower not to keep turning about in her saddle, continually looking for the Indians she knew were tailing them. Blake had warned her not to appear nervous, though she had noticed that he and Jake kept a sharp eye out, their guns always at hand. At night, when they bedded down, the men ground-tied the horses within easy reach. Even

Megan slept with a loaded rifle next to her bedroll.

When they reached the village of San Carlos without incident, Megan drew a short-lived breath of relief. If she had hoped to find reprieve from this godforsaken land in the haven of the small community, she was doomed to disappointment. Drab adobe agency buildings dotted the dusty landscape. Below the flat upon which the village was built, a handful of scrawny cottonwood trees followed the small, muddy streams. A hot wind swept the arid, barren plain, swirling the dry earth into small dust devils. The heat was stifling, the ground below her feet baked by the relentless sun. Away from the riverline, not a plant grew within sight.

More depressing than the surroundings were the people she saw here. Were these filthy, bedraggled Indians the noble savages who had roamed the plains for countless years before the white man? Megan shook her head in stunned disbelief. This was a scene straight from hell! These people hadn't just been conquered, they had been stripped of every semblance of dignity, every source of pride. The men, once mighty warriors, now slouched in the shade of the buildings. Some slept, others gambled, still others stared hopelessly ahead at nothing, their black eyes as dull as death. The only life in those obsidian eyes was a deep, abiding resentment that made a shiver run down Megan's backbone.

The men and women both wore a strange mixture of clothing, some of deerhide and some of cloth they had gotten in trade. While they might wear moccasins or breechclouts, they also wore cloth britches and shirts and skirts. Most of the men wore bands of colored cloth about their foreheads to restrain their hair, instead of the leather head-bands of other tribes. The children ran naked. No matter what the combination, Megan knew that her old torn dress was far better than anything these people owned.

Man, woman, or child, they were equally filthy. Their hair hung lank and dirty, in straggling matted strands. Their clothing was torn and stained, hanging loose on wasted bodies. The children were so thin that their ribcages resembled twin washboards framed by bony arms. And their faces, oh God, their faces! So devoid of hope! It was a struggle to keep the pity from registering too strongly on her face, especially when Megan noted that even the children were so tragically despondent. No one smiled, no one laughed, no one even spoke as the three riders entered their little village. They merely stared out of burning black eyes.

"Pathetic, isn't it?" Blake muttered, as Megan swallowed a large lump of sympathy clogging her throat.

"Pathetic or not, I'd keep a sharp eye on the horses, and especially Lobo," Jake suggested. "That wolf probably looks as good as prime beef to these poor people, as hungry as they are."

They halted their horses in front of the agency headquarters, and before they had even dismounted, a harried-looking man scurried from the building to greet them. "Welcome to San Carlos," he told them with wry humor, twisting his thin lips into a shadow of a smile. "I'm John Tell, the agent in charge here. Are you folks just lost, or is there something I can do for you?"

Swinging down from his horse, Blake helped Megan dismount. Then he approached Tell and extended his hand in greeting. "As a matter of fact, we have come in search of someone. Perhaps you can help us locate him. First, however, I wonder if there is a place inside where my wife can rest out of the sun?"

Having noticed Megan, John Tell could barely tear his eyes from her. Now he flushed obviously. "Yes, yes, of course," he stammered. "Please come inside. I'll have someone bring you something to drink. You'll have to forgive my lapse of manners. It's not often we see a lady in these parts."

Tell's office was just as dreary on the inside as it was out. His desk was littered with stacks of paperwork. Two rickety old chairs sat before it, and he gallantly relinquished his own battered desk chair for Megan's use, while he hastily cleared a corner of his desk on which to perch. An aide brought tepid glasses of apple cider to quench their parched throats, then quickly departed.

"Well, now, who might you be looking for?" Tell was cautiously eyeing the tied-down guns and the deceptively relaxed forms of the two sturdy men before him.

"We were told in Santa Fe that we might find a priest here by the name of Father Miguel," Blake volunteered. "He was working with the Chiricahua not long ago."

Tell frowned. "No, there is no priest here in San Carlos, not on the entire reservation, for that matter."

"Could he be on another of the reservations, perhaps up around Ft. Apache?"

Tell shook his head. "I doubt it. Tell you what. You folks stay here overnight, and I'll get Naiche in here. If the priest was with his tribe before they were relocated here, he will know about it."

Much to Megan's dismay, Blake agreed. They spent the night in their bedrolls on the floor of a small, empty storeroom behind Tell's office. She was appalled at the conditions of this camp, and she had learned from listening to Agent Tell that things were worse elsewhere on the reservation, in the small family encampments scattered about the large reservation. There small groups of Apache lived in squalor in their wickiups, without decent food, clothing, or blankets. Many fell ill to disease, and there was no doctor available to them.

Yet Tell had insisted that the situation would improve in time. As they had done at another reservation farther along the Gila River, he would teach these Apache to farm. They would learn to irrigate the land and make it produce food. Privately, Megan doubted that anyone could make anything grow in this arid dustbowl. It would take a magician, but she wished him luck in his venture. Without some small success, these people would soon die here, where the government had decreed that they must stay.

Five minutes after lying down, Megan began to itch. For a while, she tried to ignore it, tried to tell herself she was just nervous and imagining things. She twisted and turned and scratched until her bedding was a knotted mess. Finally she gave up, sitting up with a weary sigh. Digging her fingers into her hair, she shook her head fitfully.

Beside her, Blake shifted and groaned. "Lie

back down, Megan. As soon as we talk with Naiche in the morning, we have to leave again. This is all the rest you will get.''

"But I'm not getting any rest!" she pointed out in a hushed whisper. "I itch from head to toe! Every time I close my eyes, another place on my body begins to crawl. I don't know what is wrong with me tonight!"

"Unfortunately, I do, but it isn't going to make you feel any better to hear it."

"What?"

"This place is crawling with fleas, darlin'. Lord knows when, if ever, this place has seen a decent scrubbing."

"You mean there are bugs in here with us?" she squealed.

"Bugs, fleas, ticks, gnats, probably a few lice thrown in for good measure."

"Lice!" Gooseflesh rose on her skin and she gave a violent quiver. Megan grabbed her bedroll and started for the door.

"Whoa!" Blake grabbed the corner of her blanket to halt her flight. "Where do you think you are going?"

"Outside. I'd rather sleep on the ground than in this bug-infested excuse for a room. In all the time we have been traveling, I've never itched this way outdoors."

Blake reeled her in, inch by inch, by her blankets. "It won't help, Megan. Not here."

"What do you mean?"

"This whole camp is rife with bugs, inside and out. It comes with the filth and the poverty. We won't escape it until we leave here tomorrow. Even then, we'll be fortunate if we don't carry a few of the little critters with us in our clothes and hair." As he talked, he helped her spread her bedding down next to his once more.

"Then the first thing I want when we get far enough away is a bath," she announced heartily. "I want a clean stream, a place to air our bedding, and a bath with strong lye soap. I refuse to spend another night like this!"

"What's wrong with that delicate little packet of lavender soap you stashed away in the bottom of your saddlebag?" he teased. Even in the dark, he could see her mouth drop open. "Oh, yes, honey. I found that frivolous shawl you tucked under your other feminine pretties, too. At least you had the good sense not to waste my money on something as useless as a nightgown."

As he pulled her down next to him, she sputtered, "Blake Montgomery, you are a genuine scoundrel, going through my things like that!"

He merely chuckled and tugged her closer to his side. "Well, if I'm going to be a scoundrel, why not be a really good one? I always have hated coming in second best at anything."

Naiche either didn't know much about Father Miguel or he wasn't willing to say much. While he admitted that Father Miguel had been with his tribe for a short time, the priest had left and gone elsewhere before the agency had arrived to take the Chiricahua to the reservation. How long beforehand was anyone's guess, as the Apache's way of measuring time differed greatly from the white man's. To an Indian, the English word 'day' could mean anything from an actual day to several weeks. A 'month' could span as long as an entire season, depending on how it was interpreted. When Blake asked if Father Miguel could have gone with those Apache following Victorio, Naiche pretended not to understand a word, and refused to be questioned further on the matter.

"Where can I find Victorio?" Blake asked Tell as they saddled their horses.

"If I knew that, we'd have caught him already," the agent replied, quite put out with Naiche's reluctance to cooperate. "Your best bet would be to check with the soldiers at Ft. Bowie, around the Chiricahua's old stomping grounds, if you intend to keep looking. If I were you, I'd give it up. Victorio is more likely to find you than you are to locate him, and I wouldn't be looking forward to that if I were you, especially with the lady along."

Blake merely shrugged and answered simply, "Much obliged." Megan noticed that he did not indicate to Tell what his intentions were, or whether he was willing to forget the search for Father Miguel. Neither did he thank the man for their uncomfortable lodging. As she scratched at yet another of her numerous bites, Megan did not wonder why.

They traveled until it was nearly too dark to see, making only the most brief of stops when necessary, but they reached the Aravaipa Canyon at last. They had left the reservation lands behind by late morning, and had continued to follow the San Carlos River until mid-afternoon. Then they had veered to the south until they came to the Aravaipa Creek an hour earlier. Blake had pushed to reach this place in order to camp there. Here, surrounded by desert terrain, was a lovely hidden oasis. While the surrounding countryside baked beneath the hot Arizona sun, the Aravaipa Creek kept the small secluded canyon cool and green with vegetation.

Here the water was clean and clear, and Megan could have her bath. Here she could launder their bedding in the morning before they said goodbye to Jake and she and Blake rode on to Ft. Bowie by themselves, while their friend went on to Tucson. That this was once the stronghold of the Aravaipa Apache and the site of a massacre of more than one hundred and forty unarmed, peaceful Indians at the hands of vigilante whites and Mexicans, Blake did not tell her. He wanted her to be able to enjoy this verdant retreat, if only for the few hours they would be here. He was worried about what the hard riding would do to her health and that of their baby, and he wanted her to be able to rest while she had the opportunity.

20

About the time Megan and her two protectors were crossing into the Arizona Territory once more, on their way to San Carlos, Kirk Hardesty was reading a newly arrived telegram from New Mexico, and he wasn't happy with the news. "What in hell is this supposed to mean?" he shouted, waving the telegram in the air. "Is this supposed to make me feel better, to know where they were? Not where they *are,* mind you, since they got away. And no one but the driver is sure the girl was Megan."

Opal pushed her son into a chair. "Calm down, Kirk. There is nothing you can do about it, so it makes no sense to get all upset over it." She took the telegram from him and read it herself, as Jana and Evan listened. "It says that a woman *believed* to be Megan Coulston was seen five days ago at the Socorro stagecoach way station. That does not mean it really was Megan."

"Read on, Mother," Kirk told her. "The telegram was sent by Joe Landy. He is the same man who was driving the stage that Megan and her parents took from Abilene to Tucson. Surely he would recognize Megan again, after having her stolen from his stage!"

"Maybe," Opal conceded, "but what would they be doing all the way into New Mexico? It doesn't make sense to me. Who would Blake know over there?"

Kirk shook his head. "I have no idea." His pale gaze speared Evan Coulston. "Does Megan know anyone in New Mexico?" he asked. "Do you have relatives or friends there?"

"Not a soul that I know of," Evan replied. The idea had crossed his mind that Blake Montgomery might have been taking Megan back home to Abilene when they were spotted, perhaps thinking that her parents had gone home to wait for news of their kidnapped daughter after all this time. Evan could tell from the look on Jana's face that she was considering this idea also. "What direction were they traveling?"

"According to this wire, they had caught the stage in Albuquerque, on the run south to El Paso," Opal volunteered. "When Joe recognized Megan, or thought he did, she and an unknown man escaped, along with another man who was supposedly traveling with them."

"And no one knows who these two men were?" Jana had her own suspicions about the other man. She would almost bet it was Jake Banner.

Kirk threw Jana a disgusted look. "We know that one of them was Blake. Who the other is, is anyone's guess. Maybe one of his Mexican relatives. God knows he has enough of them on his mother's side, and they are spread all over Mexico, Texas, and New Mexico.''

"Maybe he was taking Megan to Mexico," Opal ventured.

"That still doesn't tell us what he was doing in New Mexico, or what he plans to do now." Kirk stood and began to pace. "Damn! I'd give half this ranch right now to know what he has up his sleeve. I don't trust the man, and I know as sure as I am standing here, he hasn't given up trying to get this ranch from me!"

Jana and Evan exchanged a long look. "As you said, Kirk, we might know where they were several days ago, but we have no idea where they are now, or how soon we might hear from them. I think it would be best if Jana and I moved into town. We have imposed on your gracious hospitality altogether too long already."

Opal was quick to disagree, though not too convincingly. "Oh, my, no! Why should you go to all that trouble and expense? You are welcome to stay here until Megan is found. After all, Kirk and Megan are still engaged to be married."

A pained expression crossed Evan's face. "That is precisely part of the problem. We all know what has been going through each of our minds concerning Megan and how long she has been with this man now. It would be a miracle if he has not taken advantage of her by now. Jana and I will understand if Kirk decides he would prefer not to marry Megan." Evan slanted a look at Kirk, who said nothing, though he did have the grace to look uncomfortable. "Under the circumstances," Evan continued, 'regrettable as they are, it would be better for everyone if Jana and I left. Of course we will want to stay close by, in case of news of Megan. We would appreciate it if you would let us know if you hear anything further."

Kirk offered his hand to the older man who would have been his father-in-law if not for Blake. "Of course we will," he said congenially. "I wish things could have turned out differently. Who knows, perhaps once we have Megan back again—"

He let his thought die, and turned to Jana. "Try ñot to worry, Mrs. Coulston. We'll get your daughter back safely. I won't stop looking, believe me. After all, I feel somewhat responsible since it is my cousin who kidnapped her." Kirk could afford to be nice now that he was finally about to get Megan's parents out from under foot.

Two days later, Jana and Evan returned from supper to find their hotel room had been ransacked. This really came as no great surprise, especially once they had determined that nothing had been taken. The room and everything in it had been thoroughly searched, their clothing and personal items strewn about the floor, but nothing was missing.

"They must have discovered that the documents are missing from the study," Evan told his wife. "There is no other explanation."

Jana added, "And they would not dare come right out and ask us, in case we didn't have them. They wouldn't want us to know anything about those papers, or what they contain, if we were still ignorant of them. I'm so glad we decided to keep the papers on us." She patted her bosom, where she had hidden the documents in the lining of her corset.

Anger darkened Evan's face. "Let's just hope Kirk does not go so far as to have us personally assaulted and searched. I promise you, Jana, I'll kill the first man who touches you trying to find those papers." He patted the gun he kept beneath his coat.

"What do we do now?" Jana asked, frightened by her husband's words.

Evan thought a minute. "We report this to the sheriff, as if we have no idea why someone would break into our room. Not to do so would surely be suspicious, and we are trying to allay their suspicions now. If we are very convincing, perhaps Kirk will believe that we truly had nothing to do with those papers disappearing. You know the sheriff will go running to him, telling him our every word."

"Do you suppose Kirk is having us watched?" Jana asked.

"I hope not, but it wouldn't surprise me. We are going to have to be very careful, my dear, especially if Jake Banner comes back and we get a chance to talk with him."

"He's been gone a month now, Evan. Do you think there is still a chance that he'll come back?"

Evan sighed heavily. "I hope so, Jana. I really believe that he is our only link to Megan and this Blake Montgomery. It sounds crazy, but I think Banner knows exactly what is going on."

Jana came to him and put her arms about his waist, laying her head on his chest. "It's not crazy, Evan. I think so, too. I also think he was the other man with Montgomery and Megan in Socorro that day, but I can't explain why I believe this. I just do, the same way I believe that Blake Montgomery will not harm our daughter. It is a feeling I have deep in my heart."

"I pray every night that you are right about that, my love. I just hope we hear something soon. It is the waiting and worrying and not hearing that is so awfully hard."

Back in the Aravaipa Canyon, Megan and Blake had just bid farewell to Jake. "Are you sure you don't want me to come with you?" Jake had asked. "That's some pretty wild country you are heading into. An extra gun might come in handy, especially if you tangle with Victorio's band."

"Thanks, Jake, but we really need to know what Kirk is up to, and whether Megan's parents have discovered anything yet."

"Are you sure you don't want me to at least take Megan back with me? She is of little use to you against Kirk now that he knows she is with you willingly. I could return her to her parents, explain everything, and have them take her home with them to Abilene until you get your problems straightened out."

Blake shook his head. "No. I wouldn't want to take the chance that Kirk would get his hands on her, especially now that she is going to have my child." Jake's eyebrows shot up at this new development, but he said nothing. "Then, too, I can't be sure that Megan's parents would not force her to marry Kirk, since I doubt they know how thoroughly despicable he is. He and Opal have probably charmed their socks off by now.''

Jake had to laugh at this. ''Somehow I doubt they are that gullible. Coulston didn't seem all that fond of Kirk to begin with.''

''We'll meet you in Tombstone in about a week, week and a half.''

Jake mounted his waiting horse and tipped his hat down over his eyes. ''See you there, then. Take care and watch your back.''

''That's Lobo's job, but we'll be careful,'' Blake promised. ''Now that I am about to become a father in a few months, I'll be particularly watchful.''

When Jake was gone, Megan eagerly shimmied out of her clothes. She had already laundered all of their extra clothing and their bedding with the lye soap, and it was spread out over bushes to dry in the morning sun. If there was a louse or a flea still living, it was gasping its last breath. Now it was her turn to get clean, and she intended to scrub every last inch of her body, down to the final strand of hair.

''You might as well get out of those clothes and join me,'' she told Blake, who was standing there grinning at her from ear to ear. ''You need a good scrubbing as badly as I do, and you are not getting anywhere near me until you do!''

Blake laughed. ''I must say, it's not often a man gets such a charming invitation to join a lady in her bath. I recall a day, not that long ago, when you screamed your head off when I suggested the same thing.''

"That was before I found out what a marvelous lover you are," she taunted, wriggling her backside at him as she waded into the stream. "I didn't know what I was missing then."

"Are you missing it now?" His husky voice came from directly behind her. Megan did not know how he had managed to shed his clothing that fast, but he was already turning her into his arms.

"I am missing it most dreadfully!" she confessed, placing her lips in the throbbing hollow at his throat. "I like Jake, but I thought we would never be rid of him."

It was a full hour before they got around to washing their clothes. Then, while they dried with the rest of their things, they indulged in another prolonged session of lusty lovemaking. Megan was replete and as limp as an overcooked noodle by this time, and she had no idea from where she would dredge up the energy to mount her horse, let alone ride all afternoon.

"Couldn't we stay here just a little longer?" she pleaded. "I dread the thought of getting all dusty and sweaty when I've just gotten clean at last."

"I wish we could, but we have to move on. We won't find Father Miguel by sitting around here. I'm sorry, darlin', but we really do have to go. Once we get these problems resolved, we'll have the rest of our lives to enjoy together."

"And if you never find Father Miguel? Never get your ranch back from Kirk?"

"We'll have each other," he told her tenderly. "We'll manage somehow."

*   *   *

After all the riding they had done in the past several days, Megan was still stiff and sore when they finally camped that night, but she consoled herself with the fact that she and Blake now had their privacy once more. By the end of the next afternoon, she was totally exhausted. When Blake told her they would be making camp earlier than usual, she could have shouted for joy. When they did stop, she was even more thrilled with Blake's choice of locations. Again he had surprised her, but instead of a peaceful little valley, she found hidden hot springs bubbling invitingly in the late afternoon sunlight.

"Is that actually steam rising from the water?" she asked in amazement.

Blake beamed at her like a kid on Christmas morning. "Hot bath water, just ready and waiting, darlin'. Just drag out that lavender soap of yours and hop in."

She grinned back at him. "You know, Blake Montgomery, as a fiancé you are downright wonderful. How did you ever find this place?"

"I've known about it for years, but I've never been here. We used to have an old Indian who worked for a while on the ranch when I was a kid. He told me about it, and a few other places known only to the Indians, like that little canyon we camped in. I knew it should be on our way to Ft. Bowie, but I wasn't sure I could find it, and I didn't want to say anything to you beforehand, so as not to disappoint you if I miscalculated."

"Fortunately for me, you guessed right. Oh, I can't wait to soak my aching bones in that steaming water!"

While Blake tended to their horses, Megan helped set up their camp. He had barely finished collecting an armload of firewood for the night when he heard her call to him. He turned to find her buck naked, the soap in her hand. "Last one in is a rotten egg!" she teased, then bolted for the water.

She called to him again a few minutes later, extolling the wonders of the hot water. "Hurry, darling! I can't tell you how marvelous this feels!"

"You'll be glad I took time to make this fire first," he called back. "When you get out, the night air is going to freeze icicles on your lovely little rump otherwise."

When he did join her, they made love in the bubbling water, lingering until their energies were sapped. Megan could not recall ever being so pleasantly relaxed, with such a wonderful feeling of well-being. "Oh, Blake, I think every bone in my body has melted," she sighed languorously, clinging to his neck for support.

He ceased his nibbling on her shoulder long enough to ask, "Is it the water or my loving that has made you so content, my love?"

"Both, I think, but just to be sure, perhaps you had better love me again."

"*Con mucho gusto, querida*," he murmured, lifting her far enough for his lips to find a puckered nipple. "With very much pleasure."

Her moan of desire echoed off the water and returned to them. His lips pleasured her other breast in turn, as her fingers wound tightly into his wet hair. By the time his lips wandered back to claim hers, she was writhing wildly against him, her body exciting his until they were both breathless with longing. If the water about them had not already been bubbling, it would have boiled from the heat of their bodies alone.

"Take me," she begged, her eyes smoldering sensuously into his. "Take me now!"

He entered her as softly as a sigh, his tongue and her moist mouth mimicking the actions of their lower bodies. Even in the caressing heat of the water, her silken cavern was warmer, as hot and smooth as molten lava, setting his senses aflame as she welcomed him into her body. Then she was erupting about him like a live volcano, calling out his name and going wild in his arms as the rippling contractions claimed her. Her spasms triggered his, and he was caught up in the cataclysmic rapture that held them both in its glorious grasp.

There was something in the air the next day, something different that Megan could not quite place. It was nothing she could see; rather, it was something she sensed. Blake felt it as well, for time and again she caught him looking about with a worried frown as they rode along. Even the animals were uneasy.

They had been skirting the eastern edge of a low ridge of mountains for most of the day, staying to the flatter terrain. It was mid-afternoon when the sky began to darken suddenly, ominously. Blake glowered at the clouds that seemed to have appeared miraculously out of nowhere. His curse was as low and threatening as the thunder growling in the distance. "We have to find cover, and from the looks of those clouds, it had better be soon." He headed his horse in a more western direction, toward the foothills of the mountains, though they had previously been traveling in a southeastern direction. Motioning for Megan to do likewise, he spurred his horse to a faster gait.

"We have to make it to higher ground before the storm hits!" he shouted to her as she gave him a questioning look. "These summer thunderstorms, while they bring welcome relief and much-needed water, also create flash floods that level everything in their paths. The one thing we don't need is to be caught on low ground in the middle of one of those!"

Megan and Blake found themselves in a race for time as the storm built steadily about them at an alarming rate. Dark clouds broiled in the heavens, and thunder echoed overhead. They had barely reached the beginning swells of the foothills when the first drops of rain pelted down like bullets. Within seconds they were both soaked to the skin, but Megan knew from the grim lines framing Blake's mouth that they dared not stop yet. She didn't want to, for she had caught his sense of impending peril and was now thoroughly frightened.

On and on they rode, ever upward along a twisting, water-slick path chosen strictly by their horses, since it was nearly impossible for the two riders to see in this deluge. For the first time in her life, Megan fully understood the phrase "blind faith." Once, her horse stumbled, sliding several feet downward before finding its footing again. Megan's scream of terror was swallowed by the beating rain and the rumbling thunder, but somehow Blake heard her. After that, he took the reins of her horse in his capable hands, leading her mount while she clung helplessly to the pommel and prayed for all she was worth.

Lightning speared the dark sky, making Megan cringe in the saddle. Thunder roared like a wounded beast, shaking the ground beneath them. It seemed like a century before Blake finally halted their trembling horses and pulled her quivering frame down next to his. "Are you sure we are high enough?" she asked in a quavering voice so foreign to her natural tone that she could not believe it was her own.

She felt him nod as his own head sheltered hers. "I think so. As it is, the horses are too exhausted to carry us further, so this is as far as we can go for now." His body absorbed her shiver as he held her close. "Come on, we have to get out of this rain."

Unlike some of the other mountains they had traversed, this particular range was nearly as barren as the surrounding desert. Only the hardiest of scraggly bushes and a few bristly cacti dotted its ridges. Not that Megan wanted to spend time under a tree in the midst of the worst thunderstorm she had ever known, but she had to wonder where Blake was going to find shelter on these desolate slopes.

Again she had underestimated her resourceful mate. A few minutes later, they were snuggled beneath a large outcropping of rock, viewing the storm from behind the waterfall created as water poured over the rim of the overhanging ledge above their heads. "We'll be all right, Megan," he assured her, stroking her head repeatedly in a comforting gesture. Her hair felt like wet silk slipping through his fingers, and he was reminded of their lovemaking in the hot springs the evening before. "I'd die before I'd let anything happen to you or our child."

There was a pause, then he said softly, "There is going to be a baby after all, isn't there?" It had been nearly two weeks since their first conversation on this topic.

She looked up in time to see the gentle, wistful smile on his face. "Yes, I do believe there will be," she whispered.

He said nothing more, but hugged her more tightly to him. With her head resting securely over his heart once more, Megan did not see him blink back the moisture sparkling in his vivid blue eyes, moisture that had nothing whatsoever to do with the rain coming down in sheets around them. She failed to notice that he had trouble swallowing the huge lump that had formed in his throat. Neither did she glimpse the single joyous tear that tracked a path down his cheek.

Together they waited out the storm in tender silence, witnesses to one of the finest exhibits of heavenly fireworks God had ever created. Lightning danced from cloud to cloud in a dazzling display, and sizzled in jagged arcs from heaven to earth. Thunder pealed in accompaniment to the wondrous spectacle of light, resounding and reverberating like a thousand drums, or perhaps like some great bell sounded by God's own hand. It was a sublime pageant of His power, a spectacular show solely for them, and awesome to behold.

Some time later, with the lightning now miles

away and the thunder but an echo to their ears, the sun peeped triumphantly past the dispersing clouds. It turned the falling rain into glittering jewels to grace the drab earth below. Then, to the east appeared the most magnificent rainbow either of them had ever been privileged to view. It made a full arc of the most vivid, wide hues. Just when they thought it could be no more splendid, a second bow appeared above the first, then a third spectrum above that, each more radiant than the other, until the entire eastern sky was painted with glorious color, so breathtakingly beautiful that it was beyond belief.

Blake and Megan sat there, completely enthralled, until the last ray of color faded into the blue of the sky; wondering, hoping that the unique phenomenon might be a portent of wonderful things to come in their future life together, an omen of good fortune at last.

"Do you suppose there will be a pot of gold at the end of our rainbow?" Megan murmured, strangely reluctant to break the silence surrounding them.

"I have already found my gold," Blake answered softly, his breath ruffling her hair. His hands found her belly, where their baby nestled safe within. "You are my gold. This child is my gold. As long as I have you, my life will be forever gold."

21

When the rain had stopped completely and they could crawl from beneath the sheltering ledge, Megan finally got a glimpse of the disaster they had escaped. Looking down into the little valley through which they had been riding such a brief time before, she breathed a prayer of thanksgiving that they had noticed the storm in time to reach higher ground. The valley below had become a raging river. Muddy waters tumbled and swirled as the flood raced through the land, carrying with it all sort of debris. Plants, trees, cacti had been uprooted. Animals caught unaware were caught up in the swift current. Even large rocks, so big that several men could never lift them, were carried away in the mighty rush of water. The thought that she and Blake could have been caught in the flood was terrifying.

They made camp for the night right where they

were, spreading their bedrolls in the dry space beneath the ledge. Looking about, Megan supposed it was the only dry area nearby. There was no campfire that evening, for lack of dry fuel, but Megan was too thankful to be alive to complain about her supper of cold beans and day-old biscuits. That night they snuggled together in their bedrolls, sharing their body heat for warmth.

"How long will it be before we can go on?" she asked.

"The water will recede almost as fast as it appeared," Blake explained. "We should be able to continue by late morning. The storm will delay our arrival at Ft. Bowie by no more than a day."

Blake's prediction proved correct. During the night the water had receded, and by noon they were traveling into the valley again. The ground beneath the horses' hooves was somewhat mushy. They passed carcasses of dead animals and other damage resulting from the previous day's storm, and the vultures were already soaring overhead, ready for a feast. Other than those differences, there was really little evidence that there had been a flood of such magnitude just the day before.

It was late the second day after the storm when they finally rode through the gates of Ft. Bowie. The first thing Blake did was arrange for their food and lodging for the night, and make sure their horses were cared for. Then, while Megan freshened up and changed into clean clothes in the quarters vacated for them by one of the lieutenants, Blake went to inquire about Father Miguel.

He returned shortly with their supper tray and discouraging news. The post commander knew nothing about Father Miguel's whereabouts. "He had plenty to say about Victorio and his band of renegade Apache, though," Blake told her. "They have been raiding steadily on both sides of the border for several weeks now, and leading the Army a merry chase. If Father Miguel is with them, he has his work cut out for him trying to convert this bunch."

"Do you really think he might still be with the Indians? This band, I mean?"

Blake watched as Megan ate. She was almost too tired to lift the spoon to her mouth, and a sharp twinge of guilt speared him. He had dragged her with him over hundreds of miles of the roughest territory known to man, and she had barely uttered a complaint. She hadn't nagged at him, or begged him to give up the search. Rather, she had encouraged him. She had stood beside him all this time, believing in him as no other woman would have.

Pride filled him, even as his conscience gave him another nudge. Megan was a rare woman. Any other would have dissolved into tears by now. Any other would have demanded marriage, raging at him and threatening as only a woman can. Here she was, bone-tired, filthy most of the time from long hours in the saddle, yet still willing to go on. And she was carrying his child.

Blake chided himself. He should be horsewhipped! At this time in her life, Megan should be pampered. She should have a decent roof over her head, good well-balanced meals, and plenty of rest. She definitely should not be traipsing about on horseback from sun-up to sunset, eating cold beans out of a can, and sleeping in a bedroll on the hard ground! When all of this was finally settled, he swore to himself that she would have those things and more. She would also wear his ring upon her finger and his name very, very soon.

On the same morning that Blake and Megan arrived at Ft. Bowie, Jana and Evan Coulston returned to their room after a very informative visit with Mrs. Higgins and her husband. They had learned a lot from the couple, all of it substantiating what they had learned from the documents they had found at Kirk's ranch, though neither of them breathed a word to anyone about those papers. Mark Montgomery had been a respected rancher around Tucson for many years, and his son Blake had been well-liked. Everyone had been shocked when Mr. Montgomery had died and left the ranch to Kirk. They had been even more shocked to learn that Blake had not been Mark Montgomery's son.

"I still don't believe it!" Mae Higgins had declared. "Why, I've known that boy since before he was born. His mama was expecting him when they moved onto the ranch, and I've never seen a prouder papa than Mark Montgomery when that boy was born. Besides, Mark thought the sun rose and set on Angelina's head, and so did everyone else who met her. Why, she was the sweetest little thing you'd ever care to meet, and I just can't see her hoodwinking Montgomery into marrying her if she was carrying another man's child. Angelina was not that type of woman at all. There wasn't a deceitful bone in her body."

"Even if there was, the ranch should still have gone to her son," Chad Higgins put in. "That land has belonged to her folks for as long as anyone around these parts can recall. Her granddad bought it from the Indians before Tucson was even a town, and her pa mined for gold in the mountains east of here. Yep, that place should have been Blake's, no doubt about it. There's a skunk in the woodpile someplace, and it smells like Kirk Hardesty to me. Trouble is, there's no way to prove it. Young Montgomery tried, and all he got for his trouble was a sound beating and run out of town by Kirk and that good-for-nothin' sheriff we're saddled with now, not to mention that bunch of hired guns Hardesty has working for him. That young sissy-pants can't even do his own dirty work.''

The Coulstons were still mulling all this over as they entered their hotel room. They were inside, with the door shut, before they realized that some-one else was in the room. The blinds had been pulled down and the room was in shadow. They could just make out the form of a man slouched in the easy chair near the window.

For the space of several heartbeats, no one moved. Then, finally, the man spoke. "I see you moved in from the ranch. Had enough of the Hardestys' hospitality, have you?"

Evan relaxed, though not totally. "Banner," he acknowledged with a terse nod. "We thought may-be you had left the area for good."

Jana breathed a sigh of relief upon knowing the identity of their uninvited visitor. She listened silently as Evan proceeded to question him. "What are you doing here, and why all the secrecy?" Evan indicated the drawn blinds and Jake's unannounced entry.

"Just thought I'd stop by and see if you found anything of interest at the Montgomery place. As for the secrecy, no one knows that I am back in town, and I'd prefer to keep it that way."

Evan and Jana both noted that Jake Banner referred to the ranch as the "Montgomery place." Now a quick look passed between them. The slightest of nods from Jana made Evan's mind up for him. "We might have," he answered cautiously, "but what would you do with the information if we had it?" When Jake would not commit himself, Evan went on. "You have to understand our position here, Banner. A couple of days ago we returned to find our room a shambles. Someone had searched it very thoroughly, looking for something they did not find. Were you that person?"

"Nope. I just got into town a couple of hours ago. It took a little quiet nosin' around to discover you'd left the ranch and taken a room here. By the way, did you know there is someone following you?"

"We suspected as much." Evan took a seat at the end of the bed. "You never answered my question, Banner. What would you do with any information we might have found out about Kirk Hardesty and his mother?" They had danced around the issue long enough. "Could we trade it to Blake Montgomery for Megan's release?"

Jake drew a deep breath, as if making his own mind up about trusting the Coulstons on Blake's behalf. "I sort of doubt that, at this point." When Jana gave a shaky sob, he relented. "How would you like to see your daughter again, somewhere away from Tucson?"

Jana's eyes lit up like sunshine on a clear pond. "Are you saying you'll take us to her?" she asked softly, fearful of hearing a refusal. "Have you seen her? Is she all right? You were the other man with Montgomery and Megan in Socorro, weren't you?"

Jake's face darkened. "How do you know about that?"

"The stagecoach driver who recognized Megan sent a telegram to the sheriff, and he in turn sent it on to Kirk," Evan hastened to explain. "We were still at the ranch when it arrived."

"And what was Hardesty's reaction to that?" Jake wanted to know.

"Oh, he was plenty angry that Montgomery had managed to escape again. That and the fact that he has absolutely no idea where you were heading from there."

"Then he knows I was with them?"

"No, no, Mr. Banner." Jana took over the explanation. "Evan and I figured that out for ourselves. I really think Kirk has no idea who was with them. In fact, he mentioned that it might have been some Mexican relative of Blake's. Opal thinks they might have headed down to Mexico for a while."

"Is that what Kirk thinks, too?"

Evan shook his head. "Kirk thinks Montgomery isn't about to give up that easily. He's sure Blake will try to get his ranch back again soon. He's just not sure when, or how."

A sly smile crept across Jake's face. "You slipped up, Mr. Coulston. You must have found something real interesting, 'cause you just called the ranch Blake's. Could it be you are coming around to our way of seeing things, maybe placing the blame on someone else besides Blake Montgomery?"

Evan's look was as sour as spoiled milk. "I wouldn't go that far yet, Banner. Montgomery is still guilty of plenty. He robbed that stage and kidnapped our daughter, holding her for ransom. God only knows what misery he has put her through in all this time." He wondered at Jake's smothered chuckle, but continued his tirade. "He has caused us all untold heartache. Jana has cried her eyes out almost every night, and I have been worried sick. He might have had his ranch stolen from under him, and it might be rightfully his, but that doesn't excuse using my daughter to try and get it back from Kirk and Opal. Mr. Blake Montgomery has a plenty to answer for—to me!"

"You'll have to work that out with him, Mr. Coulston." Jake rose easily from his chair. Pulling the blind back slightly, he peeked out around the edges. "Your watchdog is still out there. That is going to complicate things a bit, but if we are real careful, I think we can get you out of town without anyone knowing."

Jake turned to Jana. "Can you sit a horse, Mrs. Coulston?"

He watched the lady's face turn pale. "Not very well, Mr. Banner, but I'll manage if I have to," she said gallantly, thrusting her chin up in the same manner Jake had seen Megan do countless times. Now he knew where Megan had gotten that stubborn gesture.

"I'm sorry, ma'am, but I think you are going to have to give it a try. There is a lot of rough territory to cover between here and where we will be meeting Blake and Megan, too rough for a buggy. There are places where a wagon will not travel easily."

He started for the door. "You folks get packed." His gaze caught the stack of baggage in the corner. "Bring only what will fit in your saddlebags and leave the rest behind. I'll take care of getting your horses and the rest of your gear. You two wait until dark, then sneak out of here and meet me behind the Silver Dollar Saloon. And don't forget to bring those papers we talked about. You do have them handy, don't you?"

Jana giggled and blushed like a girl. "They are as safe as a babe in its mother's arms, Mr. Banner. Trust me."

"I *am* trusting you. I'm trusting both of you not to say anything to anyone. For all our sakes, don't make me regret that decision."

They made it out of town unobserved. Just to make sure, Jake laid a false trail, then doubled back and headed for Tombstone. It would take them three days to reach their destination, and he was sure that the Coulstons would be pumping him for information about their daughter the entire time. He wasn't looking forward to it. Evan was right. Blake had a lot to answer for, and after this trip, he would owe Jake a huge favor. Jake didn't mind helping his friend out, but babysitting an irate father and a nervous mother who was obviously scared to death of her horse was a bit much. Yes, his old buddy Blake was going to owe him quite a debt for this one!

* * *

Blake and Megan left the fort shortly after
sunrise, heading west toward the Dragoon Mountains just north of Tombstone. Tucked securely in
these mountains was Cochise's old stronghold, and
this was where Blake, going on instinct alone,
hoped to find Victorio. Of course, he said nothing
to the Ft. Bowie commander about his ideas or his
plans. The man would have tried to dissuade them,
if not order them directly to abandon such folly.

They had just begun their day's travel on the
second day out of the fort when Blake suspected
they were being followed, though again he saw no
one. It was just a feeling that made the back of his
neck tingle uncomfortably in warning, that and the
fact that Lobo appeared nervous over something,
too. Megan seemed oblivious to anything out of the
ordinary. Blake said nothing to alarm her, but his
hand rested on the butt of his rifle the entire
morning.

When they stopped for a short break, Blake
made certain that Megan did not stray far from his
side. Still, after all his caution, he was caught
unaware. A small band of Apache appeared out of
nowhere. One minute they were not there, and the
next they were forming a tight circle around Blake
and Megan. As fast as he was with a gun, it was too
late for Blake to draw his pistol, though that
probably would not have been a wise move in this
case. Blake stood stiffly, not moving so much as a
muscle, and waited helplessly to see what the
Indians would do.

Megan could not prevent the startled gasp that
escaped her lips as her wide eyes swung in a circle
about her, then flew to Blake's grim face.

He wanted to say something, anything, to reassure her, but he dared not. All he could do was stand there like some dumb statue and wait for the Indians to make the first move. After what seemed a lifetime of hearing his own heartbeats echo in his ears, one of the Apache stepped forward.

Lobo's ears went back on his head, the hair on his back bristling upright as he bared his long white teeth in a feral snarl. The Apache stopped in his tracks, eyeing the huge wolf cautiously. "Easy, Lobo," Blake said softly, not wanting to spook the animal into attacking, but wanting Lobo to stay on his guard, too. At the same time, he did not want the Apache to take offense and attack, if there were yet some way out of this perilous situation.

"Is this your wolf?" the Indian asked in Spanish, knowing that few white men knew the Apache tongue.

Blake met the Indian's eyes squarely, hoping the brave could not read the fear in his face. "*Sí.*"

"Is he tame for you? Can you make him do as you say?"

"*Sí.*"

"Tell him to let us come forward. Tell him we are friends."

"Are you, or are you our enemies?" Blake countered. "How am I to know this?"

The Indian came as close to smiling as Blake had ever seen one do. He nodded to his fellow braves, and they lowered their weapons, though Blake noted that they did not put them down. "You wander far from your safe town, white man. Why do you come into the land of the Apache?"

In answer to their small gesture, Blake placed a quieting hand on Lobo's head. "We come in peace," he said. "We come searching for a priest, a white man's *shaman* called Father Miguel." The Indian's face registered nothing, and Blake could not tell whether or not he recognized the priest's name.

Throughout this entire confusing conversation, of which Megan understood only a word or two, she had sat as if carved of stone. She was still hunched down over the open saddlebag, exactly as she had been when she had first spotted the Indians. Pure panic held her motionless, her heart pounding so violently in her chest that she feared it would burst. Even through her fear, however, she tried to gauge the extent of their danger by the expressions flitting across Blake's face. Not for the first time, she wished she had learned Spanish instead of French at that fancy girl's school in St. Louis.

Megan heard Blake mention Father Miguel's name, and she prayed that the Indians knew him, and that the good priest had made some progress in converting the Indians. She hoped he had made a positive impression on them. So frozen in fear was she, so tense, that when Scamp suddenly skittered out of the saddlebag and up her arm, Megan shrieked aloud in alarm. Immediately the Indians turned their rifles on her, their black eyes alert and wary. When the chipmunk scampered onto her head and began to chatter excitedly, the Apache braves stared dumbfoundedly for several seconds. Then, as a group, they convulsed in raucous laughter, pointing and howling with glee.

"Smile, Megan." Blake's low command came through the chorus of laughter.

Megan did as he told her, though she thought her face would crack with the effort. The muscles of her face, so stiff with panic, almost failed to obey her wishes. A trembling smile appeared on her reluctant lips. It wavered there for a moment before it finally decided to stay, wobbly though it was.

The Apache nearest Megan stepped up to her, and as Megan saw his brown hand reach out, she was sure she would faint where she sat. Again Lobo issued a low warning growl, but Blake grabbed him by the scruff of the neck, wordlessly commanding Lobo to wait. The brave's fingers touched the top of Megan's head, and the chipmunk ran up his arm and perched jauntily on his shoulder. He chirruped at the strange man as if berating him for frightening his mistress. While the others chuckled at the chipmunk's antics, Megan breathed a silent sigh of relief as the Indian stepped back again. She was overjoyed to find that the Apache was thoroughly enchanted by Scamp and content to ignore her for the time being.

The brave who had first spoken to Blake spoke again. "You have unusual animal friends. It is said you can judge a man by his way with animals. The ferocious wolf obeys you. The tiny chipmunk protects your woman. The wolf and the chipmunk make strange bedfellows. One would think they would be natural enemies, and yet they both travel with you. These animals trust you. If they can do so, then I will also, but I must first have your word that you will not try to use your guns against us." His dark eyes studied Blake's face closely, watching for signs of treachery, but he found none.

"You have my word," Blake said solemnly, hoping it was not to be the biggest mistake of his life, and of Megan's. "I also must have your word that neither my woman nor I will come to any harm at the hands of the Apache."

The Indian nodded in agreement. "You and your woman will come with us to our camp in the hills. There you will talk with our leader. Perhaps he will be able to give you news of this holy man you seek."

"May I ask your leader's name?"

"He is called Victorio in the white tongue. I am high in his command of warriors. I am called Chocto."

It was not the Indian custom to shake hands, so Blake merely returned the Indian's steady gaze. "I am called Montgomery. My woman and I will be glad of your escort into your camp. We accept your kind invitation of aid." His gaze slid to Megan who sat looking up at him, her wide eyes full of questions. To Chocto he said, "My woman does not understand our words. She speaks no Spanish— only English. I tell you this so that you will not take offense when I explain to her what is taking place, if you do not understand my words as I speak to her."

"I will trust you to speak the truth in any tongue, Montgomery, until you prove unworthy of my trust."

Quickly and quietly, Blake explained the situation to Megan. "Kind invitation?" she echoed weakly. "More like a command appearance."

"True, but what else can we do? After all, this
is what we came for, to find out about Father
Miguel. They seem friendly enough so far, if cautious. We'll just have to go along with this until we
can make a gracious exit."

"If they allow us to do so." She spoke the
words Blake had been holding back.

"Just remember to act subservient, as Indian
women are taught, but try not to show your fear.
The Apache respect courage above all else." He
touched her cheek in a tender gesture. "I'll get us
out of this, darlin'. I promise."

A tiny smile trembled at the corners of her lips.
"You always do—somehow."

22

Megan had been expecting a camp similar to the one on the San Carlos reservation. What she found when they arrived with their escort of braves was not nearly so bad. Here, in a tiny valley nestled in the mountains, there were trees to offer shade from the relentless sun. There was a clear, sparkling stream of cool water gurgling just steps from the village. The children ran laughing and playing among the wickiups. Of course, these crude lodgings of rough framework covered with woven mats, or in some cases just brushwood, were no better than the worst hovel; but they were convenient for this nomadic tribe always on the move.

As she looked about her from beneath the cover of her lashes, trying to appear the properly humble woman, she thought the people here were dressed no better than those at San Carlos. They still wore the poorest of clothing, most of it made of cloth that had long since faded from its original vibrant colors. Most of the children still ran naked, but at least their little brown faces did not have that pinched, half-starved appearance. She did not doubt that these people struggled to find enough to eat, but they were far better off than their brothers on the reservation. Here, at least the glow was not gone from their eyes. The dark eyes that watched as they rode into the camp were alive with defiance, that tiny flame of hope necessary to all living things not yet extinguished.

There were perhaps thirty wickiups in the small encampment, randomly spaced in no particular formation. Chocto led them into the center of the village. Blake and Megan remained on their horses as Chocto dismounted and disappeared into one of the huts. As they waited, Megan could feel the hatred that seemed to surround them as the villagers gathered to stare at the two whites who had dared to invade their private domain. A rapid volley of gruff conversation in the guttural Apache tongue swirled about them as the curious onlookers questioned the returning braves about their strange visitors.

"What are they saying?" Megan hissed to Blake.

"I don't know." Blake thought he had better warn Megan what to expect. "Listen, darlin'. When Chocto returns, I'll probably have to go with the men for a private pow-wow. You will be on your own, for how long I'm not sure."

Even through the lovely tan Megan had acquired these past weeks, she paled. "What am I supposed to do while you are gone? Am I just to wait here?"

"One of the women will probably take charge of you, I suppose, and show you what to do."

"How? I don't understand a word, not even if they speak to me in Spanish. Oh, Blake, I'm so scared!"

He knew it would do her no good if he were to admit that he was just as scared as she. "Just remember what I told you, and don't let them see how badly you are frightened. With a lot of sign language, maybe you can make yourself understood enough to get by until I can join you."

A few minutes later, Megan found herself standing alone beside their horses as Blake walked calmly off with the other men. Not alone exactly, for about twenty haughty-looking women and as many ragged children still stood staring at her, and the ever-faithful Lobo sat at her feet guarding her. Megan stood stock-still and stared back for some of the longest moments of her life, not knowing what to do and afraid to do something that might be wrong. These women were not armed, but Megan was sure they could be just as vicious as their men, and she was vastly outnumbered.

A small, agitated squeal from the depths of her saddlebag brought Megan out of her trance. Ever so cautiously, so as not to alarm anyone, she reached into the unlatched bag and lifted the chipmunk out, cuddling him protectively in her palm. Scamp looked about with his bright, inquisitive eyes, turning his tiny head to and fro. He spotted one of the smaller children and began to chatter at the toddler. The little boy burst into delighted giggles and babbled his baby-talk in turn. Several of the stern-faced mothers broke out in smiles. The other children twittered and eyed Megan shyly, as if to ask what else she had to show them.

Megan felt like one of those sideshow tricksters who performed magic tricks. She did the only thing she could think of, the thing that came most naturally. Mustering up a smile, she squatted down and held the chipmunk out for the children to see. Most of the children held back, some of them hiding their faces in their mothers' skirts; but a few crept closer, intrigued beyond caution. Beside her, she felt Lobo stiffen warily. Her hand on his head calmed him.

The curious little toddler was the first to come close enough to touch the chipmunk's soft, striped fur. He squealed happily, his black eyes dancing. When Scamp wriggled beneath his touch, the boy ran back to the safety of his mother's side. But now the others became brave. She let them approach, let them pet the tiny animal as long as they liked. Then she handed the squirming furball to one of the girls, and chuckled as all the youngsters gathered about, laughing and vying for the next turn.

For some reason, as much as the wolf resented the chipmunk, Lobo chose this moment to be protective of his rival. His deep growl barely preceded his leap. Megan reacted without thinking, her only thought to save the children. "No!" she screamed. Throwing herself on Lobo, she wrapped her arms about his thick neck and clung, pulling at him with all her might. "No! No!" The big wolf backed off immediately, obeying Megan's sharp command, and Megan went limp with relief.

The children were crying out in fright, their mothers screaming, until they realized that the danger was past almost as soon as it had begun. They stared at Megan in awe. Here was a woman who could charm a chipmunk and command a grown wolf. Who was this strange white woman, this one with fire in her hair? Was she human, or of the spirit world? Was she a sorceress of some kind? Were these animals of hers really animals, or were they other persons she had changed into animal form? Was she good or evil, and how much magic did she possess?

Suddenly the tables were turned, and the Apache women were more afraid of Megan than she was of them, though Megan did not realize this just now. All at once they were anxious not to anger her, concerned about what she might do. A hasty, garbled conference took place on the spot, and it was decided they should be very nice to her. A small argument broke out over who would take her into their wickiup, who would bring her food and drink, how best to approach her.

Megan did not know whether or not to trust their quick about-face. The frowns and glares of the Apache women had turned to hesitant smiles so quickly. The hatred in their eyes had become something else, something that resembled awe. Not actually friendly yet, but not unfriendly either. Megan was confused. The only thing she could figure was that they were grateful to her for calling off Lobo's attack, and this was fine with Megan. Anything was better than the bitter resentment and outright enmity that had previously been directed at her.

When the mother of the toddler smiled and motioned to her to follow her, Megan did so with a more hopeful attitude. Some of the other women followed along. Within a short time, Megan had been offered something to eat and drink. The water looked fresh enough. Megan did not have the nerve to ask what was in the wooden bowl they gave her, even if she could have understood the language. She merely stiffened her backbone, brought the greasy brown mess to her mouth, and swallowed before she had much of a chance to taste it. It was the only way she was going to get it down, and then she was not sure it wanted to stay down. If Blake hadn't warned her that it would be impolite to refuse food, she would have starved rather than eaten it.

Through sign language she managed to convey her name, which the Apache women pronounced Mee-gan. Her hostess's name was Zana, and as near as Megan could ascertain, she was the wife of Chocto. It was impossible for Megan to pronounce most of the other names, let alone remember them all. The women tried to explain to Megan how to prepare the evening meal for her "husband," but the language barrier was creating a problem. Megan threw up her hands in dismay. "Wait! Wait! It's no use. I can't understand what you are telling me. Isn't there someone in the village who speaks English? This is so frustrating!"

A young girl of about ten had just delivered an armload of kindling for the fire. At Megan's outcry, the girl stopped and turned around. "I do," she volunteered in a small, trembling voice. After speaking, she looked about hastily and ducked her head, as if fearing punishment.

Megan could only stare open-mouthed. What

she had assumed was an Indian child was actually a white girl. With her stringy dark hair and sun-darkened skin, one would never notice at first glance. Only on closer inspection would anyone realize that the filthy hair would be a medium brown when clean, and her eyes, usually downcast, were a pale blue.

The words were barely out of the girl's mouth before a woman stepped up and gave her a sharp slap to the head. Again Megan reacted before thinking. She grabbed the woman's arm before she could administer another blow. Shaking her head vigorously, she said sharply, "No! No, Homi." How she ever recalled the woman's name, Megan did not know.

Homi glared at her for interfering, but Megan glared back. Homi's eyes dropped away first, almost in fear, and she jerked her arm away as if burned.

"Tell Homi that I wish to have you interpret for me while I am here. Explain to her how much easier it will be for everyone that way," Megan told the tearful girl.

The girl did as Megan asked. A short discussion ensued, then Homi gave a short nod of assent. "She says she will allow it," the girl said.

"What is your name?" Megan asked, still stunned to find a white girl here in this camp. "How did you come to be here?"

"My name is Mindy Winslow, but here they call me Neena."

Mindy hesitated to say more, and Megan could see the fear in her eyes. "Tell me," she insisted. "How and when did you come to live with the Indians?"

The girl would not meet Megan's eyes. She stood looking at the ground and shuffling her bare feet. Finally she answered. "They raided our ranch a few months back; I'm not sure exactly how long ago. Ma and Pa were killed, but they took me with them."

"Did you have any brothers or sisters?"

"No. There was just Ma and Pa and me."

"Don't you have any other family who will be worried about what became of you?"

Mindy shook her head. "None that I know about. Pa was an orphan, and Ma never talked about her family much. I think they must all be dead."

Megan nodded. "All right, Mindy—uh, perhaps I should call you Neena in front of the women. Tell me what is in the food I ate, and if they ask, you can tell them that is what we were discussing. I don't want to get you into any more trouble. Also, convey my thanks to Homi for letting you interpret for me. And thank Zana for the meal. Tell her I enjoyed it very much."

A tiny smile flirted at the corners of Neena's mouth. "Did you really? It was rabbit and rattle-snake."

Megan nearly gagged. "Oh, Lord!" she gasped, then pasted a smile on her face. She forced back a violent shiver. "It was horrible, actually, but tell them I liked it. I just hope I can force it down again if I have to, now that I know what it is."

The evening meal was prepared, and Blake had yet to return. The grit and grime of two days' travel was almost too much to bear, with that inviting little river so close. Megan had Neena ask Zana if it would be all right to bathe in the stream. The other women thought it was a wonderful idea, and before it was over most of them had decided to join her.

It was one thing to disrobe before your parents or the man you were going to marry; it was quite another to remove one's clothes before an army of strange women. Suddenly Megan was terribly shy, and she turned rose red from head to toe. The other women thought her modesty quite funny, laughing and joking, poking one another and pointing at Megan. They proceeded to undress before her without qualm, and soon she was the only one not yet enjoying the water.

Cursing herself for her own less-than-brilliant idea, Megan reluctantly dropped the last of her clothes on the river bank and dashed into the water. For a while everything was fine. The Apache women exclaimed over her fair skin, so soft and pale where the sun had not kissed it. They marveled over her long cinnamon hair, claiming that the evening sun had become trapped within its silken strands. They were in awe again when she showed them her lavender-scented soap. Though some of them had seen soap before and knew that it could clean things almost magically, they had never before seen a bar of soap that smelled so lovely. To them it seemed another of Megan's wonders, and they jabbered to one another that Mee-gan must have used her powers to capture the wildflowers inside her soap. That she was willing to share her special prize delighted them. Surely if she were a sorceress, she was a blessed one. An evil one would not be so kind.

Megan hadn't counted on having so much

company in her bath, especially people so prone to horseplay. The women were splashing and jostling one another and having a fine time. After Megan had placed her precious bar of soap on the bank and come back into the water for a final rinse, they saw no reason not to include Megan in their games. They also had no reason to guess that Megan could not swim. Blake had promised to teach her, but somehow they had never gotten around to finding time for swimming lessons.

Megan was beginning to panic. Every time she went to take a breath, someone either pushed her into the water or pulled her under. She screamed and pleaded with them to stop, but they thought her shrieking was just part of the fun and went on dunking her. They paid no attention to her frantic splashing, and little Neena was not there to tell them differently.

Megan was weak from the constant struggle to keep her head above water long enough to breathe. She had swallowed so much water that her stomach was cramping. She was choking and crying and trying to tell the others that she was in trouble, but they were not heeding her cries. Then, suddenly, the river bottom was no longer there beneath her feet. The game had been carried to the center of the river, and Megan was too short to touch bottom and still remain above water. She went under, clawing and thrashing, and no one noticed.

Blake and Chocto were headed back to Chocto's wickiup when they heard the giggling and splashing from the river. One man to another, Chocto grinned and poked Blake in the ribs. "The women must be bathing. When I was a boy, I would hide in the bushes and watch them. They are like children grown tall. They play like young animals, pushing and shoving and pulling one another under the water. It is a good thing they are all good swimmers, or they would surely drown one another.''

Blake stopped short in his tracks, his face ashen. "My God! Chocto! Megan, my woman, does not know how to swim! If she is with them and cannot make them understand this, she could drown!''

Taboo or not, Blake raced for the riverbank, Chocto close behind. Blake's eyes frantically searched the women, looking for Megan's bright head. Just as he spotted her, he saw her go under. She did not come bobbing up again. Busy shouting and playing, the other women did not seem to notice.

He didn't even take time to remove his boots. Blake heaved himself into a long dive, aiming for the spot where he had seen Megan go under. When he came up in the center of the river, surrounded by the Apache women, they squealed in shock that a man would invade their privacy. It took Chocto's shouts from the bank to make them understand what was wrong. Blake was already arcing back under the surface, praying frantically that he would find his beloved Megan before it was too late. On his third attempt, he finally saw her. She was floating limply just beneath the water level, her long hair fanned out about her downturned face.

His arm caught her just beneath her breasts and he hauled her to the surface. He could not stop to see whether or not she was still breathing, but he did not think so. Her skin looked so colorless and she hung so lifelessly in his grasp!

Chocto was there to help him pull Megan onto the bank. It did not matter to Blake that another man was viewing his intended bride's naked body. All that mattered was getting Megan to breathe again. It was Chocto who pulled her limp arms over her head, who turned her pale face to the side and pressed his brown hands firmly between her shoulder blades time and again until she inhaled sharply and began to cough. It was he who supported her while she vomited, making sure she did not choke. And it was Chocto who gently handed her over to Blake's waiting arms and shepherded the concerned women away just as Megan began to regain consciousness.

Megan's lashes fluttered open slowly, until at last she looked up into Blake's midnight-blue eyes. "I—I'm not dead?" she squeaked, her throat raw and scratchy from her ordeal.

Blake closed his eyes against the terror that was only now receding. With a sigh, he pulled her close to his heart. "No, thanks be to God! I thought I had lost you, Megan. I have never been so frightened in my life as those moments when I could not seem to find you in the water." Tears mingled with the river water that streamed down his face from his wet hair.

She began to cry, too, and together they sat there on the bank of the river; touching, kissing, sharing their fears and their joy and defeating the terror. "Oh, Blake! I was so frightened! All I could think of was that I would never see you again, never hold our baby in my arms. How soon can we leave this place? I don't want to stay here."

"We'll leave in the morning, if you are well enough to ride," he promised. "We can be in Tombstone in a few hours."

"I'll be well enough."

"Are you sure? After nearly drowning, you should probably rest. We wouldn't want to chance anything happening to the baby. Tombstone will still be there, whenever we arrive."

"I'll be fine. I promise you. Just get me out of this desolate country before anything else disastrous happens. Between the bears, the snakes, the bandits and the bugs, the floods and the Indians, I am thoroughly sick of this wilderness. I know you need to find Father Miguel, and I hate to be such a crybaby, but I'd rather face Kirk and all his hired gunmen than spend one more day in this wasteland."

Blake chuckled softly. "Now you complain! Just when we are about to see our first town in weeks! Oh, Megan, you are priceless. Do you want to hear something else funny? I found out from Victorio that Father Miguel went to Tombstone several weeks ago. He has probably been right there, just three days' ride from Tucson all this time, while we have been running ourselves ragged looking for him in all these desolate places!"

Before they left the next morning, Megan pulled Blake aside and pointed Mindy out to him. "I want to take her with us, Blake. We've got to. I just can't bear to leave that child here."

Blake groaned. "Megan, you don't know what you are asking. Haven't you been in enough predicaments lately, without creating another for us? If they have adopted that little girl, there is no way they will let her go. We could offend them terribly just by mentioning such a thing, and the one thing we don't need is to get these Apache riled at us. They already think you are some sort of witch."

"What?" Megan was astounded. "Where did you get such a crazy idea?"

"I didn't; they did. After you had gone to sleep last evening, I sat and talked with some of the tribe for a while. The women are convinced that you are some sort of sorceress. It has something to do with your way with animals. The men don't seem to think it is so, but the women are sure of it. They believe you have the power to change people into animals. They are half afraid that if they aren't nice to you, you will do something like that to them. On the other hand, I think they envy you, too."

"That is absurd!" Megan was having trouble believing this weird tale. "Was that why they changed from hateful to sweetness and light?"

Blake nodded. "I think so, darlin'. Then, when you were so nice to them, they decided you must be a nice witch, especially when you shared your magic soap with them."

"My what?"

"The magic soap that has the wildflowers trapped inside," he explained with a broad grin.

"Oh, for heaven's sake! I've never heard of anything so ridiculous!"

"These people are very superstitious in their beliefs, Megan."

"In that case it shouldn't be too difficult to convince them to release Mindy. If they are afraid

of what I might do, this could work in our favor,"
she suggested.

"Or against us," he hastened to point out.
"Witches, while feared, have not met a happy fate
throughout history, if you will recall."

Her grey eyes grew wide at his implication.
"You mean they might try to kill me because of it?"
She had a horrid vision of being burned alive at a
stake. "But they have been so friendly so far."

"Yes, but you haven't angered them either, or
done anything against their rules. Asking them to
give up a child they probably think of as one of
their own is quite another thing altogether."

"But we have to try, Blake. Surely you see that.
Mindy does not belong here. She deserves our help
to get her back into the white world where she
belongs. I've seen the way Homi treats her. It would
go against everything I believe to leave her here
without at least attempting to free her. I'm not
saying we should steal her from them. Couldn't we
at least try to trade for her?"

Blake knew he would have no peace until they
tried. "I'll talk to Chocto and see about it," he said
with a heavy sigh. "I just hope you will not be too
disappointed if things do not work out. We are
already indebted to Chocto for helping to save your
life yesterday."

"Yes, but if it were not for the women pushing
and shoving and paying no attention to my distress,
I would not have nearly drowned in the first place.
You might point out that little fact to him!" she
added with a scowl. Then her cheeks strained with
embarrassment at the thought of the Apache brave
viewing her nude body while she was unaware and

so helpless. She was thankful he had helped, but it was so humiliating!

"I'll consider it. Meanwhile, you get the horses packed and be ready to ride out of here in a hurry if things go wrong."

A short time later they were face to face with two very angry Apache parents, who were not at all inclined to give up their new daughter. The warrior softened a little toward the idea when Blake offered to trade his beautifully hand-tooled saddlebags for Mindy. It wasn't until Blake reluctantly included his saddle in the deal that the man agreed.

Megan knew how much it cost Blake to do this. The only thing dearer to a cowboy was his horse. Megan suspected that even most wives ranked below these two things.

The deal was not yet final, however, for now Homi insisted upon being compensated also. The woman had admired Megan's split riding skirt, so Megan offered it to her. Homi accepted, but wanted more. Megan added a blouse to sweeten the pot, but it was still not enough. On a stroke of inspiration, she pulled the lavender soap from her saddlebag.

Homi's eyes lit up. "Yes," she nodded. She would be willing to part with Mindy for the magic flower soap. Of course, she expected to keep the skirt and blouse, too.

Thus it was that Blake and Megan rode out of the village with Mindy riding double behind Megan. Though still miffed at the loss of his precious saddle, Blake had insisted that he could manage to ride bareback. Luckily, Tombstone was only a few hours ride from here. Megan knew that it would be the height of humiliation for him to enter the town without a saddle beneath him, though. Therefore, because he had made such a sacrifice on her behalf, she promised him that when they neared the town, she and Mindy would lend him their saddle. Blake promptly took her up on the offer.

23

Tombstone was a rough little town, uncultured and not nearly civilized. It was a booming mining town, with gold and silver being mined in the hills all around the town. It was also the haven for every cutthroat murderer, every gunslinger, and every outlaw from either side of the Mexican border. The streets were dusty, except when it rained and made a quagmire of mudholes that were reputed to be large enough to swallow a wagon whole. False-fronted stores lined the few main streets, a few with boardwalks out front for the customers' convenience. A city of tents and crude huts surrounded the town.

Every other building seemed to house a saloon or a gambling hall. There were three hotels, two assay offices open day and night, a couple of restaurants, and a booming brothel district. There were very few homes, no sheriff's office as yet, and few decent shops for ladies. There was a laundry business, however, and a bathhouse, and some enterprising person had begun a newspaper office. There was also an undertaker who was overwhelmed with work from the nightly, and often daily, shootings that constantly broke out. Boot Hill, as the fast-enlarging cemetery just north of town was known, verified this. There was a suspicious lack of churches—not one to be found.

Megan shook her head in dismay as she and Blake and Mindy pulled up in front of one of the hotels. She supposed this was an improvement over some of the places they had seen lately, but not by much. Tombstone made Santa Fe look like heaven by comparison. Even Abilene had been years more civilized than this!

After helping Megan and Mindy off their horses and into the pitifully decorated lobby of the hotel, Blake said, "I'll get us checked in. Then you and Mindy can go up to the room and rest while I scout around and see if Jake has arrived yet." He frowned. "That brings up another matter. What are we to do about Mindy?"

"She'll have to stay with us, I suppose. Do you think we ought to get two rooms? One for Mindy and me and one for you?"

Blake nearly swallowed his tongue at this. "One for you and Mindy?" he asked loudly. "Oh, no, darlin'. You aren't sleeping anywhere but with me."

Pulling herself up to her diminutive height, Megan stared him straight in the eye. "Well, I am not about to have this poor child put in a room by herself, Blake Montgomery! She has been through quite an ordeal these last few months, and I am not about to have her feel uprooted and abandoned by us now. She is probably feeling lost and scared enough as it is.''

With a groan of defeat and misery, Blake conceded, though not graciously. He could see that they were not going to have much privacy again for a while. "I'll have them put a cot in our room for her then.''

As he started for the desk, Megan touched his sleeve. "I'm sorry, Blake, but it will just be for a little while, until we can make some other arrangements for her.''

Blake found Jake in the Crystal Palace Saloon, staring into his drink in abject misery. "What's the matter?" Blake asked, pulling out a chair and seating himself across from his friend. "You look like you have lost your best friend.''

"No, but you've come darn close in the last few days.'' Jake greeted him with a scowl.

Blake signaled the bartender for a whiskey. "What's wrong?"

"You first,'' Jake suggested. "And order us a bottle. This could take a while. What did you find out about Father Miguel?"

"You won't believe it,'' Blake announced with a wry laugh. "Megan and I nearly got caught in a flash flood a couple of days after you left us. Then we got to Ft. Bowie and learned nothing. Finally, we practically got ourselves captured by Victorio's Apache, and Megan almost drowned.''

"Is she okay?" When Blake nodded, Jake said,

"So you met up with Victorio after all. Was Father Miguel with them?"

"Father Miguel came to Tombstone weeks ago." Blake shook his head and laughed. "Now all I have to do is hope he hasn't left already. Can you beat that?"

Jake glared at him. "I can beat it hands down. Megan's folks came with me to Tombstone."

Whiskey spewed across the table as Blake broke out in a fit of coughing. "What did you say?" he demanded in a choked voice. He stared at Jake in astonishment. "Why would you do such a fool thing?"

Jake reached over and slapped Blake helpfully on the back. "Because they have the documents you've been bustin' your butt to try to find all this time," he drawled dryly. "And believe me, it was no Sunday picnic havin' to travel with those two. Mrs. Coulston sits a horse like she was ridin' on a heap of tacks, and you should have heard her shriek when she found a scorpion in her bedroll. That woman could sing opera with no problem!

"Then there's Megan's father; he's been doin' a slow boil all the way down here. I ought to warn you, he's out for your hide, old friend. You'd better hope Father Miguel is here, 'cause you're gonna need him—either for a shotgun wedding or your funeral."

Blake sat in stunned silence for several seconds, trying to take it all in. Finally he asked, "But they do have the original will? Have you seen it?" He could scarcely believe the search was over. It seemed too good to be true.

"They not only have the will, they found your parents' marriage certificate and your birth records." After hearing this, Blake could forgive his friend for sounding smug.

"Where are they now? The Coulstons, I mean."

"They've got a room in the Royal."

Blake moaned. "Just my luck. I left Megan and Mindy there not twenty minutes ago. By now they are probably having a family reunion." He pushed back his chair and stood. "I'd better get back there right away."

Jake rose too. "I'm coming, too. I wouldn't miss this for all the tea in China." At Blake's glower, he chuckled. "You owe me this much and more, old buddy. Just wait until old man Coulston finds out you've gotten his darlin' daughter with child."

They were halfway down the street when Jake thought to ask, "Who's Mindy?"

Blake explained as they walked. They stopped in front of the hotel and Blake turned and asked, "Are Megan's folks willing to give me the papers?"

Jake shrugged in that lazy way of his. "Maybe, maybe not. At first they wanted to trade them for Megan's release, but, knowing what they don't, I told them you would probably not agree to that. You'll have to meet them and see how it goes from there." He grinned wickedly. "If you want my opinion, Evan Coulston will tear your head off and feed it to you. Then, depending on what sort of impression you make, he might have mercy on you and let you have your precious papers."

Blake glared at him and stomped into the hotel. Halfway up the staircase, Jake asked innocently, "Do you suppose Megan will beg him to spare your life?"

"You bastard!" Evan Coulston let out an enraged roar and swung at Blake. His fist connected solidly with Blake's jaw, and the next thing Blake knew, he was picking himself up off the floor.

"Daddy! Don't!" Megan started forward, but Jana grabbed her arm.

"No, Megan," she said quietly, a hint of steel in her soft voice. "This is between the two of them."

Mindy hid her face in Megan's skirt and cowered. Jake stood in a corner of the room, grinning like an idiot.

It hadn't been fifteen minutes since they had entered the hotel. They had gone straight to Blake's room, where Blake had explained everything to Megan. Then Jake had gone down the hall to fetch Megan's parents, and the fireworks had begun. Megan had not even had a chance to greet her parents properly yet.

Blake levered himself to his feet and shook his head. For a city man, Evan Coulston packed quite a punch. Evan stood waiting for him, his fists raised and ready to resume the fight. Blake held up his hands, palms out in a gesture of peace. "I deserved that, I suppose, for all the misery I have put you and your wife through these past weeks, so I'm not going to fight you, Mr. Coulston. But if you raise so much as a finger to your daughter, I swear I'll take you apart with my bare hands."

The possessive tone of Blake's voice did not escape Evan, and he hesitated. "She's my daughter, Montgomery," he challenged.

"That might be," Blake countered daringly, "but she is going to be my wife and the mother of my child."

Across the room, Jana gasped loudly. "Oh, sweet Lord!"

As tense as the situation had become, Blake had to grin when he heard Megan comment crisply, "Don't go into a tizzy now, Mother, and for heaven's sake, don't you dare faint!"

Evan cast a remonstrating glare in Megan's direction. "Don't speak to your mother in that fashion, young lady. She has been worried sick over you all this time, and for good reason, it seems."

"I know, Daddy, but you don't understand everything yet. This wasn't all Blake's fault."

That his daughter could stand here and defend her captor was like waving a red flag at a bull. "I understand enough!" Evan roared. "I understand that he kidnapped you and held you for ransom. I understand that he put your mother and me through hell worrying about you! And I'm not so stupid that I don't understand that he robbed you of your innocence. The reasons don't matter to me right now. This matters!"

With that, Evan slammed his fist into Blake's jaw again. Once more Blake hit the floor. This time he sat there, stunned and angry, but unwilling to strike his future father-in-law unless it was unavoidable. "I apologize for the agony you must have endured at my hands, Mr. Coulston. You, too, ma'am," Blake said from his seat on the floor. "But I'll be double-damned if I'll apologize for falling in love with your daughter!"

Jana blinked in surprise. "You—you love her?

Why, I thought perhaps you suggested marriage because you felt you had no other choice, circumstances being what they are.''

Evan was not so quick to forgive, but the edge was off his anger now. He rubbed his aching knuckles with his other hand. ''Megan, what do you have to say about all this? I suppose you think you love this scoundrel.''

That determined little chin flew into the air. ''Yes, I most certainly do, and there is no doubt in my mind!'' she stated saucily. ''And if you dare hit him again, I'll never speak to you as long as I live!''

Evan's eyebrows rose a good inch. ''Ahemmm.'' He cleared his throat thoughtfully. His sharp gaze went from Megan to Blake, still sitting on the floor. ''Well, I suppose if you can forgive him, so can I. However,'' he paused dramatically and speared them both with a warning look, ''you two are going to be married as soon as I can arrange it. No daughter of mine is going to live in sin with a man who is not her husband.''

''Meaning that I can live in sin with him if he is?'' Megan countered, a merry twinkle in her wide grey eyes and a smile lurking on her lips.

Jana gave a sigh of distress, while Evan glowered. Jake burst into outright laughter, and Blake groaned aloud. ''Don't agitate the man, Megan. Please,'' Blake begged of her. ''My jaw is going to be twice its normal size as it is. I honestly don't know how much more abuse it can take.''

Evan smiled. Finally. He reached out a hand to help his future son-in-law from the floor. ''Montgomery, you may just be doing me an immense favor by taking that saucy little baggage off my hands," he commented with a wry chuckle. "I hope you have a lot of patience, because you are going to need it sorely."

"Thank you, sir." Blake and Evan shook hands, and then Megan was between them, throwing herself into her father's arms.

"Oh, Daddy! Thank you for understanding!" she sobbed joyfully. "I've missed you so terribly!"

Tears sparkled in Evan's eyes. "I love you, pumpkin. I hope you chose more wisely this time. Kirk Hardesty has turned out to be quite a conniving coyote."

"I know. He and his mother, too. We should all be grateful to Blake for rescuing me from a lifetime of grief with those two." Her father still wore a skeptical expression. "Believe me, Daddy. Once you get to know Blake, you'll love him every bit as much as I do."

"I think we'd settle for mutual respect, Megan," Evan said with a shake of his head as he caught Blake's eye. "You two still have a lot of explaining to do."

Jana stepped forward and gathered her daughter to her in a tender embrace. "My baby," she crooned through her tears. "I prayed every night for your safety."

"Oh, Mama!" Megan was weeping now, too. "I love you so much."

It was several minutes before anyone gave a thought to Mindy or Jake. They were all too busy with their touching reunion and introducing Blake to his future in-laws. That, and trying to answer all at once the multitude of questions that popped into each of their minds. With everyone trying to talk at the same time, it was all quite confusing. Finally they seemed to exhaust their mutual curiosities momentarily.

Jake took the opportunity to excuse himself, telling them he would see them all later. "I am going to find myself a bottle of the best whiskey this town has to offer, and a lovely lady to keep me company while I drink it." Megan thought to herself that from the glimpse she'd had of the town so far, he would have better luck finding the bottle than he would a lady. If there were a handful of true ladies in Tombstone, she would eat her only hat.

She finally had a chance to introduce Mindy to her parents, explaining to them the little girl's circumstances. Jana was immediately taken with the child, clucking over her like a mother hen from the start. Evan was equally sympathetic, and Blake went up several notches in his estimation for helping to rescue the poor child. Megan hid a satisfied smile. Not only were her father and mother already beginning to like Blake, but she could see the start of a beautiful relationship blossoming between the love-starved little girl and her soft-hearted parents. Everything was going to work out just fine.

One final problem arose when the Coulstons were about to retire to their room. "Megan, dear," her mother asked innocently. "Is this your room or Blake's? We wouldn't want to disturb him by knocking at the wrong door."

Megan's face turned a fiery red, but she answered bravely, "This is *our* room, Mother."

Jana's hand fluttered to her heart, and she looked as if she might faint from embarrassment. She was stunned speechless. Evan, however, was not. "Get your things together, Megan," he instructed sternly. "You are moving to another room."

"Daddy, this is silly. There really is no need. Mindy is sharing our room with us, so everything will be quite proper."

"It is never proper to share a room with a man, unless he is your husband," her mother insisted. "You can room in with Mindy until you are married."

Megan shared a look of dismay with Blake. Though he hesitated at first, he nodded his head. He did not want to antagonize her parents further just when it seemed they might work things out between them. "It might be best, Megan."

She shot him and her parents a disgusted look. "I really don't see why," she grumbled as she gathered her few things. "It makes about as much sense as shutting the barn door after the horses are gone."

"Nevertheless, you will not shame your mother and me. Until you are properly married, you will behave like the young lady you were raised to be. After that, what you do is entirely up to your husband's discretion."

Evan escorted her out of the room as Megan retorted, "When pigs fly!" Blake grinned at the closed door. Learning to handle that little spitfire was going to be a lifetime experience, but damn if she wasn't worth it!

Blake spent the rest of the day trying to find Father Miguel, or news of him. When he had spoken with Megan earlier, she had expressed regret that they had not been able to find the old *padre* yet. "It would be so nice to have him perform our wedding ceremony, as he did for your mother and father," she had said. "I would really rather have him marry us than anyone else, if it is possible."

Blake was touched by her sentiment. "If that is what you want, I will try to find him, if he is here in Tombstone," he promised.

It wasn't until he checked with the editor of the *Tombstone Epitaph* late in the day that he learned that Father Miguel had moved on again. Yet there was good news also. The newspaper man knew exactly where the good priest had gone, and he was positive that he was still there. Father Miguel was at the mission at San Xavier Del Bac, just a few miles south of Tucson. Built by Franciscan monks a century before, the mission had been abandoned for the last fifty years, primarily because of the Indian problem. At that time, the garrison at Tucson had been unable to offer protection to both the growing town of Tucson and the mission as well. Father Miguel was trying to reestablish the mission now, to convert the Indians to the Christian faith and start a school there for them.

Again Blake could only shake his head and laugh at the irony of it all. He and Megan had ridden hundreds of miles, most of it through the most barren territory, and Father Miguel had been practically on their back step the entire time. Of course, now they did not need the priest for the same reason. Now they merely wanted him to marry them, as he had done Blake's parents; and since Megan seemed to have her heart set on this, they would go to the mission.

Certainly it would not be out of the way, and with a little luck, Father Miguel would actually be there. Besides, there was no way they could be married here in Tombstone anyway. In the entire town there was not one preacher, priest, or minister of any faith. Tombstone did not even have a judge or a justice of the peace, or anyone qualified to perform a wedding ceremony, and Blake was adamant that they would be married properly, with no doubt about the legality of their union.

He met Megan and her family for supper at a nearby cafe. The main discussion concerned the upcoming wedding and Blake's plans to get his ranch back now that he had the proof he needed. It was decided that they would start for San Xavier the next day, after replenishing their supplies. It would take two and a half days to reach the mission.

Jana was also determined to find a proper dress for Megan to wear for her wedding before they left. She bemoaned the fact that she had not been able to bring Megan's many beautiful clothes with them to Tombstone, but she stubbornly insisted that Megan would not be wed in hand-me-downs or a common split skirt that had seen its better days.

Blake saw Megan safely to her door and left her there. The thought of an empty bed held no appeal, and he knew he would do nothing but toss and turn half the night for want of her, so instead of turning in, he headed for the nearest saloon. There, with the cigar smoke so thick you could cut it with a knife, he turned down the eager invitations of several gaudily dressed women in favor of a few drinks. Surrounded by the constant din of the blaring music, the clinking of glasses, and the loud shouts and raucous laughter of the rowdy crowd, he could barely hear himself think, which was precisely his plan. He did not want to think of Megan now, knowing he could not have her until after their wedding. He did not need to torture himself with thoughts of her wide grey eyes, her silken skin, the heat of her passion. It was three o'clock the next morning, after enough drinks to take the edge off, and a few winning hands in a poker game that had turned ugly and ended in a brawl, that he finally got to bed.

Megan was up early the next morning, after a restless night. The noise from the numerous saloons and gambling halls had gone on almost until daybreak. She had a lot to do this morning, and the first thing on her agenda was a bath for Mindy and herself. They'd had time yesterday for no more than a quick wash in the bowl. It took some fancy finagling, but she finally managed to talk the surly hotel owner into hauling up a big tin tub and several bucketsful of warm water. By the time her mother knocked on her door, Megan introduced Jana to an entirely different Mindy. The girl's hair was now a warm brown, soft and curling down her back. She would be a pretty little thing once they bought her some decent clothes to wear, which was exactly what Jana had in mind next.

Their choice of ladies' apparel was severely limited in the overgrown mining camp that had the audacity to call itself a town. In a tiny corner of a general store that sold mostly mining supplies, they found two plain gingham dresses for Mindy, some cotton underthings and stockings, and a blue sun-bonnet. These basic items would suffice until they could shop for more in Tucson. Their next problem was trying to find a suitable wedding dress for Megan.

The task had begun to seem impossible when Megan suddenly had an idea. Several stores down the street, they had passed a tiny shop with a sign in the window printed in Spanish. They had not gone inside, assuming that the establishment catered solely to the Mexican trade. Now, purely on a hunch, Megan dragged her mother back to the little store. A middle-aged Mexican couple ran the place, which displayed a hodgepodge of every conceivable item on earth. Everything from food to toys was crammed into the tiny shop, filling it from back to front and top to bottom.

Reduced once again to sign language, Megan finally made herself understood. The dark-eyed woman smiled and nodded enthusiastically, motioning for Megan to follow her to the rear of the store. From under a pile of other items, she pulled out what looked to be a length of cloth, but when she shook it out, Megan gasped in delight. It was a Mexican wedding dress! It was made of the finest woven white cotton. The bodice was fashioned to be worn off the shoulders and was tied with satin bows on either side. In place of a collar, a wide ruffle of delicate eyelet lace encircled the entire dress, covering the top third of the bodice. The same lovely lace edged the bottom of the full skirt, and ran along the outer edges of the full-length panels that split from the waist to flare out about the pristine underskirt beneath. Cinching it tightly at the waist was a wide band of satin that tied in a bow in the back.

It was, perhaps, the most beautiful dress Megan had ever seen. Far less elaborate than the pure satin gown she was to have been married to Kirk in, the very simplicity of this dress won her heart. It was perfect in every detail, and because many of the Mexican women were fairly short, it fit Megan as if it were made for her. It would go beautifully with the shawl she had purchased in Santa Fe. Megan had found her wedding dress!

24

The horses were saddled and hitched outside the hotel, the men waiting, when Megan, her mother, and Mindy came down the stairs, ready at last. Megan laughed to see that with his poker earnings, Blake had managed to buy a new saddle and saddle-bags to replace the ones he had traded for Mindy. They weren't as fancy, but they would do the job.

Just as they were ready to mount and ride out, a shout stopped them in their tracks. "Hold it right there, Montgomery!"

Megan turned to find that the owner of the voice was just as rough and ugly as he sounded. He was facing Blake angrily, his right hand inches from his holster as he assumed a threatening stance.

Blake was watching him cautiously through narrowed eyes. "You want something, Harlow?" he drawled.

"Yeah! I tried to find you after that game last night, but you had disappeared. We got a score to settle, you and me. Nobody calls me a cheat and lives to tell about it.''

Blake speared him with a level look. ''You were dealing from the bottom of the deck. What would you call it?''

The man's beefy face went purple with rage. ''So you say. I say different.''

''Then you are a liar,'' Blake returned coolly.

''That's it, Montgomery! You and me, right here, right now! You'd better be good with that fancy gun of yours, 'cause I aim to put a bullet square in the middle of your head!''

The crowd that had gathered to hear the argument now began to disperse rapidly, the curious onlookers heading for the nearest doors. Megan stood frozen next to her horse, hardly able to believe what was taking place. ''Gunfight! Take cover!'' The urgent words echoed in her head.

Blake never took his eyes from Harlow's as he quietly instructed, ''Get Megan out of here, Jake.''

The street was already clearing. Jake grabbed Megan by the arm and pulled her toward the hotel entrance. As he did so, he tossed a coin to a passing youngster, telling him he would get another later if he would take their horses around to the back of the hotel and watch their belongings. The boy looked torn between wanting the money and having to miss the gunfight if he did, but he decided in favor of the money. Evan was herding Jana and Mindy into the hotel lobby.

All this registered on Megan's stunned brain even as she tried to pull away from Jake's grasp. ''No! Let me go! We have to stop this, Jake!''

He held her firmly, pulling her inside the wide hotel doors. Her hand caught on the door frame, and she clung to it, refusing to go further. Her eyes were as round as pewter plates. "Jake! You've got to stop this!" she screamed.

Jake yanked her into his arms, wrapping them firmly about her. His broad hand came up to clamp over her mouth as she yelled and struggled against him. His harsh command cut through her panic as he told her sharply. "Megan, stop it! Shut up and settle down! Do you want to get him killed, for God's sake? How can he keep his attention on Harlow with you having a hollerin' fit?"

Jake's words brought her to her senses, but did nothing to allay her fright. Fear for Blake was making the blood pound in her ears and her knees weak. She quieted, for Blake's sake, but only Jake Banner's arms about her kept her from sliding to the floor in a quivering puddle.

As she watched through the open doorway, the two men faced off against one another in the deserted street. A strangled whimper rose from her throat, blocked by Jake's strong fingers across her numb lips. She wanted desperately to close her eyes to block out the horrifying scene before her, but her eyes refused to close. They remained locked on the man she loved, the man whose child she carried within her. Fear clutched at her heart, making it beat erratically within her heaving chest. She wished with all her being that this would all turn out to be some awful nightmare, that she would awaken any second, secure in her bed, to find it all a dreadful dream. Surely this could not be real! Blake could not be out there in the street, about to draw against this terrible man, perhaps about to lose his life and make her a widow before she was even his bride! And all over some stupid poker game!

Megan's wide-eyed gaze clung to Blake's tall form, and suddenly it was as if blinders had been ripped from her eyes. The chill of reality ran icy fingers down her spine. This man, so calm and fearsome, could not be the same man to whom she had given her heart and soul. This was some stranger out there in the street. This man was a gunfighter! A cold-blooded killer! Her shocked gaze swung to his gun, strapped so low to his thigh in its well-oiled holster. How could she have been so naive? Only gunfighters wore their guns this way!

Even his pistol was a popular model with many gunslingers. Blake's hand now rode mere inches from the butt of his Peacemaker. A hysterical laugh rose in Megan's throat at the absurdity of the name of the long-barreled Colt .45 six-shooter. A better name would have been Widowmaker.

Against her will, her eyes sought his face, searching for something familiar and reassuring, but what she saw did not ease her distress. Blake stood facing his opponent with eyes as cold as death itself; unblinking, chilling blue eyes squinted slightly against the bright light of the noon sun. He stood perfectly still, watching and waiting, his gaze never straying from his enemy's. His stance was deceptively relaxed, legs slightly apart for even balance, his arms hanging slightly away from his body, palms inward. Not an eyelash moved, not a muscle so much as twitched, his long, tapered fingers steady as they hovered near the butt of his Colt.

Harlow grumbled something in a jeering tone,

but Megan could not hear the words. Blake did not rise to the taunt, except to give the man a sneering, confident grin in return. Then, suddenly, all was motion! Harlow went for his gun, but before he could even clear leather, Blake's gun was out and firing. He drew so quickly that, even as she watched, Megan could not see the individual motion of his hand reaching for the Colt, drawing it, cocking, and firing. It was all one incredibly smooth motion, almost faster than the eye could see. Blake fired from the hip, so practiced that he did not need to aim, yet he hit Harlow squarely in the chest with just one shot, the gun nearly an extension of his hand. Harlow was dead before his body hit the ground, a stain of red spreading over his chest.

Megan could scarcely breathe. So many emotions were assaulting her all at once. Foremost, there was relief that Blake was alive and unscathed. There was revulsion at the sight she had just witnessed, and the fact that Blake had just calmly killed a man; that he had undoubtedly done so many times before in similar situations, without remorse or regret, as part of his profession as a gunslinger. She felt betrayed, and an ugly anger was rising within her at her own naiveté, at her blind trust in this man who had become her lover.

Fury was practically choking her, making her all but oblivious to what was now going on about her, to the people now filling the sidewalks and street, murmuring and milling about and discussing the outcome of the fight. She barely noticed the two men who unfeelingly picked the dead man off the street and carted him off toward the undertaker's office. Neither did she realize that Jake had released his hold on her, that he and her parents were watching her queerly as her face twisted with the force of her emotions. Pain splintered through her, making her feel as if she were about to shatter into a thousand pieces, a pain unknowingly reflected in her huge grey eyes as she stood so still and silent.

On one level she was aware of Blake approaching her; on another she was numb with emotion. When he reached out to take her by the arm, she flinched away from his touch, raising dry, aching eyes to meet his questioning look. "Don't touch me!" she hissed, barely more than a hoarse whisper, yet he heard.

His eyes narrowed into slits, and he took her arm firmly, his fingers biting into her flesh. "Come on, Megan. We're going back up to the room."

When she tried to pull away, his grip tightened. "Don't fight me. Just come along quietly and don't make a fuss." Beneath his softly spoken words was a familiar tone of warning.

Megan marched woodenly up the stairs to his room, guided by Blake's firm hand. By the time the door was shut behind them, her eyes were smoky with tears and rage, her face ghost-white except for the patches of anger that rouged her cheekbones.

Blake leaned back against the door and crossed his arms over his chest. "All right, Megan. What is it?"

She whirled about to face him. "What is it?" she shrieked. "You know damn good and well what is bothering me! You! You are a gunfighter!"

"So?" He gave a negligent shrug, though his sharp gaze upon her angry face was anything but negligent. "I'm also a bandit and an outlaw, according to you, and that didn't seem to bother you all that much."

"For crying out loud, Blake! You kill people! You hunt people down and shoot them in cold blood! I'd say that makes one hell of a difference!" Her wide grey eyes practically pleaded with him to tell her she was wrong.

"Jake is a gunfighter too, and you don't seem to hold that against *him.*"

"Jake is not the man I love! He is not the man I'm engaged to marry! He is not the father of my baby, or the man I thought I knew so well until today! I couldn't care less what Jake does for a living, or how many men he has killed!"

He shook his head. "It's not as bad as you are making it sound, Megan," he assured her. "Yes, I hire my gun out for various jobs, but mostly for protection of property or people. There have been times I've even helped a sheriff or two rid a town of some gun-happy outlaw, but I have never killed a man just for the joy of it, as you seem to think. I don't enjoy killing people, Megan."

"Would you—" her throat choked up with tears. "Would you like to explain what all that was out there in the street, then?"

"The man challenged me, Megan. He called me out."

"You could have refused."

Blake half-smiled at her as if she were addled. "It's not done that way, love, and I'd rather face a man face to face in a fair fight any day than get a bullet in the back."

"Explain something to me, if you can," she

demanded. "If you are so good with that gun of yours, why haven't you gone after Kirk? Why did you have to kidnap me and hold me for ransom? Why haven't you just killed him and taken your ranch back?"

"I thought I had explained that. If it were that simple, I would have done it long ago, Megan, but the ranch would have gone to Opal if he had died. As I said before, I couldn't very well gun down Aunt Opal, much as I would have liked to. Also, they had the law on their side, though through the most devious of means. My hands were tied until now, until I had proof that their claims were false."

He let loose a humorless laugh. "Let's not forget, too, that Kirk and Opal have surrounded themselves with about thirty loyal hired hands, most of whom are practiced sharpshooters and disreputable gunmen who wouldn't think twice about shooting an unarmed man in the back. Can you imagine what they would have done to me if given the chance? Still would, for that matter. I can't fight those odds, darlin', not even with Jake backing me up, and hope to come out of it alive. I'd find myself shot full of more holes than a round of cheese! At least now we have the means to fight them legally."

She turned sad eyes to his and asked softly, "Why, Blake? Why did you have to become, of all things, a gunfighter?"

"It was one of the best and fastest ways to make money, once I had lost my ranch. Lawyers' fees are expensive, not to mention the bill I owed Doc Shadley."

Megan was crying openly now. "You could

have done something else! Anything else!''

''But, I didn't. Megan, you have to understand the situation I found myself in. I was out on my ear, with nothing to my name but my horse, my saddle, my gun, and my boots. I barely had a change of clothes—''

''I know the feeling,'' she butted in sarcastically, reminding him of her own state until recently.

''I had lost everything I owned,'' he continued as if she had not interrupted, ''everything my family had owned for generations. If I had three dollars to my name, I was lucky. I went down to Mexico and stayed with family until I had fully recovered from my injuries, but I couldn't impose forever, and that old gold mine hadn't miraculously decided to pour forth riches suddenly.

''I was hurt, and I was angry. It made me furious that a malicious old woman and her spineless, yellow-bellied son could throw me off my own property. Of course, they had help in doing so, not only their slick lawyer and their friend the sheriff, as well as that crooked judge who made a fast fortune, but hired gunmen. I decided then and there that I would never be caught in a similar situation again. I may have to fight them through legal means to get my ranch back, but never again will I allow some jackass to stomp my bones into the ground and grind my face in the dirt. I'll be damned if that will ever happen to me or anyone I care about again.

''So I started to practice—target practice at first, though I always could pretty much hit whatever I aimed at. Then I met up with Jake, and he gave me a few pointers. I began to see just how fast and how accurate I could be with a gun. I surprised even myself. It seemed to come so easily, as if the talent had just been there waiting until I really needed it. When I thought I was good enough, I hired myself out to ranchers having problems with land and water rights or rustlers. I brought in a few outlaws with a bounty on their heads. I helped marshals and sheriffs in some of the rougher cow-towns. I even rode shotgun on the stageline for a while.''

Megan's eyebrows rose at this. ''And you made a name for yourself in the process.'' It came as more of an accusation than a statement from her lips.

''Yes, I made a name for myself, and now, every so often, some fool who thinks he is faster with a gun feels the need to prove himself by challenging me or someone like me, and usually ends up getting killed for his stupidity,'' he admitted with a grim look. ''I can't sugar-coat it for you, Megan, but it is not as bad as you are painting it, either.''

''How many men have you killed that way, Blake? The way you killed that man today?'' Her somber grey gaze leveled itself at him. ''How many notches do you have on that gun of yours?''

Teeth clenched now in an effort to control his mounting temper, Blake drew his Colt from his holster and tossed it onto the bed next to her. ''Look for yourself, Megan. There are no notches cut into the butt of my gun. I don't keep score, like some braggart who needs to prove something to himself and the world.'' When she shied away from the gun, he strode to the bed, retrieved the weapon, and advanced on her. ''I said, look at it!'' he repeated tersely. With one hand holding the back of her neck, he brought the gun up to her face.

Megan tried to twist away, but could not. "That proves nothing! You still haven't answered my question, Blake. How many men have you killed with that fast gun of yours?"

Holstering the gun again, he turned her to face him, his arms going about her to hold her tightly to him. His devil-blue eyes blazed into hers. "You don't really want to know that, Megan. You are not so much angry that I have made my way as a gunfighter, as you are that I didn't tell you about it."

"And why is that?" she shot back tartly. "Are you that ashamed of it?"

"No, Megan, I am not ashamed of what I have done. I'm not so proud of it that I go around advertising the fact to anyone and everyone, but I certainly am not ashamed to admit it. By now I thought you knew. I thought you had surely guessed, especially after some of the things Roy Banner had to say."

"Well, I hadn't, and I'm not just anyone, Blake!"

"No, you're not," he agreed softly, though there was still a tense look to his features. "You are the woman I love. You are the woman I intend to marry as soon as we can find Father Miguel, or another handy priest or preacher. You are the mother of my unborn child."

Megan was silent for several seconds, weighing what she had seen and heard against the love in her heart. Love won out. "You were right, Blake," she finally admitted. "I *was* more angry that you hadn't

told me than for any other reason, although it does
worry me. Darling, my heart was in my throat when
I saw you draw against that man. I think I would die
if anything ever happened to you. I love you so
very, very much."

"And I love you with all my heart and soul," he
told her just before his lips came down to cover
hers in a kiss that sealed their betrothal with the
sweetest of promises. "I have to tell you," he said
when they finally broke off the kiss. "If you were
thinking of backing out of our marriage, it would
have done you no good. You are going to be my
wife, come hell or high water, Megan. I'll drag you
to the church, bound and gagged, if I have to."

"That won't be necessary, my love," she
purred. "I'll marry you quite willingly."

"Even if I am a low-down gunslinger? Can you
live with that, Megan mine?"

"I'll learn," she promised. "Besides, you won't
be one much longer. As soon as you get your
inheritance back, you will be a rancher."

He agreed laughingly, then said, "I guess you
will be a rich rancher's wife after all, won't you?
Just as you had planned before I kidnapped you off
that stagecoach."

"Not quite the same, thank heavens! This time
I'll have the right man—the honest one."

The next couple of days were a trial of patience
for all of them. For Megan and Blake because of the
restrictions placed upon them by her parents' presence. For Jana because she had to fight her fear of
horses again; that and the fact that she could not
bring herself to trust Lobo. She wasn't even overly

fond of the mischievous chipmunk. For Evan because he could sense Blake and Megan's impatience to be alone with one another, and because no one was absolutely sure they would find Father Miguel there at the mission to marry the two. For Jake because he was basically a lone wolf, no longer accustomed to so much company when traveling, or so much feminine chatter. The only one who seemed to weather the ride well was Mindy, and that mostly because she was away from the Apache and looking forward to going to Abilene with Jana and Evan when they returned. The older couple, saddened that they would no longer have Megan living with them, had decided to adopt Mindy and take her home with them to stay.

At long last they arrived at the San Miguel mission. Megan eyed the huge structure with a mixture of awe at the magnificent architecture, almost unable to believe that this beautiful church had been built in the middle of the wilderness, and a feeling of anxiety when it appeared that the place was deserted. Then, almost miraculously, one of the huge doors opened and an old grey-haired man dressed in priest's robes stepped out. He came forward with a welcoming smile and glowing dark eyes. "Welcome to the Mission San Xavier Del Bac," he said. "My name is Father Miguel." They were the most beautiful words Megan had ever heard.

Barely an hour later, Megan again had butterflies taking wing in her stomach, only this time they were joyous butterflies. Her mother had performed a few miracles of her own, and now Megan stood at the rear of the chapel, dressed in the lovely Mexican wedding gown. Her freshly coiffed hair was pulled atop her head, a few kiss curls wafting about her face and nape to soften the severity of the style, her head covered with the lace shawl. She was the perfect picture of the radiant bride, except for one minor detail. Her feet were bare!

In their hurried shopping trip, they had neglected to purchase slippers, and Megan had no other shoes with her but her boots. Jana had wailed at the sight of her lovely daughter in her wedding dress with those ridiculous boots peeking out beneath. Jana's own shoes looked no better, and were much too large. Megan solved the problem by wearing nothing on her feet at all.

Now here she stood, ready to walk down the aisle and exchange her name for Blake's forevermore. A gentle smile curved her lips as she saw Blake waiting for her at the altar. He looked so tall, so very handsome standing there, his clothes brushed free of the dust of travel, his hair freshly combed and uncovered for once by his hat. He looked happy, but nervous, and she knew exactly how that felt!

Her father linked her arm through his, and the next moment she stood beside Blake, his eyes shining into hers. In deference to her and her family, Father Miguel conducted the ceremony in English, though it could have been Chinese for all Megan knew. Ever afterward, she would wonder how she could have made the correct responses, for she recalled nothing but her hand nestled securely in Blake's, his incredibly blue eyes on hers.

Blake was equally stunned. Megan had said not one word about the dress, and she looked so beautiful that the sight of her brought a lump to his throat. With her hair up that way, it brought out the perfection of her features, emphasized her large, luminous eyes. Yet even as he admired the style, his fingers itched to undo her long cinnamon hair, to watch it fall in shining waves down her back, to wrap his hands in it and bury his face in its scented length.

Before Megan could collect her scattered thoughts, the ceremony was over and Blake was gathering her into his arms for their first kiss as man and wife. "Oh, *querida*! I thought we would never get to this time in our lives," he whispered emotionally. Then he chuckled softly. "And to think that you married me with no shoes on your feet."

She laughed and blushed and clung to him happily. "You noticed."

"Yes, and I think it is a wonderful idea. I should keep you always this way, barefoot and pregnant." He cut off her retort with another kiss that had her melting in his strong arms.

They spent their wedding night in blissful privacy in a spare little room that was once a monk's quarters. The walls were two foot thick, successfully muffling their mutual cries of passionate joy as they consummated their marriage and the beginning of their future life together. It seemed strange, almost sacrilegious at first, to make love in these devout surroundings, but Blake reminded her that marriage was a sacred state. Then, with his lips heating hers and his body tempting hers so deliciously, she had no other thoughts except of him.

Later, with her head pillowed on his shoulder,

he said, "When we get to Tucson, and I can arrange it, I'll buy you a ring. A wedding band to mark you as mine to all who see, a lasting measure of my love for you. I tried to find one before we left Tombstone, but couldn't. Can you believe it? All that gold and silver coming into that town day and night, and not a wedding band to be found anywhere."

Beside him, she sighed happily. "I am content just to be your wife at last. I don't need a ring to remind me that I belong to you, heart and soul. All I need is your love, my darling, now and forever."

25

Blake couldn't just ride into Tucson as big as life, even with Megan and her parents beside him. Without a doubt, the sheriff would have had him in jail within minutes. It was even possible that Sheriff Brown would turn him over to Kirk and his men and look the other way while they took their own revenge. Blake could have been dead and buried before anyone knew anything about it. He needed time to get in touch with his lawyer. Also, Jake needed time to reach Phoenix and send a telegram to the territorial marshal in Prescott, the Arizona territorial seat, and come back with the marshal and a fair-minded judge. They couldn't chance sending a wire from Tucson, since the sheriff might find out sooner than they wanted. They needed time to prepare, for once Blake and Megan were seen together, everyone would know who was responsible for her disappearance.

The problem was, where could Blake and Megan stay until the marshal arrived? Blake needed to be close to town, yet safely hidden. Certainly they did not want to tip Kirk off to their presence in Tucson. It would be perfectly fine for the Coulstons to go back to their hotel. They had already fabricated a story about hearing of a little orphan girl who needed someone to look after her. Their absence could be explained by a short trip to collect Mindy. It was Blake and Megan who needed to stay out of sight. In no way did they want Kirk to know that anything was in the wind until they were ready to spring their trap.

It was Jana who came up with the solution to their dilemma. "Why don't we check with Mae Higgins? She and her husband have believed all along that Blake should have inherited the ranch. Maybe they would be willing to put you up for a few days, and their ranch is far enough out of town to be safe, yet not too far either."

Mae and Chad Higgins were delighted to do just that. With their four children and a fairly small ranch house, it would be a bit crowded around the table, but if Blake and Megan were willing to bed down in the barn loft, they were more than welcome to stay. Mae positively gushed over Blake and his new bride. "My lands, but it is good to see you again! And married to such a pretty little thing. Aren't you the lucky man!"

She stuffed them full of good home cooking, fussed over Megan when she discovered she was expecting a baby, and generally made them feel at home. Chad was just as welcoming. "Always said you should have had that ranch, and I didn't believe for one minute that you could be anyone's boy but Mark's. It does my heart good to know that you can finally prove it. Never did like Kirk, and that mother of his is as cold as a well-digger's knee. Always suspected something was rotten about the whole mess. Those two ought to be hanged for the thievin' varmints they are.''

Megan could finally relax, and just in time it seemed, for they no sooner settled in at the Higgins' than she began to experience the normal symptoms of pregnancy. To her dismay, she found her stomach unsettled each morning. Only dry biscuits and weak tea would do until noon. Then, predictably, she would feel fine once more. Every once in a while, she would feel faint and have to sit down until her head stopped spinning. For someone who had barely been sick a day in her life, it was quite exasperating. She could put up with the tender breasts, but the morning sickness and light-headedness were supremely irritating.

Mae just laughed and nodded her head. "It'll pass, dearie. Had the same problems with all four of mine. The next thing will be your appetite. You'll want to eat everything in sight. I swear, by the time I delivered I was as big as a barn. Felt like an elephant waddlin' around the house.''

"I can hardly wait!" Megan grumbled, earning a hearty chuckle from Mae.

"Oh, it'll all be worth it, believe me. When you hold that squirming little bundle of love in your arms, you'll forget all the trials in a hurry. Ain't nothin' like a baby to make a woman feel whole.''

*   *   *

On their second day there, Blake's lawyer came to visit, and he and Blake spent over an hour discussing their strategy. The lawyer agreed that they should do nothing to forewarn Kirk that Blake was back in town, and especially that he had the proof he needed to get his property returned to him. They would wait until Jake got back with the marshal and judge. Then they would spring the trap on the Hardestys. If everything went right, Blake could be presenting his case to the judge in ten days or so.

They had been with the Higgins family for almost a week and a half, with occasional visits from Megan's parents on the sly, when trouble came unexpectedly. Jake was expected back any time now, but that did them no good when Chad Higgins came rushing into the house one evening just before dark. "Charley just rode in! Kirk is on his way with his men and the sheriff! Charley is already saddling your horses for you!"

Blake was on his feet and running for the barn. "Megan! Get our things! We've got to make a run for it! Pack some candles if Mae has any to spare."

With Mae's help, Megan threw things into the saddlebags. She barely noticed when Scamp scurried into one before she secured it. Along with the candles and some extra matches, Mae included as much food as she could spare on such short notice, and filled their canteens with fresh water. "How on earth did they find out you were here?" she wondered aloud.

"Tell Megan's folks we are headed up to the old gold mine. Jake knows where it is," Blake told Chad. They could hear the sound of approaching horses as they headed out of the ranch yard and cut out across the fields, Lobo fast on their heels.

Their only hope was to outrun their pursuers until darkness set in. Then, under cover of night, perhaps they could lose them altogether. For a while, it looked as if their luck would hold. The last streaks of light faded from the sky, wrapping them in deep shadow. Into the night they raced. Then, as the moon rose in the cloudless sky, it became almost as bright as day. They had eluded the riders temporarily, but for how long was anyone's guess. A good tracker would have no trouble picking up their trail in the bright night, and they had no time to cover their tracks or try some tricky maneuver to outwit those who followed. Both of them knew without a doubt that they were running for their lives.

By the time they neared the mine, it seemed as if they had lost their hunters. Blake lost no time in grabbing their things off the tired horses. Then he whacked them both sharply on their rumps, sending the horses running again. Hopefully they would not stop soon, for he wanted them to go as far from the mine as possible, perhaps leading Kirk away from this area on a wild goose chase, while he and Megan holed up in the mine and waited for Jake.

He proceeded to loosen a few of the boards blocking the entrance to the mine, and helped Megan crawl inside. Then he replaced the boards as well as he could. It was dark and dank inside the mine, not at all the romantic place Megan had envisioned when she had thought of shining golden walls glistening with nuggets. It was musty and smelly, and as dark as the inside of a goat. In fact, standing there in the dark waiting for Blake, it was extremely frightening. She could hear the squeals of small animals, and she shivered wondering what they might be.

Megan nearly shrieked aloud as Blake took her arm. "Follow me," he whispered, leading her further into the black tunnel. She hoped he knew where they were going, for she could not see a thing. She stumbled more than once before they finally rounded a bend in the tunnel. They went a short way farther before Blake deemed it safe to light one of the candles.

The light was welcome, but it did not relieve the sinking feeling in Megan's stomach as she looked around at what was to be her home until Jake arrived with help. The walls, where they were not mud-brown, were a dull grey, streaked with rivulets of moisture and scarred by pick and shovel. Cobwebs hung like tattered curtains, in some places entirely across the narrow tunnel. An uncontrollable shiver raced through her, and Megan could not help but brush frantically at her clothes and hair. Her hands came away dirty and sticky with the clinging stuff. It was no consolation that Blake had fared no better.

"Don't lean against the supports," Blake warned, motioning to the age-old timbers that braced the walls and ceiling. "They are pretty rotten in places. That is one of the reasons why I didn't want to come up here before."

Megan eyed the sagging timbers with a wary eye. If one of the beams so much as groaned, she would jump out of her skin in fright, she knew. She did almost that, seconds later, when a huge rat raced practically across the toe of her boot. With a strangled scream, she threw herself into Blake's arms, nearly dislodging the candle as she did so.

He held her quivering form close to him and comforted her as best he could. "I guess the next thing I should do is scout this place out for animal life," he said. The thought that they might be sharing their abode with worse than a mere rat did nothing to console her or calm her ragged nerves. Megan refrained from asking what sort of animal life he was suggesting. Her imagination was running amok as it was, with images of huge bears and wildcats, and most particularly snakes! If he had anything worse to list, she did not want to hear about it!

Within a short time, Blake had pronounced this section of the mine free of the worst terrors, and had built a small fire to take the chill from their bones. He had cleared a space for their bedrolls near the fire. Lobo slept on the other side of the fire, and the big wolf's presence made Megan feel a little better. He would stand guard against any predators still lurking in the depths of the dark cavern.

Megan dozed from time to time, only to jerk awake at the slightest movement. She was sure Blake got little rest, if any at all, for he was constantly feeding the small fire to keep it going. It was long past midnight when Lobo raised his big head and perked his ears. A low growl issued from his throat, and the hackles on his neck rose alarmingly. Blake lay a warning finger on Megan's lips, then rose quietly to his feet. Megan did likewise, though her shaking legs almost refused to support her.

"Grab the saddlebags and go farther into the mine," Blake whispered. "Don't light a candle unless you have to. Go far enough back that no one can see you."

"Is it Kirk?" she murmured, not wanting to leave Blake and go into the dark tunnel by herself.

He shook his head. "I don't know. It might just be an animal." Almost immediately, the jingle of a horse's bridle outside the mine entrance belied his words. Then they heard the low murmur of men's voices. "Go!" he said urgently, giving her a swift kiss and a shove.

Megan did as he bid, but she went only far enough so that no one could see her lurking in the dark shadows. She could still see Blake from where she crouched. He too had backed into the shadows, though not so far as she. He was on the near side of the fire, closest to her, in order that whoever might come round the bend would be directly in the light from the fire. The fire, which could never have been completely doused in time, would now work to his advantage. Lobo was at his side, fangs bared and ready to launch himself at the unwanted intruders. It struck Megan as odd when she saw Blake heft a long piece of timber in one hand and his knife in the other. She wondered why he did not draw his gun.

Footsteps echoed down the hollow tunnel, cautious steps coming ever nearer. Then, suddenly, two men burst into the open, their guns drawn. Two more followed close behind. From the light of the fire, Megan recognized only one—Kirk. Blake recognized all four. Two were gunmen hired by Kirk; the other was Sheriff Brown.

The men stopped, unsure of themselves for a moment when they failed to find their quarry. Only when Lobo growled did they see Blake's faint, shadowy form. At least they assumed it was Blake. They seemed to hesitate, none of them eager to tangle with the huge wolf whose eyes glowed out at them from the darkness.

Kirk was the first to speak. "Call off the wolf, Blake, or I'll be forced to shoot him."

Blake did not respond; neither did he choose to calm the wolf.

"Where is Megan?" Kirk tried again. "I know she is with you. Send her out. It would be a shame to see such a pretty thing hurt, just because she is caught between us in this family feud of ours. I promise you she will come to no harm."

Blake's harsh laugh bounced off the walls of the mine. "Go to hell, Kirk!"

"If I do, I'll take you with me, cousin." Kirk aimed his pistol in Blake's direction. When he cocked it, the small noise was magnified in the rocky tunnel.

"Don't be a fool, Kirk! You fire that gun and——"

Blake's warning came too late. Megan saw the flash from the muzzle, and she heard the roar of the report. It seemed to go on and on, rumbling through the mine. She watched in horror as Blake grabbed his shoulder, and she heard her own voice screaming. Lobo, seeing his master hit, lunged at Kirk, but he was too slow. Kirk, realizing what he had done, was already retreating, his men after him. Sheriff Brown glanced around as if not sure what was happening, then turned to follow quickly after the others.

Megan was halfway to Blake when it happened. The entire tunnel seemed to tremble violently, and suddenly rocks and dirt were flying everywhere. The big old beams quivered and shook, then came tumbling inward. The mine was caving in on them!

Something hit her shoulder, and Megan fell to her knees. She was screaming and choking, almost unable to breathe because of the dirt filling the air and the panic squeezing the breath from her chest. Another heavy object fell upon her back, and as dizzying stars swirled behind her stunned eyes, darkness enveloped her.

Megan recovered consciousness only to find herself in the same hell she had temporarily escaped by fainting. Never had she experienced such utter, unrelieved darkness! And such overwhelming panic! That she was still alive was evidenced only by the throb of pain in her shoulder and the frantic beating of her own heart in her ears. It was the most terrorizing moment of her life. Even almost drowning had not been as frightening. She tried to move and could not, for something heavy was lying across her back.

A whimper escaped her quivering lips, and she began to choke again. Then, against her ear, she heard the most beloved sound on earth. "Hush, love. I'm here."

She began to cry in earnest now. She could not seem to help herself. When her sobs at last eased to an occasional hiccup, she found herself cuddled securely in Blake's arms. "Oh, Blake. What are we going to do? How are we ever going to get out of here?''

His voice sounded bleak. "I don't know. Maybe Jake will be able to dig us out, if the cave-in is not too bad. At least people know where we are, so there is still hope. At least we are both alive, which is a miracle in itself.''

"So far.'' Megan did not know whether she spoke the words aloud or merely thought them in her mind.

"Do you know what happened to the saddlebags?'' he asked. "If we could just find a candle, I have matches in my pocket. We could better evaluate our situation if we could see around us.''

"I think I had them in my hands when I fell,'' she ventured. "I'm not sure. Everything was happening so fast.''

She could hear Blake shuffling about in the dark. The next sound to her disbelieving ears was a chuckle. "I found them,'' he said, relief coloring his voice. "I also found Scamp, or Scamp found me, I should say. Scared the cotton out of me to feel that furry little monster racing up my arm and not knowing at first what it was.''

She felt Blake reach for the bags, then heard him groan in pain. Suddenly she remembered that he had been shot. "Oh, dear God, Blake! I forgot about your wound. How bad is it, can you tell?''

"We can tell better once we get some light in here.'' A moment later, a match flared, followed by the wavering light of the candle as the wick caught.

Megan's breath released in a long sigh, but her relief was short-lived. The entire left side of Blake's shirt front was covered with bright red blood. She started to shake, panic hitting her again. With trembling fingers she reached out to touch the sticky wetness, his life's blood staining her fingers. "Oh, God! Oh, dear Lord!" The words were more prayer than curse. "We're going to die in here, aren't we?"

He set up the candle securely in a heap of dirt. His hands clutched her shoulders, and he shook her hard. "Don't think that way!" he commanded. "We are alive, and I intend for us to stay that way until we find a way out of here, either on our own or with help from our friends. Now, if you can pull yourself together, I could use some help with this arm."

Where gentleness would not have, his stern demeanor helped. Shamed, she dashed away the last of her tears, leaving streaks of dirt smeared on her filthy face. She helped him out of his shirt, and cringed when the jagged wound was exposed. Luckily, now that they had the saddlebags, they also had clean cloth. A brief hunt turned up one of the canteens, and she proceeded to clean his wound. "How do we get the bullet out?" she asked shakily.

"With your fingers," he hissed on an indrawn breath of pain. "I dropped the knife when I was hit."

It was nearly as painful for her as it was for him as she worked over him by the thin light of the candle. The bullet had not gone deep, thankfully, but it kept slipping from her grasp as she probed the open gash. Blood continued to flow over her fingers from the wound. Finally she managed to work it to the surface and pry it the rest of the way out with her fingernails.

By now a cold sweat dotted her forehead,

matting her hair to her brow. Blake had bitten back groan after groan, and his entire face was awash with perspiration. Even by the weak candlelight, she could see how pale he was beneath the grime covering his face. One final time she washed the wound, wishing she had some whiskey to disinfect it, or thread and needle to close it with. Instead, she had to settle for padding it with pieces of cloth torn from a blouse and binding it with longer strips of material.

When it was done, they rested for a bit. Megan dug some food out of the bags and they ate. A short while later, Blake insisted on checking on the extent of the damage to the tunnel. A few yards ahead, they could see that the entrance was blocked; how badly was what Blake needed to ascertain. On their hands and knees, they clawed at the earth mounded across the entrance, Blake trying his best with his one good arm. Their efforts had a puny effect. In addition to tons of dirt, there were huge rocks and beams in the way, and they had to work slowly and carefully in order not to disturb things further and cause yet another cave-in.

"It's no use," Blake said at last, pulling her away from the blockage. "There is too much there for you and me to get through. We have a choice. We can either sit here and hope someone finds us, or we can try to find another way out."

"Is there another way?"

He shook his head. "I don't know, Megan. I haven't investigated the mine very far in my past visits. There might be."

"What do you think we should do?"

"I think," he said slowly, not wanting to alarm her, "that we should go farther into the mine and see what we find. Then, if we can't get through, we can come back here and wait for rescue."

"You don't think anyone will come, do you?" she asked pitifully.

He was as truthful with her as he dared. "I know someone will come, Megan. I'm just not sure when. And if they see the cave-in, they might assume that it is an old one and figure we went somewhere else to hide."

"Or they might think we died in the mine and give us up for dead," she guessed, her eyes huge in her pale face.

"Yes," he admitted. "Our best chance is to find a way out of here ourselves." A bleak look came over his face. "I just wish I knew if Lobo survived the cave-in." In their brief bit of digging, they had found no evidence of the wolf, or of any of the men, and they had no way of knowing if anyone but themselves had lived through the disaster.

Slowly, step by step, they picked their way through the eerie mine, skirting rubble and rotted timbers and deep, unexpected holes in the floor. Megan held her breath in abject fear every time they passed one of the seemingly bottomless pits, expecting any moment that the ground beneath her feet would start to crumble and she and Blake would fall headlong to their deaths. They passed numerous smaller passages, heading off in different directions, but Blake felt they should follow the main shaft as long as it lasted. Finally, they had no other choice but to take one of the smaller channels, for the main tunnel had been blocked by another slide.

Megan lost all track of time. It seemed they had been buried here forever, yet it could not have been more than a few hours. The one thing in their favor was that they seemed to have an abundant supply of air once the dust from the cave-in settled. Also, they had found Blake's rifle where Megan had left it when she had been hiding from Kirk. Whenever they came to a blockage in the underground trail, Blake used the butt of the gun in place of a shovel.

Eventually the smaller shaft also ran out. They wasted precious time in having to backtrack and try yet another avenue. When this, too, came to an abrupt halt, Megan could have cried, but she simply did not have the energy. They must have tried six or seven of the smaller tunnels, marking each with a piece of cloth so they would not try the same one twice, when they found one that worked for them. It seemed a miracle, and perhaps it was, for Blake seemed to think that the tunnel had ended here at one time. Perhaps the landslide had opened it, where man had failed.

The passageway was extremely narrow, and not braced by wood or any other material. The only way to navigate it was to crawl on their stomachs through it, not knowing what they might find on the other side, some twenty feet away and beyond the reach of the light of the tiny candle. The earth was loose, and they had to go through very slowly and carefully so as not to cause another slide and be trapped in the small passageway.

It seemed to take forever, especially with

Blake's wounded shoulder, but they eventually emerged into a larger area. This new section of the mine was more like a tiny secluded room, for there seemed to be no other entrance or exit but the one through which they had come.

As Blake held the candle up for a better look, they both let out gasps of amazement. "Oh, my sweet heavens!" Megan breathed in disbelieving awe. "Tell me I'm not dreaming! Tell me this is really gold I am seeing!"

Blake could barely speak, so overcome was he at the sight before them. Everywhere they turned, the walls were streaked with wide veins of pure gold. "If you are imagining things, *querida,* then so am I. This is beyond my wildest hopes. Unless I am badly mistaken, this is one of the richest gold strikes to be found anywhere!"

26

They had found the gold that everyone claimed was not to be found. Megan wanted to weep at the irony of it. Here they were, surrounded by more wealth than most people saw in a lifetime, and what good would it do them if they could not find a way out of the mine? She was reminded of those ancient Egyptian kings and queens, buried in their pyramids with vast wealth. Was this to be her tomb, hers and Blake's? Were they to remain buried alive, perhaps never to be found? Or perhaps found years later, nothing but piles of dusty bones in a golden grave?

That possibility haunted her all during the long hours to come, when Blake fell ill with fever. After their trek into the golden room, they had both been too tired to go farther without rest. They had decided to stay here for a short time, and tired as they were, they both slept, though fitfully. In order to conserve their meager supply of candles, they had extinguished the one they were burning, and Megan was again terrified of the blanket of utter blackness that immediately enveloped them. If they ever got out of here alive, she would never again enter a room without windows. She would revel in the sunshine, no matter how hot, and count herself the most fortunate person on earth just for the light of stars and moon to light the dark night.

When she awoke, she was aware of heat around her, even in the coolness of the mine. She soon discovered that its source came from the man who held her wrapped tightly in his arms. Blake was much too hot, and even as the heat radiated from him, he shivered and clutched her more closely to him. Fishing around in the dark, she found the saddlebag and unearthed one of the precious candles. Blake moaned in his sleep as she searched his pockets for a match. Once she had light, she carefully unbound the wrapping over his shoulder wound. To her relief, it was not any more red than before. It did not seem to be infected yet, and no alarming streaks of red were fanning out from it.

Megan prayed as she had never prayed before. She used a good deal of their invaluable supply of water to cool his fevered brow. Blake thrashed and moaned, tossing restlessly on the hard, damp earth. If she had ever needed a blanket, she needed one now. In desperation, she dragged every bit of clothing out of their saddlebags and spread them on the floor, along with the outer clothing she was now wearing. Then she rolled Blake onto them to get him off the damp ground. Clad only in her chemise and pantalettes, she lay atop him, offering him her own body heat. It was not much, but it was the best she could think of to do.

He ranted. He raved. He did his best to throw her off him. He mumbled deliriously. All the while, she held him beneath her and prayed, her tears mingling with the sweat pouring out of him. She promised God all sort of rash things if he would only spare their lives. "I don't want to die here in the dark!" she wailed pitifully to her Lord. "I want to live to hold my baby in my arms! Please don't let Blake die now! Please!" All she could envision was being alone here with the dead body of her husband, waiting to die herself of slow starvation—in the dark, for their candles would not last long. She imagined someone finding their corpses years from now. Would they be able to tell that she had been carrying a child? Would there be a tiny mound of bones cradled within her own? Did her unborn child even have bones yet?

Megan was nearly as irrational as Blake before he finally broke out of his delirium. His fever had not broken altogether, but it abated enough for him to awaken with a fairly clear mind. "We've got to get out of here," he muttered upon discovering how ill he had been. "We have got to do it soon, while my mind is still clear enough to function properly." She could not argue with that, though she wondered how long his strength would hold out. He had lost a lot of blood, and the fever had further sapped his energy.

Again they started searching the myriad of tunnels, using more and more of their candles. At one point they had to wade across a wide stretch of

inky black water. When the water proved too deep
for Megan to walk in, Blake took her upon his back
until they were across, while she held the candle
above their heads and prayed that he would have
the strength to get them safely to the other side.
Farther on, Megan glanced down to find an enormous, hairy tarantula crawling up the side of her
skirt. Her heart actually stopped beating at the sight
of the formidable creature, and it was a wonder her
shriek of terror did not bring the mine tumbling
down upon their heads again. Blake, though weary
and fevered, did not berate her. He calmly brushed
the huge spider off of her and crushed it beneath
his boot. Only once did they hear the warning hiss
of a nest of rattlesnakes, and that was once too
much for either of them. They cautiously skirted
the area and hurried on their way.

It was Scamp who proved to be their salvation
in the end. They were down to their last candle,
and it was more than half burned. Things were
looking desperate, for Megan feared that Blake
could not go on much longer. He was stumbling in
his tracks as it was, and more times than not she was
now leading him as he leaned upon her shoulder to
conserve his waning strength. Just as they were
about to give up and admit defeat, Scamp started
chirruping loudly, dashing back and forth excitedly. It was all Megan could do not to trip over him as
he scurried about her legs, then ran ahead and out
of sight down a narrow little side tunnel that
seemed almost too small to go anywhere.

They were several feet beyond the point where
the chipmunk had disappeared when he popped

out and started chattering angrily. "What do you suppose is wrong with him?" Megan asked wearily. "He is acting so strangely."

Blake looked back with fevered eyes. "I don't know, Megan. I'm too tired to care."

"Well, we can't leave him now. He has come too far with us." She backtracked to where the tiny animal had once more disappeared. As she peered into the dark chasm, it suddenly dawned on her that she was feeling warmer air on her face. The air coming from the large crack was fresher than they had become accustomed to breathing.

"Blake! Bring the light! Quickly!"

As Blake approached the spot where Megan stood, the candle flame began to waver. "Do you see that?" she exclaimed. "Can you feel it?"

He looked at her in amazement. "It's fresh air! Megan, that is fresh air! We must be close to an opening!"

With Blake once more in the lead, they entered the small passageway. As they followed it, there were places so narrow that they could barely squeeze through. Blake had to remove his gunbelt and carry it, while Megan had to hand him the saddlebags and retrieve them on the other side.

Just as their final candle sputtered its last and went out, they caught a glimpse of daylight in the distance. Megan was almost dizzy with hope, her heart racing wildly. The opening, when they reached it, was small, almost impossibly so. It measured only a little over a foot in diameter. It hung just above Blake's head, and they could see blue sky beckoning them from the other side. Just outside, urging them on, was Scamp.

They had no idea what lay beyond the hole. It could be solid ground, or it could be an endless drop through midair. Either way, they were willing to chance it. With the butt of the rifle, Blake chipped away at the edges of the hole, carefully and slowly enlarging it until it was wide enough for them to fit through. Then he boosted Megan up and partially out. "What do you see?" he asked anxiously.

"I see solid, sun-kissed ground!" she exclaimed in delight. "Oh, Blake! It is so beautiful I can hardly believe it!"

He shoved her the rest of the way out to safety. Then he slowly and painfully levered himself through the small opening and collapsed on the ground next to her. His breathing was labored, and she could tell that he was in great pain, but they were both still alive. They were lying in the bright sunlight, free at last from the terror of being trapped in the mine.

For the next few minutes they allowed themselves a brief rest. Megan checked his shoulder again, using the last of their water to cleanse it, and rewrapped it as best she could. It had begun bleeding again from all the exertion. They were not safe yet. They still had to make their way back toward town and find help. Blake could not go much longer without proper treatment of his wound.

The best Blake could determine, they were on the far side of the hill from the entrance to the mine. Help also lay in the opposite direction from their newfound exit. They would have to circle around and head for town. They would also have to do so very cautiously once they neared the mine entrance, for they could not be sure that Kirk and his cronies would not still be there waiting for them. Chances were that, if they had survived, they would be long gone. By now they probably thought that Blake and Megan were either killed or securely trapped inside, but the young couple would be careful just the same.

Blake strapped his gunbelt back around his waist with Megan's help, and they started off again. In places the going was rough, but after what they had experienced in the mine, nothing could deter them now. Slowly but surely, they made their way down and around, though Megan often had to help Blake now. He tried to use the rifle as a cane, something to lean upon, but it was sometimes not enough, and Megan continued to worry about him.

"If I pass out and you can't revive me," he told her at one point, wiping the sweat from his forehead with his good arm, "I want you to go on without me. Take the rifle with you for protection, and go for help as fast as you can."

She agreed only because he insisted, though she doubted she could bring herself to leave him alone and defenseless.

They must have been halfway around to the mine entrance. Blake was several steps behind her at the time, with Megan leading the way down a sharp, curving slope. She had reached the bottom and was about to call up to Blake, when suddenly she was grabbed from behind.

Her scream echoed off the surrounding hills, bringing Blake to attention immediately. What he saw as he looked down at her made his blood run cold. Kirk was standing behind Megan, holding her as a shield before him. An evil smile curved his lips, transforming his handsome features into a devil's mask. Kirk's gun rested directly on Megan's temple.

"Throw down your weapons or I'll kill her where we stand," Kirk demanded haughtily.

Despite her fear, Megan called out bravely, "Don't do it, Blake! He'll kill us both if you do!" The barrel of the gun dug deeper into her temple.

"*Now,* Montgomery!"

Blake tossed down the rifle, and it rattled past where Kirk and Megan stood. The beads of perspiration dotting his forehead were not from illness alone.

"Now the Colt. Nice and easy. Bring it out of your holster with your left hand. Use just your fingertips."

Blake laughed shortly and without humor. "Sorry, Kirk, but that's not possible. You see, your last shot at me hit me in the shoulder. I can't use my left arm."

Now Kirk laughed nastily. "Use your right hand then, but take care, cousin. Megan's life depends on it."

Blake reached slowly for his gun, his fingers shaking visibly both from weakness and fear for Megan's life. He knew as he did so that he would be tossing away his last chance for survival. But what else could he do? He certainly couldn't try to shoot Kirk now, with Megan held before the man. This way, at least, there was a slim chance that Kirk would let Megan live, that Jake or someone would be able to rescue her from his demented cousin. For by now Blake was convinced that his cousin was impossibly insane.

A wave of dizziness threatened him, making his vision blur for a moment, but Blake determinedly willed it to pass. Delaying the inevitable for as long as he could, he asked, "Just out of curiosity, where are your friends? It's not like you to do your own dirty work without someone to back you up."

"Too bad about them," Kirk sneered. "They were buried in the cave-in. I was the only one to make it out in time, except for you two, naturally. Of course, the good sheriff would have had to go soon anyway. He was getting too nervous to trust much longer. And the other two were just hired gunhands, easily replaced."

Blake's fingers were nearly touching the butt of his Colt when Megan screamed. She tried to throw herself out of Kirk's arms, and in the process she lost her balance. Her foot slipped on some loose gravel and she began to fall, pulling Kirk after her. He had no choice but to release her or lose his balance as well.

In that split instant when Kirk was not quite steady, when his gun wavered from Megan and began to turn toward Blake, Blake drew his Colt and fired. For a terrible moment, Blake thought he had missed, though how he could have at this range, he did not know. Kirk stared up at him stupidly. Reflex alone made him pull the trigger of his gun. Then, with a stunned look of disbelief still on his face, Kirk toppled face first into the dirt.

With one eye still on his cousin, not entirely sure the man was dead, Blake's gaze searched for

Megan. She was crouched about ten feet beyond Kirk, her wide grey gaze pinned to him, the rifle cocked and ready.

"Is he dead?"

"Are you all right?"

They both spoke at the same time.

Blake smiled weakly. "Stay where you are until I make certain." He literally crawled to where Kirk lay. Their enemy was indeed dead. No longer would they need to worry about him or his evil ways.

Megan inched her way to where Blake sat. For endless minutes they sat holding one another, grateful once more just to be alive. After all their many trials and close calls, the feeling of danger was becoming familiar to them—too familiar. Hopefully, with Kirk now out of the way, their lives would settle down. Personally, Megan thought she could stand a lot of sheer boredom in the future.

With Blake needing medical attention more each minute, they continued on their way. They were nearly to the mouth of the mine when they were met by Jake. Never had Megan been so thankful to see the gunfighter. A broad grin etched his face. "Are you two ever a sight for sore eyes!" he shouted joyously. "We thought for sure you were dead!"

"We almost were," Blake answered with a wobbly smile.

"If we don't get you to some help soon, you still might be." With rescue standing before them, Megan was quick to voice her worry. "He's been shot, Jake, and he's lost a lot of blood."

"Now, Megan, don't fu-u-sss." The words barely out of his mouth, Blake wilted into oblivion.

Megan was close to hysterics again until Jake assured her that Blake had merely passed out. Hefting his friend across his broad shoulders, Jake carried him the rest of the way down. At the mine entrance they were met by Chad Higgins, Megan's father, and several other men Megan did not know, one of whom was the territorial marshal. Leaping about and barking like mad was Lobo.

After greeting her overjoyed father, Megan knelt down and threw her arms about the wolf's neck, tears streaming down her dirt-streaked face. "Oh, Lobo! We thought you'd been caught in the cave-in!"

"He was," Chad offered. "We've all been digging for hours to try to reach you. We found the sheriff, but he didn't make it out alive. Neither did the other two we found. How that animal survived is beyond me!"

"We still haven't found Hardesty," her father injected with a frown.

"He's around the side of the hill." Megan went on to explain what had happened.

"I'm glad he's dead," Evan replied.

Chad summed it up nicely. "Couldn't have happened to a more deserving fellow."

Megan didn't get around to telling the entire story of their entrapment and escape until much later. Even then, she said nothing about the gold they had discovered. That would be up to Blake to disclose, in his own way and time.

They got Blake to town, and old Doc Shadley tended to his shoulder, clucking all the while about how he would have gone out of business years before if not for Blake and his numerous injuries. It was from him that Megan finally learned how Blake had received the scar on his cheek.

"Got it trying to show off for the girls, of course," the aged physician crowed, delighted to repeat the story to Blake's new bride. "He was about twelve at the time, as I recall, and he had been practicin' juggling with apples, but that was not good enough for him. No sirree! The day of the church picnic he decided to show off his new skills by juggling knives." Megan chanced a look at Blake and was surprised to see him blushing. "You can guess what happened," Doc continued. "One of them knives came down right across his face. Lucky it didn't put his eye out. Took seventeen of my finest stitches to put him right again, and by the time I got back to the picnic, I'd missed the meal entirely. I never have completely forgiven the rascal for that."

It was Megan's turn to blush when Blake happily disclosed the fact that they were expecting a baby sometime in the late winter or early spring. "We will be wanting you to deliver it, Doc," he said.

"I'll be right glad to, son," the doctor responded, "since I doubt you'll be making me miss another picnic supper at that time of year."

A few weeks later, Megan was as contented as a cat by a warm hearth. Blake was equally as pleased with the way everything had worked out. His wound had healed completely now; he had gotten his ranch back, and he and Megan were making it their home. There was hardly a sign about the place to show that Kirk and Opal had ever lived here, and considering the manner in which Opal had left it, Blake was glad. He wanted no bad memories in this house to haunt his wife.

While Doc Shadley had been busy patching Blake's wound, the marshal had taken Kirk's body out to the ranch. He broke the news to Opal, as kindly as he could, but there was no way to soften the blow of her only son's death. It was two days later before legal judgment was passed, and Blake could finally claim his land. He was thankful now that he and the marshal had gone alone that morning to tell Opal of her eviction from the property.

When they got there, the place had been deserted. Not a ranch hand in sight. The cook and housemaid were nowhere to be found, and every one of the hired gunmen had left. They soon learned the reason.

The house was unearthly quiet when they entered it after receiving no answer to their knock. Everything was neat and orderly as always. As they went from room to room, calling Opal's name and receiving only silence in reply, gooseflesh rose on Blake's arms. They found her in her bedroom. She had rigged a rope over one of the open beams in the ceiling and hanged herself.

They buried her next to Kirk in the family cemetery plot that same day. Later, Blake learned from one of the old ranch hands that Opal had fired everyone on the ranch, not even wanting them to stay and help bury Kirk. She had been like a crazy woman, and as soon as they had received their pay, every last one of them left as fast as possible. That, at least, explained why nothing in the house had been stolen. No one was aware that Opal had hanged herself until Blake and the marshal found her body.

Blake was glad that Megan had been spared the gruesome sight. He'd had the room cleaned from top to bottom and everything in it taken out and burned before Megan stepped foot on the property. He had done the same with the master bedroom, which Kirk had taken over, for he could not stand the sight of Kirk's things in his father and mother's old bedroom.

The ranch was theirs now, completely. Already Megan had made changes in the house, her own personal touch now reflected there. Blake had hired back many of the former ranch hands who had been loyal to him and his father. Jake had agreed to stay on for a while and help him get the ranch running smoothly once more. Recently, Blake had reopened the old mine, and the riches of the tiny golden room were pouring forth. Life was good, their future bright at last.

The judge had been very lenient. With the proof before him, he'd had no qualms about return-ing the ranch to its rightful owner. It belonged to Blake without question, and before the day was out, everyone in Tucson was well aware of the Hardestys' deceit and the fact that Blake was truly Mark Montgomery's son. The problem was Blake's part in the stagecoach holdup. After hearing testi-mony that Blake had neither personally harmed anyone nor stolen anything except Megan that day, and the fact that Megan was now quite willingly his wife, the judge relented. Also in Blake's favor was the fact that, despite his reputation as a gunfighter, he was not wanted for any other crimes in the territory. In fact, he had been quite helpful to the law in his role as a gunfighter.

As soon as Megan was settled in her new home, her parents and Mindy took the stage back to Abilene. They had been away for far too long as it was, and Evan was concerned about how his hotel business was faring without them. They promised to return next summer, after their first grandchild was born. Meanwhile, Blake and Megan had sent a letter to Santa Fe, inviting *Tía* Josefa to come stay with them for a long visit. They both agreed that the lonely old lady could stay with them for as long as she wished, permanently if she desired. Megan even said that she would learn Spanish if she had to.

Blake had not forgotten his promise about Megan's wedding band, and one evening he presented her with a shining gold band. Embossed on the top were two delicately entwined hearts, with Blake's and Megan's initials engraved side by side. It was the most beautiful ring she had ever seen, and she was especially touched when he told her that it had been made from the first of the gold taken from their special golden room in the mine.

Now, hours later, they were preparing for bed in the newly redecorated master bedroom. As she sat before the vanity brushing her hair, the light from the lamp caught the gleaming gold of her wedding band. "Oh, Blake," she sighed happily, the shine of love in her eyes nearly outglowing the gold of the ring. "The ring is so beautiful! Our lives are so beautiful! I can scarcely believe that all our dreams are finally coming true!"

He came to her, bending her and folding his

arms about her. His hands rested on her slightly protruding stomach, and through the thin material of her wrapper, he felt the small mound where their child grew. "*You* are beautiful," he murmured, his lips caressing her silken throat. "You are my precious dove, my treasured wife, the most important thing in my life."

She rose and went eagerly into his arms, her lips finding his in a long, lingering kiss that gradually grew from warm welcome to searing desire. Slowly, as if in a dream, he undressed her and himself. Piece by piece, their clothing fell to the floor, forgotten as flesh met flesh. His strong, calloused hands caressed her fevered flesh with a touch as delicate as fine silk, and hers answered with whispery strokes as light as down. Time stood still as they slowly tantalized one another with hands and lips and tongues.

White-hot flames licked at her as he cradled her breast and took the turgid tip into his fiery mouth. As he suckled and flicked the peak with his agile tongue, she cried out in yearning. "Love me, Blake! Love me!"

"Always, *querida*. Always," he promised softly, his sapphire blue eyes alight with love as he swiftly lowered her to the waiting bed and followed her down. His mouth covered hers once more in a kiss that sent her senses swimming, her blood boiling through her veins. His seeking fingertips found all her sensual, sensitive places that set her body afire with passion, rediscovering them one by one in sweet, slow torture. Then his mouth followed the course his hands had charted, his hot tongue painting her body with flame.

Megan lay writhing beneath him, her mind awhirl with desire, her hands reaching for him, needing to return the pleasure in equal measure to this man who meant more to her than her very life. Her teeth teased at his earlobe, her tongue swirling inside and causing him to quiver, even as shivers danced over her own bare skin. Her lips found the spot along his broad shoulder that was so very responsive, and again she nipped at him, reveling in the salty taste of his flesh, the musky scent of him.

His lips found the core of her desire, and she cried aloud, a soft feminine moan that drove him wild. He cradled her buttocks in his large palms, his tongue laving her, tasting her honeyed essence. Her fingers tangled in his dark hair, tugging in urgent insistence as she thrashed beneath him. Ignoring her mewling pleas, he brought her to her peak, exulting in her intense pleasure and the spasms that shook her. He joined his body with hers before the tremors had passed, feeling her tighten and pull him into her silken depths in eager welcome.

Slowly, carefully, he stoked the fires of their passion to lightning-hot pitch, his body stroking hers in the ageless rhythms of love, until they were hurled together into ecstasy's realm. Golden flames danced about them, over them, within them, melting their hearts and souls into one being—solid, inseparable, forever one—forever gold.